Faith wondered how long she'd be able to stay.

Then a horrible thought hit her. When Luke left, she and his mother would be vulnerable and unprotected. She couldn't do that to his mother. She'd have to leave when Luke did. Her shoulders slumped as exhaustion settled. She didn't want to think about moving on just yet.

The creaking sound of the door next door opening heralded Luke's arrival.

She didn't want to be attracted to Luke, and she didn't need another man in her life. She had more problems than she could handle. Like keeping herself from becoming too attached to Luke's family, like protecting these good people and like planning her next move.

With a groan she turned off the light. As tired as she was, she knew it would be a long time before her mind could banish the images of the cowboy next door.

Books by Terri Reed

Love Inspired Suspense

Strictly Confidential #21
Double Deception #41
Beloved Enemy #44
Her Christmas Protector #79

Love Inspired

Love Comes Home #258
A Sheltering Love #302
A Sheltering Heart #362
A Time of Hope #370
Giving Thanks for Baby #420

TERRI REED

At an early age Terri Reed discovered the wonderful world of fiction and declared she would one day write a book. Now she is fulfilling that dream and enjoys writing for Steeple Hill Books. Her second book, *A Sheltering Love,* was a 2006 RITA® Award finalist and a 2005 National Reader's Choice Award finalist. She is an active member of both Romance Writers of America and American Christian Fiction Writers. She resides in the Pacific Northwest with her college-sweetheart husband, two wonderful children and an array of critters. When not writing, she enjoys spending time with her family and friends, gardening and playing with her dogs.

You can write to Terri at P.O. Box 19555, Portland, OR 97280 or visit her on the Web at www.terrireed.com or www.loveinspiredauthors.com.

HER
CHRISTMAS
PROTECTOR
TERRI REED

Steeple
Hill®

Published by Steeple Hill Books™

STEEPLE HILL BOOKS

Steeple
Hill®

ISBN-13: 978-0-373-44269-0
ISBN-10:   0-373-44269-6

HER CHRISTMAS PROTECTOR

Copyright © 2007 by Terri Reed

www.SteepleHill.com

Printed in U.S.A.

The fear of man brings a snare, but whoever
trusts in the Lord shall be safe.
—*Proverbs* 29:25

To my mother, Dorothy. I love you.

ONE

The scent of pine evoked memories of better times, times before…

The doors of the bus swooshed closed. The hulking vehicle rambled away, leaving Faith Delange in a wake of acrid exhaust.

Stifling a cough, she set her bags on the ground and tugged her wool coat tighter against the December chill. Though nothing could ever guard her against the isolation and fear of being found.

A "Help Wanted" sign hanging in the window of a little diner caught her attention and her stomach growled, spurring her onward. Her leather-soled shoes slipped slightly on patches of ice and sloshed in the dirty snow.

A clear, blue sky made a perfect backdrop for tall evergreens and the rustic little town nestled amid the snow-dusted greenery. In the distance, majestic mountains rose above the trees as if stretching toward heaven. Her gaze took in the town, which looked to be a refurbished antique of the old west decorated with holiday cheer. A sense of well-being swirled around her. A spark of hope leaped to life deep within her soul.

Faith liked what she saw. Here, she could be anybody. Here, she could be safe, if only long enough to rest and eat.

Maybe here, God might answer her prayers. The beginnings of a smile tugged at the corners of her mouth.

With the side of her hip, she pushed open the door of the restaurant and walked into a replica of an old dining car. Over the striped wallpaper hung festive cutouts. A small Christmas tree sat on the counter near the cash register. A bright yellow box with the word "toys" blazoned across the front sat overflowing with wrapped presents to the right of the door. Booths upholstered in red vinyl lined the walls. In the corner, a jukebox played a slow country melody, the words of love and loss bringing a pang to Faith's heart.

A frazzled, gray-haired waitress smiled from across the room. "Come on in, honey." The waitress wiped a hand across the skirt of her apron, adding another greasy stain to the front. "Sit where you'd like."

Every head in the diner swiveled in Faith's direction. She dropped her gaze to the floor and wished people would go back to what they were doing. She just wanted to blend in, be another faceless body.

Who was she kidding? Not only was she a stranger in this small community, but she looked awful, having worn the same clothes for the last three days.

The smell of bacon drifted past her nose, reminding her of her goal. Food and a job. But the last open booth seemed a mile away from where she stood.

She tightened her grip on her tattered suitcases and started forward just as an older, grizzled man in a plaid shirt vacated a spot at the counter. Moving quickly, Faith claimed the stool and set her suitcases on the floor at her feet.

In her peripheral vision she noticed the man to her right and his openly curious stare. She tilted her head away and picked up the menu.

The waitress wiped down the counter. "What can I get for you, dear?"

Her mouth watering and her stomach cramping with hunger, Faith succumbed to the temptation to order a full meal. "I'll have the eggs Benedict, please." She set down the menu. "And coffee."

"Ethel, here, brews the best coffee in the whole state," the man stated.

Faith nodded her acknowledgement but kept her gaze forward. She didn't talk to strangers. Especially men.

Ethel beamed. "You're a charmer, L.C. Your order

will be right up, dear." The waitress moved away with a spring in her step.

The warmth of the diner seeped into Faith's skin and her coat became too much. She shrugged it down her shoulders and released her left arm from the sleeve. Gingerly, she tried to push the right sleeve down without having to raise her arm.

"Here, let me," the man, L.C., offered as he reached for her coat.

Faith jerked back at the unexpected move. She stared at him. He had close-cropped dark hair and a ruggedly handsome face with a strong jawline. The slight bump along the ridge of his nose gave his face character, and she wondered how he'd acquired the break. His clean-shaven cheeks barely hinted at the dark shadow she guessed would appear by the end of the day. Dark eyebrows slashed over the bluest eyes she'd ever seen.

Just because he was handsome didn't mean she could trust him. She knew better than most what evil could lurk behind a beautiful facade.

"I'm sorry. I didn't mean to startle you," he said, holding up calloused hands.

"Th…that's okay."

"May I?" he asked and nodded his head toward her arm.

Not wanting to draw more attention, she slowly nodded. One of his big hands caught the end of her sleeve, his fingers lightly brushing against the back of her hand, setting off a maelstrom of tingles up her arm. His other hand grasped the collar of her coat. In a smooth motion he slipped the coat down her arm. Faith winced slightly as her shoulder moved.

"Did I hurt you?" L.C.'s rich, mellow voice held a note of concern.

She swallowed and tried to find her voice. "Old injury."

"Would you like to hang your jacket up?" He motioned toward a row of hooks on the wall near the entryway.

"No, thanks." She took the coat and laid it across one of her bags.

He turned his attention back to his breakfast. Faith studied him from the corner of her eye. He wore dusty cowboy boots, faded jeans and a blue denim shirt. A cowboy? In Oregon? She'd pictured the mountains of the northwest full of lumberjacks, not cowboys.

Ethel placed a large plateful of steaming hot food in front of Faith. Faith's stomach reacted to the aroma with a loud rumble.

At the man's deep chuckle, a sheepish smile touched her lips. "I'm hungry."

"So I heard." He flashed a grin.

Heat crept up her neck.

Ethel leaned her hip against the counter in front

of the man, drawing his attention. "How's your mother coming along?"

He sighed. "Better. Reva's been tending to her, but Mom isn't happy about it. She wants me to find someone else to come in and stay with her."

Ethel snorted. "I don't blame her. Reva would be the last person I'd want hovering over me. She'd be enough to bring on another heart attack."

Faith glanced at L.C. to see how he'd take Ethel's disparaging remarks about this Reva person. His expression remained calm and composed. So not like other men she'd known in her life.

Luke shrugged. "Reva means well. Though, I came into town to put an ad in the paper for someone else to help out."

Faith almost choked on her food. He needed someone to help with his mother. For one insane moment, she almost said she'd take the job. But she needed a way to get cash fast. Just what the job in the diner would offer.

"Now, you tell her hello for me. Tell her we miss her at choir practice and I'll try to get out to the ranch this week for a visit."

"I will, Ethel, thanks."

Ethel turned to Faith. "How's your breakfast, dear?"

Faith swallowed before answering. "Wonderful." And to the man beside her she added, "And the coffee is great."

"Told you so." He gave her a crooked grin, knocking the breath from her lungs. As a teenager, she'd dreamed of smiles like his.

She'd also dreamed of a happy, normal marriage. Now all she had were nightmares.

"L.C.?"

He extended his hand. "Luke Campbell, at your service, Miss…"

Tentatively, she took his hand. The kiss of the sun had tanned his calloused fingers, a stark contrast to the paleness of her own hand. "Faith Delange."

She bit back a gasp of anxiety at giving out her real name. Having used so many aliases over the last three months she sometimes forgot who she was supposed to be.

But he'd distracted her.

A big no-no.

She couldn't let her guard down. Not for a second. She could never be sure who would be the one to give her away.

"Well, Faith, what brings you to Sisters?"

He leaned back and eyed her with an intensity that brought a heated flush to her cheeks. Her heart beat erratically at the probing question. "I'm just passing through."

"That's too bad." He cocked his head to one side and studied her. "Where are you headed?"

Good question. She didn't want to say, where I can't

be found, so she shrugged. "I'm just traveling around, seeing America." That sounded innocuous enough.

"Really?" His gaze shifted to her suitcases on the floor.

She asked quickly, "What do you do, Mr. Campbell?"

"Please, call me Luke."

Her gaze dropped to her plate. "Luke."

"I…well, for the moment, I'm a rancher."

"Why just for the moment?"

"I'm a captain in the army. My father recently passed away and my mother suffered a heart attack not long after. Thankfully, I had enough unused leave to come home and help."

Her hand went to her heart. "I'm so sorry."

"It's been hard." Luke noticed the delicate shape of her fingers, fine-boned and petite. The kind of fingers meant for diamonds. Hers were bare.

He could tell she'd been traveling hard. Her wrinkled clothes looked well-worn, and the dark circles beneath her eyes told him she needed rest. He studied her face, liking the high cheekbones, wide, generous mouth and catlike eyes. Those eyes shifted ever-so-slightly toward the door. Luke twisted around to see what she found so fascinating, but there was nothing there. "Are you waiting for someone?"

"No."

"Are you alone, then?"

She stared hard at him for a moment before slowly answering, "Yes."

"Where are you staying?"

"Oh, I'm not." She spoke quickly, "I'll be catching the next bus out." She pushed a strand of blond hair behind her ear.

He shouldn't care. He wasn't staying much longer himself. But there was something vulnerable about her that didn't sit well. "Wouldn't it be a good idea to stop and stay in one place for a while? Sisters has a lot to offer."

She glanced at him sharply and wiped daintily at her mouth with a napkin. "I can see a lot from a bus window."

"Must get terribly uncomfortable."

She shrugged.

"How long do you plan to keep traveling?"

"As long as it takes."

"Where to next?"

She thought for a moment. "Alaska."

"As in tundra?"

She gave him a pointed look. "You ask a lot of questions."

He grinned. "Guilty as charged." People tended to open up if the right question was asked. Sometimes it took a lot of questions. "I'm a curious man."

She leaned in close. "Haven't you heard the one about curiosity killing the cat?"

Following her movement, he leaned closer. "Will my curiosity kill me?"

Abruptly, she sat back. Her expression took on a pained, faraway look. "It could, I suppose. I really don't know."

"Want to tell me about it?"

Her expression became guarded. "About what?"

Every nerve ending went on alert. She was hiding something. Luke stifled the urge to press and ran a hand through his hair. He didn't need this. Her. He had enough guilt for not being there for his father to take on another person's problems.

Ethel stopped before them. "Would either of you like anything else?"

Faith's expression changed and became hopeful. "Do you have pie?"

At least she had good taste and a healthy appetite. "Good choice."

Faith liked the way Luke's eyes crinkled at the corners. But his questions still made her uncomfortable and she was thankful he let the subject drop. The last thing she needed was to have someone probing into her life. Making judgments or, worse yet, pitying her.

He pulled out his billfold from his back pocket and laid cash down on the counter.

"Here's our homemade apple pie," Ethel announced, setting the pie on the counter before moving away.

Luke rose and took a thick brown, shearling-lined

leather coat from the hook and placed a traditional cowboy hat on his head. With an engaging grin he tipped the brim. "Faith, nice meeting you. Have a safe trip to Alaska."

Safety. If only she had a guarantee she'd find it in the tundra, she'd actually head that way. "Thanks."

As she watched him walk out, a familiar sense of loneliness assailed her. Only now it was more pronounced. For a moment, talking to the man, she'd felt normal. Mr. Campbell had been kind and thoughtful. Something she'd found too little of lately. Would she ever get used to the isolation?

"How's that pie?" Ethel asked, as she refilled Faith's coffee mug.

"Delicious," she replied. "I…I wanted to…inquire about the job?"

Ethel's expression went blank.

"The 'Help Wanted' sign in the window," Faith prompted.

"Oh, lands sakes." Ethel shook her head. "I'm sorry, dear. That should have been taken down two days ago."

Disappointment rolled through Faith with the force of a thunderstorm. "Oh, I see."

"I'll go take care of that sign right now." Ethel hurried away.

Setting down her fork, Faith pulled open her handbag and brought out a small leather pouch. She tugged out the bills and let the change fall to the table. She didn't think she'd have enough left after she paid her bill to buy another bus ticket.

Okay, time to regroup. The waitressing job wouldn't have been an ideal choice anyway. She'd be too visible here, too easy to find. The town was too small.

She scoffed at the irony her life had become. Instead of tipping the server, she was the one in need of the tip. Her grandfather would be so disgusted. And he'd left her all that money. But she couldn't dip into her inheritance without throwing up a big red flag.

Pushing away the pie plate, she dropped her head into her hands. *Oh, God, please help me.*

What was the point? God had abandoned her long ago. She supposed her grandfather's steadfast belief kept her wanting to believe. But so far God hadn't heard her prayers.

Lifting her head, she stared through blurry eyes at the money lying on the table. What was she to do?

An image of Luke drifted across her consciousness and she recalled his conversation with Ethel. He needed someone to care for his mother. An idea blossomed in the back of her mind.

He didn't exactly say he was looking for a nurse, just someone to help his mother recover.

She could do that.

After all, she'd been the one to care for her grandfather after he suffered his heart attack. She'd watched the team of nurses come and go, seen the services they'd provided. She'd jumped right in when the nurses had refused to stay.

She had owed her grandfather that for having taken her in after her parents died. Gerald Emerson Delange had been a Bible-thumping, judgmental and unyielding man. But she'd loved him and no one could be as difficult to care for as he'd been.

Oh, yes, she could care for Luke's mother.

But would it be a wise choice?

She wouldn't be visible, she'd have a place to stay and the job would probably pay decently. If no one knew she was there, maybe she'd even be safe for a while.

She stretched the aching muscles in her back. She couldn't go on like this. Fatigue was making her mind fuzzy, not to mention her dwindling funds. And the longer she stayed in the open, the more chance she'd be found.

What choice did she have?

Faith paid her bill, gathered her belongings, and hurried from the diner to find Luke.

She caught a glimpse of him as he turned the corner, disappearing behind a building a block down the street. Even from a distance he made a striking picture. Instead of the expected easy-rolling gait of a cowboy, he walked with a purposeful stride. Head up and shoulders back. Very controlled. In fact, everything about Luke spoke of a forthright and self-controlled man.

I'm a captain in the army.

She had the feeling that with Luke you got what you saw. Faith liked that. It was so opposite of what she'd lived with for so long.

Desperate to catch him before he disappeared altogether, she jogged down the sidewalk, her bags jostling at her sides.

She turned the corner as Luke climbed into a dark green Bronco. An instant later, the engine roared to life. He backed his vehicle out of the parking place, the tires crunching on the snow-covered gravel. Faith dropped her bags and ran toward him.

"Luke! Luke, wait!"

The Bronco screeched to a stop. Luke rolled down his window. "Faith, are you okay?"

His deep voice washed over her, smoothing the rough edges of her nerves.

Nodding, she blinked up at him. "I…I wanted to ask you something."

He gave her a curious stare. "Ask away."

Anxiety threatened to wrap itself around her throat, but she bolstered her courage and plunged ahead. "I'd like to apply for that job you mentioned earlier."

A confused frown marred his brow. "Job?"

Faith took a deep breath. "For your mother. The helper you needed."

"I thought you were just passing through?"

"I changed my mind. The country air agrees with me." She breathed in deep, the cold air filling her lungs and making her cough. It was either the air or she was losing her mind.

She probably was nuts to be doing this, but would she be found in this out of the way town in the middle of the Oregon Mountains? And on a ranch?

No, she didn't think so. She was ninety-nine percent sure she'd be safe.

She'd worry about the other one percent later.

TWO

Hire her, Luke thought to himself immediately, and then heard himself say, "You're hired."

Her eyes rounded in surprise. "Just like that?"

Luke hesitated. He knew next to nothing about this woman and yet, when he looked into her eyes, the haunted expression that had bothered him earlier seemed to recede. "Just like that."

"I'll...get my bags."

"Here, let me," Luke offered as he opened the door. But she was already hurrying away.

Luke drummed his fingers on the door. *Okay, Lord. I trust You know what You're doing. Whatever You have planned, I'm with You.*

Still, he couldn't shake the unsettled knot in the pit of his stomach.

As Faith approached, Luke climbed out from behind the wheel and took her bags. He put them in the back and then helped her into the rig. "You travel light for someone who's been out touring the country."

"Easier to pack up and go."

Luke climbed back behind the wheel and wondered what made her need to "pack up and go."

He clamped his jaw tight. Why couldn't God have provided some nice grandmotherly type, someone he could easily dismiss from his mind?

Luke slanted Faith a glance as he pulled out onto the street. Something about the way she held herself spoke of a quiet strength he found appealing. He wasn't immune to her physical charms, either.

He liked the straight line of her nose and the stubbornness of her jaw. Her blond hair swung about her shoulders and he could almost imagine the feel of the silken strands gliding across his palm.

Resolutely, he shook the sensation away. He really didn't need this.

Suddenly, Faith moved, throwing herself on the floor and he nearly careened into a building. He eased up on the gas pedal. "What are you doing?"

Her hunted expression reappeared, making her look wide-eyed and scared. "I…think my…ear…earring fell out," she stammered and patted the floorboards.

For several seconds she continued to search the floor.

There'd been no jewelry adorning her ears. Interesting. "Find it?"

"Yes." She attempted to sit up but her purse went flying to the floor, scattering paraphernalia at their feet. Diving down, she retrieved her goods.

Luke could have sworn she'd nudged her purse off the seat on purpose. Curiosity burned in his gut. "Room and board."

He glanced down at her bent head. He noticed one hand held her purse while the other put air into the purse's opening. His curiosity cranked up a notch and his brows drew together.

She peeked at him through a veil of blond hair. "Excuse me?"

She was acting so…odd. Luke forced his attention on the road ahead of them. "I said, room and board. Plus two-hundred dollars a week."

"That sounds perfect." Her muffled voice held relief.

They passed through town and he waved at several people. Then the realization hit him. She didn't want anyone to see her leaving with him.

Why?

Luke turned the truck onto the road leading to his parents' ranch. "We're out of town. You're safe now."

Faith started and sat up. Her face flushed a deep crimson. "What do you mean?"

He nodded toward the floor. "You find everything?"

"Huh? Oh, yes. Thanks." She turned away from him, her hands clasped into a tight knot.

Seeing her knuckles turn white, he felt the need to assure her and calm her fears. "Relax, Faith. It's going to be okay."

The fearful expression in her eyes told him she wasn't convinced.

A little small talk might ease the situation. "Where are you from?"

"Back east."

"Back east is a big place," he stated with wry amusement.

One corner of her mouth lifted. "New York."

He arched an eyebrow. "It's a big state."

She slanted a glance his way. "Yes. It is."

He'd bet she came from money. The graceful table manners she'd displayed and her cultured speech oozed private school, which only left him more intrigued.

"The countryside is so beautiful and peaceful," she commented, then asked, "Have you lived here your whole life?"

"Born and raised." He didn't mention he'd left at eighteen and only recently returned.

"How long ago did your mother have her heart attack?"

"Two weeks." He'd wanted a nurse to care for his mother just in case she suffered another attack, but the doctor had assured him she would be back to normal soon. All she needed was rest and a little exercise.

And someone constantly making sure she was doing just that. Someone besides Reva May Scott.

"What does your family think of your see-America jaunt?" he asked.

She pressed her lips together and shrugged. "Who's Reva?"

She was good at changing the subject. "That's a complicated question."

He thought for a moment how best to answer. "Her father and my dad were good friends. When her mother took off after she was born, her dad started drinking. My dad tried to step in as much as possible for them."

"That was generous. So you two are like siblings then?"

He let out a short laugh. Reva would disagree. "Yeah, something like that."

"I take it from what you told Ethel, Reva and your mother don't get along."

"No, they don't. Mom tried real hard with her when Reva was a little girl, but..." He shrugged. "Reva would never accept my mom."

"That's too bad," Faith commented, her expression thoughtful. "I hope your mom will be okay with me coming home with you."

Letting up on the gas, the Bronco slowed as he turned onto the gravel drive. "I wouldn't be bringing you home if I didn't think I was making the right decision."

She turned away to stare out the window. Stretching before them in wild splendor was his family's five-hundred acres. At the end of the drive sat a two-story farmhouse, flanked on either side by a pair of large, red barns, one of which had four apartments on the second floor. A paddock and corral sat off to the right side of the barn while the other side was open grazing land with sage brush and bare trees sticking up through the layer of snow.

"Oh my, is this your ranch?" Her voice filled with awe.

"Welcome to the Circle C," Luke said with pride.

Faith twisted to look back the way they'd come. "The road is very visible. I suppose you can see cars coming long before they arrive?"

"Yes."

"Good." She sat forward. "That's good. You're pretty safe out here."

He arched a brow. "What are you afraid of?"

A huge caramel-colored animal ran along the fence.

"You raise llamas?" She turned her curious gaze on him and left his question unanswered. Again.

The depths of her hazel eyes pulled at him. He debated pressing for an answer, but there would be time enough later. "Llamas, cattle and horses."

"I've never seen a llama up close."

"They make great pets. We raise them for their coats. Raising llamas is a hobby for my mother. She used to show them, but then people started wanting to buy them so we expanded the operation.

"Our stable is small compared to others who solely raise llamas. Few people realize that Sisters is the llama capital of the United States."

"Why here?"

"Central Oregon's climate is similar to that of Peru, where llamas originate. Sisters is ideal, open and temperate."

"I agree. This place is perfect."

Luke had a feeling she meant more than just the climate. He stopped in front of the house and his golden retriever bounded up to the Bronco. Opening the door, he received a series of wet dog kisses. "Whoa, girl. It's good to see you, too."

Suddenly, the dog's ears perked up and her head lifted. She dashed out of view before Luke could re-act, and Faith became the recipient of the retriever's sloppy love.

Luke rounded the corner of the Bronco and stopped. Faith kneeled with her arms around his dog. The sight made him smile.

"She's beautiful. What's her name?"

"Brandy."

"Luke, what's going on?" A female voice brought all three heads around to face the house. Reva stood on the porch, her hands on her hips and her red lips pressed into a stiff line.

Irritation pulsed through Luke, but he shook off the feeling. It was only natural Reva would be curious, but her question seemed more accusatory than not. He glanced at Faith, who now stood with her hands clasped together and a polite smile plastered on her face.

He silently retrieved Faith's bags and guided Faith toward the house. Brandy, he noted, stayed close to Faith.

"Who is this?" Reva asked, her eyes wide, as she looked Faith up and down.

"A guest," he answered, wishing Reva wouldn't act so territorially.

Brandy growled then let out a loud bark. Luke understood the dog's urge to protect Faith. He felt the same protective instincts roaring to life in his veins.

"Tell me what I want to hear," Vince Palmero demanded of the man on the phone.

Bob Grady cleared his throat. "Sorry, boss. We lost her trail in Portland, Oregon."

Vince clenched his fist. "How incompetent can you be?"

"We'll get her. I've got men combing the city and checking the trains, buses and airport."

"Time is running out. Find her!"

Vince slammed down the receiver and pushed back his leather chair from the expansive mahogany desk. He tugged on the collar of his Italian hand-made dress shirt feeling as choked with rage as if the Armani striped tie around his neck was being cinched tight. He couldn't believe she'd done this to him. If he didn't find her and bring her back soon, his whole life would go down the tubes.

He stared at the framed photo on his sidebar. A stunning smile and hazel eyes burned into his mind. He'd loved her, offered her everything and she'd betrayed him.

She'd pay. Oh, yes. When he found her, she'd pay.

Faith's sweaty palm stuck to the banister. She wiped her hand on her pant leg as she followed Luke and Reva up the stairs to his mother's room. Although the initial meeting with Reva went well—the woman had been pleasant enough—Faith could tell that Reva didn't like having another woman in what she obviously considered her domain.

As they'd passed through the living room, Faith noted the lack of Christmas decorations. Maybe these people didn't celebrate the birth of Jesus. Whether they did or not wasn't relative to her safety.

Luke knocked on a door at the end of the hallway. Little butterflies fluttered in the pit of Faith's stomach. If Luke's mother didn't like her, then what would she do? The ranch represented a security she'd only hoped of. She wanted to stay. *Please, oh, please, dear Lord, let her like me.*

At his mother's muffled, "Come in," Luke pushed open the door and stepped aside so Reva and Faith could enter. As Faith passed him, he gave her a reassuring smile and some of the butterflies in her stomach danced for an altogether different reason.

A blast of heat hit her in the face as she stepped into the room. The bedroom was at least ten degrees warmer than the rest of the house. Sweat beads broke out and trickled down Faith's neck. The dark haired woman lying on the canopied oak bed looked wilted and weak beneath the heavy covers pulled up to her chin.

"Ugh, Reva, it's hot in here," Luke exclaimed. "I've told you a hundred times not to touch the thermostat."

"But, Luke, honey, the doctor said she wasn't to get a chill."

In long strides, Luke moved to one window and yanked it open. Almost immediately a cooling breeze entered the room.

"Oh, that feels wonderful." Mrs. Campbell sighed. "I kept asking her to turn down the heat, but she wouldn't listen to me."

Luke paused in the act of pulling the quilt off his mother and looked at Reva. The color of his eyes had darkened to a steely blue and his jaw tightened in anger. Faith stepped back.

"I was only doing what I thought best. She's still recovering from her ordeal," Reva said defensively.

"The way she makes it sound, I'm still knocking on death's door," Luke's mother muttered.

"It's only been two weeks. You know—"

"Enough, Reva."

Luke's command abruptly stopped Reva mid-whine. She made a face and sat on the edge of a small desk by the window.

Faith marveled that at least one grown man was mature enough to contain his anger.

"Mom, I have someone here I'd like you to meet." Luke's voice softened.

The eager-to-please tone and the way his voice dropped a notch brought a pang to Faith's heart. This big man loved his mother and it showed. She'd loved her parents like that. If only they were still alive.

He motioned for Faith to step closer.

"This is Faith. I've hired her to help care for you."

Faith approached the bed. The gentle eyes regarding her made her think of her own mother. It had been years since anyone had looked at her with such kindness. She knew instantly she'd like the older woman.

Taking the offered hand, she noticed Mrs. Campbell's skin felt hot and clammy against her palm. "Mrs. Campbell, Luke tells me you're recovering from a heart attack. My grandfather suffered an attack and I cared for him. I—I hope you'll allow me to care for you."

"Please, call me Dottie. I'm sure we'll get along just fine."

From behind her, Faith heard Reva snort in disbelief. She turned to stare at Reva. Such disrespect was reprehensible.

"Reva, please," Luke warned.

Studying her nails, Reva said, "Luke, dear, the housekeeping still needs to be done. Or are you expecting her to do that, too?"

"No, I'm not expecting Faith to do the housekeeping."

"Good." Reva hopped off the edge of the desk and stood. "I'm sure Blake would be happy to know I'm helping out. I'll just stay on and do the housekeeping."

Faith glanced at Luke. His annoyance was evident in the creases along his brow. Turning his gaze to his mother, he raised a brow as if to ask what she thought. Dottie grimaced with a shrug.

Suddenly, Reva was standing close, pinning Faith against the bed. Trying to gracefully disengage herself from Dottie's hand, Faith shifted to allow Reva more room. Dottie's grip tightened and for a second Faith thought she saw a trace of apprehension in the older woman's blue eyes. She guessed there was more going on between the two women than met the eye.

Though the danger was minimal, the familiar need to protect rose sharply. Patting Dottie's hand reassuringly, Faith stood her ground, becoming a physical barrier between Dottie and Reva.

"Your dad promised me I'd have a place here, Luke. He did consider me a part of the family, especially after you took off."

The muscles in Luke's jaw visibly tightened. "My father and I came to an understanding long ago." Glancing at his mother, he asked, "Mom? This is your house now."

"If she wants to do the housekeeping, I suppose that's fine," Dottie muttered.

Luke gave a curt nod. "Fine. Just stick to the housekeeping, Reva."

"Of course, dear."

Faith noticed the small, triumphant gleam in Reva's gray eyes. She decided she didn't like the woman very much. She would have to be careful and keep her distance. Faith couldn't trust that Reva wouldn't look for an opportunity to get rid of her.

"Do you smell something burning?" Dottie struggled to sit up. Luke immediately reached to help her.

"Oh, my word! My casserole," Reva exclaimed. "There's something wrong with that oven," she muttered as she headed for the door. "It's forever burning things."

"There's nothing wrong with my oven," Dottie

groused at Reva's retreating back. "I've never burned anything in it."

"Of course not, mother." Luke's smile reflected in his eyes.

Dottie smiled back, and for a moment, the two silently communicated, their bond evident. Feeling like an intruder, Faith moved to the desk and ran a hand over the polished wood.

Deep inside, she felt a familiar emptiness. She would give anything to have someone love her the way Luke loved his mother. In her heart she longed for children, a family. But the possibility of having them was out of reach. She could be discovered at any time, and then what? A shudder racked her body.

Picking up the pitcher that sat on the desk, she poured a glass of water and carried it back to the bed. "Would you like some water, Dottie?"

"Thank you, dear." Dottie smiled and took the glass. "Sit and tell me about you."

Faith pulled up a chair. She couldn't very well tell Dottie the truth. So she did what she normally did and changed the subject. "You have a very nice home, Dottie. I noticed several good antique pieces."

Dottie's face lit up. "You know antiques? How wonderful."

A safe subject. Thank goodness. Faith smiled. "Yes, I do. You have good quality pieces."

"Well, if you ladies will excuse me, I'll go get some work done." Luke kissed Dottie's cheek.

"You go on, son. We'll be just fine." Dottie settled back with a grin.

To Faith, Luke said, "If you need anything, I'll be downstairs in the office. First door on your right at the bottom of the stairs."

"Thanks."

"Sure." He ran a hand over his short hair and for a moment just stood there staring at her.

Faith raised a questioning brow.

"See you later." He smiled before sauntering from the room.

"That's the first genuine smile I've seen from Luke since he's come home."

"Come home?" Faith asked, still staring at the spot where he'd disappeared through the door, feeling a little unsettled.

"Luke's a captain in the army," Dottie announced with obvious pride in her son.

"Right." Faith smiled at Dottie.

Dottie continued, "He graduated top of his class at West Point. I'm very proud of my son. He followed his dreams."

West Point. Impressive. "I'm…familiar with the school. My grandfather's house sat on the opposite bank of the Hudson River. From the top-floor window we could see part of the academy. Had I been born a boy, my grandfather would have insisted I attend West Point rather than my mother's alma mater, Cornell."

"I'm sure your grandfather was very proud of you. Blake didn't want Luke to go. It caused a rift in their relationship for years."

"That's too bad." Faith hoped the rift had been mended before Blake's death, but she thought it tactless to ask.

As if reading her unspoken thought, Dottie said, "Luckily they patched things up between them a few years ago. Blake was very proud of Luke, too."

"Was Luke able to see his father before he passed on?" Faith asked gently.

"Yes, thankfully." Her expression became troubled. "He wasn't supposed to stay this long but…I had my attack and…well, Blake's health had deteriorated over the last couple of years, so the ranch had been neglected for the most part."

Dottie paused to take a deep breath. "The hands that stayed on have kept things going, but it was Blake who made sure the upkeep and repairs were taken care of. Dear Blake just couldn't give up control. Not even when it became impossible for him to do more than sit and watch."

Compassion filled Faith. From her own experience with caring for her grandfather she knew how hard it was to watch someone you love die. Especially when that person was as strong-willed as her grandfather had been, and as Blake must have been. Faith held the older woman's hand. "I'm so sorry for your loss."

"Thank you, dear. I take comfort in knowing Blake's with Jesus and someday we will be together again."

Conviction shone bright in Dottie's blue eyes, like beacons of light directing the way.

Faith blinked back sudden tears. She wished desperately that she could be as assured of her own place in heaven and to be reunited with her family. But why would God take her to live with Him when He'd shown no interest in her on earth?

Dottie gave her hand a gentle squeeze. "Are you feeling okay?"

Faith cleared her throat before speaking. "Yes. Fine, thank you."

"You must forgive me if I tend to rattle on."

Thinking it infinitely better for Dottie to talk, she said, "Oh, please. Rattle all you'd like."

And she did. For Faith, the next couple of hours were a breath of fresh air. They discovered many common interests such as antiques, art, theater and cooking. And Faith was more than happy to exhaust all subjects except the topic of her own life. Soon Dottie was yawning and her eyelids drooping.

"Goodness, I don't think I've had this much to

talk about in years." Dottie beamed as Faith helped her settle back into a reclined position.

"Nor have I." Faith fluffed the pillows beneath Dottie's head. "You need some rest now. I'll come back later and we can pick up where we left off."

Dottie's eyes were already closed. Unsure what she should do now, Faith wandered over to a window and stood gazing out at the expanse of land that made up the Circle C Ranch. Never in her wildest dreams had she thought she'd find sanctuary in the home of a cowboy.

Could it be possible that God was watching out for her after all?

THREE

"Have you found her?"

Vince glared with loathing at his older brother, Anthony, slouched in the leather chair facing Vince's desk. He looked awful. Like he hadn't showered or shaved in weeks. His hair was too long and his clothes ratty. Vince struggled to understand how they'd come from the same gene pool. "Not yet. I can't believe your stupidity."

"How was I supposed to know she'd divorce you and take off? I mean, what did you do to her anyway?"

Vince curled his fingers into a fist. "Nothing."

"Something," Anthony shot back.

Ignoring the barb, Vince asked, "What did you tell Fernando?"

"What you told me to. He said he'd wait until New Year's Day. If we don't return the money, he'll kill us."

Vince spread his hand on the desk and leaned forward. "He can kill you with my blessing."

Anthony's dark eyes held malice. "Just remember what I did for you."

Vince swore and moved to the window.

They'd been teens, running with the other punks in the neighborhood, dealing dope, stealing what they could just for something to do. One night they'd knocked off a liquor store, but before they could get away, a cop showed up and caught Anthony. He'd gone to jail and never ratted on his baby brother.

Anthony never let Vince forget that if he'd had a rap sheet, he wouldn't have been admitted into law school.

But after twenty years, that card was wearing thin.

"I'll find her and get your money." Vince turned toward his brother. "And then we're even."

Anthony stood and walked to the door, his tennis shoes leaving smudged tracks in the cream-colored carpet. "Yeah, whatever you say."

After he left, Vince picked up the picture of his wife. "I will find you. And you will never leave me again."

Luke couldn't concentrate.

Every time he tried to focus on the paperwork lying on the desk, his mind conjured up the image of a cat-eyed blonde. Once again his curious nature wanted to know what was going on with Faith Delange.

He shouldn't be spending time thinking about Faith. There was still so much to do on the ranch.

He'd lost two hands last week because they'd wanted to find a warmer place for the winter. His foreman, Leo Scruggs, was having a hard time finding replacements. The roof on the house and one of the barns needed fixing and a llama would be birthing soon.

Ever since he'd returned to the ranch, his life hadn't been his own. Every day he found himself becoming more like his father. And the more he enjoyed being a rancher, the more scared he became.

This wasn't the life he'd wanted. He'd wanted excitement and adventure. At eighteen, he'd taken his desires to the Lord and had been steered toward the military. Knowing he'd had God's blessing, Luke had applied and been accepted at West Point. The years there were grueling, exciting and character building. He'd walked away with a degree in engineering. But the military still beckoned, even after his five-year service obligation.

Now, he held the rank of captain and his position of authority gave him more opportunity to make a difference in the lives of his men. From the beginning, he'd felt he'd been called to share his faith with his comrades, and now Luke was looked to as a source of comfort and hope.

He'd worked alongside the chaplain to form a Bible fellowship study, and he was constantly awed by the power of Jesus's love working in the men's lives. He didn't want to give that up.

He wished his father were still here.

Luke hadn't known about his father's cancer until nearly the end.

Your father is ill, the note had read, *come home.*

He'd arrived just in time to see his father before he'd died. Guilt for not having been there ate away at him. If he'd only been a better son and kept in better touch. He'd have learned of the illness sooner and come home. He'd have been able to make his dad's final days easier.

And now, Luke was running his father's ranch and dragging his feet about leaving when all he really wanted was to get back to his own life, his unit stationed in the Middle East. He only had another twenty days of leave left.

He fired up the computer and looked up Faith on Google. A list of articles came up. Mostly charity events where Faith and her grandfather were present. One photo showed Faith in a gray business suit standing beside her grandfather who sat in a wheelchair. He was old and hunched with strong features. The caption read, "The Delanges to start a foundation for overseas missions through a local church."

Philanthropy, faith, family and money. What was she running from?

A soft knock sounded on the door.

"Come in."

The door opened and Faith stepped in. He clicked off the web page.

"I don't mean to bother you. But…well, your mother's asleep and I don't know what I should be doing."

Luke hadn't the foggiest what she should be doing now, either.

She smiled uncertainly.

Luke stood and moved around the desk. "I'll show you to your room."

Faith followed him. "I think this place is wonderful. So warm and cozy."

"My parents have lived here since they were married. I don't think Mom has bought anything new since."

Faith stopped at the bottom of the stairs. Her finger traced a carving in the banister.

"Did that when I was ten. Dad just about blew a gasket." He laughed slightly. "I can still remember how he lit into me, saying, 'If you want to carve your name into a piece of wood, there's a whole stack of firewood out back that you can carve up after you split it all.'"

"He sounds like he was a good father."

"Yeah. Yeah, he was. Strict, but always fair. Even when we didn't see eye to eye, I never questioned his love."

But his father had questioned his son's love. How

many times had Luke turned his back on the advice and instruction his dad offered? Luke would give anything to have that time back, to show his dad how much he loved him.

"That's wonderful," she stated, wistfully.

"Did you question your parents' love?" he asked.

Sadness entered her gaze. "My parents were killed when I was eleven."

"That must have been tough. Who raised you?"

"My grandfather."

"The one that had a heart attack?"

She nodded. "He passed on almost two years ago."

"Have you been traveling since then?"

Her expression became guarded. Wary. "No."

She moved away from him to stand beside her suitcases where he'd left them in the entryway.

As she bent to pick them up, he said, "Here. Allow me."

Taking her bags in hand, he led her upstairs, entered the sewing room and breathed in the scent of gardenias, his mother's favorites, perfuming the air. A dried bouquet of the white blossoms sat atop the dresser. He made a mental note to order fresh ones.

"This is lovely." Faith walked in and surveyed the room. She gently brushed a hand along the black sewing machine resting on an old wooden table. "Your mother's, I assume."

"Yes, Mom loves to sew. She's made most of her own clothes for years." Luke could remember wanting her to go shopping like other mothers, but Dottie had always been a frugal woman who insisted her own creations were as good as those found in some over-priced dress shop.

"I like your mother. She's nice."

"Thanks. She likes you, too." Luke was thankful for that. It would make leaving that much easier.

Walking to the closet door, he put his hand on the knob. "Here's a closet. It's yours to use and you can clear out the drawers in the dresser."

"Thank you. You've been so kind."

He acknowledged her gratefulness with a nod. "My room's next door and the bath is across the hall."

Faith blinked and asked, "Where does Reva sleep?"

"She has her own house to go to." Thankfully.

"Besides caring for your mother, is there anything else I can do?"

"You can relax." He thought back to her strange behavior on the way to the ranch and his observation that she didn't want to be seen. "Maybe you should tell me what you're running from?"

Her eyes got big. "I'm…I don't know what you mean?"

"Faith, it was obvious you didn't want anyone to see you leave with me. Why?"

She looked at her hands. They were shaking. He

took them in his, noticing how slender and vulnerable she felt. "Tell me this. Are you in trouble with the law?"

She lifted her head. "No."

He could see the truth in her gaze. "Okay. I'll stop pushing for now. But, Faith, if you need to talk, I'm here. You can trust me."

Faith nodded, her expression unreadable. "I'll go check on Dottie."

The second she left the room, Luke dropped his head on the doorjamb. Great. Now he was offering to be there for her when he knew he would be leaving soon. He shouldn't let himself get tangled up with her. As along as she posed no threat to his mother. He wasn't going to get involved.

He just had to stay strong, remember his goals, and not let himself get diverted from his path. Pushing away from the door, he headed out to visit the llamas and to let God know just how much he needed His strength.

After making sure Dottie was comfortably settled for the night, Faith went back to her room. She sat on the bed, elbows propped on her knees and her chin resting in her palm. The afternoon had flown by as she and Dottie talked. There hadn't been any sign of Luke, not until dinnertime. He'd come upstairs carrying two plates heaping with a delicious-smelling rice-and-chicken casserole, which she assumed Reva had cooked.

When Dottie had asked why he wasn't eating with them, Faith noticed he'd glanced at her before saying he was going to eat in his office while finishing up some work. She'd been able to eat very little of the meal.

Had she made him rethink hiring her? She hadn't meant to be so obvious in the car. But the fewer people who knew where she was the longer she'd be safe. And the longer she'd be able to stay.

She finished unpacking and was about to crawl into bed when she heard the creak of floorboards outside her door.

Old fears surged, her muscles tensed. Was someone coming for her? Would someone bust through the door?

No! She was safe. It was only Luke going to his room.

Ugh! She couldn't jump at every sound. She'd drive herself nuts for sure doing that.

When the house finally grew quiet and still, she turned off the light. As tired as she was, it would be a long while before she could banish the awareness of the cowboy down the hall.

Early morning sun streamed through the barn windows, casting long, bright rays over the horses and the stacks of hay. The smell of the animals mingled with the hay.

Luke rested his hands on the pitchfork. Every morning he came out to the barn and fed the horses. He could assign the job to one of the hands, but the chore had been his when he was younger and somehow the task helped to relieve his grief over his father's passing. Hard physical labor helped get him through the worst of the pain.

When he'd first arrived, his father had barely been alive. If only he'd come home earlier, Luke thought for the millionth time as he pitched hay into the first stall. Those last few hours together hadn't been enough time to say all the things Luke had wanted to say. He hadn't told his father how much he admired him or how grateful he was to have had him as a father. Luke would always regret the years apart. The years of silence.

Once the funeral was over, Luke had harnessed his energies to the ranch. Luke started the re-fence on the entire acreage, started repairs on the barn and the corral. Chores that should have been taken care of long ago.

His next project, he decided, would be the main house. It needed a new roof and the porch could stand some work. Staring at the structure through the double doors of the barn, he pictured a swing on the front porch. His mother would like that. Luke shook his head in wry amusement. He shouldn't be looking for more reasons to stay.

His unit needed him.

It was past time for him to wrap things up on the ranch so he could leave right after Christmas. He could hire out the work that needed to be done. And for sure hire some more hands to replace the two that had left. His foreman needed a vacation, as well.

The burden of responsibility made Luke's shoulders ache.

At least he'd done something right by hiring Faith. For the past three days she'd been a constant companion to his mother. When he left he would be assured that his mom would be in good hands.

He picked up more hay with the pitchfork just as Faith stepped out onto the porch into the sunshine. He took a deep breath and enjoyed the view, noticing the way winter sunlight danced off her golden hair, reminding him of Christmas lights. Bright and shining. Beautiful.

Her light wool coat, buttoned to the top, looked warm, but wouldn't hold up once it snowed again. She wrapped slender hands around a steaming mug and walked to the porch railing. Leaning her hips against the wood, she stared out at the scenery and sipped from the cup.

Luke knew what she was seeing; he'd stood in the exact spot too many times to count. From that vantage point, one could view the cattle grazing and the Three Sisters Mountains—Faith, Hope and Charity—rising majestically in the distance.

Studying Faith's profile, he wondered, what's your story? A part of him wanted to delve deep and find out what she was hiding from. But he'd already decided he wasn't going to get any more deeply involved.

Faith turned her head toward the barn and Luke knew the exact moment she saw him. Her eyes crinkled at the corners and her generous mouth curved upward into a stunning smile. His pulse quickened. For a heartbeat, Luke almost convinced himself she was glad to see him.

Feeling like a schoolboy caught staring at his teacher, he raised his hand in greeting, and sucked in his breath when she sat the mug down and pushed away from the railing. Mesmerized, he watched her walk across the porch and down the stairs, every movement flowing from her with graceful ease.

From around the corner of the house Brandy bounded up to Faith, who bent to nuzzle the dog's neck. A ridiculous sense of jealousy tore through Luke. He rolled his eyes. *You can't be jealous of your dog.* But he would've given anything to be on the receiving end of Faith's affection.

Faith and Brandy came forward and stopped steps from where he stood.

Luke tipped his hat. "Morning." Up close, she was even more attractive.

"Good morning, Luke."

He tore his gaze away from hers with effort and stared down at Brandy. "Seems you found yourself a friend."

Her hand stroked behind the dog's ears. "Yes, I have."

"It's good to have friends," Luke remarked, once again plagued by questions about this woman.

"Uh-huh."

The noncommittal answer made him frown. "Did you leave many friends behind?" he asked.

Visibly tensing at his words, she clasped her hands together, the knuckles turning white. "Some." The single word echoed in the barn.

"It's hard leaving behind the people you love." He said it more as a statement than a question, knowing firsthand how hard it was to walk away from the important people in his own life. And how difficult it would be to do again.

"Yes, it is," she agreed softly.

"Do you want to talk about it?"

She shook her head, her expression wary.

"I'm a good listener." What was he doing? He'd told himself he wasn't going to do this.

She gave him a tentative smile. "Thanks, I'll remember that. Actually, I was hoping you'd help me get your mother downstairs when you have a chance. She's been walking around upstairs but she'll need help negotiating a flight of stairs. The first time we try, I feel you should be present."

"Sure. When I finish here I'll be right up."

"Great. Dottie will be so pleas—" She stopped and cocked her head to one side.

The crunch of gravel sounded on the drive. But from where they stood they couldn't see the vehicle.

"Are—are you expecting someone?" Faith's voice changed.

Luke heard and saw the fear sweeping over her. "No, but people—friends—stop by all the time."

The vehicle on the drive stopped and the sound of a door opening and closing echoed in the chilly air.

In one swift, graceful motion, Faith darted to a darkened corner of the barn where she pressed her back against the wall, her hands fisted at her sides.

"Faith, you're safe here—" Luke was silenced by the finger she put to her lips and the look of terror on her face.

"Okay, God, please cover me," Luke mumbled and moved closer, positioning himself between Faith and the door. A brief look of comprehension passed across her features before they heard the heavy footfalls coming toward the barn. Each step drew the unknown closer.

Luke tensed in response to Faith's palpable apprehension. But how could he protect her when he didn't know what she was afraid of?

A small, panic-born whimper escaped her as a man stepped into view.

FOUR

Luke exhaled a rush of adrenaline and moved forward. "Matt Turner, you old dog."

As he shook Matt's hand, Luke glanced at Faith. The tension in her expression eased and her body went limp against the barn wall.

He figured Faith could use a moment alone.

Guiding Matt toward the empty corral, Luke stationed himself so he could see the barn. "What brings you out this way so early?"

Matt pushed back his black cowboy hat. "Just thought I'd come and see what my good buddy's been up to. We haven't seen much of you since you came home. Sally'd love for you to come out to the house for dinner some night."

Luke smiled at the invitation and the note of affection in Matt's voice for his wife. The couple had been high school sweethearts, clearly meant for each other. Luke and Matt had been friends since they were in diapers, and Luke should have made an effort to see the couple and their kids.

"Dinner would be great. I'd like that." Luke kept his eyes on the barn. Was Faith okay?

Faith stepped from the shadows and looked in his direction before hurrying toward the house.

What was going on? He wanted to know what had her so tied up in knots. He wanted to protect her. Help her.

But first, he had to win her trust.

Inside, Faith struggled to calm her racing heart. The panic still hadn't abated, but at least she could take a breath now. Dottie chatted away, oblivious to Faith's inner chaos. And Faith couldn't track the stream of words. She wanted to be attentive. She really did.

But her focus, her self-preservation instincts demanded her attention. She stared out the window at Luke and his friend.

How could she explain to Luke about the overwhelming sense of danger she lived with?

If she told him why she was running, what then? Would he ask her to leave? Or would he want to play the hero and promise to protect her?

She gave a silent scoff. No one could protect her. Hadn't she already learned that lesson well enough?

Maybe she should leave now, before she became too attached to Dottie, Luke and ranch life.

The thought of leaving brought sadness to her heart. She wanted to stay and make sure Dottie fully recovered.

Luke's confidence and trust in her judgment about his mother's care had warmed her. It'd been so long since she'd felt anything but the icy chill of fear, she'd forgotten how nice it was to feel heated from the inside out.

"Faith," Dottie said, concern evident in her voice. "Honey, are you all right?"

Turning toward the woman propped up against the pillows on the bed, she said, "Yes. Yes, I'm fine."

She would be fine here on the ranch. Here she was safe. Her paranoia had gotten the better of her earlier. She'd have to be more careful not to let her fear show.

Putting the episode behind her, Faith sat on the edge of the bed and made a conscious effort to concentrate as Dottie explained the basics of knitting.

As Faith cleared the dishes from dinner in Dottie's room, Dottie touched Faith's hand and gave a gentle squeeze. "Thank you, my dear. You are an answer to my prayers. You can't know how grateful I am that you're here."

Impulsively, Faith bent and kissed the older woman's cheek. More than Dottie could know or Faith could explain, being at the Circle C was like living another life. A life infinitely better than her own. "And being here is an answer to *my* prayers."

She was determined not to allow any more bouts of paranoia intrude on her peace of mind.

"Faith, why do you seem so sad at times?"

"I'm tired." That didn't answer what she'd been asked, but it was the best she could do. She tried to smile past the sudden tightness of her rib cage.

Concern marred Dottie's brow. "It's more than that." Her eyes narrowed shrewdly. "Faith, I'm here if you want to talk."

The knot tightened at the offer of a confidante. How she wished she had the fortitude to spill her secrets to this kind woman, but Faith wouldn't risk the Campbells' safety any more than she had to.

Her throat constricted, making speech difficult. "I appreciate your concern, Dottie. I'm—I'm really just a little worn out." Worn out in many ways.

Doubt clouded Dottie's eyes. "You're probably hungry, as well. You hardly touched your food again at dinner. Why don't you go down and fix yourself something to eat before you go to bed."

The thought of food made her stomach roll. Admittedly, the little she'd eaten had been very good. She made a mental note to compliment Reva. "I'll be fine. It's hard adjusting to new surroundings."

"You really should eat more. You're too thin."

Faith smiled at the familiar words. Her grandfather had often lamented that she would blow away in a strong wind. "I'll eat a big breakfast."

Dottie nodded.

Faith helped Dottie settle back against the pillows. "Can I get you anything?"

"No, dear. Thank you."

"Then I'll let you get some rest." She turned to go.

"Faith?"

"Yes?"

"God is a great listener. He longs for His children to give Him their burdens."

Faith blinked. "His children?"

Dottie nodded. "He looks at all of us as His children. And as any parent wants to do, He wants to comfort and protect. That's not to say He'll rescue us from all our troubles, but He promises to be with us, offering wisdom and guidance."

The thought of God as a benevolent and loving parent boggled Faith's mind and opposed everything she'd been taught.

Hadn't grandfather often claimed that God sat in judgment of each individual and that His righteous wrath would fall upon the heads of those who opposed Him?

A dull ache started at her temple. Was what Dottie said fact or fiction? How did she go about finding the truth? Faith rubbed her eyes.

"Oh, honey, I'm sorry. Here I am yapping away when you need your rest."

"That's okay, Dottie." Faith managed to smile. "I'll see you in the morning."

Quickly, she left the room.

In the dimly lit hallway, a hand touched Faith's arm. She gasped. Her heart slammed against her chest. She jerked back. And focused on Luke.

She sagged against the wall. The sudden fear went spiraling through her abdomen where it landed in her stomach with a burning crash. "You scared me."

"Sorry, didn't mean to." He had the grace to look sheepish. "We need to talk."

A heaviness swept over her, weighing her down. The urge to run and hide streaked through her, but she couldn't make her feet move. Deep inside she knew her only real option was to stay and face his curiosity. But did it have to be right now?

"Can't this wait until morning?" she asked.

"No, we need to discuss what happened in the barn and what, exactly, you're running from."

The tightness in her chest spread, and her breathing turned shallow. *I'm running from the outside world,* her mind screamed.

The mere thought of what waited for her out there made her head spin and lights explode in her vision.

"Faith, what's wrong?"

She heard his voice, heard the concern in his tone. The words echoed inside her head, making the already dull ache grow and sharpen. She really should have eaten more.

Between her low blood sugar, the unexpected fright of moments ago and Luke's probing, Faith was helpless against the inevitable.

She tried to answer, her mouth opened, but no words formed. The hall grew dim and her vision closed in upon itself while the world faded away.

She heard Luke anxiously call her name.

Luke caught Faith before she crumpled into a heap at his feet. He checked her pulse. The beat steady. The slow rise and fall of her chest showed she was breathing.

"Faith? Faith. Honey, wake up." Patting her cheeks didn't seem to help any.

Scooping one arm beneath Faith's legs and the other under her back, he lifted her. She was soft and light in his arms as he carried her to her room. A faint, pleasing smell of flowers scented her hair.

Trying not to jostle her much, Luke laid her on the bed then sat on the edge and rubbed her hands.

She stirred, her eyelids fluttered, then slowly opened.

Unexpected tenderness grabbed a hold of him. He tucked a lock of blond hair behind her ear, his fingers brushed across her cheek, the skin satin smooth and warm to his touch. Her eyes widened slightly and he withdrew his hand. "How are you feeling?"

"Wh—what happened?"

"You fainted."

Her teeth pulled at her bottom lip. "I guess I'm more tired than I thought." She smiled, weakly.

It was from more than fatigue.

He studied her face, liking the way her dark blond brows arched high over eyes that slanted ever so slightly upward at the corners, the way her little nose wrinkled up when she didn't like something, and especially the shape of her mouth.

Full and lush. Kissable.

Faith sat up, her body barely inches from his.

"Luke?"

Her voice held a question or an invitation, he didn't know which.

He swallowed but made no move.

She was beautiful and sensitive, strong and yet, so vulnerable. She was defenseless, exhausted, and in need of his protection, not his kisses. Plus, this was exactly what he'd been trying to avoid.

He didn't want an entanglement.

He jumped to his feet. One second longer and his resolve would have weakened. A man could only withstand so much.

"I'll—I'll just let—you get some sleep," he stammered and tried to back out of the room gracefully, but bumped against the doorjamb. "I'll—see you in the morning." He exited quickly, pulling the door closed behind him.

Smooth, Campbell. Real smooth.

Disgusted with herself, Faith flopped back onto the pillows. What was the matter with her? She'd never felt like this before. And the last thing she needed was to kiss Luke. Yet, she'd wanted to.

More than she could have ever imagined.

Uh-oh.

She must fight this attraction to him. He was her employer. She couldn't allow him to turn into anything more. Not only would her job be on the line, but her safety.

And Dottie.

Faith wouldn't want to be forced to leave her if something went…wrong.

Though her mind agreed, the rapid beat of her heart contradicted the logic.

She couldn't let her heart rule. Not in this situation. Too much was at stake.

Morning found Luke sitting at his desk, staring out the window. The Three Sisters Mountains rose high in the distance, their snow-covered peaks creating a breathtaking view.

But the beauty of nature offered him no peace. He hadn't slept much the night before. His mind wandered during his nightly devotions. He'd finally shut his Bible and dropped to his knees. Praying had always been a time of restoration and peace, a way to calm his mind before going to sleep.

But sleep proved to be elusive.

Images of Faith, her mouth inches from his, had haunted his dreams. He'd gotten up early, intent on getting some work done. After giving his foreman, Leo, permission to go into town to hire some hands, Luke meant to take advantage of this dry cold spell and start calling some roofing companies to come out and give him a bid, but so far he'd only managed to drink a pot of coffee.

The jingle of the phone pulled his gaze from the mountains to the phone on his desk. Picking up the receiver, he heard voices coming over the line.

"What do you need, Ethel?" Reva asked impatiently, having answered the phone in the kitchen.

"Just tell Luke I'm on the phone." Ethel's annoyance was clear in her tone. Ever since Reva had made Ethel's daughter, Molly, cry at their high-school graduation, Ethel had little tolerance for the woman.

"He's busy working. I'll take a message," Reva insisted.

Luke spoke up. "I've got it, Reva. You can hang up."

"But, Luke, honey, you said you didn't want to be disturbed." The whiny quality of her voice grated across his already tightly strung nerves.

"It's okay, Reva, just hang up." He waited until he heard a click. "Sorry, Ethel. What can I do for you?"

"Well, I thought I'd better call. Some man came in this morning, nosing around about that gal you had breakfast with."

Luke sat up straight. "What did he want?"

"He flashed her picture around the diner and wanted to know where he could find her. Of course, half the folks in here today were in here the other day. Everyone agreed that the woman in the picture was the one who had talked with you. A few people said they saw her get in your rig before you left town."

The worry in Ethel's voice mirrored the anxiety gathering steam in his belly.

"Did the man say who he was or why he wanted to find her?" His muscles bunched in anticipation of the answer.

"Just said he was a private investigator. He's on his way out to your place now."

An anxious ripple cascaded over him. A private investigator. He mulled that over in his mind. "Thanks for calling and warning me, Ethel. I owe you."

"You be sure to take care of that pretty little gal. I have a feeling she's in some sort of trouble."

"I will. Thanks, Ethel."

Luke started to return the receiver but he hesitated, listening to the click from Ethel hanging up and then another audible click. Anger tightened the muscles in his jaw.

He walked into the hall and raised his voice, "Reva!"

She stepped into the doorway of the kitchen wearing a tight leather skirt and high boots. Her pink fuzzy sweater looked like sticky cotton candy. "Yes, dear?"

Holding on to his patience, he gritted his teeth. "Do not call me dear. And do not listen in on other people's conversations. It's rude."

She blinked. "I don't know what you're talking about."

"Yes, you do." He spun on his heels and went in search of Faith.

After checking upstairs, he went out the front door. He saw her standing at the fence, petting the llamas. Her blond hair hung loosely about her shoulders, swishing with every move of her head. She looked both out of place and yet perfectly at home in her wool coat and jeans.

Luke gave himself a shake. There was business to attend to. He wanted to be ready when the private investigator showed up, and for that, he needed to know what he was dealing with in order to protect everyone on the ranch. As Ethel said, the girl was in some kind of trouble and he refused to go into the situation blind.

He approached the fence and several llamas came to him wanting attention. He nuzzled each for a moment, aware that Faith had also turned toward him.

"Good morning."

Her tentative greeting charmed him. "Morning."

A smile curved her lush lips and reached her eyes, making the kaleidoscope of colors sparkle. The sharp winter sunlight glinted off a thin silver chain around her neck. Luke noticed the tiny box lying against her skin.

He pulled his attention back to the animals. "That's Blondie."

"Excuse me?" Faith's expression filled with confusion.

He nodded his head toward the animal which had its nose nestled in her hair. "The llama."

"Oh." She leaned her head onto Blondie's neck. "She sure is friendly."

"Uh-huh." Luke turned away. He frowned, aware that this wasn't the first time he'd felt deprived because she was giving her affection to one of his animals. He didn't like the feeling. He told himself he didn't want her affection.

She turned back toward the mountains. "Luke, about last night."

His stomach clenched. Last night, he'd made an

idiot of himself. He'd shied away from her and their mutual attraction like a skittish colt.

But he wouldn't think about that right now. There were more pressing matters to discuss. "Faith, I need to ask you something."

"I know." She sighed heavily. "You want to know about why I panicked in the barn. But, really—I—there's nothing to tell. I don't—I don't know why it happened. I suppose I've been traveling alone for too long."

"Faith, look at me."

Slowly she turned and their gazes locked. He saw her unspoken plea to let it go. And he supposed if the situation hadn't taken on a new edge, he might have tried to accept her explanation. But, at any moment, a man would be driving up and they needed to be ready.

"Why would a private investigator be looking for you?"

Even though he expected a reaction, the change was dramatic. Her eyes widened, the color drained from her complexion and for a moment he thought she'd faint again.

In a sudden movement that sent the llamas stumbling back, she darted past him and ran toward the house. He was so startled by her action, it took a full thirty seconds before he was able to make his feet move.

FIVE

"No, oh no. Please, God, no. Oh, no."

Faith put a hand to her throat, her breath coming in short, shallow bursts. Her mind raced. If a private investigator had tracked her down this quickly, it was only a matter of time before Vince showed up. She couldn't be here when that happened.

What a fool she'd been to believe God cared. He would never provide her with sanctuary. She wasn't safe, not even on a ranch in the middle of nowhere. Vinnie's tentacles reached far and wide, and now she'd put good, decent people in jeopardy because she'd selfishly wanted to pretend to have a normal life.

Shame and dread vied for a place in her heart. She could hear the harshness of her breathing while she struggled to pull out her suitcases. After dumping them on the bed, she began stuffing the contents of the dresser drawers into the open bags. Haste made her sloppy, but she didn't care. She rushed to the closet and took the clothes, hangers and all, and stuffed them into the bags. The cases wouldn't close.

"Close. Come on, close," she muttered. Her hands shook so hard she couldn't hold on to the fasteners.

Luke appeared in the doorway. He stood with his arms held rigidly at his sides, his body tense. She could feel his gaze on her and guilt clawed at her insides, the pain only adding to her urgency. She'd put his family in danger. He'd never forgive her when he learned the truth.

The crunch of tires on the ice-crusted drive below her window filled the air, and panic seized her, its grip tight and strong. She turned her back on Luke and looked wildly around the room. She had to get out of there, but how?

She made choppy, shaky slashes in the air with her hands. "Okay, okay. Think. Think."

She couldn't think. Her brain was having a malfunction. Somewhere, deep inside, the thought that it was over came crashing through. "God, please not like this."

Luke's hands settled on her shoulders and turned her around. She tried to shrug away. "No, no. I have to get out of here." She struggled against the strength of his grip, but his hold only grew tighter.

"Shh… It's okay." He gathered her hands in his. "I'm not going to let anything happen to you."

His words rumbled through her offering solace.

What was she to do now? He said it would be okay, but it wouldn't. She was trapped.

Outside, Brandy barked wildly and a car door slammed shut.

Faith jumped.

"Let me handle this."

Luke's voice washed over her, the timbre throaty and deep. He stroked her hair, then her cheek, wiping away tears she hadn't realized she'd shed.

"What will you say?" she asked.

"I'll think of something," he said, his voice stronger now, authoritative, in command.

"But…" Would he be able to put off the P.I.? Either way, she had to leave. Once Luke learned the truth, he'd send her packing, anyway. He'd have to. To protect his family.

"Trust me, Faith."

She hesitated. Trust was given in two ways—one, by someone earning that trust, and two, by a leap of faith. At this moment Luke held her life in his hands and he wanted her to trust him. It was a combination of both that made her nod slowly.

"Later, you will tell me what's going on." His tone held a silent warning. He wouldn't be put off any longer. "Stay put and out of sight."

He gave a short nod of his head and then disappeared, his footsteps receding down the stairs and out the front door. Faith ran to the window and peeked out the corner of the curtain. Below, a short, balding man, looking very much out of place in his off-the-rack suit and tie, held out his hand as Luke came into view.

Sinking to the floor, she fingered the prayer box at her neck. "Oh, Lord, what do I do now?"

Tears once again welled up in her eyes and one by one slipped down her cheeks. How was she going to find the words to tell Luke about Vinnie?

"What can I do for you, Mr.—" Luke's gaze raked over the man, noting the muscular build beneath the dark suit and red-striped tie. The hard lines etched into the guy's face put him at about fifty.

"Mr. Costello." The man held out his beefy hand.

Luke shook the offered limb. "What brings you to the Circle C, Mr. Costello?"

"I'm looking for a woman you might have seen."

Luke kept his expression carefully blank. "Oh?"

"Her name is Faith Palmero. Tall, blonde, cat-like eyes."

A sinking feeling anchored itself in Luke's gut. He frowned. "Palmero?"

"She's probably going by an alias." Withdrawing a photo from his inside pocket, he held it out. "Here, I have a picture of her."

Aware of the man's shrewd gaze, Luke took the

snapshot and quietly sucked in his breath. There could be no mistaking the woman in the photo. Faith. The snapshot looked as if it was taken straight from the society pages.

A confident smile sparkled on her lips and her hair was piled high upon her head. Diamond earrings sparkled from her earlobes and a diamond and pearl choker accentuated the slender column of her neck.

Feeling sick, he handed the picture back. She didn't belong on a ranch in the middle of Oregon, so what was she doing here? *God, grant me wisdom now.*

"So, have you seen her?"

Snapping his mind to attention, Luke countered, "Why are you looking for her?"

"I'm sorry. Client confidentiality, you know." The man looked past Luke to the house. Luke turned to follow his gaze and saw Reva standing just inside the screen door.

Turning back around, Luke stifled the urge to grab the man by the collar. "Who's your client?"

Mr. Costello smiled tightly. "Sorry."

Luke fisted his hands. He wasn't going to let this man or anyone else harm Faith. "Is this woman in some kind of trouble?"

"So, you have seen her." Mr. Costello looked pleased with himself.

So much for his poker face. Luke shrugged non-committally and hoped Reva would stay silent.

"People in town said they saw you with her." Mr. Costello's eyes narrowed.

"I met her the other day," Luke conceded. "Seemed like a real nice lady."

"Hmm. Did she happen to say where she was headed?" The man's eyes scrutinized Luke before he darted a glance at Reva, who blessedly stayed put.

"No, she didn't." Then inspiration hit. "Oh, wait. She did mention something about wanting to see the tundra."

If he wasn't going to get any information out of the P.I., he'd just as soon wish him on his way.

"Tundra?" Mr. Costello screwed up his face in puzzlement.

"Tundra, as in Alaska." That should keep him busy for a while. Alaska was a big place and people there didn't tend talk to strangers.

"You think she went to Alaska?" The man wrinkled his large nose in distaste.

Luke steered the man toward his rented car. "Yes, I definitely remember her mentioning Alaska."

Mr. Costello stopped. "Did she have a car?"

Luke shook his head as he opened the car door. "Not that I know of."

"Uh, well…thanks. If you hear from her, would you please give my office a call?" He handed Luke a card before sliding behind the wheel of the sedan.

Luke stepped back and closed the door. *When the tundra melts.*

The sedan slowly moved down the drive and out to the road. Luke looked down at the card in his hand with the man's name and a New York address. Crumpling the card, he turned toward the house.

Reva came down the stairs, purse in hand. "Who was that man?"

Maybe she hadn't heard their conversation. Luke didn't have time now to deal with her. "Nobody that concerns you."

Her mouth drew into a pout. "Oh."

Luke stood fast under her scrutiny and relaxed when she shrugged.

"I'm off to town for groceries."

Unease slithered down his spine. "Why now?"

"Well, I can't very well cook a soufflé without butter or eggs," she chirped and hurried to her sports car.

"Wait!" he called, not liking the timing.

She either didn't hear him or ignored him as she climbed inside. She sped away faster than she should. She'd let the subject go too easily. He should have stopped her just in case she had some idea of going after the P.I. and asking questions.

He could only pray she minded her own business.

Because right now, he had to talk to Faith.

* * *

"You can relax, he's gone." Luke's voice brought Faith's head up from where it rested on her knees.

"He's gone?" That seemed too easy.

Luke stepped farther into the room. "I told him you'd mentioned seeing the tundra."

Faith's heart melted to her toes. He'd protected her and without knowing why. "Thank you."

He saluted. "U.S. Army, ma'am. Specially trained to rescue damsels in distress or small countries from military aggression."

"It sounds like a well-rounded program."

"We aim to please." He moved closer and held out his hand.

Without hesitation, she placed her hand in his and allowed him to pull her to her feet. They stood toe to toe with her hand still encased within his grasp, the heat from the contact spreading over her like sunshine on frozen snow. She looked into his face and for one dizzying moment she thought he might kiss her. Standing so close to him made her ache with yearning. A yearning that overruled her head and tore at her heart.

"Who are you?" he asked, his eyes holding questions.

Alarm shot through her, effectively shattering the moment. She withdrew her hand. "No one you need to worry about."

He gave her a level look. "What is your last name?"

Tension, like a hard solid knot, twisted in her soul. "What does it matter?"

She knew it mattered a great deal.

He set his jaw in a stubborn line. "It matters, Faith."

Unable to meet his eyes, she stared at the scar on his jaw. Luke lifted her chin with the rough pad of his index finger until their gazes locked. "Tell me."

Pulling away from him, she walked to the window and stared out at the blue sky. How much should she say? Everything?

She closed her eyes tight. If she told him everything, he'd tell her to leave. Her fists clenched at her side. Leaving was the last thing she wanted to do.

She liked living on the ranch, she cared for Dottie a great deal and…her mind skidded away from examining her feelings for Luke. Suffice it to say, leaving would be more painful than anything else she'd had to endure.

But if the danger had moved on to Alaska, did she have to say anything?

With Vinnie's private investigator looking for her in the frozen north, she was safe on the Circle C. Why spoil it with tales of her sordid mistakes from the past?

"You know—how sometimes—you imagine something and then when you're faced with the reality of it, it doesn't live up to the image in your mind?"

When Luke didn't respond, she turned to face him. The expression on his face showed his confusion but she also knew she had his attention. "Being here on your ranch, caring for your mother and—" Unready to finish the thought aloud, she dropped her eyes to the buttons on his shirt.

She took a deep breath and lifted her eyes to meet his gaze. "It has far surpassed anything my feeble mind could conjure up."

Luke's brows creased. "Faith…"

She held up a hand in a gesture of entreaty. "Please. I want the past to stay in the past. I just can't drag it all out for your inspection. It's not important."

"Faith, if you're in some kind of trouble with the law, you need to tell me."

"No. It's nothing like that. I haven't done anything wrong. I mean, it's just not important."

"You were scared out of your mind. You honestly expect me to believe it's not important?" He stepped closer, filling the space between them.

"It's not," she insisted and clasped her hands together to keep them from trembling. "You sent that man to Alaska. He won't be back and no one knows I'm here. No one needs to know I'm here. Please try to understand."

"I don't understand. Who do you *not* want to know you're here?"

He took her hands and held them tight. An anchor

in the storm. The simple gesture weakened her already wobbly knees and tears welled in her eyes. "It's a family matter, Luke. It has nothing to do with you." He was such a good man, he could never understand someone like Vinnie. "It just doesn't matter."

With the pad of his thumb he wiped away a stray tear coursing down her face. "It does matter. You matter, Faith."

The sincerity in his voice, in his eyes touched her deeply. If her heart weren't already in a puddle at his feet, it would've melted. She had to tell him the truth. Or at least a watered down version. "When my grandfather died, I came into a great deal of money. Money that other people thought they had a right to. The pressure just became too much for me. Now, those people are trying to bring me back."

"Who are these people?"

"Investors. Charitable organizations. People my grandfather promised money to but didn't include in his will. They have no legal standing, but it doesn't stop them from making my life miserable."

"You didn't want to give them the money?"

She hated the look of disapproval in his eyes. "It wasn't that. The situation was very complicated and overwhelming. No one had proof that grandfather had made any promises. I didn't know who to believe."

He took a deep breath and she held hers, waiting to see if he'd decide to let her stay or to send her on her way.

"Who's Palermo?"

There was no way to avoid telling him. "My ex-husband."

His jaw tightened. "I see."

"Are you going to make me leave?"

"Of course not," he replied. "You're welcome to stay as long as you want. You'll be safe here." He turned to go.

She had to know or it would eat her alive. "Luke?"

He turned back toward her, his gaze intense and focused. "Yes?"

"Why—why did you protect me?"

"I like you," he stated simply.

"Oh." She hadn't expected the admission but it filled her with joy. Tears gathered at the back of her eyes again.

Luke tipped his hat and strode from the room.

Softly, she whispered, "I like you, too."

What kind of idiot am I? Luke tightened the stirrup strap with a hard yank, drawing a snort from his horse, Winter.

"Sorry, boy," Luke muttered to the big, black beast.

It's a family matter.

My ex-husband.

The idea of Faith being married made something inside Luke cringe and grow hot. A curious burning sparked low in his abdomen and slowly worked its way up into his chest. He dropped his head to Winter's neck.

I'm struggling here, God. Really struggling. I need to stay focused on what I want. On what You want for me.

An image of Faith, her tear-filled eyes looking at him so defenselessly slammed into his mind. His heart ached. Resolutely, he pushed her from his mind.

My career, Lord. That's what I should be focused on. I want to get back to my life, my ministry. The men need me.

More images of Faith barged into his consciousness.

The first time he'd laid eyes on her, standing in the doorway of the diner, her expression wary. Haunted.

Faith nuzzling a llama. The soft smile curving her lips. The look of contentment in her eyes.

The panic when he'd told her about the P.I.

The way her eyes had widened when he'd admitted he liked her.

Frustration ripped through him, leaving an aching wound in its wake. Muttering, he shook his head. "Cut it out. You're leaving and she has no place in your life."

A verse of scripture came to him. Luke closed his eyes. 'Bear one another's burdens, and thus fulfill the law of Christ.'

He'd been trying to live that verse through his work in the military. Now he was to take on Faith's burden, too?

He couldn't turn his back on her.

Not like he'd done with his father. His chest squeezed tight. If he'd cared more for his parents than himself and his career, maybe his father wouldn't have gotten so sick. And his mother wouldn't have had a heart attack.

His shoulders weighted down with guilt and remorse for his selfishness, he led Winter out of the stall. He needed to ride and clear his thoughts, but as he mounted Winter he glanced up and saw Faith at the window.

Her image was forever branded in his mind.

Faith went to the window in Dottie's room, again. She scanned the distance for any sign of Luke. It'd been hours since she'd seen him gallop off, kicking up mud and snow. She hoped he wasn't angry with her, or worse, disappointed. His opinion mattered to her. Though why, didn't make sense.

"Is something the matter, Faith?" Dottie asked, pausing in her daily routine of walking around the upstairs to get some exercise.

The late afternoon sun danced on the glistening snow. "Oh, no. I was just thinking how beautiful it is outside."

"It is nice out. I think we should go out and enjoy what's left of the afternoon while we can." An eager smile lit Dottie's features, making her appear healthy and younger than her fifty-eight years. "I heard the weatherman say we'd be seeing more snowfall within a few days."

"Then let's enjoy today while it's clear."

"Sounds good to me. Shall we go outside?"

"Let's."

It might even help take her mind off her troubles.

Taking Dottie by the arm, Faith helped her down the stairs. After the first venture outdoors with Luke's help, Faith had managed to help Dottie herself, thanks to Dottie's returning strength.

They could hear Reva in the kitchen and by silent agreement they went out the front door. As they went down the porch stairs, Faith scanned the road in the distance. A pickup truck carrying bales of hay went by. On the left side of the drive, beyond the fence, the llamas stood in small groups, grazing on scattered hay. The corral on the right side of the drive stood empty.

"I love days like this." Dottie turned her face up to the sun. "Blake used to say the clean, fresh winter air made the move to Oregon worthwhile."

"You didn't always live here?"

"Oh, no. Blake and I were originally from Salt Water, Texas. We moved here right after we got married." Dottie started down the drive toward the llamas. The snow had been shoveled off to the sides to form small mounds.

Faith fell into step with her. "Do you still have family in Texas?"

"We do. Both Blake and I have siblings still living there. Sometimes I miss not having family close by and I think Luke missed out, too." Regret crept into Dottie's voice. "We weren't able to have any more children."

"I'm sorry."

"Oh, don't be. God blessed us with Luke, and Blake, bless his heart, thought of Reva as a daughter."

"And—you didn't?"

"No. No, we never really connected. Not even when she was little." Dottie sighed. "Her family lived on the next ranch over. She was always coming around, getting into things. Especially after her mama ran off. Then things went from bad to worse. Her dad drank himself to death."

"No wonder she turned to you and Blake."

Dottie nodded. "That she did. And Blake had always hoped that one day Luke would stop thinking of Reva as a nuisance and marry her."

Surprised by that tidbit, Faith had a better understanding of why Reva viewed her as a threat.

Reaching to nuzzle the first llama to reach them, Dottie cooed, "Ah, here are my beauties."

"Hi there, Blondie." Faith stroked the neck of a light-colored llama that had nudged her shoulder.

Dottie laughed. "That's Ricky. Blondie is over by the barn."

"Oops, sorry boy."

"You know, someday, I hope I'll have some grandbabies to spoil." Dottie gave Faith a sidelong glance over Ricky's head.

Faith stared ahead, choosing not to interpret Dottie's look. Instead, she fought down a sudden wave of jealousy for the woman Luke would someday marry and have children with. "You know there's only fifteen days left until Christmas."

Dottie's gaze clouded. "I'd forgotten. I usually have decorations up right after Thanskgiving, but—" Dottie sighed. "I haven't been in a very festive mood."

"That's understandable."

Taking Faith's arm, Dottie said, "But it's time to throw off the melancholy and get ready to celebrate the birth of Jesus. When Luke gets back he can get the decorations from the attic."

"That would be wonderful," Faith agreed.

This Christmas would be a celebration. She was free of Vinnie and with people she cared about.

What more could she ask for?

SIX

Luke stretched out his legs, his muscles tight from today's ride. He watched Faith sitting across the living room, her hands clenched tightly. She was still upset. The paleness of her skin concerned him. But she had no reason now to be afraid.

The private investigator was more than likely flying over the Canadian border by now.

For his part, the ride this afternoon had done nothing to dispel his frustration, because his thoughts had centered on Faith, alternating between the trouble she was hiding from and his growing attraction to her.

"Did you enjoy your dinner, Luke?" Reva leaned her hip on the arm of the chair he sat in. Something about the way she'd been overly sweet this evening set off warning signals in his brain.

He gave her a considering look. "Yes, you did a fine job, as usual."

With a satisfied smile, Reva walked back into the kitchen.

Hoping to catch a moment alone with Faith so they could talk, he asked, "Are you heading upstairs, Mother?"

"No, actually. I'm feeling very perky this evening," Dottie said.

Faith glanced up with a wan smile and rose. "If you don't mind, I'll go to my room now."

Concern arched through Luke. "Do you need anything?"

"No, thank you. You both have been more than kind," she stated and went upstairs.

Luke debated following her. He really wanted to know more, but decided he had to let it go. He couldn't get too involved. "Can I get you some tea, Mom?"

Settling back in the cushy chair, Dottie patted his arm. "No, I'm good." She picked up the remote. "I'll just catch up on the news."

"I'm going to check on Lucy. I'll be back in a few." He turned to go.

"Luke?"

He stopped. "Yes, Mom?"

"Tomorrow would you bring in the Christmas decorations from the attic?"

His heart squeezed tight. Christmas without his father here was going to be tough. "Are you sure?"

Though her eyes misted, she nodded.

"Then of course."

"I think it will be good for Faith and I to decorate. Take her mind off whatever troubles her."

Family business. "I'm sure she'd like that."

"I like her," Dottie stated.

"Me, too, Mom."

A sage smile lifted the corners of Dottie's mouth. "Good. Now off with you."

"Okay, Mom." He hoped she wasn't getting any ideas about matchmaking. The last thing he needed was to have to be on guard from his mother's machinations.

When he walked into the kitchen, Reva was washing dishes. Now was a prime opportunity to talk to her. He leaned against the counter. "Tell me you didn't talk to the P.I. when you went to town."

Her hands stilled for a moment. She turned to face him and arched a dark blonde eyebrow. "Are you talking about the man that was here earlier?" Her mouth twisted sarcastically. "I didn't listen to your conversation."

He couldn't tell if she was telling the truth or not. "Thank you," he replied.

A gleam entered her eyes. "Interesting though that a private investigator would come to the Circle C. What did he want?"

"Nothing to do with you. And let's keep it that way."

Her mouth smiled but her eyes turned hard like slate. "Whatever you say, Luke. I only want to make you happy."

He frowned, not liking that statement. "You don't have to try to make me happy. That's not your job."

Inclining her head, she said, "I misspoke. I only want to be of help."

"We appreciate your help and we pay you well for it," he stated to clarify where their relationship stood.

"I'd want to be here even if you didn't pay me," she stated, her gaze softening, beseeching.

Uncomfortable, he headed to the door. "Good night."

He didn't trust Reva not to go snooping now that he'd piqued her curiosity. Tomorrow, he decided, he'd go into town and make sure the P.I. wasn't still hanging around.

"Costello found her."

Bob Grady's triumphant tone over the phone did little to appease Vince Palermo. "Where?"

"On a ranch in Sisters, Oregon. The guy that owns the place says she went to Alaska, but she's there."

"What's the guy's name," Vince snarled.

"Luke Campbell. Do you want us to grab her?"

"Not from the ranch. That would draw too much attention. Whatever you do, don't let her ditch you again."

"We won't. I've got a plan."

"Good. We'll talk again." Vince hung up and stared out the window of his fortieth-floor office. The Manhattan skyline was shrouded in shades of gray that matched his mood. Time was running out. His fingers curled into tight fists.

He had to get his wife back or he'd lose everything.

Faith toyed with her red cloth napkin, feeling unsettled and insecure in the Turners' home.

Get a grip and enjoy the evening. She forced her hands still. The Turners were very gracious people and their small house was decorated with festive red bows and green sprigs of pine that grew in abundance in this area. Tea lights flicked from the center of the table and reflected in the gold-rimmed dishes full of savory foods that scented the air.

The cozy setting and friendly atmosphere was foreign to her. In her grandparents' home, dinners were formal or taken in her room. Christmas decorations were a form of art not something taken from outside.

With Vinnie, Christmas had been a lonely time. His family gatherings had been loud and chaotic but for Faith, she'd always sat on the sideline, wishing for some type of connection.

The type she'd found with the Campbells.

Though a week passed without incident, no more

P.I.'s, or anyone else showing up unannounced, Faith remained on edge.

She longed to go into town to explore the quaint old-west town decorated for the holidays. But she couldn't afford to be seen. She'd gotten good at coming up with excuses. Too good. And she hated always having to say no to Luke and his mother.

Even when it came to attending Sunday service.

But staying alone on the ranch with only Brandy as her protection had stretched her nerves taut and made her decide that this coming Sunday she'd risk being seen and go with them to church.

However, tonight Luke and Dottie had insisted she join them at the Turners' house for dinner and not wanting to be left alone, she'd agreed.

"A Christmas toast." Matt Turner raised his glass of sparkling cider high.

Faith picked up her glass. The light amber liquid sloshed around the bowl but thankfully didn't spill over the side.

"To a Merry Christmas. May we each find the blessing God has waiting for us." Matt's craggy face beamed at his wife.

"Hear, hear." Sally raised her glass in one hand while she held on to Jason, her two-year-old son, who sat on her lap shredding a paper napkin. White bits of paper fell to the floor at Sally's feet but she seemed oblivious to the mess.

Her dark eyes reflected the soft candlelight and her thick, brown hair had been pulled back into a braid that hung over one shoulder. Specks of paper stuck to her braid.

"What does 'hear, hear' mean, Mama?" six-year-old Gloria asked from her place at the table, next to Faith. In her little hand she held her plastic cup up high like the adults and her big brown eyes were wide with curiosity.

"It means I agree with Daddy," Sally replied.

"Why are we holding our cups up and what's toast got to do with it?" Gloria asked, her little nose wrinkled in puzzlement.

Luke's deep chuckle rumbled through Faith as their gazes met across the table.

Matt answered. "It's a tradition. You hold your glass high, say a toast, or a better phrase would be a blessing, and clink the glasses together."

"*Gently* clink the glasses together," Sally interjected.

Faith's gaze went from one Turner family member to another. The love so obviously shared in this family overflowed, warming her heart. A lump formed in her throat. She ached with longing for a family of her own. Children to cherish, a husband to love. Maybe one day. One day when Vinnie was no longer tracking her.

"Dottie, will you be making pies again this year

for the Christmas festival?" Sally asked as they all began to fill their plates.

Faith looked to Luke for an explanation.

"Every year the church has a big festival on Christmas Eve. The whole community gets involved."

"Maybe with Faith's help, I could make some pies," Dottie announced.

Luke raised his eyebrows at his mother.

"Of course I'll help," Faith said and ignored the voice inside her head that cautioned she might not still be here by Christmas. If that investigator found out that she hadn't gone to Alaska, he could come back to Sisters. And then she'd have no choice but to leave.

"That was so much fun," Dottie exclaimed as Luke drove home from the Turners'.

"It was. Thank you for insisting I tag along," Faith replied.

Luke smiled at her through the rearview mirror, glad to see the animation in her face. She'd been so nervous when they'd first arrived at the Turners'. But she'd quickly succumbed to the exuberance of the Turner family. Luke was grateful for his old friends and their welcoming of Faith.

He turned the Bronco on to the driveway.

"Uh-oh," Dottie muttered. "Reva's here."

Luke pulled to a stop beside Reva's red car. He'd

told her she didn't need to make dinner because they had other plans. Obviously she hadn't believed him. He helped his mother out of the car and preceded Faith and Dottie into the dark house.

"Reva?" he called out as he flipped on the lights.

She sat at the kitchen table. Luke recognized the hard light in her eyes and the grim set to her mouth. She was spoiling for a fight. He turned his attention to his mother and Faith. "Go on up."

Faith gave him a worried look before nodding slowly. His mother's mouth pressed into a tight line as she preceded Faith up the stairs.

As soon as they were out of sight, Luke turned to Reva. "Did I miscommunicate to you that we had plans tonight and wouldn't need you to come over?"

Reva crossed her arms over chest. "Where were you?"

Luke pulled out a chair and sat down. He held tight to his irritation. "Reva, don't you think it's time you started finding out what you want to do with your life?"

"I know what I want," she said, her gaze boring in to him.

Luke sighed. "You and I are never going to happen."

"Why not?" She reached out to put her hand over his. "I could make you happy."

He pulled his hand away. "Reva, don't do this."

Her expression crumbled, revealing the little girl that used to follow him around.

"But I love you, Luke."

He ran a hand over his face. He hated to hurt her, but he figured being brutally honest was the only way to get through to her. "I don't love you. Not like a man loves a woman he wants to marry."

She closed her eyes for a moment and when she opened them rage shone in the gray depths. "It's because of her, isn't it?"

He didn't have to guess who she meant. He had come to care for Faith, but her presence didn't change his feelings for Reva. "No. This has nothing to do with anyone but me. I don't love you. I never will. Now, I think it's time for you to go home."

Reva rose, and without another word, she stalked from the house.

Luke turned off the downstairs lights and then went upstairs. Faith was waiting for him in the hall. She still wore the black pants and white blouse she'd worn to dinner, but she'd released her blond hair from the rubber band that had held it back earlier. She looked so appealing in the muted light of the hall.

"She's pretty upset," she commented.

Her anxious expression pulled at Luke. "I know. Reva and I needed to have that talk. I should have done it a long time ago. I doubt she'll be back."

There was understanding in her eyes that made the harshness of what he'd done bearable.

"It's hard to say words that you know are going to hurt someone," she said.

"Yes. It is." He tucked a lock of hair behind her ear. "It's late. You should be in bed."

"I'm a little too keyed up to sleep, yet. I thought I'd make some tea. Would you care for some?"

He too was keyed up. "That would be great."

They headed back down to the kitchen. Faith put on the kettle and took two mugs from the cupboard. "Herbal?"

"Whatever you're having is fine."

She stuck a tea bag of his mother's favorite chamomile in each cup. They waited for the water to boil.

"Faith, tell me about your family."

Tilting her head to one side, she considered him for a moment. "What would you like to know?"

He wanted to know about her marriage. Did she still love her ex-husband? But he couldn't put voice to the question. Instead, he shrugged as she handed him a mug. "Start with your parents."

Taking a seat, she placed her steaming mug on the table and ran her finger over the rim. "My parents were—eccentric. Father loved to take pictures of everything he saw, and Mother loved to write about everything she saw. They made a good team. My grandparents thought their lifestyle was—well—that it was scandalous that they chose to spend their lives running around the world, sharing their experiences through pictures and articles. Grandfather wanted Father to take over for him. But Father would always say he had no head for business."

"Did they publish their work?"

"Oh, yes. In several of Grandfather's travel magazines. But they did it mostly for their own enjoyment."

"Your grandfather was a publisher?" She'd said a great deal of money, he just hadn't realized the scale she was talking about.

"Among other things. He always said media had the pulse of the nation. He'd started out with just a newspaper when he was a young man. He slowly worked his way to running half the newspapers, radio stations and television stations across the country."

"He was very powerful." And with that power came pressure. The pressure she was running from. He was beginning to get a clearer picture.

Faith nodded. "For a time."

"What happened?"

"Grandmother said that he slowly lost interest. His health began to slip and he didn't have Father's interest so he began selling his assets." She scoffed. "He was old school and didn't believe women could run multimillion-dollar corporations."

"So where did you fit in?"

She gave a small laugh. "When I was very small I went with my parents everywhere. I don't remember it too much, but I have impressions of exotic places that surface occasionally. About the time I turned eight, my grandparents demanded my parents bring me home for some schooling. My parents, bless their souls, believed I would get a better education staying with them, but since my grandparents funded most of their trips, they had to do as they were told. So I was sent off to private school."

"That must have been hard on you."

"I suppose. But Mother and Father came home often to visit. They would bring all sorts of odd souvenirs from the places they went. As I grew older, I went through a period of resenting them, but I grew out of that. I'm just glad they were able to live their lives the way they wanted."

The sadness in her voice made Luke's hand tighten around his cup. "It wasn't fair of your family to separate you from your parents."

Faith glanced at him then quickly looked away. "I suppose not."

"You said your parents died?"

She nodded. "A car accident. On my eleventh birthday, of all time. They—" Faith looked up at him with sad eyes. "They were on their way home to see me."

Setting his mug down, he reached over and covered her white knuckles with his hands. "I'm so sorry."

"It was a long time ago." She stared down at their clasped hands. In a low whisper Luke heard her say, "I never got to say goodbye."

Understanding her pain, Luke's heart ached for her. "When I heard my father was dying, I was afraid I wouldn't arrive home in time."

She lifted her head. "But you did."

"Yes, but there still wasn't enough time to tell him everything I wanted to say."

She nodded. "That's how I felt when my grandfather died." Tears rapidly filled her eyes. "I knew his death was coming but—I just wasn't ready." A tear spilled from her lashes and rolled down her cheek. "He'd had a heart attack five years earlier, after my grandmother passed on, that caused so much damage. He wouldn't have surgery and slowly he got worse until finally his heart stopped."

Luke stifled the urge to take her into his arms. He knew once he did he might never let go. "You were with him."

A small, sad smile touched her lips. "Yes. I was the only one he couldn't scare off. Grandfather was a prickly man on the outside but—I loved him a great deal."

"Tell me about him."

Faith moved restlessly, tucking and untucking her legs beneath her.

"Grandfather was—traditional."

"Like in women are women and men are men?"

"Exactly."

They shared a smile. "Did your grandfather believe in God?"

Her mouth twisted. "Oh, yes. He was definitely a God-fearing Christian."

"And he taught you to fear God," Luke stated gently.

"Yes, he did. He made sure that terror of God was deeply instilled." She quickly added, "But I knew Grandfather loved me. He just had a hard time showing his affection."

Luke ached for the little girl she'd been. Growing up without her parents, having her controlling grandfather warp her view of God. Faith deserved to be cherished and loved. "Fear of the Lord isn't about terror. It's about awe and respect. How can we love and obey a God we're terrified of?"

Her eyebrows drew together in puzzlement. "But isn't that why people obey God? Because they are afraid He'll strike them down if they don't?"

"God strikes down those who oppose Him, but not before giving them a chance to come to Him. And He always gives second chances. He gives humans free will to choose. Follow Him and receive all the blessings He freely gives or turn away from Him to live without the blessings."

She seemed to absorb his words, he wasn't sure she believed him. "Thank you."

He frowned. "For what?"

"For understanding. For giving me a job and a place to stay."

Her hazel eyes were direct, without guile. He liked that about her. "You're welcome."

For a moment silence stretched between them as their gazes remained focused on each other. Not awkward, but active. Two people finding something of interest in the other. Luke liked looking at her, seeing the beauty within her made his heart beat harder.

She slightly raised one eyebrow, bringing an end to the intimacy of the moment. "What made you join the military?"

He gave a mirthless laugh. "I didn't want to turn into my father."

A crease appeared between her eyebrows. "Why?"

Pride. He shrugged. "At eighteen, I guess I wanted a different, more adventurous life than my parents."

"And did you find that life?"

With a nod, he answered, "Yes. I started—"

Brandy raced into the kitchen barking wildly, the hair at her nape raised. She skidded to a stop at the back door, her nails scraping on the tile. Her barks deep and guttural, frantic.

Faith scrambled out of the chair. "There was someone at the window."

SEVEN

Heart pounding, Luke moved swiftly to the door and turned off the kitchen light, then turned on the outside porch light.

"Don't go out there," Faith pleaded.

His gaze searched the dark for the trespasser.

After a few moments, Brandy's barks tapered off and she paced, the fur on the back of her neck still raised.

Faith, her complexion pasty white, stood in the doorway of the kitchen, her body shaking. He went to her and took her hands. "Do you remember what the man looked like?"

"I don't know. I just saw a flash of movement."

"Could it have been Reva?"

Her brow furrowed. "I suppose. But why would she—?"

"She was angry when she left."

Faith looked unconvinced. "Should you call the police?"

"Luke?" Dottie called from the top of the stairs.

"Here, Mom." Luke moved into the entryway.

His mom stood on the landing, her robe hastily thrown on. "What's got Brandy in such a twitter?"

"Someone was outside," Luke replied.

"One of the hands? Is there a problem?"

"I don't know, Mom."

Faith touched his arm. "You go make your call. Dottie and I will be upstairs."

He could see fear lurking in her hazel gaze. "You're safe. I'm not going to let anything happen to you."

She nodded and ascended the stairs and led Dottie back to her room.

Luke called the sheriff's station. Thirty minutes later, Sheriff Bane and a young deputy arrived. After shaking hands with the sheriff and being introduced to Deputy Art Unger, Luke said, "Faith thought she saw someone at the kitchen window."

He told him about his conversation with Reva.

"Nothing like a woman scorned. Let's take a look." The sheriff grabbed a long, black-handled flashlight from his car and walked around the back of the house. The bright beam revealed footprints in the snow beneath the window. Sheriff Bane shifted his weight on to one leg and hovered his other foot over a clear print. "I'd say a size eleven or twelve boot. Too big for Reva. These are pretty deep, so I'd say a heavy man." He peered through the window. "Tall, too, to be able to see through this window."

The young deputy scribbled notes on a small pad.

Sheriff Bane swung the beam along the ground. "Prints disappear on the gravel drive. Who else is on the property?"

"My foreman and the hands live in the four apartments above the stables."

"Could it have been one of them?" the sheriff asked.

Shaking his head, Luke answered, "I don't think so. Brandy wouldn't have flipped out the way she did. Except—"

"Except?"

"I have two new hands, but Brandy knows them."

"Let's go see if they noticed anything or anyone lurking around," Sheriff Bane said. "Art, take a post outside."

Luke led the sheriff to the second-floor apartments in the bigger of the two barns. A light shone under the first door. At their knock, the door opened and Leo stood there in stocking feet. His frame was lean and lanky in jeans and a plaid shirt hanging open over a white T-shirt. His graying hair stuck up in tufts and his blue eyes regarded them sharply. "Hey, boss. What's up?"

"Can we come in?" Luke asked.

Leo stepped back and held the door wide. Though sparse on furniture—a refrigerator, stove, a small dining table and lone chair, a recliner and TV—the tiny space was cluttered with trophies, saddles, plaques on the walls and stacks of magazines and newspapers.

Luke had been nearly twelve when his dad had hired Leo. He could still remember being in awe of the cowboy who'd come to live on the ranch. Leo had been a rodeo star in his youth and he had stories that had kept a boy entertained for days on end.

"Mind telling me what this visit is about?" Leo asked.

Luke explained the situation.

"I ain't seen anyone around. I know the boys went to town tonight. Haven't heard them return." He shrugged. "That's not to say they haven't. I don't hear so well these days."

Luke hadn't thought about how Leo's health might be. Leo and his father hadn't been that far apart in age. Now, Luke felt a twinge of concern for his foreman. Maybe soon it would be time to talk to him about retiring.

The sheriff asked Leo questions about the other hands.

"Charles has been on the ranch for about three years now, ever since his wife left him. The two new guys came highly recommended by the Krofters, a couple of ranches over."

The sheriff took their names and then asked Leo to let Luke know if he saw anything out of the ordinary.

"Will do, Sheriff." Leo clapped Luke on the back. "Don't worry, boss. Nothing's gonna happen that I don't know about."

As they turned to leave, the sheriff paused. "What size boot do you wear?"

Luke opened his mouth to protest, but froze when Leo replied.

"An eleven."

No way would Luke believe Leo had been spying on them, and he said as much to the sheriff once the door closed.

"We can't rule out anyone," the sheriff replied as he moved down the hall to knock on the doors of the other three small apartments.

"Seems your hands are still out for the night. Do they do this often?"

Luke shrugged. "I don't keep tabs on their personal time. I'll talk to them tomorrow."

"Good enough." The sheriff and his deputy walked to their car. "I'll keep my eyes and ears open around town. And I'll have a talk with Reva." The sheriff opened the car door.

Relieved that he wouldn't have to deal with Reva himself, Luke replied, "That'd be great. Thanks."

He watched the car disappear down the drive before heading back inside.

"Did they find anyone?"

He came to a stop at the bottom of the stairs. Faith stood on the top landing. Her blond hair hung loosely over one of his mother's old terry robes tied securely at the waist.

He shook his head. "No. Whoever was out there is gone."

She stared at him a moment before inclining her head. "I'll see you in the morning."

"Good night," he said and watched her slip into her room. Then he grabbed a blanket from the hall closet and sat on the couch.

Brandy rose from her bed and nudged him with her nose before flopping down on the floor beside him. Within moments Brandy's soft snore was the only sound in the house.

Quiet enough to let Luke's mind wander to the beautiful blonde upstairs.

Reva May Scott hated country music. It was too depressing and too close to her life. But in a small town like Sisters, there wasn't any escaping the soulful ballads and honky-tonk tunes played on the jukebox in the corner of the Rib Eye Bar and Grill.

She sat on a stool at the long wooden counter in the bar area of the restaurant, feeling conspicuous as a single woman among so many couples out for a good time on a Friday night. She lifted her martini glass and took a sip. The sweet and sour concoction hit her taste buds with a snap. She didn't think the thing tasted that much like a Granny Smith apple, but the green color was sure pretty.

Especially on a dismal night like tonight.

It wasn't the weather bringing her down. In fact, she rather liked the dry air, snow-covered ground and biting temperature of winter in central Oregon. Much better than the drizzling rain on the west side of the state.

No, tonight was dismal for a different reason.

All she'd ever wanted was to be a part of a family. To belong to someone who would love, honor and cherish her. Just like all the marriage vows of all the people whose weddings she'd gone to over the years.

Silly words. Silly sentiment. Still, she wanted it.

She took another drink, letting the tangy liquid slide down her throat and the vodka take the edge off her hurt at Luke's rejection.

She'd had her heart set on Luke for so long she couldn't remember when she didn't love him. Oh, he'd never professed any sort of romantic feelings for her, but she'd kept believing that in time he'd come around, just like his father had said. She'd hoped if she was close enough, did enough, then one day Luke would vow to love, honor and cherish her and she'd finally belong.

But not now. Not with Faith in the picture.

Anger burned in her belly, fueled by the alcohol.

That private detective should have hauled Faith off after Reva told him she was on the ranch and not on her way to Alaska.

But no. The creep had just smiled and left town.

Something had to be done. It just wasn't fair that this strange woman could come in and take Reva's place in Luke's life.

"Hey, beautiful, what are you doing sitting here all by your lonesome?"

Tensing at the unexpected intrusion, Reva slanted a glance toward the man who'd sidled up to the bar beside her. Recognizing him as one of the hands on the Campbell ranch, she relaxed. Not that she re-membered the guy's name. He was new and not Luke. "Hey, yourself. Where are your buddies?"

"Oh, they'll be along. We each had stuff to do." He inclined his head toward her near-empty glass. "Can I buy you another?"

She wasn't stupid. A free drink was a free drink. "Why not?"

"Another for the lady and I'll take a beer," the man said as he sat on a stool.

"Thanks…uh. I'm sorry I don't remember your name."

His dark eyes danced with amusement. "That's okay. I remember yours. Reva."

She shrugged. His name wasn't important. He wasn't important. He wasn't Luke.

She picked up the fresh drink the bartender had placed in front of her.

"So what are we celebrating?"

Reva shook her head. "We're not."

"I didn't see you at the ranch today."

She snorted. "And you won't. Not while *she's* there."

He leaned closer. "You don't like the new lady?"

"No."

"You want her to disappear?"

Like a cloud of smoke. Poof. Gone. Reva giggled, the drink making her a bit woozy. "That'd be nice."

His voice dipped low. "I can help you with that."

"You can?" She leaned closer. "Tell me how."

Sunday morning roared in with a heavy dumping of new snow and a drop in temperature. After a quick breakfast of toast and coffee, Faith dressed for church and met the Campbells in the living room. Luke had on a tie with his cotton oxford shirt, jeans and cowboy boots. He looked like the perfect gentleman rancher.

He helped his mother into her long down parka over her wool dress. Her black sensible shoes and thick tights made Faith worry that she'd dressed inappropriately. Her own tennis shoes, khaki pants and striped turtleneck were as dressy as she had.

"Here you go," Luke said, now holding out the new parka he'd bought for her in town.

She slipped into the jacket, mindful of Luke's warm breath on her nape. "Thank you."

"Zip up. It's cold out there," he stated as he opened the door.

Faith shivered as much from the cold as from nerves about being seen in town as she slid into the back of the Bronco. Immediately, the fresh snow that had fallen on her head melted and dripped down her neck. Luke helped Dottie in before going around the front and hopping into the driver's seat.

"Now, let's hope the main road has been plowed," he said.

The Bronco eased forward down the drive, the tires crunching over gravel and ice. When they came to the main road, Luke stopped and let the vehicle idle. "Okay, ladies. The road is not plowed. I think we can make it, but we could get stuck."

That didn't sound appealing to Faith. Even with the heat on high, she was still cold.

Dottie sighed. "I'm not up to a walk in the snow if we do get stuck."

Faith met Luke's gaze in the rearview mirror. She wrinkled her nose. "Me, neither."

"All right then," Luke said and threw the Bronco into Reverse.

Once he parked the car back in front of the door, they all hurried back inside.

Luke immediately built a fire in the fireplace and Faith went to set some water to boil for tea. Dottie sat in her recliner and covered up with a blanket.

Faith admitted to herself she was thankful she wasn't leaving the ranch. Once the water was ready, she brought out three steaming mugs and the basket with teas.

Dottie snagged a chamomile and Luke took a black tea. Faith dipped a spicy-smelling bag in her water.

"If you're up for it, mother, I thought I'd invite the boys in for dinner tonight and give them their Christmas bonuses."

"That would be fine. Faith and I can create some gourmet meal. What do you think, Faith?"

"That would be wonderful," she replied, enjoying being included.

Luke set his mug down. "I'll go make sure the guys are all available. Though I don't imagine any of them will be leaving the ranch tonight."

Or anyone coming to the ranch, Faith silently added.

She could only hope the snow continued to keep the outside world from intruding.

"Wow, that was some meal," Jerry Ridgeway exclaimed, sitting back in the ranch's dining-room chair with a satisfied grin.

"You could say that again." Another ranch hand, Mac Stone, agreed while wiping at his mouth with a green cloth napkin.

"I'll say it," Charles Fry stated and rubbed at his gut in a satisfied gesture. "Fine meal."

Leo nodded his approval. "We have a keeper here, Dottie."

Dottie laughed. "Careful, Leo. You'll scare her off."

Luke glanced at Faith, who blushed under all the praise. She sat near his mother at the opposite end of the table. The festive Christmas decorations and delicious food foreshadowed the upcoming holiday. With Faith here, Christmas might not be as sad an occasion as Luke feared it would.

Faith seemed to have no idea of her effect on everyone in his house. The hands all seemed as smitten with her as his mother, who adored her. He didn't care to examine his own feelings for her.

Tonight they'd invited the hands to a pre-Christmas dinner so he could give them their Christmas bonuses. Even though Mac and Jerry were new, Luke had given them each a bit of extra cash.

Now, he pushed his chair away from the table. "That *was* a wonderful dinner, Faith."

"I'm glad you liked it. Your mother told me chicken and dumplings were your favorite." Her smile was tentative.

His mother beamed at him from her place at the head of the table.

Pleasure and unease seeped into his veins, heating the blood pounding through his suddenly racing heart. His mother definitely was trying her hand at matchmaking. "Thank you."

His gaze locked with Faith's. For a split second he forgot to breathe. In her eyes, he saw a myriad of emotions—yearning, wonder, and a hint of appre-hension.

He wanted to explore the yearning and wonder, and rid her of any apprehension. But now was not the time.

For the past few days life had calmed down. No more Peeping Toms. Leo and the hands all promised to keep a vigilant eye out for any intruders. Reva hadn't shown up since his talk with her and the sher-iff had called to say he'd questioned Reva about Friday night. Apparently, she had been in town at a bar the whole time.

Luke stood, breaking the eye contact with Faith and busied himself by gathering the empty plates.

Noticing her look of surprise, he gave her a self-conscious grin. "I'll help clean up, okay?"

"Uh, sure. That'll—be great." She pushed her chair back and stood.

Luke reached for an empty platter in the middle of the table just as Faith reached for it, too. Their hands brushed against each other and each let go as if burned by the same electrical current. The platter dropped noisily to the table and Luke jerked his gaze to Faith.

She slowly raised her gaze. "Slippery plate."

Laughter filled the room, relieving the tension. Luke chuckled and nodded. "Very."

Luke left the slippery plate to Faith and turned to carry his stack of dishes to the kitchen. He met his mother's mirthful gaze and knowing smile, and the significance of helping with the dishes suddenly struck Luke.

His father had helped his mother every night, claiming it was their time together. Luke had, on occasion, watched silently from the doorway as his parents worked side by side. Doing dishes had become an intimate act that he'd never wanted to intrude on. Anticipation catapulted his heart into triple time.

The rational part of his brain screamed a warning. He didn't want to get too comfortable in this domestic scene, but he was unable to resist.

His mother gracefully rose from the table, the twinkle in her eyes shining bright. Leo scrambled to pull out her chair.

"Thank you for dinner, Mrs. Campbell, Faith," Jerry said as he rose. "This sure beats microwave or restaurant food."

Mac and Charles rose as well, each adding their thanks.

"Any time, boys. We're glad to have you on the ranch," Dottie replied.

After the three men left, Dottie patted Leo's hand. "Would you like to join me for some tea?"

"Sure would," Leo answered.

Luke hesitated, not sure how he felt about his mother and Leo becoming chummy.

"I'll start some water," Faith offered.

Dottie gave her a grateful smile. "Thank you, dear."

She and Leo went into the living room.

Luke helped Faith clear the table while he wrestled with the thought of his mother socializing. It wasn't like she and Leo were going on a date or anything. Just two old friends having tea in the living room.

Get a grip. He wasn't his mother's keeper.

"You really don't have to help." Faith set the kettle on the stove to boil.

"Oh, but I want to." He picked up a dish towel. "You wash and I'll dry."

Faith arched a blond eyebrow. "And just why do I have to be the one to get dishpan hands?"

"You're the woman," he teased with a grin.

"Ah, that's rational thinking coming from a mere man." She rolled her eyes with an answering grin and turned on the faucet.

Within moments, steam rose from the hot spray of water.

"Here, I'll wash," Luke offered, realizing that as a society woman, she probably wasn't used to washing dishes.

She waved him off. "I was just kidding. I'll do it. It's not that big a deal. Besides, the chore is kind of soothing."

"Really?"

"Yes, really." She slipped her hands into the water and scrubbed a plate before handing it to Luke to dry.

A lock of hair fell forward into Faith's eyes and she blew at the stray wisp. Unable to resist, Luke reached out to brush back the strands and caressed her cheek. She turned to look at him, her gaze bright and trusting. He wanted to sink into her gaze, to taste her lips, to hold her close. His head dipped and gently he pressed his lips to hers, the contact sending jolts of sensation ricocheting through his system, making his toes curl inside his cowboy boots.

"Oh, don't mind me. I'll just grab a couple of cups and be out of your way in no time."

His mother's voice yanked Luke back to his senses. He straightened. Color rose high in Faith's cheeks. She quickly turned back toward the sink and plunged her hands into the water.

Luke leaned against the counter and took several steadying breaths.

"Would anyone else like some tea?" Dottie cheerfully asked.

"No, no thank you, Mother," Luke managed to answer, sounding somewhat normal.

"Well, you know, tea has a very calming effect."

Faith made a strangled sound and Luke stared at his mother through narrowed eyes. Dottie blinked at him. He glanced at Faith. Her cheeks turned bright red and her lips were pressed together in a tight line. She thrust a plate into his hands.

They continued in silence until Dottie left the room.

The second his mother was gone, Faith turned on him. "What was that all about?"

"What?" he asked innocently.

"You know perfectly well what." She stood with her soapy hands on her hips, sparks flying from her eyes.

"I'm sorry. It won't happen again."

Her mouth dropped open and then snapped shut. Abruptly, she turned back to the sink and Luke thought that was the end, but she whirled back around. "You're right it won't happen again, Luke Campbell. Next time you kiss me, you'd better mean it."

She threw a wet sponge at him, hitting him square in the chest, before marching out of the kitchen.

Luke stared at her retreating back in astonishment. Then a slow grin spread across his face as the implications of her words sunk in.

"Of all the insufferable, pigheaded, arrogant…"
Faith punched her pillow, creating a nice round dent

in the soft, downy feathers. The lingering effects of Luke's kiss coursed through her veins.

She groaned aloud and punched the pillow again. He'd had the gall to apologize. And say he wouldn't kiss her again. Faith buried her head beneath her pillow and willed herself to calm down. She really didn't want his kisses, so why was she so upset?

A soft knock startled her into a sitting position. Slowly, she got off the bed and walked to the door leading to the hall and paused with her hand on the knob. "Yes?" she whispered.

"Faith, we need to talk," Luke said.

"We can talk tomorrow."

The door wasn't locked but he wouldn't enter unless invited. Vinnie wouldn't have bothered to knock, he'd have just barged in. But she could trust Luke. He wouldn't hurt her. Especially, physically.

Any emotional hurt would be her own fault.

EIGHT

The next day, after his chores, Luke found his mother and Faith sitting in the living room each with knitting needles and yarn in hand.

"Hello, ladies."

"Can I make you a sandwich?" Faith asked, her gaze somewhat shy as she rose.

"I can get it," he said and moved into the kitchen to wash up.

"I don't mind," she countered, her expression sincere as she followed him.

He relented. "That would be great, then."

Remembering how they'd parted last night made Luke's pulse quicken. He wanted to talk to her about the kiss and what it meant. Or didn't mean. Or what they wanted the kiss to mean. But with his mother watching he chose not to approach the subject now.

"Reva hasn't shown up again this morning," Dottie commented as she too entered the kitchen.

Luke turned his attention away from watching Faith make his sandwich and addressed his mother. "I don't know that she'll be back."

"Oh? Did something happen that I should know about?"

With a shrug, Luke replied, "I laid my feelings for her out on the table. She was pretty mad."

Dottie whistled. "Well. It had to be done."

"Here." Faith handed him a plate with a thick ham sandwich.

"Bring that in to the living room and talk with us," Dottie said.

Luke helped his mother to her favorite chair, and then sat next to Faith on the sofa, leaving mere inches between them.

Faith arched her eyebrows high and nodded to the rest of the sofa. "Is there something wrong with that end?"

He shrugged. "Not at all. Just more cozy here."

He liked the way she blushed. Her complexion turned a pretty shade of pink and her eyes sparkled. It wasn't nice to tease, but it was such fun.

Luke noticed his mother's interested stare and gave her an innocent look before taking a bite of his lunch.

"You behave yourself," Dottie admonished with a pleased smile.

"Always," he answered with a lopsided grin.

Faith snorted beneath her breath. He nudged her with his elbow. "What?"

She turned her face toward him and it took a great deal of effort not to lean in close and taste her lips. Instead, he gave her a slow smile and savored her blush.

His mother's voice drew his attention away from Faith. "I think I saw a raccoon this morning."

"They're seeking warmth. I'll make sure I let Leo know so he can plug any holes in the llamas' barn."

Dottie motioned toward the bookshelf against the wall. "Luke, hand me those photo albums, please."

"Ahh, Mom. You're not going to start showing my baby pictures are you?"

"But, of course." Dottie bestowed an innocent look on him. Faith burst out laughing.

Luke glowered in mock outrage. "You think that's funny, do you?"

Still laughing, she nodded.

"Well, I'll give you something to laugh about." He set his plate on the coffee table and then his hands found the tender spot on her rib cage and began tickling. She squirmed beneath the onslaught.

His mother's rich laughter stilled his hands.

Stunned, Luke couldn't ever remember being compelled to tickle anyone, let alone doing so in front of his mother. Embarrassed to his toes, he picked up his plate and stared at the big Douglas fir tree by the window. "The tree looks great by the way."

Mirth still danced brightly in Dottie's eyes. "Yes, it does. Thanks to Faith, the whole house is ready for Christmas. I can't believe just five more days. I need to go to town and do some shopping."

"I'll take you tomorrow, if you'd like," Luke offered.

"Perfect. Maybe we can talk Faith into coming as well," his mother said, her expectant gaze on Faith.

She swallowed and her expression showed the panic going on inside her head. Luke had already assured her the P.I. had left town, so why was she still so worried? "Or we can pick up anything you need," he offered.

Her relieved smile didn't reach her eyes. "I'll make a list. The pharmacy has a refill that needs to be picked up."

"I can do that." He rose. "I need to check on Lucy."

"She's due soon, isn't she?" his mother asked.

"After Christmas."

"Lucy?" Faith asked.

"One of the llamas is about to be a mama," Luke explained as he retrieved the photo albums his mother had requested and handed them to Faith. "Have yourself a good laugh."

Faith took the offered books and looked up at him. Traces of panic still lingered in her gaze and Luke hesitated. Part of him wanted to gather her close and reassure her that everything would be all right. He wouldn't force her to go or do anything she didn't want to.

A bigger part of himself ordered him to stand down. He was getting too entangled. She was his employee! And that was a road he didn't want to travel. He forced himself to look away and breathe deeply.

After kissing his mother's cheek, he headed toward the door. On the threshold, he paused and looked back. Faith still watched him, her expression tinged by a sadness he didn't understand. He ached for her and felt a compelling pull to do whatever it took to make her relax.

Employee or not.

"And this picture was taken at Luke's sixth birthday party."

Faith stared at the snapshot of Luke wearing a miniature cowboy hat, leather chaps and showing a gap-tooth smile for the camera. Her fingertips brushed over the image.

Today she'd seen a glimpse of the little boy he must have been and she liked the playful side he'd displayed. She didn't know what to make of him. He'd protected her, kissed her and now teased her outrageously. He made her head spin so fast she became dizzy any time she tried to hold on to an emotion or thought.

She tried to analyze what she was feeling. She was attracted to Luke, there was no denying that. In her eyes he was everything a man should be, handsome, but not too pretty, gentle, yet with a quiet strength that made her feel protected. He'd been sensitive to her feelings so many times. He'd earned her trust.

But she couldn't allow herself to fall for him. He was a port in the storm of her life. And one day Dottie wouldn't need her any longer and Luke would return to his military career. And she'd…

She pushed aside her confusion and concentrated on the photo album.

"This is my Blake." Dottie pointed to a picture of a handsome man holding a small infant.

The resemblance between Luke and his father was uncanny. Faith touched the image. "You must miss him a great deal."

"Yes, I do. He was a good husband and father. Luke is a lot like him."

Faith smiled to hear the subtle suggestion in Dottie's voice. She didn't have to work too hard to know Dottie wanted her son to settle down and start a family. It's what every mother wanted for her children. Faith had no doubt he'd make a fine husband and father.

"Luke was an adorable child."

"That he was. He was also headstrong and willful." Dottie chuckled. "I can't wait for the day when he has his own kids and I can sit back to watch the fun."

She could picture Luke holding an infant, his strong, gentle hands cradling the tiny body. "Luke will make a good father."

"Do you like children, Faith?" Dottie's steady gaze pinned her to the sofa.

"Yes, but…I don't have a lot of experience with them." Almost none. Vinnie had refused to start a family, and now she was very thankful. Adding a child to the situation would have been so unfair to the child. But in the future? She dared not even dream that far ahead.

"Do you like my son?"

Dottie's blunt question startled her. "Uh, yes. I do like Luke. He's a decent man." Not to mention caring, sensitive and attractive.

"I think he likes you, too." Dottie's wistful expression made Faith's heart pound.

"He's a good employer," Faith said, hoping that would put their relationship in perspective, for both her and Dottie.

Dottie's slight smile told her she wasn't convinced.

"What are you two doing?" Reva hovered just inside the doorway from the kitchen, a bucket of cleaning supplies in her hand. The tight pink sweater she wore optimized her cleavage.

Surprised to see Reva and thankful for the distraction, Faith answered, "Looking at some old photos." She hesitated a moment, sympathy for the other woman twisted in her chest. "Would you care to join us?"

Reva's expression shifted, and for a brief mo-

ment, Faith saw longing in her gray eyes. She understood what it was like to be on the outside looking
in, wanting to belong.

How many times had she herself looked at
Vinnie's family and wanted to belong? They'd never
let her in. And in retrospect, she was again thankful.
Had she been attached to his family, would she have
had the courage to flee when she needed to?

"Oh, Luke has shown me those before," Reva
said airily, her chin going up slightly as if challenging them to dispute her.

"That was nice of him," Faith offered with compassion aching in her heart.

Reva smiled tightly and moved away from the
door but instead of going back into the kitchen, she
disappeared down the dark hall.

"I'm surprised she came back." Dottie sighed. "I
wish she'd get her own life."

Now that Faith knew Reva's situation and had
heard Luke tell her the exact same thing, the wari-
ness Faith had felt for Reva evaporated. "She seems
lonely."

The shrill sound of the phone echoed through the
house.

"Would you mind getting that, dear?" Dottie
leaned back in her chair.

"Sure." Faith stood.

Just then Reva came sailing back into the room.

"I'll get the phone," she threw over her shoulder before disappearing into the kitchen.

A moment later she reappeared. "It's for you."

Dottie began to rise, but Reva shook her head. "Not you, Dottie. The phone's for Faith. You can take it in the kitchen." Reva left the room and went back down the dark hall.

Faith couldn't seem to make her feet move. She could feel the blood rushing from her head. Who could be calling?

"Do you want me to find out who it is?" Concern etched lines in Dottie's forehead.

"No, that's okay." The last thing she wanted was for Dottie to think something was wrong. She forced herself to walk, dread creeping into her soul with each step. "It's probably just the pharmacist. I refilled your meds yesterday." Though why they'd be calling now, she didn't know. The pharmacist had assured her the refill would be ready for pick up tomorrow.

In the kitchen the phone lay on the counter, Faith stared at the instrument with apprehension before picking up the receiver and putting it to her ear. "Hello?"

There was a moment of silence before a deep, muffled voice she couldn't identify spoke. "I'm coming for you, Faith. You can't get away from me. No matter where you go, I'll find you."

The line went dead.

Icy talons of fear pierced Faith's skin, causing goose bumps to rise. She dropped the receiver. It clattered noisily on the counter and she backed away. Blood and fear pounded in her brain, her vision blurred.

Tears welled in her eyes and she bit her lip. A trickle of blood seeped into her mouth, the coppery taste making her gag. She hadn't tasted her own blood since the night she'd run away. Violent shudders racked her body and her breathing became shallow.

She had to leave.

But how? Where would she go? Part of her wanted to give up. When would it ever end? Would she ever find the peace she so desperately sought?

The thought of leaving the Campbells' weakened her knees, but for their sake, their safety, she had to go. Her sanctuary was nothing more than a house of cards. God wasn't watching over her. She had to take care of herself and protect those around her. Never mind her selfish dreams.

"Faith, honey, are you all right?" Dottie called from the living room.

It took several tries before she managed to answer, "I'll be right there."

Her mind frantically reviewed her options. She could walk to town and catch a bus. But she'd have to ask Luke or Dottie for some cash. Or she could take some money from her trust fund. Since Vinnie already knew where she was, that seemed the best option.

Only she wouldn't be able to get at the money unless she went to the bank. She'd have to go to town with Luke tomorrow.

Calming herself down enough to rejoin Dottie, Faith settled back on the couch, aware of Dottie's scrutiny.

"You look a little pale," Dottie commented. "Is something wrong?"

"I think I need some fresh air. Would you like to go outside?" Faith asked, hoping to distract Dottie.

Dottie slowly stood. "I'd love to see my babies."

They bundled up and then stepped outside. The snow from the previous evening had dusted the gravel drive, making the uneven surface look more like a sea of scattered marshmallows rather than chunks of stones.

They approached the fence and the llamas meandered over. Brandy came bounding out of the barn to give Faith and Dottie wet kisses before running back to the barn and disappearing inside.

"Luke must still be in with Lucy," Dottie commented.

Faith ran her hands through the soft fur of the animal named Ricky and wished the soothing texture could smooth the edges of her nerves.

"He likes you," Dottie stated. "Ricky is usually very standoffish."

"The llamas are much friendlier than I heard they were," Faith said.

"Faith, Faith!"

Reva's high-pitched call sent the llamas scattering. Reva came hurrying out from the house and down the road, her frosted curls bouncing about in disarray. She'd donned her black, fur-lined parka.

Reva gave Dottie a tight smile. "You're looking the picture of health."

"I feel good." Dottie smiled back brightly and Faith was sure Reva's eyes narrowed slightly before she turned to address her.

"I almost forgot. This was delivered for you on Friday." Reva held out a white envelope.

Faith took it and frowned. "Who delivered it?"

"Oh, some local rug rat. Said some man in town paid him to ride his dirt bike out here."

"When?" Faith looked toward the road. A boy had biked to the ranch and she hadn't seen or heard him? A small tremor raced from Faith's toes to her hand and her throat tightened. She was getting too complacent, too comfortable.

"I don't remember. I'm not your secretary," Reva groused.

Faith inclined her head to acknowledge that. "Well, uh—thanks."

"Aren't you going to open it?" A thread of impatience vibrated in Reva's tone.

Faith didn't want to. A sense of foreboding invaded her senses. First the phone call, now this?

Sliding her fingernail beneath the seal, she slowly opened the envelope and pulled out the folded piece of paper. Her hand shook as she unfolded the note. The words, written in bold, black ink, were in stark contrast to the white paper.

You can't hide from me.

Dizziness clouded Faith's vision, forcing her to lean against the fence for support.

"What is it?" Concern laced Dottie's voice.

"Yes, what is it?" Reva echoed.

Faith's mind worked to come up with a plausible explanation. "It's—just—hmm—personal."

She hated dodging Dottie, but she couldn't tell her the truth. The note was meant to scare her and it was doing a good job. But the note and the phone call wasn't Vinnie's style. He wouldn't give her a chance to run, he'd show up unexpectedly.

It had to be from the private investigator.

Maybe he thought he could flush her out with the note. She glanced down the road. There were no cars visible, but that didn't mean he couldn't be out there somewhere, waiting. She couldn't wait for tomorrow. She had to leave tonight.

Anxious to get back inside and plan her next move, Faith turned to Dottie. "Would you mind if we go back in? I'm feeling a little tired."

"Of course not, dear." Dottie hovered over Faith as if she were the invalid. "We'll get you to your room so you can lie down."

"Oh, yes. You do look a little under the weather." Reva smiled sweetly before walking away.

"That woman has no heart," Dottie muttered, taking Faith's arm.

Faith shrugged and let Dottie lead her back to the house. After hanging up their coats, Faith asked, "Do you wish to go upstairs?"

"Yes, I think I'll take a rest, as well," Dottie answered.

Faith settled Dottie in her room and turned to leave.

"Whatever it is, Faith, tell Luke."

Stunned, Faith gaped. "I—don't—what?"

With an amazingly strong grip, Dottie took her hand. "Honey, something's got you scared. First, that phone call this afternoon, and now this note. You're pale, and you're shaking like a leaf in the breeze. You don't have to tell me, but tell Luke. He can help you."

Faith closed her eyes. Everything inside screamed for her to do as Dottie suggested, but she couldn't. It wasn't his problem to solve. She kissed Dottie's cheek. "Goodbye."

"Excuse me?" Dottie's anxious expression tore at Faith's heart.

"I mean I'll see you later."

She went to her room to plan. She'd have to make do with the little money she had until she could get to a bank.

Now, if she could just get out without anyone questioning her. Her mind kicked into overdrive. Reva would be leaving the ranch to return to her own home soon.

Fleetingly, Faith contemplated asking Reva for a ride, but discarded the idea. It would be better if no one knew how or why she left. That way when Vinnie did show up, they could honestly say they didn't know what had happened to her. She couldn't leave until dark and when no one would miss her right away.

Once Dottie was upstairs and settled for the night, she'd leave. Luke would be with the llamas or the horses as he always was after dinner, so she'd have to be careful going down the drive.

She'd be leaving the Circle C Ranch tonight and leaving behind a part of her heart.

NINE

From the corner of his eye, Luke saw movement.

He sank back into the shadows and waited. The light of the moon reflecting off the snow illuminated a figure scurrying behind his Bronco. A second later, the person emerged from around the front.

Adrenaline pumped through his heart, energizing him. On quiet feet, he moved through the shadows, closing the gap between him and the mystery person. Approaching from behind, Luke judged the person to be of medium height and slight of frame.

He couldn't make out the face, obscured from his view by a dark cap pulled low over the collar of a dark jacket. The person's pace accelerated, soft tennis shoes crunched slightly on the packed snow on the edge of the gravel drive.

With grim determination, he closed in on his target. No one tried to make off with something from the Campbell ranch. Then he recognized the suitcases.

Confused, he frowned and grabbed Faith by the scruff of the neck and turned her around. "What are you doing?" he demanded.

Faith dropped the bags and squeaked, "Luke."

"For crying out loud, Faith." Apprehension tightened his chest, making his voice gruff. "Where are you going?"

Her chin came up in a defensive gesture that set his teeth on edge. "I don't have to answer to you."

"Oh, yes you do." He grabbed the bags. "We'll discuss this inside."

"Give me my luggage." Faith struggled unsuccessfully to take the bags from his grip. Finally, she fisted her hand. "You have no right to stop me, Luke Campbell."

Anger and an odd sense of hurt flashed within his chest. Had the friendship they'd begun to build mean nothing? "Oh no? I think I have every right. As your employer, I deserve two weeks' notice." He thought she might be on the verge of tears, but he couldn't tell for sure.

"I don't have two weeks!"

Her exclamation left him more bewildered and he softened his tone. "As your friend, I'd like to know what's going on."

She turned away from him and the moon's glow lit her features, exposing her drawn, scared expression. That did it. He would get answers out of her tonight, even if he needed to throw her over his shoulder and carry her inside.

"Come on, Faith. We're going in."

He could tell by the tightening of her lips that she wanted to protest. Giving her no chance, he turned on his heel and carried her bags toward the house. He let out an exaggerated sigh when she didn't immediately follow, but when he heard her quiet footfalls behind him, he released a quick breath of relief.

Bossy, controlling, arrogant.

Faith couldn't come up with enough names to silently yell at Luke's retreating back.

Didn't he realize she had to go for his sake? *No, of course not, you dolt.* He didn't know what lurked out there, waiting to pounce. She hadn't told him.

She stoically followed him into the study. The overhead light came on bathing the room in a yellow ambient glow. He went around the wide walnut desk and set her bags down on the muted sage green carpet before seating himself in his black leather captain's chair.

"Please, shut the door."

His tone made her think of the one time she'd been sent to the dean's office in prep school for talking in class. Luke had that same reasonable look on his face that Dean Snoddgrass had had, and it made her feel small and insecure. But she was a grown woman, not a child.

And she'd vowed after Vinnie, she would never cower before a man again.

Drawing herself to her full height of five-feet, eight-inches tall, she closed the door and moved to sit on the striped cushioned divan by the window. Looking at Luke, she clasped her hands in front of her and waited.

"You do that when you're nervous." Luke leaned forward, his look intent.

"Do what?"

"Clasp your hands together until the knuckles turn white." He nodded toward her hands.

Abashed, she looked down and realized her knuckles were indeed turning white. Unhooking her fingers, she spread her hands, palms down, on her thighs.

"So tell me," he said.

Biting her lip, she hedged. "Tell you what?"

For a long, silent moment he closed his eyes, and when he opened them she knew he'd reached the end of his patience. "Tell me what's really going on."

"I don't have to tell you anything." Surprised at herself for baiting him, she steeled herself for his reaction. Her heart told her Luke was a man who had control of his temper, yet when his palms landed on the desk, making a loud noise, she flinched.

"I can't help you, Faith, unless you tell me what you're so afraid of. And don't tell me it's investors or charitable organizations," he said through gritted teeth.

"Who said I wanted your help?" Though that was exactly what she wanted.

She wanted to break down and let him take care of everything. It was so hard to be strong and brave. And alone. But she cared too much about him to continue to risk his safety.

He came around the desk, moving slowly and deliberately. She tensed, steeling herself as old fears rushed headlong into her mind. Was she wrong about him? Would he be like Vinnie and use his physical power to bend her to his will?

Luke knelt down beside her and took her hands in his. Relief swept through her and burning tears gathered at the back of her eyes. He'd proven himself gentle and self-controlled before. She was ashamed for doubting him.

"Whatever your burdens are, God can help you. Tell him. And if I can help you, I will."

Each word he spoke was a plea to her heart. She could feel the tears gathering steam and fought them with all her might. God wouldn't help her. What right did she have to put Luke in danger? What right did she have to his help? She tried to speak. "I—I don't—"

"Please, Faith."

The tenderness of his voice battered down her defenses and she broke, like a water pipe bursting. Large, wet tears streamed down her face and sobs racked her body. The brave front, the unyielding control she'd kept herself under, shattered like crystal hitting the floor. Jagged edges of pain and fear cut into her, leaving her wounded and bleeding inside.

The past had caught up with her, the uncertainty of the future stretched out before her and the world seemed more cold, more desolate than before.

Luke gathered her into his arms and suddenly warmth enveloped her, a soothing balm to her tattered soul. The embrace was comforting and the pressure secure. His hand stroked down her back in a calming tempo. The rhythmic movement continued until the tide of tears ebbed and the flow dried up. She lifted her head from his shoulder and their gazes locked.

The air around them seemed to shift and change, the embrace became a caress and heat scorched her palms where they rested against his hard chest. Faith took a shuddering breath, unsure what she should do.

Luke's smile was as intimate as a kiss and the effect left her off-kilter.

Gathering her strength, she sniffed. "I don't usually cry on men's shoulders."

"No, I don't suppose you do. I would imagine you don't let anyone close enough." He tucked a lock of hair behind her ear, the gesture raising goose bumps on her skin.

"I'm sorry." How she hated that sentiment. She'd

sworn to herself she wouldn't say those words any-more. For too many years those little words spared her some pain, but not humiliation.

Luke shook his head. "You have nothing to be sorry for."

Everything was turned upside down. Her strength deserted her. "You don't understand."

"Make me understand." His words caressed her.

"Where do I begin?" she whispered, her voice raw.

"Start with tonight. Why were you leaving?"

A sense of the inevitable overwhelmed her and her head dropped to his chest. Luke's finger under her chin brought her gaze back to his. From deep inside she dredged up the courage to tell him. "He's coming."

"Who?"

Taking a deep breath, she blurted out the truth. "My ex-husband."

Instantly, an oppressive weight lifted from her, making her light-headed. And just as quickly, she felt guilty for her utter selfishness. Her motivation for telling him wasn't to protect him and his family but to lighten her own load.

She expected him to recoil, to draw away from her, but he touched her cheek with the back of his finger, his voice soft. "He's who you're running from?"

She nodded.

"How do you know he's coming here?"

"He called."

It sounded ridiculous and it still didn't seem right. It just wasn't Vinnie's style to give any warning. He usually struck when least expected.

"Are you sure the voice was his?"

Faith frowned. "I—the voice was muffled, but who else could it have been?"

Luke stood and began to pace. "What did he say?"

"Well—" She bit her lip in concentration. "If I remember correctly, he said, 'I'm coming for you, Faith. You can't get away. No matter where you go, I'll find you.'"

"Could the call have been from someone else?" Luke sounded unconvinced.

"I don't know." Faith realized her hands were clasped tight again. Quickly, she separated them.

"The P.I., maybe?"

She shrugged. "I had the same thought, but why would he do that?"

Then she remembered the note. She pulled it out of her pocket and offered the folded piece of paper to Luke. "This was also delivered here."

He took the note and read it in silence. His jaw tightened and the small scar on his chin blanched.

"You said this was delivered?" He looked up from the note and studied her.

She nodded.

"By who?"

"A boy."

"When?"

"Sometime Friday."

"What did he say?" The questions came like rapid fire.

"That some man paid him to ride his bike out and deliver the note."

"You talked to the boy?"

He should have been a lawyer, she thought. "No, Reva did."

His eyes narrowed. "I'll talk with her tomorrow." Stroking his chin, he seemed deep in thought.

This is it, she thought, he's going to tell me to leave. What choice did he have? He had to do it to protect Dottie, himself and all the rest of them. Faith closed her eyes, confused why the knowledge hurt so much. She'd been on her way when he'd stopped her, so what did it matter?

It mattered because before it had been her decision, now it would be his.

"Why is your ex-husband looking for you? The money you were talking about?"

Opening her eyes, she met his intense stare. How did she explain the crazed mind of Vince Palmero? "No, not the money. He wants what belongs to him."

Luke moved to his desk and leaned his hips against the edge. "Meaning?"

Faith stood and did some pacing of her own. She retraced her steps several times before she finally found it within herself to go on. "Meaning, he is a possessive man who never lets anything be taken away from him."

Unable to face Luke, she continued her trek back and forth across the room. "You have to understand that I was his ticket to a life he'd only been able to view from the outside. Through me, he was able to enter New York society. When I left him it was the ultimate betrayal. To him, I am a possession. Nothing more than a showpiece, bought and paid for through marriage. The money is just a bonus."

The ache in her tightly clenched hands barely registered against the ache inside. She faced Luke, not sure what to expect. His dark eyes were hooded and hiding any indication of his thoughts. Doggedly, she continued. "I am his property, Luke, and he won't rest until I'm back in my gilded cage." She shuddered. "Or dead."

"Neither one of those things is going to happen, Faith."

He sounded so sure, she longed to believe him. "He's not going to stop looking for me. I should leave now while I can before he comes here. He's unpredictable. I'm sorry I put you and your family in danger."

Ignoring her words, he asked, "What have the police done?"

She lifted her hands in the air in a helpless gesture. "The police? Are you kidding? In New York, you have to prove abuse for a divorce to be granted on the grounds of cruel and inhumane treatment. So my lawyer filed for separation, and then a year later I was granted a divorce based on that. But in the meantime, Vinnie began stalking me."

She gave a mirthless laugh. "Or I should say he had others stalk me. Again, for an order of protection to be granted, I had to prove *he* was stalking me. One officer I talked to had been sympathetic and suggested a bodyguard."

She clenched her fists. Ineffectual rage at the system burned hot in her soul. "Brian, the bodyguard, ended up in the hospital with a bullet in his back. Of course, there were no witnesses and the police said they had no evidence implicating Vinnie. It was then I realized the only way to protect myself and everyone near me was to run. Unfortunately, that was the one night Vinnie decided to make his move. He must have had someone watching me because he showed up just as I was leaving."

She hated even thinking about that night. "He— he hurt me badly. But I still got away. And once again since there were no witnesses, just my word against his and he had an alibi—his family—the police's hands were tied."

Nothing she said seemed to faze Luke. He still

leaned motionless against the desk, his expression indecipherable.

She repeated her earlier words. "I should leave."

Suddenly he pushed away from the desk, tension emanating from him in waves. He shook his head. "Running isn't the answer. Just because there are no walls, you're still in a cage."

"But Luke, you don't seem to understand. He's coming *here*. I've put you and your family in danger. I have to go."

A sinking feeling told her he wanted to play the hero and an image of Brian, on the ground, blood seeping from the wound in his back, skittered across her mind. "I couldn't stand it if I were responsible for some harm done to you or your mother."

"Nothing is going to happen to any of us, Faith." He stood in front of the window and stared out at the black night.

"Do you honestly believe you can protect us from Vinnie?" She continued on even though he kept his back to her and didn't respond. "You would tower over him, but what good is that when faced with a gun?"

Still no response. She frowned and said, "My only option is to keep running." She moved around the desk to pick up her bags.

In the reflection of the window, she noticed Luke had closed his eyes and his lips moved with silent words. She stilled. He was praying. She was awed by the thought that he was asking God for help. "No use praying on my account. God wants nothing to do with me."

He turned then. "That's not true, Faith. God loves you very much. And we will figure this out. I need to know everything you can tell me about Vinnie."

"Luke, this isn't your problem. This isn't a military operation for you to understand and execute. This is my life."

"And I need to get a handle on the situation so we can determine the best course of action."

"I'm not asking you to help me, Luke. I'm asking you to let me go. Just forget you ever met me."

He shook his head. "I can't do that. God brought you into my life for a reason."

"It was chance that brought me into your life, not God."

"Do you really believe that?"

"I don't know what to believe anymore." Since she'd landed in Oregon and met Luke, she'd felt closer to God, thought she'd felt His presence through Luke and Dottie. But why now after all these years?

He considered her words. "Tell me what happened with your marriage."

To humor him, she complied. She avoided his gaze as shame washed over her. "Vinnie wasn't what I thought he was when I married him."

"What did you think he was?"

"I thought he was a good man." She shrugged. "When my grandfather died, I was so lost and alone. I fell apart. Vinnie worked for the law firm that handled Grandfather's estate. He was so—smooth. At first, kind and sympathetic. He stayed by my side during the funeral and the following days when so many people came around demanding money. I mistook my gratitude for love. When he asked me to marry him it seemed like the right thing to do. By the time I realized how wrong I'd been about him, it was too late. He'd wanted what marrying me could bring him."

She glanced at Luke. He sat attentively listening. No one had ever really listened to her before.

"He'd known just how to play me. I was so gullible."

"Go on," Luke prodded gently.

"He never quite fit in to the New York social circles. Oh, he got invited to the best parties and had access to the most exclusive clubs, but he couldn't change the fact that he'd grown up in a blue-collar home in the Bronx. And he became obsessed with me. He wanted to control my every move, who I talked to, where I went. I found myself becoming more and more isolated from the world until I felt like a prisoner in my own home."

"So you broke free."

She gave a mirthless laugh. "No, not right away, but I should have. Instead I thought I could change him, make him see how unhealthy his behavior was getting. But the more I tried, the worse he got." A shudder rippled down her spine. "One day I tried too hard."

"What did he do?" Luke's voice sounded gruff and his expression fierce.

Her throat constricted making her unable to continue. She shook her head, wanting to run, to get away from the memories.

"Did he hit you, Faith?"

"He—he hurt—me." She remembered the look of rage on Vinnie's face, the sound of his fists slamming into her body, and the pain. The pain that still lingered in her shoulder and her heart.

"Did you tell the police this?"

"Vinnie kept me under lock and key most of the time. I couldn't go to the police. Besides, he was smart enough not to hit where it would be obvious. At first I tried to understand and believed his promises that it wouldn't happen again." She clenched her fists. "I'd turned into one of those women you see in made-for-TV movies. He may have hurt me in so many ways, but he never crushed me."

She could see the anger in his eyes and the tightening of his jaw. "Faith, you were right to leave him. God would not expect you to stay in an abusive relationship."

Fresh tears gathered in her eyes. She'd been taught that marriage was for life. No matter what.

His expression softened. He took her hands again. "God loves you, Faith. God did not author the evil that has touched your life. The Bible urges believers to separate from those who hurt them and to create a safe place for themselves. And you've done that, Faith."

"If God loves me, why did He allow it?" Old anger surfaced, clogging her throat. She didn't understand. She'd tried to be good. A good daughter, a good granddaughter, a good wife. Still He'd taken her parents and then her grandparents away. He hadn't protected her from Vinnie.

Luke squeezed her hands and looked at her with an earnestness that touched her soul. "I don't have the answer to that question, Faith. He never promised there wouldn't be difficult, awful times in our lives, but He promised to be there with us. He knows you and He has cried with you. He has felt your hurt and your anguish. He's not sitting up in the sky judging you, looking for ways to hurt you. He loves you. He wants you to put your trust in Him."

The crystal blue of Luke's eyes shimmered. Faith swallowed as the tears gathered in her own eyes. She wanted to believe Luke's words, she just felt so uncertain and lost.

"Faith, it wasn't chance or coincidence that brought you here. I know in my heart that God has a plan for you. You just need to lay down your doubts and trust."

"That's easier said than done."

Luke smiled tenderly. "It takes a leap of faith."

"I suppose it does."

She held his gaze and the moment stretched. In the depths of Luke's eyes, she could see and feel the mercy and grace of God's love. She felt warmed and cared for and she would take the memories of this moment with her, because, sadly, the situation had not changed. "Luke, I appreciate your words, I really do. But it doesn't change the fact that I need to leave. And I need to leave now."

He shook his head. She could feel the tension inside of him. He stood and paced. When he stopped he looked at her with a determined light in his eyes. "We don't have to decide anything tonight. Tomorrow, after we've had a chance to think things through, then we can—" He paused and stepped closer. "We, together, will figure out a way to protect you. You can't keep running for the rest of your life."

She stood. "I don't think—"

"Please, promise me you'll rest tonight and tomorrow we can deal with all of this."

Leaving in the morning would be easier. Luke could take her to town; she could stop at the bank and then catch the next bus. "All right."

Luke looked relieved. He moved to his desk and pulled something from one of the drawers. When he came back to her, he held a leather-bound Bible in his hands. "My father gave this to me when I was a teenager. I'd like you to have it."

"Oh, Luke, I couldn't." Her grandfather had had a beautiful Bible that he'd read from and in those last few weeks she'd taken to reading the psalms to him.

"Please." He put the book in her hands.

Awed by the gift, Faith ran her finger over the inscription in the bottom right hand corner. TO MY SON, LUKE CAMPBELL.

"I think you'll find the answers you seek in there."

Faith's gaze shot to Luke's. How did he know? "I wouldn't know where to begin."

"I've always been partial to the book of Luke myself." He grinned.

She laughed. "That sounds like a good place to start."

Luke's expression turned serious. "In the morning, we'll come up with a plan."

"I need to stay longer."

"Oh, nice joke. When are you coming back?"

"It's no joke, Rog." Luke could picture his friend's chocolate-brown forehead creased with lines and his black eyes narrowing as silence stretched over the phone line. Though Roger Tumble was his commanding officer, their friendship had been immediate and tight. Each attributed the deep bond to their mutual commitment to God.

In his soft southern drawl, Roger commented, "How much time?"

"End of January."

"I'll send you the paperwork. Your mom not doing well?"

"She's good. Something else has come up."

"Now, that sounds intriguing. Care to share?"

Luke stared out the window of his office and watched snow fall against the dark sky. Light-colored flecks floated down to earth, blanketing the ground. Good thing he'd stopped Faith from leaving or she'd be trudging through the snow right now. "Not really."

"Don't tell me this has anything to do with a woman?"

Luke sighed. "It does."

"I could have sworn you were a confirmed bachelor. So tell me."

Luke grimaced. He wasn't ready to discuss the issue of Faith yet. Not when his emotions were all over the place. "When I see you."

There was a pause. "If that's what you want. Give your mother my best."

"I will. How's the weekly Bible study going?"

"So, so. It's not the same without your leadership."

Luke felt a blast of guilt for leaving the guys in the field for so long.

He'd worked so hard to build a foundation of ministry in his unit; he didn't want it to flounder.

But right now Faith needed him more.

"Thanks, Roger. I'll talk with you soon." He hung up and sat back.

For most of the night, he'd wrestled with his conflicting thoughts about Faith, about the secrets she'd kept and about the potential danger she'd brought to his house. He was angry. Sure. Her presence put his mother in harm's way. Though, the threat was slim compared to the war he'd been fighting on the other side of the world.

But more, he was hurt that Faith hadn't confided in him sooner.

Earlier he'd contacted the sheriff and filled him in. Sheriff Bane had checked out the P.I. The Sheriff had assured Luke that Costello had left town. Sheriff Bane said he'd keep an eye out for any other strangers. Also, he'd promised to send a car along the main road at intervals.

After talking to the sheriff, Luke had contacted a local lawyer who said he'd see what he could do legally to protect Faith.

Now all he had to do was convince Faith to stay put and to keep his own heart from falling victim to her.

TEN

Rats! Large rats with heavy feet in the attic. Faith's pulse raced. Panic rushed in.

Something. Someone was on the roof. Trying to get in. Vinnie?

She scrambled out of bed. She was shaking so hard, she had trouble pulling on her robe and putting her feet into her tennis shoes. At the bedroom door, she paused and listened. The quietness of the hall suggested all was well. But she knew what she'd heard. She hurried to Luke's door and knocked. No answer.

Biting her lip to keep the panic from overwhelming her, she cautiously went downstairs. Faint streaks of the dawn light splintered through the cracks in the curtains. The frigid air left from the night clawed at her, prickling her skin.

With her hand on the knob leading outside, she paused. The noise she'd heard earlier became recognizable. She stepped outside and followed the steady beat of a hammer around the house until she was standing just below her bedroom window.

On the ground was a pile of clean snow, obviously cleared from the roof. She arched her back and craned her neck to see onto the roof. A male was crouched with a hammer in his hand.

Her shoulders sagged with relief. "Luke, what are you doing?"

The hammering stopped and he stood. "Blocking the vents so the raccoons don't nest," he replied.

The dawn light bathed Luke in its frosty glow. He had a cap pulled low over his ears. His usually clean-shaven face showed the night's growth of beard, making him more rugged and handsome. Traces of snow clung to his work boots and his thick plaid shirt didn't look nearly warm enough.

"It's barely five o'clock in the morning. I nearly had a heart attack!"

"Sorry," he called. "I couldn't sleep."

"It's freezing, not to mention that roof is slick with ice. You're going to kill yourself up there. Come down."

He regarded her for a moment. "Worried, are you?"

Heat crawled up her neck. "As I would be of anyone standing on an icy roof."

With a grin, he stated, "I'll be done soon. Then we can talk."

"Fine," she replied and pulled her robe tighter against the chilly air.

She'd let him talk her into staying last night, but she was determined to leave today. No matter how much she didn't want to.

The sharp winter sun beat down on Luke. Even though the temperature barely reached thirty degrees, beads of sweat rolled down his back and disappeared into the waistband of his jeans.

He'd long since removed his flannel shirt, opting for just a long-sleeved thermal. And now he used the edge of the material to wipe his brow as he stood to stretch his tired muscles. His gaze took in the beauty of the land.

The looming Cascade mountain range covered in lush forests of Ponderosa Pines dusted white was breathtaking. The high desert, though flat, stretched out with a beauty of its own, whether in winter or during the blush of spring or the heat of a dry summer or the turning of the leaves in fall. It didn't matter the time of year, he loved this land.

Luke knelt down and picked up a tile, turning it over in his hands the same way his conflicted thoughts turned in his head.

He should be back with his unit, fighting the good fight to keep freedom a reality for all human life. Helping the men to keep their faith.

Yet, he wanted to stay here where his life began.

He wanted to fulfill the dream his father had for him. But which father?

His earthly father had wanted him to run this ranch, to carry on the Campbell name and pass on the legacy of love that his parents had built. Blake Campbell had never made his wishes for his son a secret.

His Heavenly Father had wanted Luke to join the military, to serve his country as well as serve God. Luke had never made his faith a secret and he'd gladly done as he felt the Lord wanted of him, never once feeling unsure of his path.

But now Luke *was* unsure. Why had the Lord brought Faith into his life? And why was he so glad?

The tile fell from his hands like a hot coal. Was he falling for Faith? The emotions bouncing around his head and his heart were unfamiliar. And, frankly, it scared him. *Lord, what's happening? Is this part of Your plan? But why?*

He liked Faith and respected her. He admired her courage and strength, was proud of how capable and willing she was to try new things. Her sense of humor and quick wit captivated him. And yes, he was physically attracted to her. Any male with a beating heart and blood in his veins would be. Kissing her had only solidified that attraction.

But falling for her? No way.

Picking up his hammer, he pounded the nails in

the last vent with more force than necessary. He had to get perspective here.

It would only complicate matters if he were to pursue any type of relationship with Faith beyond that of friend. She had baggage in her past that needed to be dealt with, and he had a life to sort out. It wouldn't work for them to get involved.

He was a man used to being in control. He could control himself, all of him, including his emotions.

Awareness brushed over him as Faith walked outside again. As if the world had suddenly slowed on its axis, he stood to watch her walk to the fence. Three llamas trotted instantly to her side.

Sunlight danced off her girlish ponytail, making her look young and carefree. His throat constricted, trapping his breath in his chest, painfully expanding his lungs. It pleased him to see she wore the down parka he'd picked up for her in town. Much better suited to the climate than the thin wool coat she'd arrived in.

Suddenly the fence railing inches from Faith exploded with a dull thud, splintering the wood into flying junks. The llamas scattered. Faith yelped and crouched low, covering her head with her hands. Close to her feet, dirt and snow sprayed out as something hit the ground.

Gunfire!

Panic seized Luke's lungs. His gaze frantically

searched for the shooter as he stepped forward. On the main road a dark green pickup screeched away.

Luke's foot slipped on the slick roof and he realized he'd made a mistake. He went down hard on his backside, then onto his back. His hands flayed hopelessly in search of something to grab, his body plummeted down the roof, the edges of each tile biting into his flesh. His teeth ground together in sharp pain.

From below him, he heard Faith's cry of alarm.

The gutter rushed at him and he grabbed hold, but one end of the metal gave way with a loud wrenching creak. His grip failed and he was free-falling again.

Then he hit the snow-covered ground with a dull thud and a loud groan. The last thing he saw before his eyes slid shut was the hunk of gutter swaying over his head.

He was dead.

Fear constricted Faith's heart, forced the air from her lungs. She ran to him, to his limp body on the snow-covered ground.

"Oh, please don't let him be dead."

Putting her fingers against his neck, she felt a strong pulse beating a steady rhythm and momentary relief eased her panic.

He wasn't dead.

"Luke? Luke, can you hear me?"

She quickly searched his body for broken bones.

There didn't seem to be any obvious fractures. But his head…she stifled a sob.

"Luke—" her voice trailed off and tears sprang to her eyes. "God, let him be all right, please."

With jerky, harsh movements, she wiped away her tears. *He's not going to die,* she admonished herself gruffly. God would not do that to Luke.

He needed help and she was his only hope. She stood and turned to run, but a hand wrapped around her ankle nearly toppled her over. She screamed before noticing Luke regarding her with pain-filled eyes. Immediately she knelt beside him.

"I have to go—get h-help." Her voice broke.

"I'm—okay," he croaked on a deep breath before wincing.

Faith smoothed a hand over his brow. "You're hurt."

"Minor scrapes and bruises."

"You might have a broken back or neck, even."

"The snow broke my fall," he quipped. "Are you okay?"

A ripple of terror ran through her. "Yes. Thankfully he was a bad shot."

"Not meant to kill, only scare."

"Well, then, he did a good job. Let me go get help." She moved to rise again, but his hand gripped her arm.

"You help me."

"Luke, you shouldn't move, not until the ambulance comes."

He closed his eyes. "I've fallen off that roof more times than I can count. It just knocked the wind out of me."

"I don't know." She looked him over, unconvinced. "I still think I should get a doctor."

With a groan, Luke pushed himself up on to his elbows. His eyes scrunched up tight and his mouth thinned. The scar on his jaw paled. His visible pain made her nauseous.

With infinite care, he sat. The rip in his shirt revealed a raw cut on his shoulder. So much red. The sight of his blood turned her stomach. It could have been so much worse. For both of them.

And that's when it hit her.

If anything happened to Luke she knew her heart wouldn't survive.

She helped him stand and when his arm settled around her shoulders, she staggered slightly as she bore the brunt of his weight.

They entered the house and Faith steered him to a chair at the kitchen table. "Do you have a first-aid kit somewhere? We need to clean your wounds."

Grimacing, he lowered himself to the chair. "I need the phone."

She handed the phone over and clenched her hands together as he called the sheriff to explain what had happened.

When he hung up, she asked, "Do you think they'll catch him?"

"We can pray so." He started to rise. "I have a first-aid kit in my room."

She rushed to support him as they made their way upstairs. "Should I get your mother? She was sleeping when I came outside."

"If she didn't hear anything, let's not upset her."

Pushing open the door of his bedroom, she realized she'd never before seen his domain. His masculine scent swirled around her, heightening her already taut senses.

He pointed to the closet. "My first-aid kit's in there."

The kit sat on the floor of the closet next to his cowboy boots. She also grabbed a soft-looking blue flannel shirt off the hanger. On the verge of closing the door, her gaze snagged on a blur of green.

It hit her like a punch in the stomach.

These were his military clothes—camouflage fatigues with his name sewn on the breast pocket and a dark green suit. Even in the dim light of the bedroom, the medals and ribbons were eye-catching.

At the reminder of his life outside the ranch an ache in the vicinity of her heart stole her breath away. Resolutely, she turned away, telling herself she shouldn't be upset. She'd known from the beginning that Luke was only a temporary fixture in her life. One day soon he'd be leaving, going back to a job where worse than a fall from a roof could happen. Where his life would be in danger every second.

Masking her distress, she moved back to the bed and set the kit down. The case easily opened with a click and she pulled out the supplies she needed. Unable to meet Luke's gaze, she handed him two painkillers. "I'll go get you some water."

Luke shook his head. "Not necessary." He popped the pills into his mouth and swallowed them dry.

The large cut on his shoulder needed her attention first. She helped him to remove his shirt and forced her gaze to stay on the cut, not on the width of his shoulders and muscles on his arms. Thankful for something to keep her mind and hands busy, she doused a cotton pad with an antiseptic. Before applying the pad to his skin, she said, "This may sting."

He nodded and she placed the soaked pad against his flesh.

Luke closed his eyes but made no noise.

Taking her lip between her teeth, Faith continued to bathe the wound, wondering at his ability to take the pain. Once the area was free from the dried blood, she used butterfly bandages to close the gap.

Tenderly, she began to tend to the various other bloodied scrapes. A nasty looking scar on his right shoulder caught her attention. The skin puckered and drew inward around what appeared to have been some sort of hole. Faith went rigid.

An image of her bodyguard flashed in her mind. With shaky hands, she touched the imperfect flesh. Hoping it wasn't what she feared, she asked, "What is this?"

Luke shrugged. "Got too close to a pitchfork one day."

"A pitchfork," she repeated, her voice breaking.

His head swiveled around and he stared at her for a long tense moment. Faith looked back at him steadily, knowing his flippant remark was meant to deflect, but she was unwilling to push for the truth.

Still holding her gaze, he stated flatly, "It's a bullet wound."

Having the truth confirmed did nothing to ease the distress she felt. She placed her hand over the scar as if she could somehow erase the proof of his mortality.

Feeling his gaze on her again, she lifted her eyes and met his intense look. In a voice barely above a whisper, she said, "Tell me about your life in the army."

He cocked his head to the side. "You want to know about the good parts or the not-so-good parts?"

"All the parts."

"War is ugly." A bleakness entered his expression and the look tore at her heart.

"Where were you when 9/11 happened?" she asked.

"At the time I was stationed in Birmingham, Alabama."

"And then?"

"Afghanistan. Operation Enduring Freedom. I agree with why we went, but I still have to live with the memories."

With a gentle touch she caressed his cheek, wishing she could take away his pain. "How *do* you live with the memories?"

"I release them to Jesus."

She marveled at his trust and dedication to the Lord. She didn't completely understand, but she admired his faith. Maybe one day she'd be as certain of God as Luke was.

"I'm sorry you had to see any fighting at all," she commented softly.

He gave her an odd look.

"What?"

The moment stretched and then finally he spoke as if she'd opened the floodgates to a dam, his words tumbled out, his voice a rough, raw rasp. She could see his torment, could hear the anguish in his tone.

He told her of secret missions long before the tragedy in New York, most in far-off places and some surprisingly closer to home. He talked of lives he'd saved and those he'd taken, and with each story he grew more distant, more mechanical.

Her heart cracked in her chest and she knew any minute it would shatter into a million pieces; her anguish at his private torment was tearing her apart.

She touched her fingertip to his lips, stilling his words.

"Why do you stay in the service?" she asked, gently.

"I joined because God led me there. I stay out of obedience to what He has called me to."

The simple honesty in his eyes struck her profoundly. She'd never experienced that kind of certainty in her life.

She helped him into the flannel shirt. Careful not to put pressure on his wounds, she wrapped her arms around him, needing to somehow comfort his soul, as well as his body. For a heartbeat he resisted.

"Let me," she whispered.

He melted against her, coming to rest in the cradle of her arms.

It was a heady feeling, this sense of protectiveness and willingness to give of herself, one she'd never fully experienced before. Oh, she'd cared for her ailing grandfather, but this…this was different. More intense, more…consuming.

She smoothed her hand over his hair. His head rested against her shoulder and the warmth made her feel strong and sure. After a long, silent moment, he lifted his head. The spot where his head had been grew cold, but the look in his eyes warmed her heart.

"Faith, I've never told another person these things before," he wavered. He sounded stunned and a bit frightened.

His openness, his trust was a precious gift. One she didn't deserve, but one she would cherish. "Thank you."

He reached for her and winced.

"You need rest." Purposefully, she made her voice brusque. She'd allow things to get too personal as it was.

Waving away her concern, he said, "Need to see the damage outside from the gunshots."

"We shouldn't go outside," she stated, her heart pounding with fresh panic.

He stood, his jaw tightening. "You shouldn't go outside. Not yet. I need to figure out how to better protect you."

As he moved past her and out the door, tenderness welled inside her chest. She would be forever grateful to God for bringing Luke into her life, for showing her that not all men were the same. Some could be generous, giving, loving. But her feelings for Luke left her no other choice. She had to leave.

No matter how much it would hurt.

Luke stared at the bullet hole. Or rather what remained of the shattered wooden fence railing. Hot coals of anger burned in his gut right alongside ice-cold terror at how close those bullets had come to taking out Faith.

The shooter was no amateur. At the distance that

truck had been, he had to have had a high-powered rifle, and the lack of retort suggested a silencer.

The jilted ex-husband?

Luke didn't think so. Not from what Faith had said about him.

A hired assassin? Then why the scare tactic?

Luke's lip curled in disgust. Her husband didn't want her back, he wanted to hunt her down. The man enjoyed the chase.

Luke fisted his hand. He hated the helpless, sitting-duck feeling stealing over him. Action. That's what he needed. Take action. Find Vinnie Palmero and end this situation. Then Faith would be free to go back to her life.

Luke frowned, not liking how the thought of Faith leaving stabbed at him.

Faith needed to leave and resume her life so that *he* could resume his life.

With that in mind, Luke headed to his office and called the sheriff's station again and was told the sheriff was on his way to the Circle C Ranch.

While he waited he did a Google search on Palmero. There was, he found, very little info. His name in the New York Bar Association, a few court cases, a wedding announcement for his marriage to the Delange Heiress.

And one interesting tidbit. An article about a man named Anthony Palmero who had been arrested and put in jail for the robbery and murder of a store clerk. The article mentioned that the younger brother, a lawyer named Vince Palmero, had worked tirelessly to get his brother paroled. He'd been successful. Anthony Palmero was paroled after serving ten of his twenty-year sentence.

Luke wasn't sure how this all fit together with Faith's situation. Funny that she hadn't mentioned Anthony.

Two cars pulled up outside; the sheriff with an entourage.

Luke went out to meet them.

Sheriff Bane and Deputy Unger emerged from the first car. Two other uniformed officers stepped from the second vehicle. Luke knew them, Deputy Jason Russell and Bill Smith, the county's local crime-scene tech. He acknowledged them with a nod.

"Did you find the truck?" Luke asked as he shook hands with the sheriff.

"Yes. Abandoned on the other side of town. It was stolen sometime during the night from some tourists renting a condo at the Black Butte Resort. The vehicle had been wiped clean."

Luke wasn't surprised. Leo and Jerry came out of the llama barn. Luke filled them in on the morning's events. "Where are Mac and Charles?"

"Mac's visiting his mother over in Bend. I haven't seen Charles today," answered Leo.

"I'll see if he's in his room," Jerry offered.

"I didn't realize Mac was local," Luke stated.

Leo shrugged in answer.

"So that's where the bullets hit?" the sheriff asked as he moved closer to the fence.

"Faith was standing there, where Jason is," Luke commented, pointing.

Deputy Russell whistled. "That was close."

"Okay, Bill. Do your thing," Sheriff Bane said, stepping back to give Bill room to find the slugs. "I'll be posting Jason here outside the gate. He and Deputy Unger will be taking turns. No one will go in or out with out passing them first. I've contacted the New York Department of Justice. They're checking on Palmero. As soon as I learn anything I'll let you know."

"Thanks."

"How's Faith holding up?"

"She's spooked," Luke replied.

"Keep her close to the ranch. If her ex-husband is anywhere in the vicinity, he'll have a hard time getting to her if she's here."

"That won't be a problem." He hoped.

"Good."

"Got them," Bill exclaimed and held up the two small metal bullets between his latex-covered fingers. He bagged the slugs.

"Not much else for us to do now," stated the

sheriff. "I'll keep in touch." He, Bill and Deputy Unger climbed into the sheriff's car.

Luke thanked them and watched as they drove out of the drive. Deputy Russell parked his vehicle just outside the Circle C entrance.

"The guys and I will also take turns patrolling the ranch," said Leo, his weathered face showing concern.

Luke nodded his thanks. Grateful for the support.

For now they were safe. But the thrumming of warning pulsing through his veins questioned that reasoning. The threat remained out there, lurking.

And Luke was anxious to meet it head on.

ELEVEN

From the living-room window, Faith watched the uniformed men talk with Luke. The need to confide in Dottie rose sharply. Dottie deserved to know the truth.

Faith took a deep breath. "There's something I have to tell you."

"What it is, dear?" Dottie put down her knitting.

She told Dottie about her ex-husband, about the months of running and finally about Luke's offer of protection.

Dottie listened intently, her gaze never wavering.

Faith wound up her tale and waited for recriminations from Dottie, for the anger and hurt that would come for putting the Campbell family in such danger.

But Dottie surprised her by reaching out and taking her hand. "You poor child. To think you've been alone and scared for so long. I knew when you came here something weighed on your mind. And on your heart."

Faith couldn't comprehend Dottie's compassion. "You aren't mad at me?"

"Of course not. This situation will take care of both of you and Luke's problems."

"Both of our problems?" Faith repeated, confused. What problem did Luke have?

"Yes, Luke needs you as much as you need him." Dottie nodded sagely.

"He does?"

"Of course, dear. He just doesn't know that he does, but I think he's beginning to realize it."

Baffled, Faith felt like she was walking through a maze. Luke needed her? Whatever for?

"My son has been searching for fulfillment for most of his life, Faith. He thought he'd find it in the army. And I'm not saying he didn't find some. I know the military is a great adventure for him, but when he comes home on leave, I see the emptiness. You can't hide some things from a mother." Dottie laughed softly, the corners of her eyes creasing.

"No, I suppose not," Faith agreed, sharing Dottie's smile and turning to watch Luke out the window. The sheriff and his men dispersed, leaving Luke and the hands talking.

Dottie touched her arm. "Since he's been home this time, he's slowly changed. The emptiness isn't so visible. And with you here, he seems—happier."

"Really?" Faith couldn't stop the hope seeping into her heart, the pleasure welling up inside.

Dottie gave her a knowing smile and patted her hand. "He laughs and smiles more readily. In fact, he makes getting you to laugh his mission. And when he doesn't think you're looking, he watches you like a lost soul who has spotted a beacon in the dark."

Faith wanted to believe her, she really did, and in the past few weeks she'd learned how to dream. But in the back of her mind, she knew she was quite possibly setting herself up for more disappointment and heartache.

If only she could focus on the positive.

Wasn't Christmas a time of blessings?

Luke entered the house, his jaw set in a grim line. "Mom, did Faith fill you in?"

"Yes, dear. How horrible. But I know you'll take care of everything."

"I appreciate your confidence," Luke stated and motioned for Faith to follow him into the hall.

Faith rose and met him in the hall. "I'm sorry I've brought all this trouble here," she said, before he had a chance to speak.

His expression softened. "Don't be. I'm glad you're here."

Thinking of what Dottie had said, with her heart in her throat, she asked, "Why?"

"You're safe and my mom's happy."

That wasn't enough. Disappointment tightened a knot in her chest and must have shown on her face.

He held up a hand. "Look. Right now is complicated."

She tried to smile. "I know."

"I'm going to do what I can to put an end to this situation."

She tensed. "What do you mean?"

"Palmero wants to play a game of cat and mouse, I'll give him a game of cat and mouse."

Fighting back the anxious ripple skating across her skin, she put a hand on his arm. "Please don't do anything rash. I couldn't stand it if something happened to you."

He touched her cheek. "Nothing's going to happen to me. Or you."

She pressed her cheek into his palm, so desperately wanting to believe him. But her heart warned her he shouldn't promise things he had no control over.

Later that night, Luke left his office to find Faith sitting on the floor of the living room with Brandy. The light from the fire touched her face with its amber glow. Her gaze was fixated on the Christmas tree.

He took a seat on the leather recliner near them. "The tree is beautiful."

A slight smile touched her lips. "When I was a

kid, we'd put up a twelve-foot-tall tree in the entry-way of my grandparents' house and the staff would decorate it in gold and white ornaments that didn't mean anything. I like this tree so much better. Each ornament has a story to tell of your family."

He'd never thought of that, but she was right. He could look at any one of the dangling doodads and remember a past Christmas. "This will be the first one without my father."

Her gaze held compassion. "But your memories will never disappear."

"True." He leaned forward as a way to put emphasis to his words. "Vinnie is still in New York."

She blinked. "How did you find that out?"

"I called his office."

Her eyes grew big. "You talked to him?"

"I asked his secretary if he was available. She said he was on another line and would I care to hold. I hung up. My intent was to verify his whereabouts, not engage him. Yet."

"But that doesn't mean he didn't hire someone to try to shoot me."

"True. And I'm sure he did. Now, we just have to figure out who. Sisters is a small community but we attract a lot of tourists. Especially with Black Butte and Sunriver resorts in the area. And with Bend, Redmond and La Pine so close—" He shrugged. "That's a lot of territory for someone to hide in."

"Great. That's reassuring."

"It's realistic. I don't want you to attend the Christmas festival at church on Christmas Eve. Leaving the ranch is too chancy."

She pinned him with an intense look. "I'm tired of running. I want to go. If something happens to me, then it was meant to. But I want to go to church on Christmas Eve."

He should have guessed she'd say as much.

Independent, brave. Strong-willed and oh, so appealing.

Whoa! Not going there. Too much was at stake. Stick to business, Campbell. "Sheriff Bane won't like it."

"I don't care."

Her courage and determination revealed a core of steel. This was the woman who'd left a bad situation in order to protect others. A woman fighting to maintain control of her life. "Fine. I'll stick close to you."

Her mouth quirked up at the corners. "I can live with that."

Silence stretched for a moment. A log shifted in the fireplace, letting off a smooth hiss.

"What are the good parts?" she asked.

"The good parts?"

"Of your military career."

For once an easy answer. "My ministry."

Her eyes widened. "You have a ministry? You're a pastor?"

He laughed. "No, I'm not a pastor. I started a Bible fellowship study group in my unit. We began with a few guys, but over the years it's grown. I've been helping the chaplain develop other groups in other units."

He couldn't keep the excitement out of his voice. "I'm hoping to develop a national ministry in all areas of the armed forces. The leaders of the national Promise Keepers are very encouraging. They're giving me good advice and help. I think this will really be a positive undertaking."

"That's very ambitious." Faith turned away. "You must be anxious to get back."

Luke was about to say yes, but hesitated. He wanted to return, to finish what he'd started… He stared at her profile, fighting for control of his heart.

Faith turned to look at him. "What?"

"You are so beautiful," he said truthfully.

"Luke." Her tone scoffed at his words and her gaze dropped to her lap.

"You are."

"I'm glad you think so." She lifted her gaze back to him, her eyes sparkling in the twinkle of lights from the tree. "You're beautiful, too."

He smiled, pleased she thought so, though he couldn't remember anyone ever telling him that before. On impulse, he bent closer, his lips hovering over hers. He heard her sharp intake of breath and felt her lean toward him. Their lips met, warm and yielding. His world narrowed to this particular moment in time.

With Faith in his arms, their lips joined, his heart pulsing, he couldn't decide where he ended and she began. For this one instance, they were one and everything inside of him wanted to hold on to her forever.

Outside, an earsplitting shriek broke the night air, jarring Luke away from Faith's mouth.

No! It wasn't time yet.

Distress and fear drove him to his feet. There hadn't been any of the usual signs.

"What is it?" Faith asked, her voice filled with panic. She clutched at him.

"Lucy." He freed her hands from his shirt. "Stay here."

He ran for the door and vaulted down the porch stairs, nearly colliding with Charles, who'd come running from the barn.

"Something's wrong. Lucy's in labor, but it's gone bad. The vet's not going to make it here in time." Charles's anxiety showed in his tone. Without waiting for a reply, he turned and ran back to the llama barn.

Luke hurried after him. Faith ignored his command and followed.

"What's happening?" Jerry came running down

the apartment stairs, his gaze searching for danger. "What's wrong?"

"Lucy's having a difficult birth," Luke explained.

Jerry visibly relaxed and rushed into the barn. "Oh. Okay. What can I do?"

The scene in the barn stole all of her attention. Faith's hand went to her mouth at the sight of the large brown llama lying on her side. The animal's head thrashed about and her swollen belly looked misshapen and painful. Lucy's legs kicked wildly while she tried to right herself to a standing position.

Leo knelt beside Lucy speaking in soothing tones, but his calming words made little difference.

Luke was on his knees beside the animal, his hands assessing the position of the baby. "Charles, towels, blankets, warm water and the first-aid kit. Hurry! We have to help her with this baby now."

Faith jumped out of the way as Charles quickly rushed after the items requested. She took her bottom lip between her teeth, then ventured, "Can I help?"

Without sparing her a glance, Luke gave her instructions. "Get behind her head. Talk to her, try to calm her down. Jerry, steady her flank."

Glad to have some direction, Faith moved and sat behind Lucy's thrashing head. Her hands sought to calm the beast and with gentle ministrations, Lucy's head slowly came to rest on Faith's lap. "There now, you'll be all right soon. Luke will take care of you."

Charles returned, bearing the supplies. Luke glanced up and nodded with his head. "Good. The baby's breech and trying to come backward. Jerry, hold Lucy's legs. Faith, keep talking to her. And watch out because she'll probably start spitting."

"Uh—okay." Unsettled by that bit of information, Faith continued to talk to Lucy. The words were nonsense. Lucy didn't understand, but Faith hoped the llama's wide-eyed stare meant trust.

Concentration etched lines in Luke's forehead. When he put on a pair of rubber gloves, Faith faltered in her one-sided dialogue. Luke met her gaze, tension radiating from his clenched jaw and worried expression.

"We have to turn the baby." He answered her unspoken question.

For a moment, she felt faint at the implications of his words. She looked away and began to sing a lullaby she remembered her mother singing to her when she was a child.

Lucy twitched and bellowed as Luke and Leo worked. Unable to watch, helpless, Faith continued to sing and stroked the llama's head.

Then suddenly, Luke's voice mingled with her own, the deep timbre crooning with sweet words of encouragement.

Lucy's head began to whip around and green spit flew from her mouth. Faith moved back slightly to avoid the spray and gave Luke a harried glance, only to quickly turn away. His arms were buried to his elbow within Lucy's womb and Leo was manipulating from the outside.

Time crawled by, yet for Faith, the world ran on fast forward. Her heart rate accelerated with Lucy's every cry and sweat ran down her temple, but she didn't want to stop caressing the animal to wipe the moisture away.

Suddenly Lucy jerked and struggled to stand. Frightened, Faith scrambled away. Lucy managed to get all four feet under her and hoist herself up.

"Here we go," Luke said, his voice sounding strained.

Chancing another glance toward Luke, Faith's breathing stopped. He had moved with Lucy and now ˙squatted nearly beneath her. Tugging and grunting, he pulled at the baby llama until it slipped from its mother's womb with a swoosh. Lucy collapsed, her body limp and her breathing slow and shallow.

A sense of awe filled Faith. She watched Luke hold the baby close to his chest for a moment with tears in his eyes, then he grabbed at the towels and wiped the baby down. Wrapping a blanket around the newborn, he handed it over to Leo who guided the infant to its mother. Soon the baby was hungrily nursing. Lucy gave an audible sigh.

"Good job, boss," Charles commented as he gathered up the used supplies and then quietly left the barn.

"He's beautiful," Faith whispered.

Luke grinned at her. "He's a she."

Pride and trust swelled within her breast for this man who'd taken her in and given her a home. "You saved them both, Luke. I knew you could."

In a moment of clarity, love for Luke filled her, overflowing.

But immediately doubts invaded her mind. Could she trust her heart to really know love? Was she responding to the moment and calling it love?

"You helped." The tender look he gave her made her heart pound and a blush worked its way up her neck, the heat flaming her cheeks. Did he feel the same? Was he coming to care for her?

The baby llama pulled away from Lucy and rose on wobbly legs. Faith stared in astonishment as the baby began to walk slowly around, sniffing at her mother. Lucy raised her head and met her offspring's nose.

Fascinated with the bond forming right before her eyes, Faith whispered, "That's so sweet."

"It is sweet."

She shifted her gaze back to him. The moment stretched, their silent communication vibrated in the air.

"I'm naming the baby Faith, so we'll always have something to remember you by," he stated softly.

Her heart twisted.

Nothing could have reminded her more eloquently that her time here was borrowed. He rightly assumed that once the danger passed they'd go their separate ways. Luke didn't love her. What could be more clear?

It was one-sided, this emotional charge she kept feeling. The realization was bitter to take, yet on some level, it was better this way.

Thankfully, she hadn't said the words that would change things between them. The growing closeness she felt now could only be defined as friendship. Nothing more, nothing less.

She tried for a light smile, but could feel the corners of her mouth quiver. "I'll go back to the house. I'm exhausted."

"Thank you for your help tonight." His quiet, somber words echoed off the barn walls.

All she could do was nod and hurry away before the ache in her heart showed on her face.

From the shadows, a man watched Faith hurry inside the house. He could have grabbed her then, but didn't want to chance it, not with so many people roaming about.

His jaw tightened with frustration. He'd thought for sure the bullets would scare her off the ranch where she'd be more vulnerable since Reva's ideas didn't work.

A lot of money had been promised if he could deliver the woman. He needed that money.

In the next day or so, he'd find an opportunity. Soldier man couldn't stay with her around the clock. He glanced at the window that just lit up. Faith's room. Hmm. Maybe a midnight grab?

Naw. Too risky.

There had to be a way to get Faith alone.

"Buck broke through the south pasture fence again. Charles is herding him into the north pasture with the cows," Leo stated when he found Luke in the barn cleaning up after the vet's late-afternoon visit.

Luke sighed. "Ugh, that bull!" Glancing out the barn door at the low sun, they'd be missing dinner tonight. "Well, we best get to it now before it gets too dark. Buck doesn't play well with others."

"I'll go round up Mac and Jerry and get the supplies loaded in the truck."

Luke stepped inside the house to inform Faith he wouldn't be home for dinner. The aromatic scents of tomatoes and spices filled the air. The sight of Faith at the stove, her hair tied back, her cheeks flushed from the heat, made his insides clench. Steeling himself against the attraction ricocheting through him, he said, "Faith."

She jumped and the spoon clattered inside the steaming pot she'd been stirring.

"What's wrong?" she asked, her voice sounding panicky.

"Nothing's wrong." He immediately assured her. "A bull broke through a fence. You and Mom go ahead and eat."

"You're not going to try to fix the fence in the dark, are you?"

He shrugged. "It has to be done. We have a portable floodlight."

"You'll be careful?"

"Always. Lock the door behind me and if you get scared, call me on my cell."

"We'll be fine." She gave him a smile that he was sure meant to inspire confidence.

"I'll leave Brandy with you," he stated. Faith and his mother would be safe. Deputy Russell was down at the end of the drive. There was no reason to worry. Still, he paused outside the door until he heard the lock slide into place.

Moonlight streamed through the slit in the curtains, the white glow illuminating Faith's path as she paced the kitchen. In the oven she had a plate warming for Luke, but he hadn't returned from fixing the bull-trampled fence. Maybe something happened to him?

No, she couldn't think that way. She was becoming way too attached; to the ranch, Dottie and especially, Luke. Eventually, they would part ways.

When all was said and done, Faith wondered what would become of her. Where would she go? Not back to New York where memories of Vinnie would haunt her, never back there. There wasn't anywhere she wanted to be other than where she was. Already in the short time she'd been in Oregon, she'd made true friends, Dottie, Sally and Matt Turner and of course, Luke.

Her fists clenched in useless frustration. In this house she was accepted for herself, not for her money or her position in society. Here she belonged.

She glanced at the clock. Where was he? The four walls of the kitchen closed in on her. She needed to get outside and breathe some fresh air. She left the house to visit her namesake.

Baby Faith came directly to her, as did Lucy. Both animals nuzzled against her, making her feel wanted and loved.

"Well, at least you love me." Faith knew self-pity was an undesirable quality, but at the moment she felt the need to wallow. Luke didn't love her. She had to accept that.

Faith sang softly to the llamas, her voice clear and bright in the night air. She sang a sad song of love found and love lost.

From behind her, a hand closed over her mouth. Her song turned into a muffled scream.

Close to her ear, a male voice, gloated, "Got you."

Terror roared in her brain. She tried to break free, her elbows driving backward, her legs kicking. An arm snaked around her waist, beneath her rib cage and tightened as she was pulled backward. She twisted and scratched at the hand across her face. Her heels dug into the ground, but she was no match for the man pulling her out of the barn.

From inside the house, Brandy's frantic barks echoed in the quiet of the night. Why hadn't she brought Brandy out with her? *Please, let Dottie look out the window and see what's happening.*

She was slammed up against the side of a dark sedan, parked behind the barn. The door handle jabbed painfully into her hip. The hand at her mouth released. She took a breath to scream, but her air supply was cut off when the man jammed his forearm across her throat, knocking the breath from her.

She heard the sound of pulling tape and then a wide strip of adhesive was slapped over her mouth. Her hands were yanked behind her and taped together. She was pulled away from the car, the door jerked open and she was thrown in. The dome light didn't come on. Faith couldn't make out her attacker's face.

The man captured her feet and taped them together. Then flipped her over so that she landed across the floor of the back seat. A musty-smelling blanket was thrown over her.

A moment later the engine rumbled to life and the car moved slowly forward down the drive, then stopped. Hope flared through her. The hiss of the electric window going down was drowned out by the sudden blare of music from the radio.

The driver had to shout to be heard. "Hey, Deputy."

"Evening. Where you headed?"

"Bend. My mom took a turn for the worse."

Shock jerked through Faith. Mac, the ranch hand with the ill mother? Why was he kidnapping her?

She thumped her tied feet against the floorboards and screamed into the tape across her mouth. She tried to sit up, but she was wedged between the front and back seats at too awkward an angle.

The radio went up a notch. Faith didn't hear the deputy's response before the car began moving again. Then the radio shut off and the roar of the ice-crusted road beneath the car tires reverberated inside Faith's brain along with her pleas to God for help.

TWELVE

"I'll go tell Charles to bring Buck back," Leo stated as they were finishing up with the fence. Puffs of breath visible in the floodlights marked the chilly night air. The ground crunched beneath their feet as they moved about.

"I thought Mac was already doing that," Luke replied, replacing his tools into the back of the Bronco.

Jerry lifted the wooden slats they hadn't needed and carried them to Leo's truck. "I thought he went to get some more nails, but it turned out we didn't need any."

"More nails? I have a ton in here," Luke gestured to the workbox in the back of the Bronco. "When did he leave?"

"Fifteen, twenty minutes ago."

Charles came riding up on a small ATV. "Hey, Buck's not one to be patient. Any chance you all are about done here?"

"Where's Mac?" Leo asked.

Charles shrugged. "I haven't seen Mac since I rode out."

Luke didn't like the uneasy feeling coming over him. "I'm going to head back to the house. You guys finish up here."

"I'll come with you," Jerry said.

Luke didn't want to take the time to argue. He climbed in and drove quickly over the rough, ice-crusted ground back to the ranch. As soon as he pulled up he knew something was wrong. His mother and Brandy were waiting on the back porch.

"She's gone!" his mother exclaimed.

"What happened?" Luke's heart pounded in his head like a hammer hitting a post.

"I don't know. Brandy was barking so wildly. Like she did the other night. I came downstairs and I couldn't find Faith."

"The deputy," Jerry said.

"Go inside and lock the door," Luke instructed his mother. "I'll find her."

To Jerry he said, "I need you to stay and keep an eye out. Let Leo and Charles know what's up when they return."

"Sure thing," Jerry stated.

Luke hesitated, then decided he'd better go armed. He wasn't sure what Mac was up to, or why, but Luke didn't want to go into the situation unprepared. He ran up to his room where he kept a Glock in a small lockbox under his bed. Once in his Bronco, he sped down the drive, the tires slipping. He skidded to a halt at the end of the road. The deputy got out of his car and came over.

"Did you see anyone leave here?" Luke asked, his voice sharp.

The deputy nodded. "Yeah, Mac left just a bit ago. Said his mother took a turn for the worse, so he was going to Bend to see her. What's up?"

The news slammed into Luke's chest like mortar fire. How could he have been so blind? "Call the sheriff. Give him a description of Mac's car. I think he kidnapped Faith."

Without a word, the deputy ran back to his cruiser. Luke turned out onto the road, his mind frantically going over the options.

If he was going to try to get her out of the state, he'd either drive or take a private plane. Driving was too risky. He'd know the police would be looking for him. Roberts Field Airport in Redmond was about fifteen miles outside of Bend, which had smaller commercial planes. Bend Municipal Airport just northeast of Bend handled Lears and more private planes. The closest major airport was in Portland. Mac wouldn't take her to a major one. Too many people. Of the other two, Luke had a fifty-fifty shot. He chose Bend Municipal.

Luke drove as fast as the slick roads allowed. He prayed he'd find Faith before it was too late.

The shrill ring of a phone jolted through Faith. Already tense muscles tightened even more. Her body ached from being on the floor of the car. She strained to hear Mac as he answered.

"Yeah, I got her. We're about ten minutes out. What? You never said anything about that. Let me check."

The car slowed, the sound of loose road debris hit the underbelly of the car as they came to a stop, the engine left to idle. The blanket was pulled off of her. Mac twisted around in his seat and loomed over Faith. Her body went rigid. Her heart pounded fiercely against her rib cage.

Mac grabbed her by the throat, and rubbed his hand along her neck and collarbone before releasing her.

Relief rushed through her veins, making the world spin.

"No," Mac said once he was back in his seat. He put the car in gear. "Too bad, dude. That's your problem. You didn't say I had to get anything else. I've got the woman and you've better have the hundred grand."

So a hundred-thousand dollars bought Mac's betrayal. Disgusting.

Faith closed her eyes and continued to pray.

* * *

Luke's Bronco skidded to a stop in the parking lot of the airport. He bolted from the vehicle. A blanket of powdery snow covered everything but the black tarmac where a small twin-engine plane prepared to take off.

Luke's gaze searched the airport and landed on a Cessna on the far side of the tarmac.

Mac's sedan was parked by the plane. Mac emerged from the driver's side and opened the back door. He leaned in and seemed to be struggling with something. Mac's fist rose then slammed down before he dragged something out on to the ground. A body.

Luke's heart jumped to his throat. Faith!

Automatically shifting into military mode, he took off at a dead run.

Mac had picked up Faith's bound form and hoisted her into the cabin of the plane.

The pilot gestured wildly toward Luke. Mac jumped in and slammed the door closed. The rotators whirled, the sound rushing into Luke's ears as he reached the side of the plane. He yanked at the door handle. It wouldn't budge. He could see Mac urging the pilot on. The plane started to move.

Luke drew his weapon and ran hard to get in front of the plane. He aimed at the wheels and fired.

The plane slowed and limped off the runway into the thick snow. Luke rushed to the plane.

The pilot jumped out his hands in the air. "Hey, man. Don't shoot me."

"On the ground, hands behind your head," Luke commanded. "Mac! Come out. Keep your hands up."

For a second, he thought Mac was going to comply, but then he dived for the door on the other side of the cabin. He hit the ground running.

Luke found Faith curled up on the floor behind the plane's front seats. A large nasty bruise dominated one cheek. Pulse-pounding dread drowned out the sounds of everything but the faint hiss of her breath. She was alive, but he'd failed to protect her. He'd never forgive himself.

He gathered her up and carried her from the plane. He took her to the sedan and laid her gently on the seat. Taking out a pocketknife, Luke cut the tape binding her arms and legs. Carefully, he removed the tape across her mouth. She didn't so much as flinch.

He pulled out his cell phone and dialed 9-1-1. He told the operator what was needed and hung up.

"Please, God. Oh, please." He stroked Faith's hair back from her face. "Faith. Come on, Faith."

Helplessness, heavy and dark centered in the middle of his chest. All his battlefield first-aid training was useless in this situation. His heart hurt so badly he thought he'd be ripped in two. He should have protected her better.

Sirens filled the night air as the local police, sheriff and an ambulance descended on the tarmac.

Within moments a paramedic crouched beside the open door. "Sir, we need to help her."

Luke let the paramedics move her to the ground where they assessed her condition.

"You okay?" Sheriff Bane asked as he came to stand beside Luke.

"Me, yeah." His gaze stayed riveted to Faith. "Mac got away."

"We got him."

Rage twisted in Luke's gut. "I want to talk to him."

"I'm sure you do," Bane stated. "But we'll follow procedure."

Luke wanted nothing more than to put his hands around Mac's throat and squeeze. "How did Palmero get to Mac?"

"When I know something, I'll let you know."

The paramedics lifted Faith onto a gurney and slid it into the ambulance.

"I'll be at the hospital," Luke told the sheriff before jumping into the ambulance.

He took Faith's hand and leaned close to her ear. "You're going to be all right. I promise."

The ride to the hospital seemed to take forever. Faith lay so still and pale. She looked okay, except for the purple mark on her face where Mac had punched her. That awful reminder of how Luke had failed to protect her made him want to retch.

At the hospital, Faith was whisked away by the medical personnel. Luke paced the sterile waiting room and refused to consider that she wouldn't be all right.

"Are you Luke?" an older man, wearing a white doctor's coat, asked as he approached.

"Yes. Faith?"

"She has a concussion and is a bit disoriented, which isn't uncommon after head trauma. There was no sexual assault."

Luke swallowed back bile at the very idea that she could have been raped.

"She's asking for you."

A wave of relief crashed over Luke. "Please, lead the way."

Faith's face brightened when he walked in the room. The dark bruise on her face tore at his conscience. He rushed to her side. "It's good to see your smile."

"I'm just thankful to be out of that car. What happened to Mac?"

"He's been taken into custody." Luke held her soft hand. "Don't worry about him. He's no longer a threat to you."

"That doesn't mean there won't be someone else. Vinnie got so close."

A cold knot formed in Luke's gut. "Yes. He won't again," Luke vowed. "I'm sorry I failed to protect you."

"Oh, no, Luke. This isn't your fault. You had no way of knowing."

He shook his head. "I should have been more careful."

"Please, don't feel guilty." Her eyebrows drew together. "Mac was getting a hundred-thousand dollars for me. But he got a call and it sounded like he was supposed to get something else."

"Like what?"

She sighed. "I don't know. It all seems so surreal."

"Then don't think anymore about it." He squeezed her hand. "For now, you need to concentrate on getting better."

"The doctor said I'll have to stay the night."

"I'll stay with you."

She squeezed his hand. "No. You need to go home and be with your mom. I'll be safe enough here. I'm just going to sleep anyway."

She would be safe, but still Luke didn't want to let her out of his sight.

"Please, go, Luke. I'll be fine."

"I'll have the sheriff post a man outside your door."

"If that makes you feel better," she said softly.

"It will. I'll be back first thing tomorrow."

She smiled and let her eyes drift shut. Luke kissed the back of her hand before quietly leaving the room.

He sagged against the wall outside of her door. He'd never been more afraid in his whole life than he had been in the last hour. So much for not becoming attached to his employee.

He called his mother and told her that Faith was well and that he'd be home soon. But first he had a stop to make.

At the sheriff's station, Luke was led into the sheriff's office to wait. The room was small but functional, with a desk, computer workstation and a bookshelf full of manuals and such. Luke ignored the guest chairs and stood by the window to stare at the dark sky.

"Thank You, Lord, for giving her back to me. I won't let You down again," he whispered.

The door behind him opened. Sheriff Bane walked in, his gaze disapproving. "I said I'd call when I had information to give you."

"What has he said?"

"Nothing." Bane sat behind his desk. "He lawyered up."

"Let me see him." Luke clenched his fist. "I'll make him talk."

Bane gave him a droll stare. "And throw the arrest out the window? I don't think so."

"Did you at least confirm Palmero hired him?"

"Like I said, he's not talking."

Anger boiled in Luke's veins. "Palmero's behind this."

Bane nodded. "From what you've told me, I agree. But proving it will be hard unless Mac cooperates."

"What about the pilot?"

"He claims he was just hired by Mac."

"Where was he supposed to take them?"

"His flight plan said Boise."

"Then Mac must have had other transportation arrangements there," Luke said.

"We're looking into it." Bane stood and came around the desk. "I promise you, I'll let you know the minute I have anything concrete. But for now, the best thing for you to do is take care of your family."

His family. Faith had become part of his family these past weeks. The certainty sent his heart reeling with awe and tenderness.

"Can you put someone at the hospital to protect Faith?"

"Already ahead of you on that one. Deputy Russell should be there now."

Luke left the sheriff's station and headed back to the ranch. Tomorrow he'd bring Faith home.

And he wouldn't ever let her go.

The ranch came into view. Sprawling and beautiful, just like the first time she'd laid eyes on the Circle C. A sense of coming home infused Faith as Luke turned onto the gravel drive. For the moment she wasn't going to fight the attachment or the sense of well-being. For now she'd soak it up.

The front door opened and Brandy shot out like a cannon and bounded down the porch stairs, barking happily. Dottie came to stand by the railing, a welcoming smile on her face. The mother Faith had so often longed for.

Luke parked and came around to open the passenger door. Brandy practically knocked him over in her effort to greet Faith. She accepted the dog's sloppy love before Luke nudged Brandy aside and held out his hand. Faith grasped his big strong hand and let him lead her to the house. There was nothing sisterly about her reaction to Luke. Her heart sped up and her senses fired little fissures of heat over her skin.

He didn't let go until they were on the porch. His mother gave her a fierce embrace.

"I was so scared," Dottie said with a sniff.

"Me, too," Faith answered.

Once inside the house, Dottie led Faith to the couch. "Here now. Let me get you some soothing tea," Dottie cooed and bustled into the kitchen.

Relaxing back into the cushions, Faith closed her eyes, aware of Luke hovering nearby.

"Would you like to go to your room?" Luke asked.

"I'm fine here," she replied. "Shouldn't you and Dottie head to the festival? It's Christmas Eve, after all."

"We're not going anywhere," he stated and sat beside her, his warmth reaching her without his even touching her. She opened her eyes to study him. His hair had grown since that first day and now showed signs of curling. The brightness of his blue eyes held her. She tried to decipher what emotions lurked in those liquid pools but couldn't. Maybe she was too tired and overwhelmed, or maybe he was just that good at hiding his feelings.

"Are you sure you're okay?" he asked.

"The doctor said I was." She reached out for his hand. "Thank you for what you did."

His fingers closed over hers, warm and reassuring.

"Here we go." Dottie returned, carrying a tray with a teapot and three cups. She set it on the coffee table and poured them each a cup.

Faith didn't want to release her hold on Luke to take the offered cup, but had no choice. She held the warm mug in her hands and tried to allow calm to seep through her.

Dottie sat in her recliner. "Luke, honey, I hate to ask, but would you be willing to take the pies we made to the church by noon? I called Sally and asked her to let them know we wouldn't be coming today, but they could still use the pies."

Luke inclined his head. "I'll see if Leo can drive them out."

"That would work."

"You two can still go," Faith said. She didn't like that her situation was preventing Dottie from doing something she'd been looking forward to.

"Nonsense." Dottie waved away her words. "Why don't we see if there's a Christmas movie on TV." Dottie picked up the remote. "I just love that one with Jimmy Stewart and the angel."

Thinking she'd found two earthly angels of her own right here, Faith smiled. "I do, too."

Luke stood. "As much as I want to join you, I have some calls to make."

Faith watched Luke stride from the room, taking his warmth and energy with him. She set her mug down and settled back as Dottie flipped through the channels.

For a moment Faith stared at the television, the flicker of shows hypnotic. Sleepiness overtook her. Her eyelids drooped. The doctor said she should rest, that her head would hurt for a while but she would recover.

Recover enough to leave.

But deep inside, she knew her heart would never recover once she left Luke behind.

Luke sat at his desk and waited on hold while the operator connected him to Roger's direct line.

"Tumble," Rog answered, his drawl unmistakable.

"Rog, it's Luke."

"Hey, how ya doing?"

"I've been better," Luke replied, then told Roger all that had happened.

Roger whistled. "You have had a lot going on. How can I help?"

"I don't know that you can. I wanted to check on that paperwork."

"It's coming your way. I have good news on another front. George Peterson has stepped up to the plate and is doing a great job leading the fellowship studies. He's even talked with the guys from the Promise Keepers and is moving forward with your plans. I figured you'd be okay with it."

Luke sat back. He hadn't expected that news. And he wasn't sure how he felt about it. Regardless, he said, "That's fine. Hey, I'll give you a call later. I've got to go."

"Sure. Let me know if I can do anything."

"I will."

Luke stared out of his office window at the mountain range and tried to make sense of all that was happening. He couldn't.

His old life didn't seem to be waiting for him.

He should be grateful that someone was following through with his plans but…

He fought back hard feelings. He'd developed the program; he'd spent countless hours building the Bible study. He should be the one to see it grow, to see his plans fulfilled. He shook his head, disappointed in himself for feeling…jealous.

It wasn't his plan or his Bible study. It belonged to God. He'd started it, yes, but because God had called him to it. And now Luke wanted the glory?

He hung his head in remorse. "Forgive me, Lord."

Taking a deep cleansing breath, he scrubbed his hands over his face. Now what? What plan did the Lord have for him now?

The phone rang, jarring him out of his thoughts. "Hello?"

"Matt here. Sally said you all weren't coming into town today. I was hoping to talk with you. I have a proposition for you."

"Can it wait until next week?"

"Not really. I just need an hour. Could we meet at the diner?"

Luke drummed his fingers on the desk. He was going to have Leo run into town, but…he'd just make sure the guys kept a vigilant eye out. "Yeah, that'd be fine. I have to take some pies over to the church at noon, so how about we meet at twelve-fifteen?"

"Sounds great. Thanks," Matt said and hung up.

When Luke entered the living room, Faith was fast asleep on the couch. She looked so vulnerable and sweet. His heart spasmed with a wellspring of tenderness. He grabbed a blanket from the closet and laid it over her.

He whispered to his mother, "I'll be taking the pies into town."

At the flicker of surprise in his mother's eyes, he added, "I'll make sure Leo knows I won't be here. He'll look out for you two."

Dottie patted his hand with approval.

Luke found his most trusted hand with the baby llama.

"Hi, boss," Leo greeted him.

"Hey, I have to run into town. Can you keep an eye out?"

"Sure, thing. Glad to see that young girl back safe and sound." He shook his head. "Still can't get over Mac being so rotten. Makes for a strange Christmas."

Luke gave a dry laugh. Very strange indeed.

After talking some more with Leo, Luke left the barn to load the pies in the back of his truck. Brandy whined when he wouldn't let her in the back with the food.

"You'd eat them for sure, girl."

She barked as if to deny the accusation.

When Luke opened the driver's side door, Brandy leaped inside and sat in the passenger seat. Her normal spot when he took her with him.

"Hey, girl, not this trip," Luke said. "Come on out of there."

Brandy laid down in response. Her paws hung

over the edge of the seat and her tail thumped against the door. She stared at him with big pleading eyes.

"Stubborn dog," Luke muttered and climbed in.

After dropping off the pies, he parked outside the diner, cracked the window for Brandy and headed for the door.

He sat at the counter and immediately Ethel set down a steaming cup of coffee. Nodding his thanks, he sipped from the strong brew, aware of the waitress's steady regard. Raising his brows, he asked, "Is something the matter?"

"Well, I don't rightly know. That investigator fellow was back here this morning and he had a friend with him this time."

Coffee sloshed onto the counter and Luke set the cup down. A horrified feeling settled over him, making his voice rough. "What did his friend look like?"

Ethel tapped a finger against her chin. "Well, now. Thin, average height, sort of slick. You know, city type."

Pressure throbbed behind his eyes. Luke's hands fisted on the countertop. "What did they want?"

Ethel narrowed her eyes. "I'm not sure, but Reva was cozying up to them, and if you ask me, that bodes trouble for sure."

Apprehension slithered across Luke's flesh, causing bumps to pucker his skin. He stood. "How long ago were they here? Any idea where they were headed?" Luke couldn't keep the urgency from his tone.

Ethel's worried expression matched what Luke felt. "They left an hour ago. Didn't hear where they were going. But Reva's working at the General Store now. You could go ask her."

"Call Sheriff Bane and tell him to send a car to the ranch." He was practically out the door before he thought to call over his shoulder, "Thanks, Ethel."

"Anytime, honey," she said as the door closed behind him.

The General Store, so called because it carried everything from groceries to hardware, sat a block down Main Street. Luke entered the store and headed straight for Reva. She stopped stacking the cans of soup to smile at him.

Luke backed her into a corner and growled, "All right, Reva. What kind of game are you playing?"

Her smile faltered for a brief second. "I—I don't know what you're talking about."

"Don't toy with me, Reva. I know you were talking with that private investigator. What did you tell him?"

"Why, just the truth." She stepped around him and continued stocking the shelves.

Luke clenched his fists in an effort to control his rising temper. "And what truth would that be?"

"Oh, just that Mr. Palmero's *wife* could be found at the Circle C."

Wanting nothing more than to shake her until her tongue rattled loose, he ground out between gritted teeth, "Do you know what you've done?"

She stared at him, the picture of innocence. "I just steered a husband to his wife."

"She's his ex-wife, Reva. And what you've done is put Faith and my mother in danger."

Anger and fear raged in large waves to the forefront of his consciousness. He'd promised to protect Faith and again he wasn't there when she needed him. "Are they on their way there now?"

"I suppose." Reva's brows drew together. "You don't really think he'd harm them, do you?"

"Your concern is a little late." Disgusted, he whirled away, but was stopped short by Reva's voice.

"If only she'd gotten scared and left, this wouldn't be happening and you'd still be mine."

Without turning back around, he asked, "What do you mean?"

"If she would have just run like she was supposed to. I mean, how stupid to stay when she was warned to leave!" Bitterness cloaked her words, making her sound petulant and petty.

He turned to stare at her. "The note and the phone calls. Those were your doing. You lied to the sheriff when he asked you about them."

"I was losing you, Luke. I had to do something. Those weren't my ideas, they were Mac's." She stepped toward him, her hand reached out beseechingly.

Luke shook his head in disbelief. He'd never have thought her capable of such treachery. "You never had me, Reva."

Running from the store, Luke headed for his truck. Speeding through town, he picked up his cell phone and dialed the house, but the phone only rang and rang. Fear and anger took turns seizing his gut. Brandy barked wildly, as if urging him to go faster.

Dear God, I can't lose Faith. I'm begging You, protect my family. Don't let me be too late.

If anything happened to his family, he didn't know if he'd be able to stop himself from killing Vince Palmero.

THIRTEEN

Bundled against the crisp air, Faith stared in silent contemplation, her gaze taking in the snow-covered peaks and trees off in the distance but not really appreciating their beauty. From the back porch of the Circle C, the mountains looked as if she could reach out and touch them.

Her fingers fumbled with a ball of yarn and knitting needles as her mind tried to grasp what Dottie was saying from her seat beside her, but all she could concentrate on was not thinking about the official-looking letter lying on top of a stack of mail that sat on the little side table.

The seal said U.S. Army and Faith's stomach churned. Was Luke being sent on a mission? Would he go, when he'd promised to stay until her problems were resolved?

Resolved? Ha! She doubted she'd ever see resolution. She'd always have the threat of Vinnie hanging over her head. He knew his way around the law too well.

Picking up the ball of yarn from her lap, she went back to practicing the stitches Dottie had shown her. She was trying to make a cap for Luke to give him tomorrow on Christmas Day. But she kept having to back stitch because she couldn't concentrate.

"Well, well, well. If this isn't a sight to remember. My dear little wife turned country bumpkin."

The ball of yarn fell from her hands and rolled across the porch and disappeared off the side.

Faith looked up and the all-too-familiar sneer jarred her to the very core. Vinnie. Her worst nightmare had come true.

Under his long trench coat, his silk designer suit, usually sharply pressed, showed creases. His jet-black hair, normally slicked back with gel, fell forward in stringy strands. The prized Italian loafers were scuffed. She'd never seen him so disheveled or so desperate.

"Who are you?" Dottie demanded to know, her eyebrows slammed together in a frown.

Ignoring Dottie, Vinnie stepped onto the porch, his voice dripping with sarcasm. "No tearful greeting, Faith? I thought for sure you'd be ready to come home by now. This little rebellion of yours is getting quite tedious."

Desperate to avoid the inevitable, Faith looked at

Dottie and tried to tell her with her eyes not to antagonize him. The older woman's narrowed gaze sent fresh shivers of alarm down Faith's spine. Where were Leo and the other hands?

A fierce countenance replaced Dottie's usually mild demeanor. It reminded Faith of a mama bear defending her cubs. "You're not wanted here. Leave this instant or I'll call the police."

Faith laid a hand on Dottie's sleeve and shook her head.

"Oh, I don't think you'll be calling anyone," Vinnie gloated.

Dottie's eyes widened and Faith turned to find herself staring down the barrel of a gun. Swallowing, Faith mustered all her bravado. The need to protect Dottie overcoming any tendency towards cowering, she met Vinnie's gaze and held it without wincing.

His dark eyes danced with glee and his thin lips spread into a feral grin, making Faith's stomach lurch.

"Put the gun away, Vinnie. You don't need that." Her voice trembled ever-so-slightly, giving away her inner turmoil. She wished Luke hadn't gone into town. But then again, if he were here, he'd be in danger, too.

Anger burned hot in Vinnie's eyes. "No one betrays me and gets away with it. Come on, Faith. Get your things and let's go."

Vinnie motioned for her to get up.

"Wh—what right do you have to order her about

like that? We're not alone here," Dottie piped up, her voice angry. Yet fear underlined each word.

Annoyance narrowed his gaze on Dottie and he swung the gun toward her. "You mean the two men in the barn? They've been taken care of."

Heartsick by the implication of his words, Faith's stomach convulsed. She had to stay strong and not let her fear show. Wanting to bring his attention back to her, Faith stated quickly, "We are no longer married. I don't belong to you."

His attention once again zeroed in on Faith. Possessiveness lit his black eyes with a feral gleam. "You do belong to me."

From inside the house the phone rang. Each ring stretched Faith's nerves.

She took a deep breath, drawing on strength she'd learned from Luke. "No, I don't."

"What?!" His face turned a frightening shade of red and the vein at his temple pulsed into a squiggly, purple line.

"You heard me. I want you to leave." Her voice wavered and she watched his face contort with rage.

Cursing graphically, he stepped threateningly closer, the gun raised and pointed at her chest. "You've made me chase you all the way across the country, forced me to spend good money on flunkies, made a fool of me."

"Leave, Vinnie," Faith repeated, her bravado

rapidly retreating, replaced by a gnawing fear. He was unpredictable. She shouldn't push too hard.

"Oh, no, no, no. I'm not leaving here without you. You've caused me too much trouble, Faith, for me to let you go." The black of his eyes took on a sinister gleam, the centers hollow, with no sign of a soul.

"She's not going anywhere with you. My son will be back any second and he won't let you take her away." Dottie sounded so sure, so confident. Her belief in her son rang in every syllable.

For a brief moment, Vinnie's gaze narrowed in speculation on Dottie, then swung back to Faith. His lips spread into a sadistic grin. "If you don't want this old woman to die, you'll pack your things and leave with me now."

Icy talons of fear gripped her heart. She knew he'd shoot Dottie and walk away without any remorse.

"Don't—please don't do this." Faith stood and placed herself in front of Dottie, using herself as a shield for Luke's mother.

Fury consumed his demeanor. His face twisted and he lunged for Faith, knocking over the small table and kicking aside the chair she'd been sitting in. Faith raised her hands to ward him off, dreading the violence to come, but she resolved to protect Dottie. At any cost.

Vinnie's thin hand closed around her neck and

sent her backward with a hard shove. She landed with a painful thud in the chair Dottie had just barely vacated. Faith twisted around and caught a glimpse of the older woman—moving faster than she thought possible—disappearing inside the house. She prayed she'd call the police and not come back out.

The cold metal of the gun pressing into her temple brought Faith's gaze back to Vinnie. His fingers dug into her neck and he said in a harsh rasp, "You're mine, Faith. I'll destroy this place and everyone in it, do you hear me?"

His grip tightened, choking her, and she could only nod as she gasped for breath. Darkness threatened to overtake her, but she fought the blackness. She had to stop him. She couldn't let him hurt the Campbells. Praying the police were now on their way, she knew what to do. It'd always worked before. She forced the words out. "I—I'm s-sorry."

The pressure on her neck eased slightly. Vinnie cocked his head and stared at her as if she were a cockroach he'd like to squash.

Heart rebelling against the scene they were about to play out, Faith whispered again the hated words that had saved her many times during her marriage. "I'm—sorry." She knew that to him those two little words meant she was wrong and he was right.

Leaning in closer, his breath hot and sticky against her cheek, he whispered, "I can't hear you."

Desperate anger helped her draw strength from past experience and forced her voice to a louder octave, "I'm sorry."

"Ah, that's better. But what are you sorry for, Faith?"

Briefly she closed her eyes, hating him for finding her, hating herself for having been dumb enough to marry him in the first place. "For—running—away," she ground out.

Abruptly, he pushed away from her and stood, his feet braced apart, the gun still aimed at her. "Tell me," he barked.

She knew the drill. Everything inside her objected, but it was what she had to do. "I—shouldn't have run away from you. You're—you're wonderful, Vinnie, you're everything a girl could ask for. I was—was a fool not to see that. You were there when I had no one and—and I will always be—grateful to you."

With lightning speed, his hand shot out and grabbed the front of her shirt, yanking her to him. "I don't believe you. I think you like it here."

Desperation clawed at her, this wasn't the way it was supposed to go. Her stomach knotted in fear. "No, no—I—I don't."

"You're lying to me, Faith. I don't like it when you lie. You know how angry that makes me."

Remembering his displeasure, the fear and humiliations that went with it, she cringed. "Yes. Yes, I know."

"Let's go." He grabbed her arm and dragged her toward the porch stairs.

Mind working frantically to get past the overwhelming fear, she latched on to one thought, *stall him.* "Wait," she screamed.

He ignored her and gave a vicious yank. She stumbled, going down hard on her knees. Pain exploded up her legs and wood splintered into her palms as she tried to break her fall.

"Get up," Vinnie yelled.

Faith looked up and saw his raised fist. Reacting instinctively, she scrambled away. Behind her she heard his frustrated curse and looked back to see him stalking menacingly toward her.

Panic gripped her. Keep talking, she told herself. "V-Vinnie," her voice came out a croak, so she tried again. "Vinnie, l-listen to me. You're wrong, I don't like it here." The lie nearly made her retch.

He continued toward her.

Beyond desperate now, she elaborated on the lies. "I—I don't belong on a ranch, I see that now. I belong in New York with you. This hick town can't compare with the excitement of the city and—and these cowpoke people mean nothing to me."

She held her breath as Vinnie stopped and stared at her, mentally gauging her words. She could tell he wasn't convinced, but she'd gained time.

Slowly, she stood and continued, the lies bitter on

her tongue. "I—I love you Vinnie. It's al-always been you, you know that. And you love me. You're coming here proves it. I guess I—just needed to have this show of affection to realize how—much."

The subtle change in his expression told her the words were starting to work. He was getting wrapped up in the lies. Dizzy with relief, she continued, hoping to keep him distracted long enough for the sheriff to arrive. "Don't you know? I'd be nothing without you. I really am sorry for causing you so much trouble, though you hired some good detectives. That was very smart of you. You're so smart, Vinnie."

His chest puffed up at the praise. "Yes, I am."

"Of course you are." Bile rose in her throat at the awful sickness of it all.

From her peripheral vision, Faith saw a movement at the stairs. She turned slightly and widened her eyes at the sight of Luke stepping up on the porch. Quickly looking back at Vinnie, she hoped he hadn't followed her gaze with his own.

But he had. The pit of her stomach dropped to see him whirl away from her and raise the gun. "You're a dead man," he shouted.

Faith reacted. Throwing herself at Vinnie, she used her fingers to claw at the gun in his hand. He shoved her away from him with a hand to her chest, sending her into the wall with jarring force.

Luke raised his hands in supplication, his expression neutral. Faith watched in horror, not believing Luke would stand there like an open target. Almost as if he dared Vinnie to shoot.

"Are you a cop?" Vinnie asked, sneering.

Luke shook his head. "No, this is my ranch."

"So, you're the wife-stealer. I ought to shoot you right now and be done with you."

Faith struggled to keep from crying out.

Luke shrugged. "You could. But there's no need. You can have her. I'm done with her. You heard her, she loves you. How can I fight that?" Luke inched forward, so slowly and carefully the movement was hardly noticeable.

Faith's mouth dropped open. He couldn't possibly believe the things she'd said to Vinnie, could he? Or had he figured out the sick game she was forced to play?

"You're right, she does love me," Vinnie postulated, his hawklike features settling into a smug expression. "Come on, Faith, we're leaving." Vinnie held out one hand while the other still aimed the gun at Luke's chest.

Faith stared at Vinnie's outstretched hand and then swung her gaze to Luke, who stared back at her, his blue eyes cold and remote. His stance was almost casual, as if they were doing no more than talking about the weather. How could he be so relaxed?

"Go on, Faith, your husband wants you to leave."

Luke's words sliced a gaping hole into Faith's heart. I don't want to leave you, she wanted to scream.

Faith stepped forward, but refused Vinnie's hand. She heard his sound of disapproval, but ignored him. Holding her head high, knowing she'd escape again the first chance she got, she marched in front of Vinnie toward the porch stairs. Tears gathered in her eyes as she passed Luke, but she forced her gaze straight ahead.

Two steps down she heard a noise. She turned back in time to see Luke launch himself at Vinnie. The agility and grace of Luke's body as he struck out amazed her. The rapid-fire movements of Luke's limbs connected with Vinnie's wiry frame, causing a yelp of pain.

She sagged against the railing in overwhelming relief. Luke wasn't going to let Vinnie take her. He was living up to his promise. She felt shame for doubting him. Vinnie turned the gun toward Luke and in a blood-pounding moment her elation turned to terror. She cried, "Nooo."

Unbelievably, Luke stepped in closer, his hands closing around the barrel of the gun. The two men moved in unison, their chests close together as they fell to the porch floor.

Faith covered her mouth with her hands. Fear

for Luke washed over her in giant waves, making her nauseous.

The loud retort of the gun split the air, the acrid smell of gun powder burning Faith's nostrils. Shudders ripped through her body at the thought that she might have lost Luke to Vinnie's gun.

Her heart stopped beating. *Please, God.* Neither man moved for what seemed an eternity, then suddenly Luke rolled away and stood. In his hand he held the gun. Faith whimpered in relief. *Thank You.*

She rushed to his side as he bent to check Vinnie's pulse. "Is he—?"

"He's alive," Luke stated and met her gaze.

"Drop the gun."

Startled, Faith jerked her gaze around to find the source of the command as Luke's arm came around her waist. Three men stood near the side of the house. Two held guns aimed at them. Both men were dressed in long trench coats and shiny dress shoes. Faith blinked as her mind registered the smaller man without a weapon. He wore jeans, a leather bomber jacket and his dark hair fell forward over his brown eyes. "Anthony?"

"I said drop the gun," the man on the right barked.

Luke laid the gun on the ground and slowly rose, his arm pulling her behind him. "You know these men?" Luke asked over his shoulder to her.

"Yes. No. I mean—Anthony is Vinnie's brother."

She tried to step forward, but Luke held her still, his body protecting her. "What's going on?"

The bigger of the two men shoved Anthony forward and he stumbled to a halt. "Sorry, Faith. I never meant to drag you into this."

"Drag me into what?"

"Enough chitchat," the older of the other two men stepped forward. His demeanor made it obvious he was in charge. "Get it."

Anthony grimaced. "Faith, I need your prayer-box necklace."

"What? Why?" She resisted the urge to reach inside her shirt collar and finger the box.

"I wrote down a number on the back of the prayer. I need that number," Anthony explained, his gaze showing desperation.

"So that's what you were doing in my room." She remembered the day she'd walked in to the bedroom that she'd shared with Vinnie a week before she left. Anthony had been going through her jewelry. She'd figured he'd swiped something to pawn for money to support his gambling habit, but nothing had been missing.

"I need that number or they're going to kill me," Anthony pleaded.

"How do you know that once you give it to them, they won't kill you, and us, anyway?" Luke demanded harshly.

"You don't," the older man stated. His ruddy complexion grew redder with the cold air. "Now get it. I'm freezing here."

"Faith, please. Just do as they ask. Where is it? Inside?" Anthony stepped closer.

"What's the number to?" Luke asked.

"Now if we told you that, we'd really have to kill you," the younger man quipped.

"Shut up, Junior," the older man barked. "Just get the number. I'm running out of patience."

The slight squeak of the porch door sounded seconds before the loud bang of a shotgun. Faith yelped, Anthony dove to the ground with his arms covering his head, the two men swung their guns toward the house and Luke bent to grab the gun from the ground.

Dottie, looking fierce holding a twelve-gauge shotgun aimed at the chest of the older man, moved to the top of the stairs. "Throw your guns on the ground or you'll take one in the chest."

The older man lifted his hands, his gun aimed in the air. "Now, listen here, I just want what's mine."

"You heard the lady, put down your weapons." Sheriff Bane came from around the house, a gun in his hand, as well.

Faith clutched Luke's arm, feeling like she'd somehow been plopped down in the middle of some gangster movie. The distant wail of a siren grew louder, bringing hope of an end to this daylight nightmare.

The older man swore and dropped his gun. The big guy did as his boss. Within moments, the place was swarming with uniformed police officers and men in navy vests with the letters FBI emblazoned across them in bright yellow. Luke helped Faith to the porch, where he took the shotgun from his mother before going to talk with the sheriff.

Faith watched the activity with numb detachment. The two strangers and Anthony were cuffed and put into a cruiser. The private investigator was also apprehended. Leo and Charles had been found tied up in the barn. Vinnie only had a leg wound. Paramedics worked to stop the bleeding.

Unsure how she felt about Vinnie surviving, Faith clenched her hands together. On the one hand she was grateful Luke wasn't responsible for a death. Yet, with Vinnie alive, her nightmare still lived on. She knew he wouldn't stay in jail forever and then he'd come looking for her again.

She dug out the prayer box from inside the collar of her shirt. Carefully, she opened the lid and pulled out the rolled paper. She stared at the numbers across the back. What were they to? She hurried to where the FBI agent who seemed to be in charge stood giving orders.

"Excuse me," she said as she approached.

"Ma'am," he responded. "Agent Tanner at your service. Can I help you?"

"Yes, sir." She held out the paper. "This is what the men were looking for. Do you know what it is?"

Luke stepped close but didn't touch her. She wished he'd put his arm around her, she needed his solid strength.

"Yes, ma'am. This is a numbered bank account. Mr. Fernando and his associates run a gambling and drug operation in Miami. Hopefully, this will be enough to put them away for a long time."

"How did you know they were here?"

He lowered his voice. "We have a man on the inside of the operation."

"What does Vinnie have to do with any of this?" she asked.

"From what Mr. Campbell, here, tells me, your ex-husband was stalking you. Other than a means for Fernando to find you, Vinnie wasn't involved with the operation. But he will be dealt with on the stalking issue. Now if you'll excuse me."

Agent Tanner left, taking the two men from Miami and Anthony with him. Luke went to talk with the sheriff.

Needing something to do, Faith righted the chairs and table. Beneath her feet, she heard the crunch of paper and saw the mail scattered about.

Bending down, she began to pick up the pieces

of paper and froze as her hand closed around the official-looking envelope. Sadness gathered in her heart. She knew she had to give the letter to Luke.

Her gaze settled on him. He bent down close to where Vinnie was stretched out on a gurney. She frowned. What could he be saying to Vinnie? The ambulance attendants stood a good distance away, leaving Luke alone with the wounded man.

She could see the same hardness in Luke's face that she'd seen earlier, but there was also a menacing quality to his expression that sent a chill down her spine. This was the man who'd spent the last decade in the military.

From the wide-eyed, scared look on Vinnie's face, Faith could only assume that whatever Luke was saying was having an impact on her ex-husband.

Luke moved away from Vinnie and the attendants lifted the gurney into the ambulance. She released a sigh of relief when the vehicle rumbled down the drive. A powerful sense of momentary freedom infused her, but did nothing to dispel the ache in her heart.

With the letter in hand, she walked down the stairs and over to where Luke stood talking with the sheriff. Both men turned at her approach and Sheriff Bane tipped his hat before ambling away.

Luke's penetrating gaze caught Faith off guard. She swallowed back the urge to fling herself into his arms and ask him to hold her until she felt safe again. Instead, she said, "Thank you, again."

He nodded, his gaze never wavering. She couldn't ascertain what he was thinking, so with a trembling hand she held out the envelope and felt a part of her shrivel up into a tight ball. He would open the letter and go to wherever he'd been assigned.

For a long moment neither moved. He looked at the envelope then back to her face. His hand reached out and closed over hers. "Faith, I…"

"It's okay, Luke," she interrupted him, wanting to spare him from having to say the words or her from hearing them. "We both knew this moment would come."

She withdrew her hand, leaving the envelope in his grasp. With a heavy heart, she said, "You're— you're free to go back to your life now. I don't need your protection any longer." Just his love.

He nodded, his expression shuttered. "I see."

Do you? she wondered, tears burning the backs of her eyelids. She refused to give in to the pain tearing at her heart. "I'll leave in the morning."

"Whatever you'd like. Just let me know how I can help you," he responded in clipped, formal tones.

Rapidly losing the battle with her tears, Faith nodded and hurried back to the house.

FOURTEEN

Luke knelt beside his bed, his head bowed and eyes closed. *Heavenly Father, I'm asking You for guidance. I know what my heart wants, but I will do what You want.* He waited and listened with his whole being for some reply. Moments passed. *Okay, Lord. Let me be more specific. Do I tell Faith that I love her and ask her to stay even though she's made it clear she wants to leave? Or do I let her go and return to the military?*

He waited for the excitement, the sense of adventure that always came when he thought of his career. They didn't come.

Realization hit him full in the chest. He didn't want to return to his military life. Relief swept away the guilt he'd felt for leaving his men to flounder. He shook his head. They weren't his men, they belonged to God. And now someone else was leading them. *Forgive me, Lord, for being so arrogant.*

But that still left the question of Faith. Would she be content to be a rancher's wife? Did he dare ask her to be?

Lord?

Luke's mouth quirked. Free will. Sometimes the Lord left the decision to His children. Well, he knew what he wanted and the only way to get it was to ask.

Twilight had come and gone. Dusk settled over the ranch, the darkness a relief to the grim events of the day. On Christmas Eve, Faith had expected to be in church singing worship songs, not in her room, fighting off an ache that clenched her stomach into a hard knot. Around her, clothes lay in heaps. Her open suitcase sat on the bed.

For so long, tension and fear had been her constant companions. But now all she felt was a deep, wrenching pain. A tear slipped down her cheek, leaving a wet trail in its wake. She was doing the right thing by not staying at the ranch. She'd already put the Campbells through enough. And this time when she left, she wouldn't be alone. God would walk with her every step of the way.

But she loved Luke. Her heart and her mind knew the truth. And if she didn't tell him, she'd live the rest of her life with regret.

Dear God, I want to be with Luke. It doesn't matter to me if it's on the ranch or a military base some-

where, I just want to be with him. I love him. He's told me You have a plan for my life. Please let it include Luke. I ask this in Your Son's precious name. Amen.

Determination dried her tears and lifted her chin. There was unfinished business between her and Mr. Campbell and it needed to be resolved now. Tonight. On Christmas Eve.

She stepped into the dimly lit hall and ran straight into a moving object. The world teetered, and for a precarious second she thought she'd find herself on her behind, but two strong arms gathered her close, pulling her up against a hard muscled chest.

She knew those arms, that chest. Knew the heady scent that wrapped around her like a cozy blanket. Savoring the embrace, she tilted her head back to look up into Luke's face.

"Sorry," he said, dropping his arms, leaving her feeling vulnerable and cold.

For a moment silence stretched between them. Faith gathered her courage. "Luke, I—"

"Faith, I—" he said over her.

Laughing softly, she held up a hand. "Please, let me say this."

With a slow nod, he stood perfectly still, his gaze intense. "Luke, I—I just want to be sure you under-stand that the things I said to—to Vinnie were un-true. I said what I did because—"

He pressed a finger to her lips. "I know."

"You do?" she said against the rough pad of his finger.

His hand moved away, leaving a warm spot on her mouth. She licked her lips, tasting the faint essence of him.

"I'll admit, at the time I was taken by surprise. Hearing those words hurt, but—that lasted only a second. I know you were protecting yourself and I know how you protected my mother. And when you attacked Vinnie, I knew you were protecting me." He placed a hand over his heart. "I can't begin to tell you how that made me feel. You're one courageous lady, Faith."

Ducking her head, she could feel her cheeks heating at his praise. Gently, his finger crooked beneath her chin and tilted her face up. The tender expression on his face knocked the breath from her body like his size had nearly knocked her from her feet.

"I know you want to leave in the morning but I just—I—" He took a quick breath and shifted his feet. "I was doing a lot of thinking tonight. And I came to some conclusions. First and foremost, I have to stop running from who I am. I've become everything I thought I didn't want to be. There's no use denying the truth any longer. I'm a rancher, just like my father."

"Oh, Luke." She knew how much he loved his father.

"Ironic, isn't it? I joined the military to keep from

becoming my father and here I am wanting nothing more than to follow my father's path."

"I'm sure he would be proud to know that."

Luke nodded. "Yes, he would have been. He was a wise man. He'd said once that each person had to find their own way home, wherever that home may be. It took me a while, but I've finally come home."

Barely daring to breathe, she asked, "Wh—what about your career?"

He took her hands in his. "I'm not going back. That season of my life is over. God has set me on a new road. I belong here."

"But your ministry?"

"Is not limited to the military. I started something that others can finish. Now, it's time to do good closer to home."

Biting her lip, Faith's mind raced. If he wasn't leaving, did that change things between them? "Luke, I—"

"Faith, please." He squeezed her hands. "Let me finish."

She almost protested, wanting to say the words burning on her tongue, but the agitated look now in his eyes kept her silent. She nodded.

Dropping her hands, he began to pace. Three steps left, pivot, three steps right, pivot. For a long tense moment, Faith watched his restless movements until she couldn't stand it any longer. Softly, she prodded, "Luke, what is it?"

As he passed in front of her, he abruptly stopped, his handsome face intent and his eyes dark in the dim hall. "I know I can't offer you what you had in your old life. You deserve better than being the wife of a rancher and I don't blame you for wanting to leave."

Heart racing, Faith interjected, "But, Luke, I—"

"No, Faith, I need to tell you." He took a shuddering breath. "I don't want you to leave."

Urgently, her heart brimming with tentative hope, she asked, "Why?"

Determination etched in every line, every angle of his body. "Because Faith, these weeks with you have been the best in my life. Because, you fill a void inside of me that I didn't know I had."

She tried to stop the trembling that suddenly began in her knees. Was he trying to say what she hoped he was saying? Did she dare believe that God would grant her the desires of her heart?

Capturing her hands, he said, "You belong in my life, Faith." He pressed a kiss to her palm. "I love you."

The doubts, the fears, all melted away with the utterance of those three little words. Savoring the joy welling up inside, she closed her eyes. "Luke, I—"

No more words could slip past the tightness in her throat.

He dropped his gaze. "It's—it's all right if you don't feel the same. I understand."

"No, Luke. You don't understand."

In a shaky voice, she told him what was in her heart. "I don't want to leave. Don't you know? I love you, too. I have for so long."

"Are you sure? Do you mean it?"

"Don't ever doubt it," she said fiercely and repeated, "I love you, Luke."

Swiftly, he took possession of her mouth. At once wild and urgent, Faith lost herself in the fire igniting between them until a dark, awful thought intruded. What would happen when Vinnie returned?

Regaining control of herself, she pulled back, breaking the contact.

Eyebrows furrowed in concern, Luke asked, "What's wrong?"

"What about Vinnie?"

"What about him?"

"When he gets out of jail, he'll return with a vengeance." Old fear surfaced, clouding her happiness.

Tenderly, Luke stroked her cheek. "Sweetheart, you don't ever have to worry about him again."

"But how can you be sure?"

He gave a mirthless laugh. "Oh, I made it very clear what would happen if he ever came within a thousand miles of you."

The memory of the fear in Vinnie's eyes as Luke

bent over him pricked her curiosity. "What did you tell him?"

"You don't want to know. Let's just say it involved the removal of vital body parts."

Faith gaped. "You didn't."

He shrugged sheepishly. "Well, something to that effect."

Giggling, she shook her head. Amazingly, she believed she'd never have to fear Vinnie again. Not with Luke by her side and God watching over them.

"I know it's not officially Christmas yet, but—" He took her hand and led her down the stairs to the living room.

He went to the tree and picked up a beautifully wrapped present. "Merry Christmas."

Her hands shook as she took the gift. Overwhelmed by his generosity and by her lack of a gift for him, she blinked back sudden tears. "I haven't finished your present."

"Your presence is gift enough," he stated softly.

Love for this man filled her soul to overflowing.

"Go ahead, open it," he urged.

Eager to see what was inside, she quickly dispensed with the wrapping and opened the box. She gasped. "Luke!"

His boyish grin filled her with joy.

She lifted the intricately designed butterfly ornament from where it lay on a bed of tissue. As she lifted it high, the glass, multicolored wings caught the light from the tree and reflected on the walls, filling the room in a kaleidoscope of color.

"It's beautiful!"

"Add it to the tree."

A tear slipped down her cheek as she hung the butterfly on a branch.

Luke gathered her close. "Now we'll have a memory of when you joined our family."

"Joined?"

Luke dropped to one knee. "Marry me, Faith."

No longer able to stand she dropped to her knees. Joy bubbled from the depths of her soul. Looks like God was giving her a Christmas blessing after all.

"Yes, I'll marry you."

* * * * *

Dear Reader,

Thank you for reading *Her Christmas Protector*. I hope you enjoyed Faith and Luke's story as each struggled to understand God's plan for their lives. So often we think our lives are one way and that change won't or shouldn't come, but when we're open to God and His blessings, we find that He knows what's best for us so much better than we do. And how much better could it be to discover that plan at Christmas?

Christmas is such a wonderful time of year. The decorations, the music and the holiday cheer. It can also be a lonely and sad time for those without family or friends. My hope is that we would all be open to God's leading and extend His love to those in need during the joyous time of celebrating Jesus's birth. He came so that all would be saved. He came to love everyone, not a select few. He came at Christmas time.

May your Christmas be filled with cheer, blessings and God's abounding love.
God Bless,

QUESTIONS FOR DISCUSSION

1. What made you pick up this book to read? How did it live up to your expectations?

2. Did you think Faith and Luke were realistic characters? Did their romance build believably? Talk about the secondary characters. What did you like or dislike about the people in the story?

3. Was the setting clear and appealing? Could you "see" where the story took place? How did you imagine it?

4. For Faith, she had to realize that God loved her and was with her, even through the bad times. Can you share an instance when you had a hard time remembering that God loved you and was with you even though it didn't seem as if He was?

5. What was the motive behind Luke's decision to join the military? Discuss a time in your life when you made a decision because of your parents. Was Luke's motivation worthy? How did God use Luke's decision?

6. Do you believe that God would not want someone who is a victim of abuse to stay in a bad situation? Why or why not?

7. Did you notice the scripture in the beginning of the book? What application does it have to your life?

8. Did the author's use of language/writing style make this an enjoyable read? Would you read more from this author? What did you particularly like about the writing?

9. What will be your most vivid memories of this book?

10. What lessons about life, love and faith did you learn from this story?

There was something about the young woman—something he couldn't put his finger on. He'd hardly glanced at her when he'd hauled her from the family sleigh, but now he took a longer look through the veil of falling snow.

For a moment her silhouette, her size, and her movements all reminded him of Noelle. How about that. Noelle, his frozen heart reminded him with a painful squeeze, had been his first—and only—love.

It couldn't be her, he reasoned, since she was married and probably a mother by now. She'd be safe in town, living snug in one of the finest houses in the county instead of riding along the country roads in a storm. Still, curiosity nibbled at him, and he plowed through the knee-deep snow. Snow was falling faster now, and yet somehow through the thick downfall his gaze seemed to find her.

She was fragile, a delicate bundle of wool—and snow clung to her hood and scarf and cloak like a shroud, making her tough to see. She'd been just a little bit of a thing when he'd lifted her from the sleigh, and his only thought at the time had been to get both women out of danger. He couldn't quite figure out what, but he could feel it in his gut.

The woman was talking on as she unwound her niece's veil. "We were tossed about dreadfully. You're likely bruised and broken from root to stem. I've never been so terrified. All I could do was pray over and over and think of you, my dear." Her words warmed with tenderness. "What a greater nightmare for you."

"We're fine. All's well that ends well," the niece insisted.

Although her voice was muffled by the thick snowfall, his step faltered. There *was* something about her voice, something familiar in the gentle resonance of her alto. Now he could see the top part of her face, due to her loosened scarf. Her eyes—they were a startling, flawless emerald green.

Whoa there. He'd seen that perfect shade of green before—and long ago. Recognition speared through his midsection, but he already knew she was his Noelle even before the last layer of the scarf fell away from her face.

His Noelle, just as lovely and dear, was now blind and veiled with snow. His first love. The woman he'd spent years and thousands of miles trying to forget. Hard to believe that there she was suddenly

right in front of him. He'd heard about the engage-
ment announcement a few years back, and he'd
known in returning to live in Angel Falls that he'd
have to run into her eventually.

He just didn't figure it would be so soon and like
this.

Seeing her again shouldn't make him feel as if
he'd been hit in the chest with a cannonball. The
shock was wearing off, he realized, the same as
when you received a hard blow. First off, you were
too stunned to feel it. Then the pain began to settle
in, just a hint, and then rushing in until it was unbear-
able. Yep, that was the word to describe what was
happening inside his rib cage. A pain worse than a
broken bone beat through him.

Best get the sleigh righted, the horse hitched back
up and the women home. But it was all he could do
to turn his back as he took his mustang by the bridle.
The palomino pinto gave him a snort and shook his
head, sending the snow on his golden mane flying.

I know how you feel, Sunny, Thad thought.
Judging by the look of things, it would be a long time
until they had a chance to get in out of the cold.

He'd do best to ignore the women, especially
Noelle, and to get to the work needin' to be done. He
gave the sleigh a shove, but the vehicle was wedged
against the snow-covered brush banking the river.
Not that he'd put a lot of weight on the Lord over

much these days, but Thad had to admit it was a close call. Almost eerie how he'd caught them just in time. It did seem providential. Had they gone only a few feet more, gravity would have done the trick and pulled the sleigh straight into the frigid, fast waters of Angel River and plummeted them directly over the tallest falls in the territory.

Thad squeezed his eyes shut. He couldn't stand to think of Noelle tossed into that river, fighting the powerful current along with the ice chunks. There would have been no way to have pulled her from the river in time. Had he been a few minutes slower in coming after them or if Sunny hadn't been so swift, there would have been no way to save her. To fate, to the Lord or to simple chance, he was grateful.

Some tiny measure of tenderness in his chest, like a fire long banked, sputtered to life. His tenderness for her, still there, after so much time and distance. How about that.

Since the black gelding was a tad calmer now that the sound of the train had faded off into the distance, Thad rehitched him to the sleigh but secured the driving reins to his saddle horn. He used the two horses working together to free the sleigh and get it realigned toward the road.

The older woman looked uncertain about getting back into the vehicle. With the way that black gelding of theirs was twitchy and wild-eyed, he didn't blame her. "Don't worry, ma'am, I'll see you two ladies home."

"Th-that would be very good of you, sir. I'm rather shaken up. I've half a mind to walk the entire mile home, except for my dear niece."

Noelle. He wouldn't let his heart react to her. All that mattered was doing right by her—and that was one thing that hadn't changed. He came around to help the aunt into the sleigh and after she was safely seated, turned toward Noelle. Her scarf had slid down to reveal the curve of her face, the slope of her nose and the rosebud smile of her mouth.

What had happened to her? How had she lost her sight? Sadness filled him for her blindness and for what could have been between them, once. He thought about saying something to her, so she would know who he was, but what good would that do? The past was done and over. Only the emptiness of it remained.

"Thank you so much, sir." She turned toward the sound of his step and smiled in his direction. If she, too, wondered who he was, she gave no real hint of it.

He didn't expect her to. Chances were she hardly remembered him, and if she did, she wouldn't think too well of him. She would never know what good wishes he wanted for her as he took her gloved hand. The layers of wool and leather and sheepskin lining between his hand and hers didn't stop that tiny flame of tenderness for her in his chest from growing a notch.

He looked into her eyes, into Noelle's eyes, the woman he'd loved truly so long ago, knowing she did not recognize him. Could not see him or sense him, even at heart. She smiled at him as if he were the Good Samaritan she thought he was as he helped her settle onto the seat.

Love was an odd thing, he realized as he backed away. Once, their love had been an emotion that felt so strong and pure that he would have vowed on his very soul that nothing could tarnish nor diminish their bond. But time had done that simply, easily, and they stood now as strangers.

＊ ＊ ＊ ＊ ＊

Don't miss this deeply moving
Love Inspired Historical story about
a young woman in 1883 Montana who reunites
with an old beau and soon discovers that love
is the greatest blessing of all.

HOMESPUN BRIDE
by Jillian Hart
available February 2008

And also look for
THE BRITON
by Catherine Palmer,
about a medieval lady who battles for
her family legacy—and finds true love.

Love Inspired. HISTORICAL

INSPIRATIONAL HISTORICAL ROMANCE

THE McKASLIN CLAN

Thad McKaslin never forgot Noelle, and her return to the Montana Territory rekindled his feelings for her. Will Noelle see how much Thad cares for her, or will her need for independence make her push him away?

Look for

Homespun Bride
by

JILLIAN HART

Available February 12.

LOOK FOR TWO NOVELS FROM THE NEW LOVE INSPIRED HISTORICAL SERIES EVERY MONTH.

Steeple Hill ®

REQUEST YOUR FREE BOOKS!

2 FREE RIVETING INSPIRATIONAL NOVELS
PLUS 2 FREE MYSTERY GIFTS

Love Inspired®

SUSPENSE

YES! Please send me 2 FREE Love Inspired® Suspense novels and my 2 FREE mystery gifts. After receiving them, if I don't wish to receive any more books, I can return the shipping statement marked "cancel." If I don't cancel, I will receive 4 brand-new novels every month and be billed just $3.99 per book in the U.S. or $4.74 per book in Canada, plus 25¢ shipping and handling per book and applicable taxes, if any*. That's a savings of 20% off the cover price! I understand that accepting the 2 free books and gifts places me under no obligation to buy anything. I can always return a shipment and cancel at any time. Even if I never buy another book from Steeple Hill, the two free books and gifts are mine to keep forever.

123 IDN EL5H   323 IDN ELQH

Name _____ (PLEASE PRINT)

Address _____ Apt. #

City _____ State/Prov. _____ Zip/Postal Code

Signature (if under 18, a parent or guardian must sign)

Order online at www.LoveInspiredSuspense.com

Or mail to Steeple Hill Reader Service™:

IN U.S.A.: P.O. Box 1867, Buffalo, NY 14240-1867
IN CANADA: P.O. Box 609, Fort Erie, Ontario L2A 5X3

Not valid to current Love Inspired Suspense subscribers.

Want to try two free books from another series?
Call 1-800-873-8635 or visit www.morefreebooks.com

* Terms and prices subject to change without notice. NY residents add applicable sales tax. Canadian residents will be charged applicable provincial taxes and GST. This offer is limited to one order per household. All orders subject to approval. Credit or debit balances in a customer's account(s) may be offset by any other outstanding balance owed by or to the customer. Please allow 4 to 6 weeks for delivery.

Your Privacy: Steeple Hill is committed to protecting your privacy. Our Privacy Policy is available online at www.eHarlequin.com or upon request from the Reader Service. From time to time we make our lists of customers available to reputable firms who may have a product or service of interest to you. If you would prefer we not share your name and address, please check here. ☐

LISUS07

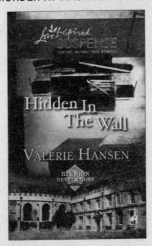

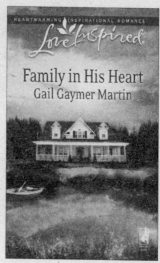

Love Inspired
SUSPENSE
RIVETING INSPIRATIONAL ROMANCE

A thug attempted to abduct Julia Daniels at gunpoint in broad daylight. And whoever was after the widowed mother would stop at nothing, including shooting a police officer. Handsome deputy sheriff Eric Butler was on the case, but he needed the truth about who she was running from. Yet how could Julia tell him when it meant putting all their lives in grave danger?

Look for
Deadly Texas Rose
by LENORA WORTH

Available January wherever books are sold.

Steeple
Hill®

LIS44275

TITLES AVAILABLE NEXT MONTH

Don't miss these four stories in January

FAMILY IN HIS HEART by Gail Gaymer Martin
Nick Thornton could tell Rona Meyers was a special person, so he'd offered her a much-needed job. And as he got to know her, he couldn't stop wondering if God was offering him a new beginning and a second chance at love.

NEXT DOOR DADDY by Debra Clopton
A Mule Hollow novel

When rancher Nate Talbert prayed for a change to his reclusive life, he got new next-door neighbor Pollyanna McDonald. But the menagerie of pets that she and her son cared for was driving him *crazy*. Could he handle the chaos that surrounded her?

THE DOCTOR'S BRIDE by Patt Marr
Everyone in town was trying to find Dr. Zack Hemingway a wife. Yet the one girl who caught his eye wasn't interested. Why was Chloe Kilgannon hiding from him? This doctor knew it would take some good medicine to get to the heart of the matter.

A SOLDIER'S PROMISE by Cheryl Wyatt
Wings of Refuge

Pararescue jumper Joel Montgomery had the power to make a sick little boy's dream come true. He was determined to follow through even if it meant returning to a place he'd rather forget. And meeting the boy's pretty teacher made his leap of faith doubly worth the price.

LICNM1207

Stephen—the only man she'd ever kissed, had ever wanted to kiss…!

She craved more, far more, knowing what heights this man could take her to. Her knees went weak with the memory of a solitary moment of bliss. She wanted the pleasure again. She wanted Stephen.

He broke the kiss, cradled her head against his shoulder. Even through her hard, unsteady breathing she felt him shudder.

Nothing had changed. Not in six years.

"I have to go." His voice was low and harsh.

It took her a moment to remember he was leaving Branwick for York. But he'd be back, wouldn't he?

"You will come back?"

"On my honor."

The second kiss nearly knocked her senseless. Foolishness beyond belief, but if not for the girls napping on their nearby pallets, she'd be sore tempted to pull him down in the dirt and strip him bare…!

Dear Reader,

Harlequin Historicals is putting on a fresh face! We hope you enjoyed our special inside front cover art from recent months. We plan to bring this "extra" to you every month! You may also have noticed our new look—a maroon stripe that runs along the right side of the front cover and an "HH" logo in the upper right corner. Hopefully, this will help you find our books more easily in the crowded marketplace. And thanks again to those of you who participated in our reader survey. Your feedback enables us to bring you more of the stories and authors that you like!

We have four incredible books for you this month. The talented Shari Anton returns with a new medieval novel. *Knave of Hearts* is a secret-child story about a knight who, in the midst of seeking the hand of a wealthy widow, is unexpectedly reunited with his first—and not forgotten—love. Cheryl St.John's new Western, *Sweet Annie,* is full of her signature-style emotion and tenderness. Here, a hardworking horseman falls in love with a crippled young woman whose family refuses to see her as the capable beauty she is.

Ice Maiden, by award-winning author Debra Lee Brown, will grab you and not let go. When a Scottish clan laird washes ashore on a remote island, the price of his passage home is temporary marriage to a Viking hellion whose icy facade belies a burning passion…. And don't miss *The Ranger's Bride,* a terrific tale by Laurie Grant. Wounded on the trail of an infamous gang, a Texas Ranger with a past seeks solace in the arms of a beautiful "widow," who has her own secrets to reveal….

Enjoy! And come back again next month for four more choices of the best in historical romance.

Sincerely,

Tracy Farrell, Senior Editor

Knave of Hearts

SHARI
ANTON

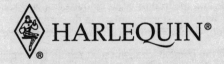

HARLEQUIN®

TORONTO • NEW YORK • LONDON
AMSTERDAM • PARIS • SYDNEY • HAMBURG
STOCKHOLM • ATHENS • TOKYO • MILAN • MADRID
PRAGUE • WARSAW • BUDAPEST • AUCKLAND

ISBN 0-373-29147-7

KNAVE OF HEARTS

Copyright © 2001 by Sharon Antoniewicz

This edition published by arrangement with Harlequin Books S.A.

Visit us at www.eHarlequin.com

Printed in U.S.A.

To the Schwagers:
Lady Chris, of the flaming hair and enchanting smile,
and Sir Ron, her dark and stormy knight.
Hark, the summer cometh!
And we couldn't ask for better playmates.

Prologue

April, 1109

Stephen wished he could cheer his half brother out of his morose mood. He'd tried and failed, probably because by getting angry and confronting King Henry, Stephen bore some blame for getting Richard into trouble to begin with.

Within Wilmont's richly furnished chambers in Westminster Palace, Richard slumped in a high-backed chair, a goblet of wine dangling from his fingertips, a frown on his face. No wonder. He'd been forced to accept the guardianship over the widow and orphan of Wilmont's greatest enemy, a man who'd damn near succeeded in getting Richard killed.

Stephen still had trouble believing events had taken such a strange turn, but King Henry was adamant and they must all deal as best they could with this unpalatable situation. For his part, Stephen would leave at sunrise for Normandy, to assess the extent of young Philip's estates and determine if the boy's relatives posed a threat. The errand should take a month, or maybe a week or two more, to complete.

Which left Stephen this one night to secure a betrothal bargain with Carolyn de Grasse, the heiress who awaited him in a bedchamber on a lower floor of the palace.

Stephen gave Richard an affectionate shake on the shoulder. "Get some sleep. I will see you come morn."

"Do try to stay out of trouble," Richard said.

Stephen didn't take offense. 'Twas the several goblets of quickly quaffed wine talking. Of his two siblings, Gerard, the eldest brother and powerful baron of Wilmont, was the more overbearing and quickest to censure. Despite his brothers' tendency to overprotectiveness, Stephen wouldn't trade either of them for all the riches in the kingdom.

He just wished they wouldn't take every opportunity to remind him of his tendency to give in to his whims of fancy, which they considered his weakness. 'Struth, bound by duty, his brothers possessed neither the time nor inclination to follow the flight of an eagle simply to see where it landed. Staid fellows, both. A repugnant fate Stephen intended to forswear.

He chided Richard. "Pray tell, how can I get into trouble by spending the night with the woman I plan to wed?"

For the first time in hours, the corner of Richard's mouth twitched in amusement. "Oh, I can think of a way or two."

"Never fear. I have not yet failed to thoroughly pleasure a woman whose good opinion I wish to enjoy," he boasted, and was rewarded with a wider smile and a grunt of disbelief. "Now I must go. 'Twould not do for me to be late for a tryst with my betrothed."

"Lady Carolyn is not your betrothed, yet."

"Give me an hour and she will be begging to marry me."

To the heartening sound of Richard's soft chuckle, Stephen left Wilmont's chambers and strode down the palace passages and stairways, wishing Gerard was here to help Richard.

Unfortunately, Gerard wasn't on good terms with King Henry at the moment, so he'd sent Stephen and Richard to court at Westminster in his stead. While keeping a careful watch for any shifts of power that always accompanied large gatherings of England's nobility, Stephen had also taken the time to study the current crop of unwed heiresses.

A man in his position needed to marry, to continue the family line and provide heirs for his holdings. Stephen intended to do his duty, but on his own terms. That he'd finally found a woman damn near perfect for his needs, Carolyn de Grasse, he considered a heaven-sent twist of fate.

A few years older than his own two and twenty years, newly widowed for the second time, Carolyn wanted a young, virile man as her third husband. She wanted a man to pleasure her in bed and sire her children, then otherwise make himself scarce so she could oversee her lands with no husbandly interference.

Stephen kept the "scarce" condition firmly in mind— the best part of the arrangement to his way of thinking. He could fulfill his duty to his family and provide an heir to his estates, all without becoming staid.

Since he'd already proven his prowess to Carolyn yesterday, leaving her languid and sated, he harbored no worries over tonight's outcome. He would pleasure her once more, explain the need for his upcoming journey, and secure her agreement to accept no other man as her husband in his absence. When he returned from Normandy, he'd present his suit to her father.

From the nearby abbey came the peal of deep-toned bells, announcing the hour of matins. Midnight. Right on time. He tapped lightly on the chamber door and softly called Carolyn's name. Receiving no answer, he pushed on the latch, and finding the door unlocked, eased it open.

The flame from a thick tallow candle cast enough mellow light for him to inspect the chamber. Sparse, Stephen judged the furnishings. Truly, he'd have thought the room unoccupied if not for the human-size lump curled in the middle of the bed, huddled completely under a wool coverlet.

It didn't bode well that Carolyn had fallen asleep. He'd expected her to remain awake with anticipation. But then she'd left the door unbolted and a candle lit for him to see by, and she *was* in the bed waiting for him to come to her.

Planning a seductive awakening, Stephen slid the bolt, then shucked his tunic and sherte and tossed them onto the small oak table. As he sat on the only stool in the room and removed the first of his boots, a soft gasp came from the direction of the bed.

Bare-chested, boot in hand, Stephen stared at the woman propped up on an elbow. Within the space of a heartbeat he noted hair of sable brown, not auburn. Skin of ivory, not porcelain.

Hellfire. Not Carolyn.

He recognized the woman who stared at him with eyes the color of polished pewter. He hadn't seen her in five, no six years, but he knew the lovely lady's name as well as his own.

Marian de Lacy.

They'd lost their innocence together, he and Marian, in her father's stables. During secret trysts filled with eager, exploring touches, in a fever of sense-banishing youthful lust, they'd discovered the thrill of robust, if unskilled, coupling.

Stephen searched for a way to end the shocked silence, but came up with nothing better than a nod and her name.

"Marian."

She glanced at the door, then at his discarded garments.

"Sweet heaven, Stephen. What are you doing here?" she asked in a loud whisper.

Knowing women as he did, Stephen suspected that blurting out the truth might not be wise. A man did not tell a former bed mate that he'd come to make love to another woman and hope to escape unscathed.

"I...um..."

Marian shushed him, then eased out of bed while arranging the coverlet into a jumbled heap. When she stood, her sable hair tumbled over her shoulders and down to below her rump, only partially veiling her lush curves. She wore a chemise of cream linen, without sleeves, cut low to her bosom and high on her calves.

Her hips were more rounded than he remembered, her breasts fuller. She padded toward him on bare feet, sleepy-eyed and delectable. All the vision wanted was a stray piece of hay caught in her tumbling, wavy tresses and they could be right back in the stables enjoying each other's bodies.

His loins stirred, a familiar and natural reaction to seeing a near naked woman, especially when remembering how he'd hastily divested this female of a similar filmy chemise to fondle her firm, dusky-tipped breasts.

To press her smooth skin against his. To ease his aching member into Marian's slick, velvet softness.

Stephen dropped his boot and stood, his arms rising to invite an embrace. Marian stopped beyond his reach and pointed to the door.

"Out," she whispered, the command as clear as an angry shout.

So much for a tender reunion.

Stephen placed his hands on his hips, drawing her gaze downward to his waist and below, where evidence of his thoughts now strained at his breeches. She stared at the bulge long enough for him to know she remembered well what they'd been doing, in boisterous fashion, when last together.

"Is that any way to greet an old friend?" he asked.

"Shh!"

He failed to understand her insistent hushing. "Why must we whisper?"

Marian glanced over her shoulder at the bed. "So we do not wake my daughter."

Stephen noted the heaped coverlet, under which must lie a child, a little girl. He banished a moment of unease by recalling, with great relief, that his and Marian's union hadn't borne fruit. For a while after their affair he'd wondered over that particular consequence, fearing Marian's father might come roaring into Wilmont demanding a wedding—or Stephen's head. It hadn't happened. He'd been spared.

He'd also taken the incident as a warning and forever after been careful about where he spilled his seed.

The bundle on the bed shifted, the child the result of another man's spilled seed.

Marian must now be married. No wonder she was so angry at his intrusion—and he had intruded. He'd taken it upon himself to enter the chamber in search of Carolyn.

Was it possible that sometime after he and Carolyn had arranged this tryst, the palace seneschal had moved her into another room, giving this one to Marian? And Marian's husband? Was that why the door hadn't been bolted?

Stephen sat and pulled on his boot. He'd never been caught in a compromising situation with another man's wife and didn't intend for that to happen now. Too, he had yet to find Carolyn and secure the betrothal bargain tonight.

Dare he ask Marian if she knew where Carolyn had been moved to? He stood and shrugged into his sherte and tunic, preparing for a hasty escape if Marian took his inquiry badly.

"My pardon for the intrusion, Marian. I obviously mistook your chamber for that of another. Do you happen to know where its former occupant might be?"

She stared at him, long and hard. "You look for Carolyn?"

Wary, he nodded.

Without a hint of surprise or anger, which might be expected of a former lover, she said, "Then you are in the right chamber. Unfortunately, my cousin is not here." She waved at the door. "Kindly wait without."

Marian and Carolyn were cousins? They shared these quarters? Stephen pushed aside further questions. Those were for Carolyn to answer, not Marian.

"As you wish. Truly, I did not mean to disturb you, Marian, only talk to Carolyn."

Marian scoffed. "Talk?"

"Aye, talk," he said. "If you will recall, you and I managed to do some of that, too."

"You talked. I listened. For all my devoted attention you dismissed me without so much as the courtesy of a farewell."

True enough. She'd listened, fascinated by his tales of the many places he'd been, and especially about those he yet wished to visit. He'd forgotten how good a companion she'd been, but then, he truly hadn't thought about Marian in years. He'd been too busy traveling to all of those exotic places he'd told her about. She was wrong about dismissing her lightly, however. Surely, someone had explained to her why he'd left her father's estate so quickly.

"We were denied the chance to part company as we should. I am sorry for that," he said.

He took a step forward, knowing he shouldn't touch her, yet reached out to brush at a lock of silky hair that threatened to cover Marian's eyes. She jerked back and looked away. Her recoil hurt, sharper and deeper than it should. His offending fingers curled into his palm.

"Rather too late for apologies, is it not?" she asked.

Apparently so, and for that he was sorry, too.

"Fare thee well, Marian."

Chapter One

July, 1109

Marian didn't have to look up from her embroidery to know which of her twin daughters entered the hut. Audra's leather sandals slapped the hard-packed dirt floor with the purposeful steps of someone much older than five summers. Had it been the other twin, Lyssa, the footfalls would have landed light and quick.

Flipping her raven braid behind her, Audra sat at the table and propped her chin in her hands. Well acquainted with her daughter's pout, Marian pursed her lips to withhold a smile. Apparently, Lyssa was doing something Audra didn't approve of. Not unusual.

Bowing to the inevitable, Marian asked, ''Where is Lyssa?''

''Playing on the stone fence.'' Audra's tone suggested Lyssa receive a scolding, which Marian wasn't about to do. Though she didn't completely approve of Lyssa's daring, she could hardly deny the girl one of the few joys in her life.

As different as night and day, were her girls. Though

they looked so alike most people couldn't tell one from
the other, their temperaments distinguished them as no
physical trait could. Audra would never scramble up on
the stones and walk along the top of the fence, not for
fear of falling off but out of disdain for such unladylike
behavior. Lyssa inevitably forswore dignity when a
fence wanted climbing, a mud puddle must be run
through, or a twin sister needed irritating.

Most often the twins balanced each other. Lyssa
sometimes heeded Audra's cautions, which prevented
the bold twin from courting disaster. Audra sometimes
got caught up in Lyssa's gleeful view of life, which kept
the solemn twin from becoming dour.

Usually, as happened last night, when Lyssa's headaches stole away the sparkle in her eyes, Audra sat next
to her twin's pallet, quietly holding her sister's hand.

With an inward sigh, Marian acknowledged that the
long, vexing trip to Westminster with Lyssa had proved
a failure. They'd endured the journey's physical hard-
ships, the sorrow of leaving Audra behind and the annoyance of Carolyn's almost constant company, all for
naught. Marian had so hoped the London physician
would provide a cure for Lyssa's headaches. Though
Lyssa obediently downed the powders and herb mixtures
the physician claimed would help, the headaches still
struck hard and without warning. In the three months
since returning home, Lyssa had suffered two bouts of
pain no treatment seemed to ease.

If Lyssa felt well enough to walk along the fence this
morn, Marian wouldn't call her down until necessary.

She slid the needle into the pristine white linen, wishing she could set the altar cloth aside and join her girls
out of doors. Unfortunately, the altar cloth she decorated—a gift from her uncle, William de Grasse, to the

Archbishop of York—must be completed and taken to Branwick Keep today.

So she'd comply. Uncle William asked so little of her in return for his protection. 'Twas the least she could do for the man who'd seen to her welfare when she'd desperately needed shelter and succor.

"Do not fret, Audra. Lyssa will come down from the fence when she is ready. You have finished your chores?"

Audra's head bobbed. "Aye. I fed the chickens and Lyssa tied the goat to graze. Truly, Mama, when you finish the altar cloth we can leave for the keep. Shall I tell Lyssa to come in to make ready?"

"Not quite yet." Marian again stifled a smile, this time at Audra's sigh. "Go out and enjoy the sunshine. I shall call you both when I am finished."

Audra got up and slowly headed for the door. Then she stopped and turned. "Mayhap we should gather eggs for his lordship. He enjoys them, does he not?"

Audra knew very well William did, and Marian thought her daughter's ploy to get Lyssa down from the stone fence just might work. That William would be delighted with the gift of the eggs only made the offer more appealing.

"He will be well pleased, Audra."

The girl wasted no time in grabbing a basket and scurrying out of the hut, calling her sister's name.

Marian gave in to both her mirth and curiosity. She set aside the altar cloth and took the few steps necessary to see out the open door, yet not be noticed easily.

Lyssa took the bait of an egg hunt and scrambled down off of the fence. Their black braids bouncing on the backs of their brown tunics, the girls hurried toward the long grass beyond the garden where an egg or two would likely be found.

Sweet heaven, how she adored the tykes, despite the trials of raising them on her own. Now, she couldn't imagine life without them, when once, as a young and naive girl, she'd envisioned her life far differently.

Marian shook her head. What was past was past. She usually managed to get through weeks on end without thinking of those days before the twins were born—until lately. The memories came more often, she knew, because she'd seen Stephen again.

Stephen—standing before her in the palace bedchamber, partially disrobed, his arms outstretched.

The knave. He'd fully expected her to step into his embrace as if the years gone by had never happened, as if they'd parted on the best of terms. Knowing full well the impact of his charms, and having heard tales of his recent amorous exploits from Carolyn, Marian didn't doubt Stephen simply accepted female adoration as his normal due.

Thankfully, she'd been too shocked at seeing him and too concerned over protecting Lyssa that she hadn't done his bidding. Under other circumstances... No, never again would she willingly court such heartbreak.

Marian took a steadying breath, fetched the altar cloth and resumed stitching. The last gold cross was nearly done.

The motions she was sure she could do in her sleep soon lulled her into a familiar calm, heedless of all but the slip of needle and slide of thread through linen. So intent was she on finishing the cross she didn't hear the jangle of horses' tack until the travelers were nearly at the front gate.

The girls called a greeting to whoever was passing by. The altar cloth put aside, Marian got up to observe.

Stunned, her feet rooted to the floor when she saw *him.* Panic swelled and threatened to clog her throat. *Breathe!* her body shouted. She could barely obey.

Stephen of Wilmont, mounted on a magnificent black horse, smiled down at the twins who gave him their rapt attention.

Marian squelched the urge to scream at the girls to come into the safety of the hut, or to shout at Stephen to be on his way. Neither the girls nor Stephen would understand her panic at seeing the three of them together.

The threat he presented nearly overwhelming her, Marian took refuge in glancing over his escort.

Two chain-mail-clad knights rode horses of brownish red, of the same renowned Wilmont stock as Stephen's. Six helmeted foot soldiers, carrying spears and shields, flanked two wagons pulled by teams of sturdy oxen. As did most nobles when traveling to a keep where they intended to visit a long while, Stephen arrived bearing crates and barrels—filled with his belongings, extra food, gifts for his hosts—and furniture. Above the sides of the last wagon she spied the half moon of a round table. Towering above it all were the thick, unmistakable four posts of a huge bed. Stephen's bed.

The girls giggled. Lyssa climbed up onto the wall, the better to talk to the man who beamed down at her. Audra dared a couple of stones to rise higher, to get a better view of the noble lord who, for whatever reason, stopped to speak with them.

Marian remained rooted, not daring to go outside until she brought her fears under control. Stephen had no reason to harm the girls, or to suspect they were other than the daughters of a peasant. The realization calmed her some.

She wished she could hear clearly what they spoke of, but all that reached her ears was Stephen's deeply timbered tone and the girls' high trills.

Why couldn't he have found some other adventure to pursue to keep him away longer, or better yet forever? After a month had passed, then two, she'd been sure another woman had caught his fancy, enticing him to forget about marrying Carolyn.

Now, a full three months after their meeting in Westminster, Stephen arrived in full splendor, apparently intent on winning Carolyn, so sure of his welcome he planned on a prolonged stay and brought along his bed.

Stephen had obviously taken great care in his choice of garments today, wanting to impress, and impress he did. Over a bloodred, long-sleeved sherte he wore a gold-trimmed, black silk tunic. A girdle of gold links wrapped twice around his waist. Impressively noble garb on a magnificently formed male.

He possessed coin aplenty, or so Carolyn claimed. His brother, the baron, had gifted both Stephen and their half brother Richard with several holdings apiece from which to draw income. Enough coin for Uncle William to take Stephen's suit for Carolyn's hand seriously, though Marian suspected Stephen's being the sibling of a powerful baron was more a factor in William's acceding to Carolyn's pleas to hear Stephen's offer.

Carolyn, on the other hand, cared little for the coin or Stephen's rank. A gifted Adonis, Carolyn had dreamily termed the young man with the comely face, exquisitely formed body, and lack of desire to interfere with her wish to be sole overlord of Branwick when she inherited.

Truly, Marian's youthful lover had most definitely

come into the fullness of his manhood. Stephen had grown tall, wide across the chest and narrow in the hips. Unlike most Norman nobles, he wore his hair long in Saxon fashion, the wind-tossed black tips skimming his broad shoulders.

No boyish innocence remained in his striking features. His clean-shaven jaw jutted forward at a determined but not arrogant angle. A noble brow hooded his deep-set eyes of sparkling, spring green—both predatory and mesmerizing—that darkened to nearly emerald when lust reached feverish heights. His mouth, so quick to smile, with lips full and warm and mobile—

Marian's heart stuttered, an unwanted reminder that those lustful bouts with Stephen remained so vivid and affected her so forcefully, even from across the full length of the yard. Even over the passing of years. She thought she'd been fully prepared to see him again if necessary, had steeled her heart and mind against his appeal. 'Twas galling to admit she'd failed so utterly.

Audra swept a hand behind her, palm up, stopping when her fingers pointed at the hut. Inviting Stephen inside?

Dear Lord, have mercy, no!

Stephen glanced at the doorway. Marian stepped back. A foolish gesture. He couldn't see this far inside the hut from the road.

Coward, a niggling voice chided her. If Stephen were here to stay, if he married Carolyn, he would learn where Marian lived, that the girls were hers. What sense putting off what couldn't be avoided?

Her secret was safe. She'd told no one, and no one could guess merely by noting that the girls and Stephen shared but the one physical trait of shining, raven-hued hair.

Marian took a step forward.

Stephen shook his head, an aggrieved smile on his face. With a courtly bow to the girls, he backed his horse from the fence, signaled to his escort, and resumed his journey to Branwick Keep.

Marian sank down on the stool and covered her face with her hands, so relieved that she moaned.

The twins came into the hut at a run.

"Mama, he is here!" Lyssa cried. "Stephen of Wilmont has come to marry Carolyn!"

"He comes to ask Lord William's permission to marry her, you mean," Audra corrected Lyssa, once again proving that Audra missed none of the servants' gossip. She set the basket of eggs on the table. "Will William like Stephen over Edwin, Mama, as Carolyn does?"

To Marian's bewilderment, Carolyn preferred to marry Stephen of Wilmont over Edwin of Tinfield. True, Stephen was young, unlike Carolyn's first two husbands. Stephen had no wish to usurp Carolyn's place as ruler of her dower lands and eventually Branwick, as she feared Edwin might try to do. Stephen pleased Carolyn in bed, a fact Carolyn had been eager to point out to Marian, if not to her father.

That Carolyn had the chance to marry Edwin, a man she'd been fond of for years, held no sway with Carolyn in her choice of husbands.

William was inclined to allow his daughter some say in her third marriage. He'd chosen both of her first two husbands and saw how miserably and quickly those marriages had ended!

"'Tis for William to decide," Marian finally answered.

"Can we go now, Mama? We have the eggs!" Lyssa said proudly.

Marian glanced at the altar cloth. "Not yet," she said, grateful for the short reprieve.

Mayhap, if fate proved kind, she could slip in and out of Branwick Keep later today without hardly a soul, especially Stephen, knowing she was there. No sense flirting with further distress when it would likely find her soon enough.

With Branwick Keep in view, Stephen shifted in the saddle, the better to swipe at the road dust on his tunic and breeches. There wasn't any hope for his boots, so he didn't bother with them.

"Nervous?"

The question came from the man who rode at Stephen's right, Armand, one of Gerard's favorite squires and a pleasant companion on a long journey.

Stephen shrugged an indifferent shoulder. "Not unduly."

After all, one Norman noble thought and acted much like another. He usually handled himself well around the likes of barons and earls, and King Henry—the most headstrong Norman in the kingdom. 'Struth, his last encounter with the king hadn't gone at all well. Still, William de Grass, lord of Branwick, shouldn't present a challenge.

"I would be, knowing I was minutes away from confronting and being judged by the father of the woman I hoped to marry," Armand admitted with a shiver.

William was also ill and quite frail, which had kept him from accompanying Carolyn to Westminster. Stephen saw no difficulty in having his way with Carolyn's father.

"I doubt the proceedings will lead to a confrontation, rather to a meeting of the minds."

"His lordship might be of a mind to deny you. You *are* late."

Long overdue, by several weeks. He'd been stuck in Normandy longer than planned. Then he'd spent several more weeks helping Richard. Then he'd stopped at Wilmont to report to Gerard. The four to six weeks he'd planned to be gone had stretched into three full months. Carolyn might not be pleased by his extended absence, but Stephen didn't see how he could have done anything differently and still do right by Richard.

And he'd done right by Richard—now settled at Collingwood, playing lord of the manor, getting along well with his ward and perhaps a bit too well with his ward's mother. Stephen withheld judgment on that affair—'twas Richard's decision to make the woman his bed mate or not.

Still, Carolyn's reaction to his tardy arrival might be a problem.

"Then I shall have to placate his lordship somehow. Mayhap the keg of Burgundy wine will prove an acceptable bribe for forgiveness." Stephen smiled. "Or perhaps I should have accepted Audra's offer of refreshment in her parents' hut. They might have told me how to best treat their lord."

Armand answered with a wry smile. "Can you imagine the reaction of the parents if a Norman noble deigned to grace their hut? The poor peasants might have died of heart failure!"

Harlan, the white-bearded, crusty old knight on Stephen's left, huffed. "Unnatural, I say, for a peasant tyke to make such an offer, and with the manners of the high born, too. Girl is headed for trouble if her parents continue to allow such behavior."

A valid observation, Stephen acknowledged. A peasant who forgot his or her place was most often severely reprimanded if caught by one of high rank who took offense. Audra's actions had amused him, but another lord might have backhanded the girl, or worse, for her presumption. 'Twasn't his problem, yet the thought of anyone mistreating the little girl didn't sit well.

Seeking a reason for Audra's unusual behavior, Stephen wondered aloud. "Mayhap the girls are being trained for service in a noble household, and so are taught such manners?"

Armand let out a laugh. "If so, then Lyssa is not taking to her lessons well. What a scamp!"

Harlan shook his head. "'Twould never happen, not with twins. What noble household would have them?"

Stephen knew of one. "Gerard would take them at Wilmont."

"Name me another."

Stephen conceded the point. The superstitions people held about twins would prevent their acceptance in most noble households. People feared what they considered an abomination of nature, so much so that dispensing of one of the twins at birth wasn't unheard of among high and low born alike. Apparently, Audra and Lyssa's parents didn't fear the girls might become pawns of the devil and had allowed both girls to live.

As had the parents of another set of twins. Corwin, Stephen's best friend, was twin to Ardith, who had married his brother Gerard. No one at Wilmont would dare accuse either of consorting with the devil, at least not to their faces. The little girls might not be so fortunate.

Cute tykes, destined to be lovely women. Their father

would need to keep his wits about him as they grew up, to protect them from the randy bucks sure to come around, not caring if the object of their fancy was a twin or not.

"We are spotted," Armand said, ending Stephen's musings.

An imposing timber palisade surrounded Branwick Keep. Near the gate, several guards gathered to observe his company's arrival.

"Harlan, have the wagon drivers stay tight to each other," Stephen commanded. "Once inside, halt the soldiers and wagons in the outer bailey. Armand and I will go up to the keep and send someone down to you with further instructions."

"As you wish, my lord."

Stephen gave his tunic a last, quick brushing. He'd dressed the part he must play, the wealthy noble come courting. Gold thread sparkled on his tunic. Silver studs shone bright on the leather of his steed's bridle and saddle. Enough show of wealth to make an impression without being pompous.

Stephen far preferred to travel on his own, or with one other companion, yet conceded when Gerard insisted on providing this escort and the wagonloads of goods. Though he truly hated it when his brother acted the baron, at times Gerard knew best how to approach an uncertain situation.

Little could be more uncertain than a woman's reaction if she felt insulted, and Carolyn could well bear him ill will for taking so long to come to Branwick.

Only look how angry Marian had been because he hadn't bid her farewell, and that six years ago! Even with three months to mull over her reaction to him, he still didn't understand how she could hold harsh feelings against him for so long. Over the lack of a fare-thee-well. Over that which hadn't been his fault.

Pushing aside the vision of Marian's beauty, even in her anger, Stephen crossed the bridge over the deep ditch surrounding the palisade. The guards waved him through the gate.

"A good sign, do you not think?" Stephen asked Armand. "I had a moment's dread that Carolyn might have left instructions for the guards to deny us entry."

"We have only gained the outer bailey," Armand said in a droll tone. "Do not count yourself welcome until the lady allows you entry to the hall."

Stephen heard the creaks and groans of the wagons fall silent. Harlan would keep the soldiers and wagons in hand until told where to send them.

Much as in any Norman keep in England, Branwick's outer bailey teemed with people. Merchants' shops, a smithy and the stables all lined the palisade, with guards patrolling the plank walk fastened high on the timbers. Men-at-arms practiced with swords, maces or lances in the tiltyard.

Stephen passed through the gate of the second curtain wall into the inner bailey, noting the mouth-teasing aroma of roasting meat wafting out of the kitchen. Servants scurried about, in the midst of morning chores, a few of them taking note of the new arrivals.

On a high, earthen motte sat a three-story, stone keep, the home and refuge to the lord of Branwick and his daughter. Though Carolyn possessed dower lands from her first two husbands, she preferred to live at Branwick Keep, which she would one day inherit and then pass along to her children. Stephen's children, if all went well.

He rode to the stairway that led up to the great hall

on the second floor. As he dismounted, a short, thin, gray-haired man came scurrying down the stairs.

William de Grasse? Probably not. According to Carolyn, her father was too frail to leave his bed, had been ill since last winter.

The man bowed slightly. "I am Ivo, steward of Branwick. You are Stephen of Wilmont?"

Stephen handed his horse's reins to Armand. "I am, but how did you know?"

"Oh, my lord, Lady Carolyn was most exacting in her description of you, so accurate the guards at the gate knew your identity immediately and sent word to us."

"Ah, I see. Then Carolyn knows I am here."

"Most certainly, my lord. She awaits you in the hall."

The steward's words were given graciously, but something in the man's tone warned of something amiss, and Stephen feared he knew what it was.

He glanced over at Armand who, having relegated their horses to a stable lad, pushed his mail cowl back from his head. He ran his fingers through his sandy-colored hair, only half attempting to hold back a knowing grin.

"Then we should not keep her ladyship waiting," Stephen told the steward and took to the stairs, Ivo and Armand following close behind.

Stephen opened the huge oak doors at the top of the stairway, stepped into the great hall and searched for Carolyn. She sat at a table on the dais at the far end of the hall, sipping from a silver goblet, paying scant heed to the man sitting next to her on the bench. Upon seeing him inside the doorway, she rose and came around the table, then stood statue still, waiting for Stephen to come to her.

His intended's beauty would take any man's breath

away. Regal in her bearing, Carolyn's gown of sapphire showed both her coloring and figure to great advantage. Braids of shining auburn hung forward, over her breasts, down to beyond her waist. A stiffened band of sapphire stitched with gold hugged her forehead. Stephen waited for her bow mouth to curve into a smile, and was disappointed.

If she was angry, however, she hid it well behind a mask of indifference. Not until he reached her did Stephen notice a tinge of annoyance surface.

"You came, finally," she said.

Stephen grasped her dainty hand and brought it to his mouth. "I rushed to your side the moment my duty was done. My apologies for having worried you."

She arched an eyebrow. "Worried? Nay, Stephen. I have found worrying over any man a useless waste." She pulled her hand away. "You and your company will wish to get settled."

Annoyed by her formality, striving for a charm that usually came naturally, Stephen tilted his head and gave her his most engaging smile. "Once done, you and I shall renew our acquaintance—"

"Mayhap after evening meal," she said. Carolyn beckoned forth the man she'd been sitting next to at the dais.

The man, whose dark hair was quickly succumbing to gray, took his time answering her summons. Norman, Stephen judged the man from both his self-assured demeanor and elegant tunic. Old, but not soft of mind or body.

Carolyn smiled up sweetly at the older man. "Edwin and I were about to go riding, were we not, your lordship?"

Edwin shrugged, giving Stephen the impression this

was the first Edwin had heard of the plan but wasn't inclined to refuse her.

Carolyn's smile disappeared. "I hope you find your chamber to your liking, Stephen. Ivo will see to your needs."

Incredulous, Stephen watched the pair leave the hall, Edwin trailing in Carolyn's wake.

"An interesting turn of events," Armand said lightly.

Stephen agreed. "Who is Edwin?"

Ivo didn't bother to hide his amusement. "Edwin of Tinfield, your rival for Lady Carolyn's hand."

Chapter Two

Stephen slowly recovered from hearing another man competed with him for Carolyn, and a man nearing his dotage at that. Granted, Edwin of Tinfield was well preserved, but going gray nonetheless.

Knowing Carolyn loathed the thought of marrying an older man, Stephen doubted she seriously considered Edwin's suit. Or did she? She'd smiled at him rather prettily. Because she liked the man—or to display her annoyance with her tardy suitor?

More importantly, did Edwin of Tinfield have William de Grasse's favor and blessing?

"I require an audience with his lordship," he told Ivo.

The steward waved a hand toward the farthest corner of the room where stood a drapery-enclosed bed. "William is resting. Mayhap you can have a word with him before evening meal. Until then, we shall settle you into a chamber. If you will permit, my lord, I shall have your possessions brought up to the keep."

Stephen bit back his vexation at having an order shunted aside. Though he outranked everyone at Branwick, including its lord, 'twould not further his cause to berate the steward. One never knew when an underling's goodwill might be needed.

Stephen nodded his consent for Ivo to send for the supply wagons still waiting in the outer bailey.

Studying the bed in the corner of the hall, Stephen wondered why the man preferred to have his bed down here in the hall instead of his upstairs chamber. Apparently, William still suffered mightily from whatever illness had prevented him from accompanying his daughter to Westminster.

The lack of parental presence there had afforded Stephen rare freedoms in pursuing Carolyn. Her only familial companion at court, and not a hindrance to his pursuit of Carolyn, had been Marian.

Marian had revealed her relationship to Carolyn as cousins, and Stephen knew enough of the family lines of England's nobles to conclude they must be related through their mothers. Still, William must hold Marian, or possibly her husband, in high enough regard to have allowed his daughter to travel in the couple's care.

After leaving Marian, Stephen didn't have the time or the inclination to inquire after Marian's husband. He'd barely had time to find Carolyn. She'd been so high flown on the king's wine he hadn't pressed his advantage, simply escorted her to her chamber, all the while explaining his need to leave for Normandy. She'd been sober enough to agree to pass along his intention to secure a betrothal bargain to her father.

'Struth, he'd been relieved to find Carolyn in no condition for a tryst. Memories of Marian, her sweet charms and eager body, had refused to leave his head. He might have seriously blundered if he tried to make love to one woman while thinking erotic thoughts of another.

Here at Branwick, knowing Marian was far from sight

and out of reach, safely ensconced with her child and husband in some distant manor or castle, he would have no such trouble. If Carolyn wasn't too angry. If Edwin didn't interfere.

"Now what?" Armand asked.

Very aware he hadn't been received at Branwick in the manner he hoped to be, Stephen had half a notion to tell Armand to ready the company to leave, but dismissed the idea. True, Carolyn insulted him by going off riding with Edwin, but marriage to a woman who needed little tending suited his needs too perfectly. Besides, how could he go home and tell his brothers that Carolyn preferred the company of a man nearly double his age and of lower rank? Wouldn't they have a good laugh?

"We wait for William to wake up or for Carolyn to return from her ride," he said, seeing no choice in the matter.

"You are taking this setback rather well."

Stephen didn't see much choice in that, either. He couldn't very well go chasing after Carolyn, nor shove the bed curtains aside and shake his future father-by-marriage awake.

"Where would be the fun in life if there were no challenges?" he chided Armand. "Keeps boredom at bay. Come, I hear wagons arriving."

Harlan, indeed, arrived with the baggage carts. Under Ivo's direction, Wilmont's soldiers and Branwick's servants hauled Stephen's belongings up the narrow, winding stairway to a bright, large bedchamber on the third and top floor of the keep. A slight musty odor hinted that the chamber hadn't been occupied in some time. Considering the tapestries lining the walls, the huge brazier and ornate furnishings—with no bed in evidence—Stephen guessed this must be the lord's bedchamber.

His mood brightened. Only an honored guest would be granted the privilege of using William de Grasse's chamber. Mayhap Carolyn wasn't taking him lightly after all.

Harlan assured Stephen that he and Wilmont's soldiers had been assigned quarters in the armory with Branwick's guards. The horses and oxen would be cared for in the stables. The food had already been taken to the kitchen, and the kegs of fine Burgundy wine hauled into Branwick's cellar.

Acting as Stephen's squire, Armand would sleep on a pallet on the floor, a pallet easily moved out of the bedchamber if—when—Stephen required privacy.

Soon only he and Armand and a young maid remained in the chamber. Armand squatted down and drew bed linens and fur coverlets from a trunk to hand over to the maid. Stephen peered over Armand's shoulder into the open trunk.

"Are the gifts packed in here?"

Armand moved several of Stephen's tunics aside.

"Thinking to give them to Lady Carolyn already?"

"Only one, and not the best, which she does not get until our betrothal is agreed to." He pulled out a wooden chest with delicate brass hinges and clasp, its top beautifully carved with a floral design. "This chest should prick Carolyn's curiosity about what I might have brought along to put into it."

"A shrewd maneuver."

"I hope so."

Armand rose and closed the trunk. The maid wandered over, finished with making up the bed.

"Will there be aught else, my lords?" she asked.

Stephen recognized the invitation on her face. He'd seen it countless times on the faces of women of low and high birth alike. Odd thing was, the pretty little maid looked forthrightly at Armand, whose cheeks colored slightly.

Well, how interesting! Stephen surmised that if on some night he asked Armand to sleep elsewhere, the squire need not sleep alone.

"Nothing now," Stephen answered, drawing the maid's attention. "To be sure, if your services are required, I shall send Armand to you straightaway."

The maid curtsied. "You need only seek me out," she said, then sauntered saucily across the chamber to the door, where she shot Armand a half shy, half seductive look before leaving.

Such an invitation shouldn't be ignored. The lass was certainly pretty enough, and just about the right age to give Armand a rousing tumble. About the same age as Marian had been when Stephen gleefully answered her enticing smile.

She'd been so ripe and eager, and he so randy and ready. Only Marian hadn't been a maid, but the daughter of Hugo de Lacy, a Norman knight.

Armand cleared his throat. "I wonder what gifts Edwin has already given Carolyn?"

Jerked back to thoughts of his intended, Stephen said, "Much the same as I will gift her with, I would think. Delicacies for her table, baubles for her to wear. I can only hope Carolyn prefers my baubles over Edwin's."

"Carolyn cannot help but love the brooch. For a woman who does not wear many baubles, my lady Ardith has exquisite taste."

"No argument there," Stephen agreed, thinking of the shiny silver brooch his sister-by-marriage had unmercifully nagged him into buying.

Ardith, sister of his best friend, Corwin, and now three

years married to Gerard, was a gem of a woman. Gerard had never been forced to ply her with gifts, for she considered Gerard's love beyond price and all she required for her happiness.

The two of them, to Stephen's way of thinking, challenged the norm of noble marriages. Loving couples were a rarity. More normally marriages were arranged to bind alliances or secure wealth. Long ago, Stephen had concluded that his own marriage would be for convenience sake, as his parents' marriage had been.

His parents' marriage hadn't been joyful. Indeed, they'd barely tolerated each other. The problem lay, or so Stephen had concluded, within expectations. His parents had married extremely young, had met on the day of their wedding, neither knowing what to expect of the other.

His marriage to Carolyn might not be based on love, but each knew what to expect. There would be no misunderstandings, and therefore no disappointments. He'd give Carolyn the security of a marriage, sire her children, then make himself scarce, just as she wanted.

Best that way, at least for him. It simply wasn't within him to do as his brothers did—spend the bulk of his time in one place with one woman, doing the same things day after day, season after season.

The bedchamber suddenly seemed smaller, containing less air.

Stephen put the ornate chest on top of the trunk. "Let us go down and see if William has awakened, shall we?"

With her girls at her side and the altar cloth over her arm, Marian entered Branwick Keep. During a quick perusal of the great hall she determined Stephen was elsewhere. Relieved, she hoped if she hurried her chore she might escape the keep without seeing him.

Marian approached Branwick's steward. "Good day, Ivo. Is his lordship awake?"

"Aye, my lady, he is, and your visit is well-timed. He is in want of cheering."

The consternation on Ivo's face said William's mood needed lifting beyond the normal frustrations of his illness.

"What troubles him?"

"Carolyn behaved in less than gracious manner earlier. His lordship is not pleased she went riding with Edwin instead of showing proper deference to our guest."

The guest must be Stephen. Marian bit back questions over what had transpired upon his arrival. 'Twasn't her place to question Carolyn's actions. Nor did she wish to become involved, in any manner, in Carolyn and Stephen's situation. Though the thought occurred to Marian that Carolyn's inattention didn't bode well for Stephen's suit. Not a displeasing thought.

"And the guest?"

"Stephen of Wilmont." Ivo glanced at the stairs. "He wishes an audience with his lordship. When your visit is done, I will fetch him."

Grateful for the inadvertent information and reprieve, Marian hurried toward the bed where her uncle spent the bulk of his days, garbed only in white linen shertes, propped up by bolsters. She paused at the foot of the bed.

"Uncle William?"

"Ah, Marian. Come."

She pushed aside the curtain at William's right side, the side less affected by his apoplexy. His blue eyes sparkled with intelligence and curiosity beneath eyebrows as bushy white as his hair.

"What brings you?" he asked, as was his habit, making Marian feel a bit guilty for not visiting more often. He knew her reasons and accepted them.

"The altar cloth, of course. Did you not wish to have it in your possession today?"

Marian didn't wait for an answer, just snapped the cloth open and let it drift down over the woolen blanket that covered his legs. He ran the fragile fingers of his good hand over the cloth.

"'Twill do," he said.

"'Twill do?" Marian rejoined. "Uncle, if you hope to bribe your way into heaven, your gifts to the archbishop had best be of better quality than a mere *'twill do.*"

"'Tis beautiful, Mama," Audra proclaimed.

Lyssa elbowed her sister hard enough to jostle the eggs in the basket Audra held. "Tsk. Uncle knows that, Audra. He jests with Mama."

William raised a bushy eyebrow at Lyssa. "Do I now?" he asked gruffly, to which Lyssa answered a confident, "Aye."

He leaned over slightly and whispered none too softly, "Mayhap you are right, child, but do not tell your mother. If I praise her work too highly, she may become lax in her efforts on my behalf and I shall never get into heaven." Lyssa giggled. He waved Audra closer. "What have you in the basket?"

Audra set the basket on the bed. "Eggs, six of them," she said proudly.

William leaned back, his expression aghast. "Six! Whoever shall help me eat so many?"

Audra's smile was sly as she glanced at her twin. "If

the cook boils them hard, we can help you eat them, my lord.''

''Ha! Off to the kitchen with you then. Be sure to tell the cook we want them well boiled.''

Marian gave credit where credit was due. William treated her daughters as well as he knew how. Even now, as the girls celebrated their fifth summer, he didn't often use their names for fear of getting them wrong. He accepted the twins where others didn't. The girls had been born in Branwick Keep, and everyone should be used to them by now. Yet, many kept their distance, fearful of getting too close to two such identical little beings.

'Twas hard to fight superstition, so mostly she and her daughters kept to themselves and ignored those whose fear overruled their sense.

''What think you of Stephen of Wilmont, my lord?'' Lyssa asked.

The tyke's question surprised Marian as well as William.

''I do not know,'' he answered. ''I have not yet talked to the man. Since you asked, I gather you have formed an opinion.''

Lyssa's head bobbed. ''He stopped to greet us at our stone wall. He is ever so handsome and has a kind smile.''

''He also minds his manners,'' Audra added. ''He must be wealthy, too. He wears a silk tunic and his horse's bridle is studded with silver.''

Marian pursed her lips to hold her peace. William had asked the girls to express their opinion. If she tried to shoo her daughters on their way too soon, William would wonder why. His body might be frail, but his mind was as sharp as ever.

William glanced from one girl to the other. ''I see. I

will take your observations into consideration. Now, see to our eggs if you please.''

The girls dipped into quick curtsies then hurried out to do William's bidding. Marian picked up the altar cloth to fold it.

''I should be away, too. Now that you have approved of the cloth, I will have it wrapped for transport.''

''You know of the family of Wilmont?''

Marian saw no sense in denying it. She could too easily be found out a liar.

''My father once purchased horses from Wilmont's stock.''

''Fine stock.''

''That it is.'' The lords of Wilmont bred quality horse-flesh, the finest in the kingdom. Those who could afford the steep price settled for no less. '''Tis nearly time for evening meal, my lord. Shall I have your meal brought to you?''

''When the eggs are done. Sit a moment, Marian.''

Until William gave her leave to go, she must remain. Hoping Ivo wouldn't fetch Stephen until after she left, as he'd said, she perched on the edge of the bed.

''I have noted,'' William said, ''that in the months since you returned from Westminster, you have never expressed an opinion of Carolyn's desire to marry this Stephen of Wilmont. Surely you, too, must have one.''

She did, but one she chose not to share. In the end, only Carolyn's wishes mattered. So Marian had made peace with her inner turmoil, hoping if the marriage came to pass Stephen would take Carolyn off to some distant manor of his, so she wouldn't be forced to witness their union for very long.

''The matter of who Carolyn marries is truly none of my concern. That choice is hers, with your approval.''

"Did you see him in Westminster?"

Marian hoped the rush of warmth coursing through her didn't manifest on her cheeks. She'd seen far too much of Stephen's smooth, bare chest. Been close enough to notice his arousal, ready for a romp in bed with a woman. With Carolyn.

"I did."

"And?"

"And, my lord, I think you should form your own opinion without hearing mine to influence you."

"You do not like him."

I loved him—desperately.

Marian rose from the bed, turning aside to hide what pain might inadvertently show. Her memories of Stephen and their time together came in quick, vivid flashes.

She'd mistaken his male lust for love. After all they shared, or rather what she'd believed they shared, Stephen left her without a word of farewell and never returned. Abandoned her to face disgrace and shame—

Marian silenced a young maiden's outrage at the injustice, for she'd passed by her chance for justice. When she'd found herself with child, she refused to name her lover. If she had, her father would have demanded a marriage. By then, she had come to realize that putting Stephen to harness would be as like to capturing the wind. His free spirit would balk at the forced marriage.

He might marry her, but he would never be a true and steady husband, one who would gladly share life's joys and sorrows.

Better no husband at all than one who resented being a husband. Better no father for her children at all than one who wouldn't be there when needed.

She'd never regretted her decision, not even when her

father banished her for wanton behavior and insolence. Thankfully, Carolyn had witnessed the sorry debacle and intervened, and brought a rebellious and very pregnant Marian home to Branwick.

Here at Branwick, only Carolyn and William knew the whole of the story, but neither of them knew who'd sired her girls. They'd never asked and she never told.

Marian turned back to the uncle who'd given her succor, her expression indifferent—she hoped.

"I met Baron Everart of Wilmont and his son, Stephen, when they came to Murwaithe to deliver horses. At the time, I considered Stephen brash, something of a scoundrel, and suffering from wanderlust."

William's smile covered only half of his face. "A rogue, hmm? 'Tis what Carolyn says she wants." His expression turned thoughtful. "I met Stephen's father a time or two, a powerful yet decent man. The brother, Gerard, is well respected. I know little of Stephen. Dare I hope he possesses some sense?"

Marian kept her peace, unwilling to offer more of an opinion on Stephen's character. She doubted Stephen had changed over the years, but 'twas not her place to belittle him. Nor did she wish to rouse William's curiosity over just how well Marian knew Stephen of Wilmont.

"You will have to judge for yourself, William."

"I suppose I shall." He shifted against the bolster. "Have Ivo send in my body servants. I wish to dress for evening meal. You will stay, of course."

Marian fought a flash of panic, realizing William intended to be carried to the table to preside over supper, likely in honor of Stephen. Sweet mercy, she wanted no part of it.

But the girls were off having the eggs boiled and

would be greatly disappointed if not allowed to eat them with William, and she *had* neglected her uncle of late.

Though she determined earlier she couldn't completely avoid Stephen, she wished as little contact with him as possible. Perhaps he'd be preoccupied with charming Carolyn and impressing William, too busy to notice her or the girls. Highly unlikely. Still, she could hardly refuse William's simple request.

Resigned to an uncomfortable evening, Marian took leave of William. "I will inform Ivo."

Marian closed the curtain, came around the foot of the bed, and stopped abruptly.

Near the high table, standing beside Ivo, looking every bit the handsome, high-born noble, stood Stephen.

Marian hoped her dismay didn't show as readily as Stephen's surprise. His spring-green eyes widened. He cut short whatever he'd been saying to Ivo.

She dismissed the fluttering around her heart as simply recognition by a healthy woman of an attractive man. Once, she'd thought herself in love with Stephen, but no longer. She now knew the difference between lust and love. No matter that his body drew hers, like iron to lodestone, she'd not give him the chance to once again ruin her life.

Best she get this first encounter done and over, keeping in mind that this Norman lord could destroy the life and peace she and her girls had found at Branwick.

Chapter Three

What was Marian doing at Branwick?

He'd envisioned her at home on some distant manor with her husband and child, far from where she could distract him.

Such a distraction. Gowned in dove gray, the linen's weave rough and suited for workaday wear, Marian gracefully floated toward him. So beautiful. He'd thought so from the first moment he set eyes on her—standing beside her mother on the steps of Murwaithe, awaiting presentation to the baron of Wilmont and his youngest son.

The two of them had made an effort to resist an instant and powerful attraction. On the third day of his visit, however, they gave in to their lust—and once done, easier done.

"Stephen, I fear your audience with my uncle must wait a few moments," she said, her voice matter-of-fact, and yet melodic. She turned to Ivo. "His lordship wishes to sit at table for evening meal. He asks you to send his body servants to him."

"At once, my lady. I gather you and our guest have met."

She glanced Stephen's way before she admitted, "We have."

Most assuredly they had. So many years ago and so well met. For two days they'd taken every chance to place eager hands and warm mouths on each other's bodies. Well met, indeed.

Stephen bowed in her direction. "Lady Marian and I have known each other for several years. Mayhap she and I can renew our acquaintance while I await his lordship's convenience."

Ivo's eyebrow arched. "Only a moment ago you were ready to tear down the draperies from around his lordship's bed."

Stephen shrugged off his former impatience. True, he needed to talk to William, but the mystery of Marian's presence proved too enticing to resist further examination. Obviously she was visiting Branwick, but why and for how long? With or without her child and husband?

Had she ever tumbled in the hay with her husband? How odd he should wonder. Even odder he should realize he'd never tumbled in the hay with any other woman.

"'Twould hardly further my cause if I disturbed his lordship at an untimely moment," he explained to Ivo. "I shall wait until he is fully prepared for my visit."

Ivo took his leave.

Stephen took a longer than normal breath, remembering the unease of his last conversation with Marian. Part of that unease, certes, had been their state of undress and seclusion in a bedchamber. Yet, even though they stood in Branwick's hall, with servants scurrying about to prepare for evening meal, with Armand hovering nearby, Stephen's body and mind were firmly engaged by the woman standing before him.

"I do not see you for many years, then you appear in the most *unexpected* places," he said, then could have bitten his tongue for evoking the faint blush that bloomed on her cheeks.

He'd seen her turn vivid scarlet once before, her face and chest fully involved. She'd been astride him at the time. He hadn't known those many years ago what that meant, but he did now—a female reaching her full pleasure. Try as he might, he couldn't tamp down the pride of realizing he'd brought Marian to her peak without knowing what he was doing. He truly hadn't—which meant Marian must be one of those women who reached bliss with little effort on her bed mate's part.

So much for pride.

Marian's husband must be delighted with so easily pleased a lover for a wife, if he cared at all. Many men didn't, which made no sense. Pleasured bed mates made for eager bed mates.

"I hear Carolyn did not receive you well."

The edge in Marian's voice both rebuked him for reminding her of their meeting in a bedchamber, and turned the conversation back to Carolyn—whose rebuff had been witnessed by enough people that the tale would have spread swiftly to all in Branwick.

Stephen hadn't a doubt he would be back in Carolyn's good graces by the end of evening meal. He must be, despite the distraction of Marian, whose good graces wouldn't be so easily obtained.

Knowing full well it wasn't true, but not willing to admit to anyone but himself that his intended bride had purposely deserted him, Stephen prevaricated. "Apparently I intruded on Carolyn's previously made plans for an afternoon ride."

"Mayhap your visit with William will go better. He cannot get up and walk out on you."

Marian turned as if to leave.

"How fares William?" he asked, partly because he wanted prior knowledge of the man's current mood. Partly because Carolyn had already turned her back on him and he hated the thought of Marian repeating the insult.

"His mood or his health?" she asked.

"Both."

"His mood is decent and his health is improved."

Not much to go on.

"I gather his illness does not keep him abed permanently."

She hesitated a moment before answering. "The apoplexy drained his strength and restricts his movements. He remains abed, for the most part, because he does not like having servants carry him about. My uncle's body may be sorely afflicted, and one must listen carefully when he speaks, but have a care not to mistake his slur for lack of intelligence."

"My thanks for your help."

"I do not tell you this to help you, but for William's sake. I would not have him upset because you treated him in thoughtless fashion."

Marian's admonishment stung. Surely, she knew him better. True, he possessed the devil's own temper when crossed unfairly, and a nobleman's natural expectation of deference. He wasn't so high flown with himself, however, that he'd treat William as a lesser man because of his affliction.

On the edge of his vision, Stephen saw two young men slip behind the draperies, one carrying a pitcher and washbasin, the other bearing what must be garments. They would soon have William suitably robed.

"Your caution is unnecessary," he told her.

"Is it? I do not remember you as the most considerate of lads."

It irked him that Marian hadn't forgiven him for a lapse of manners nearly six years ago, a lapse not his fault. Nor had she seen fit to accept his tardy but sincere apology, having told him it came too late. 'Twas as if she thought him both brainless and unfeeling.

Damned if he'd apologize again. If the woman chose to hold a youthful mishap against him, so be it. He didn't need her good opinion. 'Twas Carolyn he must win over, not Marian.

"I intend to treat William de Grasse with no less than his rank and intelligence deserves. 'Twould not further my interests to do otherwise."

She blinked, then said softly, "Nay, you would not treat a man of rank with disregard. I should have known better than to think you would."

He didn't know how to answer, and indeed Marian didn't give him the chance. She spun around and walked toward the door.

"You do have a way with the ladies today," Armand commented.

Stephen winced, having forgotten Armand stood so close as to overhear. Thank the Lord the young man could be trusted not to reveal this latest debacle.

Women. He thought he understood them, how their minds worked. Indeed, not until today had he questioned his ability to talk to a female in perfectly reasonable fashion. How had he managed to fail so completely with two women on one day?

Ivo came toward him. "His lordship awaits you."

Grateful for what he hoped would be sensible meeting of minds, Stephen followed the steward to the right side of the bed.

Carolyn's father appeared much as Stephen expected: aged, white-haired and withered. But, possibly due to Marian's cautions, Stephen noted the sharp clarity and unmistakable self-assurance within the man's deep-set brown eyes. Carolyn had inherited her father's eyes, his intelligence, and most probably his stubborn nature.

Stephen nodded to William de Grasse, who occupied a bed with the dignity befitting a king upon his throne. "Good tidings, William. 'Tis good we finally meet."

"You find your bedchamber to your liking, your lordship?" he asked, the words slightly ill formed.

"I have traveled widely, both in England and without. I find no lack in Branwick's hospitality."

William's head bobbed slightly at the compliment. He folded his right arm over the unmoving left. "Your travels kept you away overlong, Stephen of Wilmont. So much so that my daughter cast aside her good manners and left the hall in a snit. I will, certes, speak to her about her rudeness, though you *did* sorely test her temper."

Stephen withheld a request to ignore Carolyn's behavior. 'Twas a father's right to reprimand his children, no matter their sex or age. Stephen could only hope for light discipline so Carolyn wouldn't be more upset with him than she was already.

However, he wasn't about to apologize to either father or daughter for helping his brother.

"Carolyn's expectations aside, I took charge of a task for my brother, Richard. The duty took me longer than anticipated."

William said nothing, only looked at him expectantly.

Stephen allowed that a fuller explanation might be in order. A man might understand what a woman might not and, given Carolyn's hard feelings, he needed William's good opinion.

"King Henry settled the guardianship of an orphaned boy on Richard. I offered to inspect the boy's lands in Normandy and assess any threat of interference from his paternal relatives. There was resistance, not over the boy, but over control of the fees and rents from the boy's inheritance."

"You arranged a bargain?"

He had, except Richard hadn't liked the bargain. In the time it had taken Stephen to bring the boy's uncle to England to exchange Philip for more coin and goods than Richard could ever hope to gain in one fell swoop, his brother had grown fond of his ward and wouldn't give over.

"Nay, only brought the two parties together so a bargain could be reached."

"Then your brother's problem is resolved."

"So I believe."

William frowned. "You do not know?"

The accusatory tone didn't sit well.

"The last I saw of the boy's uncle, he was returning to Normandy without taking his nephew. Richard considered the matter done, so I left Richard's holding for Wilmont, to report on the situation to our brother, Gerard."

"I see."

Stephen heard disapproval. That William thought Stephen left his brother without hope of further aid wasn't to be borne, no matter how much he wanted William's goodwill. He did, however, try to keep his anger under control. 'Twas his loss of temper that had gotten Richard into trouble, and Stephen sensed he was in quite enough trouble now without inviting more.

"Should Richard need further help he need only send to Gerard, who will bring every resource of the barony of Wilmont to play, if warranted. Gerard also knows where to send for me if I am needed. Though I thank you for your concern over my brother's welfare, I assure you 'tis not necessary."

William waved a dismissing hand in the air. "I have no doubt Gerard of Wilmont can take care of any problem that may come his way. 'Tis you I have my doubts about, Stephen."

Very aware of his less than steady reputation, and knowing it was one of the reasons Carolyn considered his suit, Stephen asked warily, "How so?"

"Let me say that I do not consider you a suitable mate for my daughter."

Not suitable? He was a knight of Wilmont, a member of one of the most powerful families in the kingdom. His wealth far surpassed that of William de Grasse. If he had a mind to, he could gather more men-at-arms than necessary to lay siege to Branwick and take it by force. Surely the man knew Stephen of Wilmont to be a better match for his daughter than lowly Edwin of Tinfield.

Had the apoplexy somehow affected William's mind more than anyone at Branwick, including Marian, wanted to admit?

"Your daughter considers me suitable."

"My daughter also believes herself capable of overseeing Branwick and her dower lands without assistance." William tilted his head. "If Carolyn considers you more suitable than Edwin, then why is she out riding with him instead of attending you?"

Stephen couldn't comment on Carolyn's ability to manage her and her father's lands, but he was fairly sure of why Carolyn had dragged Edwin out of the keep.

"To test my resolve. Carolyn wants to know if I insult easily, and if I can give back as good as she gives. I suspect her elderly husbands could not."

The corner of William's mouth twitched. "I gather you believe you can?"

"Aye, I believe I can."

"We shall see."

William's attention swerved to the sound of little feet pounding across the rushes.

Stephen turned in time to see the twins pull up short behind Armand. He recognized them as Audra and Lyssa, the peasant girls he'd seen earlier.

His first thought was to shield them against their lord's anger at being interrupted. The smile on William's face belied all trace of ire.

To Stephen's amazement, William beckoned the girls forward. "Back so soon?"

Lyssa nodded. "Cook plopped the eggs into the soup kettle to boil."

Stunned that the girls had been allowed to interrupt, Stephen glanced down at the basket Audra held. Six hard-cooked eggs lay nestled within.

William looked up behind the girls. "Where is your mother?"

"Wrapping the altar cloth." Audra held up the basket. "Can we eat these while they are yet warm?"

William patted the bed, an invitation the girls readily accepted. Before Lyssa hopped up on the bed, she flashed Stephen a sunny smile.

"Would you care to share our eggs, Lord Stephen?"

Stephen doubted William would appreciate it, and decided to take his leave while the old lord was in a good mood. He chucked Lyssa under the chin, grateful that at least one female at Branwick considered him worthy of her regard.

"My thanks, little one, but I would not think to deprive you of your treat. We shall continue our talk later, William."

Stephen left the bedside, Armand at his heels. He headed for the door, hoping a brisk walk might help clear up some of his confusion.

Apparently William de Grasse had gleaned information, and little of it good, on Stephen of Wilmont from someone. Carolyn? Possibly. Marian? Hellfire, had she carried her irritation with him too far, belittled him to her uncle? Somehow he couldn't bring himself to see Marian as vindictive.

Why were two little girls allowed the freedom of the great hall without the supervision of their mother? Strange, that. Children simply weren't allowed to interrupt their lord for any reason, but the twins had been joyously welcomed.

Like Richard with his ward. Or Gerard with his sons. Could it be…?

"Armand, see if you can find out if Carolyn has any half sisters she has not told me about."

Marian chose to sit at a trestle table near the door even though she and the girls were entitled to seating near the dais. Once this meal ended, soon now, she could make her escape without too many people taking note.

She sat between the girls to keep order and ensure they both ate appropriately. Her intent to concentrate on the twins worked for the most part, but 'twas hard not to glance occasionally at the four people seated at the dais.

Strapped into a chair, William held sway over the meal with a vigor that usually eluded him. He would sleep hard and long this night. To his left, Edwin of Tinfield carried the greater part of the conversation. The two men had known each other for many years and never lacked for conversation.

To William's right sat Carolyn, and next to her, Stephen.

Carolyn was getting over her case of the sulks, though she'd resisted mightily at the beginning of the meal.

Marian wasn't surprised. She knew firsthand how effortlessly charming a companion Stephen could be, and this evening he made an effort to charm Carolyn. His smile, his gracious manner, his way with words could soften the hardest of female hearts.

As if his charm were not enough, Stephen had given Carolyn a gift—a wooden chest. The chest sat on the table in front of Carolyn, and must be lovely, for every so often Carolyn ran her fingers over the top or lifted the lid. Carolyn hadn't yet smiled at Stephen, but she would eventually succumb, and Marian wanted to be gone before it happened.

Petty, she knew, but sitting here watching her cousin and her former lover take a meal together proved more hurtful than she'd imagined. She shouldn't be upset. She'd decided long ago she didn't want Stephen, that he wasn't a man she wanted to be married to. She shouldn't be angry at Carolyn for considering Stephen's suit, or miffed that Stephen found Carolyn beautiful and worthy of being his wife.

She shouldn't be angry at Stephen for glancing her way only once that she knew of. Their gazes had met, and held, then she'd turned away to signify her disinterest. Yet she barely ate for wondering if his stunning green eyes had focused on her again, and for how long, and if he liked what he saw.

Stupid, pointless, but there it was.

"Mama?" Audra whispered.

Marian looked down at her daughter, only to have Audra direct her attention to Lyssa. All thoughts of Stephen fled as she noted Lyssa's half-closed eyes. Marian inwardly cursed her inattention, for not noticing Lyssa's lack of chatter during the meal.

She lifted Lyssa into her lap and cradled her daughter's head against her shoulder. "Audra, go quietly up to the dais and inform his lordship we must leave."

Audra slid off the bench and walked toward the dais. William saw her coming and motioned her forward. Marian slid around on the bench, prepared to get up as soon as Audra returned.

"Why did you not tell me you hurt?" she whispered in her daughter's ear.

"I did not want to leave so soon." A tear slid down Lyssa's cheek. "Cook made apricot tarts."

Marian inwardly sighed and hugged Lyssa, unable to utter a reprimand for ignoring the pain for so silly a reason. The mind of a child simply didn't function reasonably when a treat was in the offing, less so when that little head near burst with pain.

Hearing Audra's running footsteps, Marian looked up to see her daughter followed by Carolyn and Edwin. So much for her plan for a quiet leave-taking. Now everyone in the great hall watched.

Carolyn's smile was as tender as her smiles could be. She bent down to put a hand on Lyssa's forehead. "Leaving us so soon, my dear?"

Lyssa heaved a sigh. "I tried to wait for the tarts."

Carolyn's smile widened. "Tarts, hmm? Well, I do believe I can arrange to save you one or two. Perhaps when you next come to visit my father you can have your tarts."

"Audra, too?"

"Of course, dear."

"On the morrow?"

"We shall see," Marian said, injecting motherly caution.

Carolyn straightened. "Send word on how Lyssa does. Father will want to know."

Marian nodded and shifted her feet to rise.

"My lady, if you would permit?" Edwin extended his arms, obviously offering to carry Lyssa.

"I can—"

"His lordship asked me to be of assistance, which I am most pleased to do."

Carolyn placed a hand on Edwin's arm. "Mayhap you should order forth a cart."

Edwin's arms folded over his chest, a dark eyebrow rose. "Carolyn, I assure you, I am not yet so feeble I cannot bear one little girl to her pallet, even if that pallet be in the hamlet."

"I am sure Father's request to lend assistance meant for you to find a servant to carry Lyssa, not bear the burden yourself."

Edwin smiled down at Lyssa. "I doubt she weighs more than a sack of feathers." Once more he extended his arms, and Lyssa went to him readily, hugging him about the neck, her head on his shoulder. "There, you see? No burden at all."

Carolyn raised her hands, palms up, and backed up a

step. "As you wish, but have a care for your back and do not bounce the poor tyke."

Edwin rolled his eyes heavenward. "Lead on, Marian."

Marian rose from the bench, thinking the walk would go faster if she carried Audra.

"Nay, none of that."

Stephen's command thrummed through her, stopping her in midreach. She glanced up at the dais. Uncle William had sent far more assistance than needed or wanted.

Stephen bowed to Audra. "My little lady, might I have the honor of seeing you home?"

Audra giggled then, mindful of her manners, curtsied prettily. "You may, kind sir, if Mama says you may."

Her heart sinking, Marian knew she truly had no choice in the matter. Besides, arguing would only take up time and she needed to get Lyssa tucked into her pallet.

"You may," she said, still wishing she could refuse, especially when Stephen swept Audra up to sit on his hip.

This was wrong, a sight she'd thought never to see, Audra snug and secure in Stephen's arms. Marian forced herself to turn away, to lead the men carrying her girls out into the night.

At the gate she stepped into the guardhouse to fetch a torch, which the men would need to see their way back to the keep. She set a quick pace toward her hut.

From behind her she heard Stephen and Audra talking, their voices audible in the night air, but the words muffled. The desire to separate the two lengthened her strides, which the men had no problem matching.

Marian passed the spot at the stone wall where Stephen had halted this morning, talked to the girls and ruined their mother's peace. She ran for the door, and once inside, lit the candle on the table.

Edwin entered and glanced around.

Marian pointed to Lyssa's pallet. "There."

The moment Stephen entered with Audra, the already small room shrank to crowded. He took up too much space, breathed too much air. Stephen, too, glanced around, but more slowly—noting the simple furnishings and lack of luxuries, she was sure.

Edwin eased Lyssa onto her pallet. Stephen hadn't yet put down Audra, who seemed in no hurry to be put down.

Marian handed the torch to Edwin, then busied herself with Lyssa's bolster and blanket. "My thanks, sirs, for your aid. You will want to start back to the keep while there is yet a little light."

"And before the tarts are gone," Audra added.

Stephen tugged on Audra's braid, smiling. "Certes, we must collect our share of the tarts, and ensure Carolyn has set yours aside."

Finally, he set Audra on her feet.

The men said their farewells and closed the door behind them. Marian took a long draw of air, the scents familiar and comforting, but not quite the same. The unique aroma of male, of Stephen, lingered. On the morrow she would open wide the door to let the summer breeze freshen the room. On the morrow she would reclaim the peace and safety of her own home.

Chapter Four

Edwin carried the torch, leaving Stephen to walk along-side with no more to do than avoid the ruts in the road and ponder his growing puzzlement over Marian.

Dare he question Edwin?

Upon Edwin and Carolyn's return to Branwick, William had presented the two rivals for his daughter's hand to each other, then chastised Carolyn for not doing so earlier. From then on Carolyn had been the model of a proper, if sullen, chatelaine of her father's keep.

Edwin hadn't said a word to Stephen since, not that Stephen attempted to further their acquaintance either. He didn't particularly want to know Edwin any better than necessary to assess his rival's strengths and weak-nesses where Carolyn was concerned.

'Twas obvious from their easy ways at supper to see William favored Edwin. Stephen had already decided the battle must be won through Carolyn, to so thoroughly capture the lady that her older suitor would despair of hope. He'd made progress to that end with the gift of the chest at supper. She liked the gift, had even made a point to show it to Edwin.

Unfortunately, Edwin didn't seem the sort to despair easily.

'Twould probably be best to prod Edwin into a conversation about their mutual quest to win Carolyn, but his curiosity over Marian wouldn't leave Stephen alone.

"Adorable girls," Stephen commented.

Edwin didn't even glance sideways. "They are."

"A shame about Lyssa's headache."

"She suffers them often, I hear."

Stephen digested the news with a pang of sympathy for both daughter and mother. A wee one should not suffer so, and it must be hard on Marian to see her daughter pained.

Marian's daughters.

His suspicion that the twins might be William's had come to an end at evening meal. Those little faces matched Marian's too well to be other than her own offspring, but not until seeing them sitting together did he notice the resemblance. Too, Carolyn had made a remark about the twins being her nieces.

Why did the family live in the hamlet? Marian's kinship to William certainly warranted residence in the keep, unless he thoroughly disapproved of Marian's husband.

Where was the girls' father, who should have been at evening meal with his family? Obviously off somewhere.

Stephen kicked at a rock, sending it far down the road, beyond the light of the torch. "Has no cure for the girl's headaches been found?"

"Not for want of trying. Marian took Lyssa into London to see a physician. 'Twould seem his potions cannot prevent or ease the headaches."

Then Lyssa had been the blanket-wrapped bundle on

Marian's bed in the palace bedchamber. Audra must have remained behind at Branwick while Marian visited a physician with Lyssa.

"You have known Marian for some time, then?"

Edwin finally graced him with a glance. "For some years. Why so curious?"

"I knew Marian as a girl, but have not seen her in recent years. My concern—" Stephen stopped and looked back toward the hut, now out of sight, and put to words what bothered him ever since closing Marian's door. "I do not like leaving Marian and her children alone like this. 'Tis not wise. What if some knave decides to take advantage of her husband's absence? She and the girls should have remained at the keep for the night."

"Marian is a widow. She and the girls have lived alone in that hut for several years."

A widow? No husband. No protector for the girls.

"All the more reason she should live in the keep."

"I hear she prefers living in the hamlet. 'Tis odd William allows it, but then the whole tale of how she came to Branwick is odd."

"How so?"

"Carolyn brought her to Branwick after her husband died. The girls were born here, and a few months later William allowed her to live in the hut." Edwin paused before adding. "I often wondered why she did not return to Murwaithe. Must have been some bad feelings with her family, I suppose."

He remembered Hugo de Lacy as a proud, rather pompous man, and his wife as pleasant enough. He'd not sensed any animosity between parents and daughter.

"Something must have happened to cause a rift between Marian and her parents around the time of her marriage, then. I remember them as being fond of one another.''

''An old friend is she?''

Something in the way Edwin asked brought the swirling questions in Stephen's head to a halt. Stephen doubted Marian wanted anyone at Branwick to know how friendly they'd been—nor did he. Certainly not Carolyn. Especially not his rival.

''Marian's father bought horses from mine.''

'Twas all the explanation Stephen intended to give. He resumed the walk, anxious now to return to the keep and find out what tidbits Armand might have gathered.

When Edwin didn't follow, Stephen halted. ''Something amiss?''

''You cannot win, you know. You might as well pack up your belongings and take them back to wherever you brought them from.''

Stephen had fought in enough battles, on English soil and Norman, to recognize the strategy—dispirit the enemy by breeding doubt of success.

''Beg pardon, Edwin, but I am in no hurry to be on my way. I believe I shall leave my bed where it is until Carolyn makes her decision.''

''Tis not merely Carolyn's decision. She cannot marry where her father does not approve.''

Stephen shrugged with what he hoped showed unconcern. ''I will grant you the advantage of having known William longer, and you seem to be in his good graces. But I have youth on my side.'' He smiled and ruffled his hair. ''See Edwin? Not one strand of gray.''

Edwin laughed and shook his head, then resumed walking. Stephen fell into step within the torch's light, acknowledging once more that Edwin wouldn't fall into despair easily.

"A strand or two of gray would serve you well."

"With Carolyn? Not so."

"Believe as you will."

Stephen had reason to believe as he did, for Carolyn made quite clear her preference for a young man as her third husband. Yet, Edwin seemed to think his age made no difference. The man could go on thinking so, to his detriment.

After turning over the torch to a guard, they entered the great hall to find the trestle tables folded up and stacked against the walls for the night. Stephen spotted Harlan and a few of Wilmont's soldiers seated on the floor with a group of Branwick's guards, cups of ale in hand and tossing dice.

William was yet strapped into his chair, now settled near the hearth. Carolyn sat on a nearby bench, an open book in her hands.

A place of peace, quiet—boredom.

The place wanted for music, or games, or a wrestling match. At least Harlan had found entertainment with his dice. Stephen looked around for Armand, and not seeing him, guessed his squire must have found more interesting amusement, too.

"What is this?" Edwin complained, the words snapping Carolyn's head up. "I had thought to come back to sweets, at the least."

"Do not be churlish, Edwin. You must know I set several aside for the two of you as well as for Marian's girls." Carolyn waved a hand in the air, hailing a serving wench. "Tarts and ale for our guests."

The wench bobbed a curtsey and scurried off.

Stephen slid onto the bench beside Carolyn, ignoring Edwin's raised eyebrow.

"How very thoughtful of you, my lady. As I told your

father earlier, I find Branwick's hospitality most note-
worthy."

"My thanks."

The compliment garnered him a half smile. 'Twas
progress from her ill humor at supper.

He glanced down at her book—a prayer book—one
to be admired.

"Your psalter is beautifully illustrated," he said, the
comment genuinely meant. The lettering was both simple and graceful, and the picture of the Holy Mother,
surrounded by cherubs, had been drawn by a skilled and
loving hand. "From where did you purchase it?"

"'Tis a gift from Edwin."

A costly gift, surely, but not a gift a man gave a
woman he was wooing. Did Edwin know nothing about
women? Maybe he knew something about one particular
woman that Stephen didn't.

He would never have guessed Carolyn preferred to
read a psalter for her leisure, yet Carolyn sat in the great
hall reading instead of taking to her solar to choose
which baubles to place in her new wooden chest.

"The Swiss monastery at St. Gall is renowned for
beautifully illustrated books," Edwin commented.

"Never been there," Stephen admitted. "Mayhap one
day I should visit."

"In need of a psalter, Stephen?"

"Nay, but it would account a fine gift for my mother.
She cherishes fine works of a religious nature." He refrained from voicing his belief she cherished them overmuch.

The tarts and ale arrived. Edwin assured William that
Marian and girls were settled for the night. Stephen contemplated drawing Carolyn away for a private talk, then
decided it too soon, for she hadn't yet let go completely

of her sulks. 'Twould also be too obvious a ploy for privacy to commit in front of Edwin.

"You look tired, my lord," Edwin commented to William.

The old man waved the concern away. "I spend too much of my day abed as it is. Besides, Carolyn and I were discussing the improvements she wishes to make to Branwick."

Carolyn closed her psalter. "My suggestions are quite sound, Father. I believe you should approve every one."

"And again I ask, where would the coin come from to pay for all of these improvements?"

"I know how you abhor moneylenders—"

William huffed. "Thieves. Every one."

"—but many of the repairs must be made before winter. We can delay some until after we sell our stock of fleece. The price should rise soon and—"

"If it does not, then with what will we repay the moneylenders?"

Carolyn pursed her lips, and for a moment Stephen thought she would end her argument. He silently urged her on, cheering her persistence. How many times had he stood before Gerard, arguing a point, striving to make his brother see reason? At times, it worked. To his delight, Carolyn's chin rose.

"Father, I realize you find it hard to make decisions based on others' observations and opinions. If you were able to take to horse and ride the estate, you would agree that all of the items on my list deserve immediate attention."

"Surely not all."

"Ivo agrees with me."

"My poor steward likely gave in to you to save his wits. But you are right, since I cannot see for myself I must depend upon the opinion of others. Edwin and I have discussed—''

''Without telling me? You would heed Edwin's opinion over mine?''

William didn't answer, simply stared hard at Carolyn. She noticeably reined in her temper. Stephen knew the feeling and was tempted to defend Carolyn. Truly, though, she didn't yet need help, had held her own quite admirably.

''I see,'' she finally said, her voice calm now yet strained. ''Am I to assume you have made a final decision then?''

''Not as yet. I thought to seek yet one more person's opinion.'' William's challenging gaze swung around. ''What of you, young Stephen? Have you the knowledge of land use and husbandry to offer an opinion?''

'Twas a challenge, insultingly delivered. The old lord wanted to know how, as a husband to his daughter, Stephen would council Carolyn. 'Twas also clear William thought Stephen incapable of a knowledgeable opinion, just as he thought Carolyn's knowledge faulty.

Stephen knew perfectly well how to manage an estate, several of them in fact. All of his holdings were doing quite well, too.

''On what matter would you like an opinion, William?''

''What might be your view on moneylenders?''

The answer placed Stephen squarely between Carolyn, who urged obtaining a loan, and William, who wanted nothing to do with those he considered thieves. No simple yea or nay would suffice if he wished to please both daughter and father.

''I have not had occasion to use their services, however, I believe if the need for ready coin is urgent, a lender should be considered. I know two London Jews who my family has dealt with in times of dire need. Both are forthright in their bargaining and are content with a modest return on their loans.''

William's eyes narrowed. ''So you would risk the loss of Branwick?''

''Never. A lender should only be consulted if Branwick is already at risk from want of ready coin. Without knowing the particulars of the improvements Carolyn has suggested, nor having any notion of the health of your coffers, I would not presume to judge Branwick's state of need.''

Stephen thought he'd slipped from a dangerous situation neatly, until William continued.

''As I was about to say before Carolyn's outburst, Edwin and I discussed the replacement of the millstone. Apparently the stone is cracked so badly it cannot be trusted through harvest. 'Tis a heady expenditure, but must be done lest we be short of flour for winter. On the remaining items I am undecided.'' William turned to Carolyn. ''On the morn, give Edwin and Stephen copies of your list. Mayhap one or the other can find a way to give you all you wish at a price I am willing to pay.''

In so few words, casually delivered, William had declared a contest. Stephen clearly understood that whichever suitor presented the best overall plan at the least cost would be highly favored as Carolyn's next husband.

Armand entered the bedchamber with a smug, satisfied look about him that even the dim candle glow didn't diminish.

Lounging on the bed, stripped down to sherte and breeches, Stephen didn't have to ask where and with whom Armand had found amusement.

"So how is the little maid?" Stephen asked.

"Her name is Dena, and she is lovely."

At the hint of defensiveness, Stephen abandoned the urge to tease the squire further.

William's audacity yet rankled. 'Twasn't fair to take his ire out on Armand. Though it annoyed him, he'd participate, if only because Edwin hadn't protested the contest, thus making Stephen look peevish if he did.

"Was Dena also informative?"

"Somewhat." Armand threw the bolt on the door and began to shrug out of his tunic. "The twins are not Carolyn's half sisters, but her cousin's daughters."

"So I learned for myself. I also learned that their mother is a widow. Did Dena say how Marian came to be at Branwick?"

"Nay, but then I did not ask. Shall I?"

Stephen thought to say yes, then changed his mind. The mystery was still there, but would keep for the nonce. More urgent matters pressed on his mind.

"No need."

Armand shrugged a shoulder. "As you wish. Anyway, I did ask Dena about Edwin of Tinfield, thinking you would wish to know about your rival. On that score, she was most informative." He tossed his tunic down onto his pallet at the foot of the bed, then lowered onto a stool to dispose of his boots. "Edwin's prime holding is not far from here, so he has known William de Grasse and his family for a long time. Apparently Edwin lost his first wife about the time Carolyn lost her first husband. He applied to her father for a marriage bargain, but William had already pledged Carolyn to another."

"So now Edwin tries again."

"Only this time Carolyn pleaded with her father to let her choose her third husband, or at least have some say.

William must have felt some pang of sympathy because he agreed. He has, however, allowed Edwin to spend much time at Branwick, even though Carolyn balks at Edwin's age.'' Armand grinned. ''Dena says the arguments between the pair are spectacular, most of them over how much freedom a woman should be granted within the bounds of marriage. Edwin taunts Carolyn with her unladylike beliefs. Carolyn taunts Edwin about his gray hair. A mismatched pair, I would say.''

Another mark against Edwin. Still, even if William didn't force Carolyn to marry Edwin, he could certainly refuse to allow his daughter to marry Stephen of Wilmont—all because of this damn contest.

Stephen rubbed his eyes, thinking about the list he'd receive on the morn. Gad, he'd left his estates under his stewards' and Gerard's direction for too long to know costs of materials and labor readily. 'Twould pose a problem, though not an insurmountable one. William couldn't expect him to know the price of goods and services in this area, for costs differed greatly depending upon ready availability. Ivo could supply figures.

His greatest problem was getting to know Carolyn better. He needed to know what pleased her outside of the bedchamber—which he already knew.

She obviously liked to ride over the countryside, but did she also like long walks? Did she prefer bold colors to pale, ale to wine, a psalter to a wooden chest?

Not William, nor Edwin, nor Ivo would be of help on that front. Nor would Armand's Dena, for servants often saw their betters in a different light than would those of closer rank and status.

He knew of only one other person at Branwick who matched Carolyn's status and could supply the answers he needed. Marian.

Marian of the pewter eyes and sable hair. The widowed mother of adorable twins, who lived in a hut on the edge of the hamlet. He still didn't like the arrangement, the three of them out there alone and unprotected, no matter how long they'd lived on their own.

Marian's continued vexation at him rubbed a raw spot on his innards, more troubling than he should allow. He hadn't meant to seem indifferent to her all those years ago; there simply hadn't been time when leaving Murwaithe for fare-thee-wells or a parting kiss. Yet she still held him in contempt for that one act of discourtesy.

Could he somehow make it up to her now? Would she then soften her manner toward him, talk to him without an edge to her voice? Grace him with a smile?

'Twasn't as if Marian had pined for him overlong. Judging by the size of her girls, they must be somewhere around the age of four, so Marian she must have wed within a year or so after their affair and given her husband children.

Had Marian's husband known she wasn't a virgin before they married?

Stephen frowned.

If Marian had confessed her lack of virginity to her father, she might have had to settle for a less than suitable husband. Could it be she blamed Stephen of Wilmont for some degradation he knew nothing about? 'Twould certainly explain her high vexation, and also explain Edwin's comment about the possibility of hard feelings in Marian's family. Perhaps she'd come to Branwick after her husband's death because she couldn't return to Murwaithe for some reason.

''What plan for the morrow, my lord?''

Armand's question jolted Stephen back to the immediate problem of William's challenge. He briefly related the conditions to Armand.

"Should not be a difficult task," Armand commented. "You did a similar study several years ago for Gerard, did you not?"

The king had settled a large grant of land—confiscated from a traitor to the crown—on Gerard for bringing the miscreant to justice. Gerard kept only one holding, then gifted Stephen and Richard with the rest. Seeing the opportunity to be off on an adventure, Stephen offered to inspect all the newly gained holdings and report back on their condition. He'd taken Corwin along, and the two of them enjoyed a grand time visiting one estate after the other. Some of the estates had suffered greatly under their former overlord.

"Similar, but different. Wilmont's coffers run deep, and Gerard was willing to borrow funds, if necessary, to make urgent repairs. William is neither so wealthy nor so broad-minded."

"Broad-minded enough to allow Carolyn the freedoms he does. Mayhap he will be easier to please than you fear."

'Twas possible. Unfortunately, since arriving at Branwick he hadn't been able to please anyone except one little girl who'd smiled brightly at him before coming down with a severe headache.

Despite Marian's obvious wish not to, he'd like to make amends with the girl's mother. Not because Marian could influence William's opinion of him, if she chose, but for his own peace of mind.

Except, given Marian's hostility, returning to her good graces might prove more difficult than winning William's contest.

* * *

Marian couldn't believe her eyes. She'd cracked opened the shutters to judge the time by the rising sun, then wondered if her wits had fled.

'Twas just past dawn, yet Stephen sat on her stone wall, staring at her hut. Garbed in a dark-green tunic, brown breeches and boots, he looked like a man of the forest, a wanderer—or a brigand.

Stephen hadn't been out there all night, had he? Surely not. Then he must have left the keep before the chapel bell pealed to bid all to morning Mass.

She gave a moment's thought to staying safely within the hut before she pulled on her boots and tossed a hooded cloak over her unbound hair and gray gown. The girls would sleep awhile yet, and she wanted Stephen gone before they woke.

He slid off the wall as she slipped out the door. She walked toward him, getting only close enough to talk quietly so they'd not wake the girls.

"How fares Lyssa?"

His inquiry tugged at Marian's heart. Stephen didn't know he asked after the health of his own daughter. Then again, the inquiry might not be truly Stephen's, but William's. 'Twould be like her uncle to send someone out at dawn to ask after Lyssa.

"She was up twice in the night, but has slept steadily for the past few hours. The worst has passed."

"Poor tyke. 'Tis not right a little one should suffer so. On our way back to Branwick last eve, Edwin told me you had taken her to a London physician to seek a cure. That was Lyssa in your bed that night, was it not?"

She'd tried very hard to put that night in Westminster Palace out of her mind, as well as other nights in Stephen's company, and certainly didn't want to talk about any of them now.

"Aye, 'twas Lyssa. She had finally fallen asleep and I did not want you to wake her." Marian glanced back at the hut, her refuge. "I should go back in now, and you had best be on your way or you will miss Mass."

He smiled, a hint of mischief in the upward curve. "I suppose I should, or William will have one more thing to hold against me."

The question that skittered through her head must have shown on her face.

"He does not like me," Stephen said. "William thinks me too young and not worth my daily bread, to hear him tell it. Certes, not worth the hand of his daughter."

William could be blunt, but he was rarely outright rude. "My uncle told you this?"

"Not only did he say he considered me an unsuitable match for his daughter, but he has devised a contest designed to prove his belief." Stephen turned around and placed his hands on the wall, his head turning as he perused the view of Branwick's fields and woodlands before him. "Edwin and I will each receive a list of improvements to be made to Branwick. We are to inspect the holding and devise a plan to make the most improvements at the least cost. He did not say so but he expects me to make a muck of it."

Hoping her uncle might be right, which meant Stephen would be on his way soon, she asked, "Will you?"

He spun around. "Oh, nay. In truth, I am not overly worried over the contest, merely annoyed. I am concerned, however, over you."

Her confusion heightened when he took two steps toward her and grasped her shoulders. She could feel the heat of his hands through her cloak, enjoy the pressure of the familiar squeeze of his fingers.

"I was up a time or two myself last night," he said. "After we left here last eve, I worried over leaving you and the girls out here, unprotected. Edwin told me you have lived as such for several years, yet I do not understand why you do not live in the keep, as you should."

She wished his fingers would be still, that her own arms didn't yearn to wrap around him. She locked her arms firmly across her chest to muffle her pounding heart.

"I prefer the hut to the keep. Truly, we are in no danger."

He looked skeptical, so she pointed toward a hut not far down the road.

"In yon hut lives the blacksmith, whose two lads are nigh as big as bulls. If I scream, you had best prepare to defend yourself."

A smile touched the edge of Stephen's mouth. "I am a Wilmont trained knight. I do believe I can manage against the blacksmith's lads." His amusement disappeared. "Marian, I must confess the ill will you bear me sits heavy on my mind. I had hoped we could make amends. At Westminster, I tried to apologize for whatever heartache I might have caused you. Will you listen now?"

This was why Stephen had come. Not to inquire about Lyssa or relay concern over their safety. Marian backed up a step; Stephen's hands fell away.

"'Twas a long time ago. You need have no concern—"

"I believe I do." He waved a hand at the hut. "You deserve far better than a hut outside the walls of your uncle's keep. I remember a girl filled with gaiety and a sense of adventure, but the woman barely smiles. I fear our liaison caused your downward change of fortune. What happened after I left you?''

Marian quelled the panic before it could rise. Stephen didn't know about the twins. He begged answers she refused to give.

''The life I now have is of mine own choosing. Let it be, Stephen. Best you go back to the keep before you are missed.''

She fled the man and the memories. Not until she opened the door did he call out her name. The urge to turn around nearly overcame her good sense, but she closed the door behind her and threw the bolt.

Marian leaned against the door, trembling, listening for the sounds of his footsteps. Not hearing them, she dared a peek out the shutters. Stephen had vanished, as if he'd never been there.

But he had been and he'd be back. As sure as she drew her next breath, she knew Stephen wouldn't let the matter be.

Her daughters, Stephen's daughters, yet slept. How angelic they looked in their sleep. Audra with her thumb in her mouth; Lyssa without the furrow of pain on her forehead.

She'd been up most of the night holding a cold rag on Lyssa's brow and wished she could do more for the darling who'd given her so much joy. Somewhere in the wee hours, with her eyes heavy and guard down, the thought had crept in that she'd denied Stephen the joy of watching the girls take their first steps, hearing their first words.

Heaven help her, she still couldn't help wondering if she'd made a grievous mistake in keeping them apart.

Chapter Five

Needing a long, hard ride after his unsatisfactory talk with Marian, Stephen decided to begin his inspection of Branwick at the farthest reaches of the estate. All he need do is have someone point him in the right direction.

All through Mass he'd reviewed his talk with Marian and realized he went about it wrong. He should have apologized first, then tried to find out what he apologized for. She couldn't still be angry with him over a discourtesy; it had to run deeper, much deeper.

He gave the horse's cinch a hard tug. The stallion protested with a toss of his head and an irritated snort, as he always did.

"Problem?" Edwin asked from two stalls away, where he prepared his own mount for an outing.

"Nay. He is simply peevish."

"Ah. Then the two of you make a suitable pair this morn."

Stephen heard Edwin's amusement, didn't appreciate it, but didn't fault the man for making the remark. He might have taunted Edwin with a similar comment if their moods had been reversed.

The list Carolyn had given both men consisted of

twenty items, some within Branwick's walls but most without. A few items required long rides and an overnight stay at two of William's lesser holdings. None of the items seemed beyond the ordinary repairs or improvements regularly necessary or much desired on any holding of good size.

The only item to pique his interest was the repair of the thatched roof on Marian's hut. Surely William would agree to the repair without a qualm or thought for cost. Or William might not, forcing Marian to reside in the keep where she belonged.

Irritating woman.

Edwin backed his horse out of the stall. "Where shall we begin?"

"*We?*"

Edwin sighed. "We must inspect the same places and you have no notion of where most of them are. Why not go together if only to keep you from getting lost?"

"I should think you would rather I got lost."

"Nay, I would rather win this contest fairly, not because you rode over a cliff."

Damned if the man didn't sound sincere, and damned if Edwin didn't know Branwick well enough to act as a novice's guide.

Still wary, Stephen asked, "Just you and me?"

"On my word, Stephen, you have naught to fear. I will not help you, but neither will I hinder you. The sooner over, the sooner you are gone."

Stephen relented. This would be a good opportunity to observe Edwin, though he'd still watch his own back. Edwin seemed an honorable man, but was a rival. One didn't trust one's enemy to adhere to honor when the prize was great.

"I had planned to begin at whatever site is farthest

from Branwick yet reachable within the day. Agreeable?''

Edwin smiled. "A good hard ride should work the peevishness out of both rider and mount. Ready?''

"Lead on.''

Edwin wound his way through the crowded inner bailey, picked up speed in the outer bailey, then dashed out the gate, Stephen at his heels. Once out, Stephen gloried at the freedom of flying over the countryside, at a speed that tasked the horses' stamina and the riders' ability. By the time Edwin slowed to spare the horses, Stephen's mood was much improved.

He pulled up alongside Edwin. "Where do we go?''

"The bridge.''

Stephen recalled Carolyn's list. "Carolyn deems one of the supports rotted and in need of replacement. Is the bridge heavily traveled?''

Edwin hesitated before answering. "At times.''

Stephen chided himself for asking the question. 'Twasn't Edwin's intention to give further aid than ensuring Stephen didn't get lost. Fair enough. What information he couldn't glean from observation, he'd ask of Branwick's steward.

For the better part of the next hour, they rode in silence over a decently kept road which wound through well-tended fields and dense woodlands. He observed the wealth of game, from fluttering doves to an elegantly racked buck. A hare scampered across the road and into the wheat field, safely hidden now within the tall sheaves of gold.

"Ah, for a falcon,'' Stephen said, drawing a wistful smile from Edwin.

"Aye, 'twould be a good day for a hunt if we had not

another task before us. I hear tell Wilmont's mews are beyond compare.''

"My brother does love his hunting birds. To my great fortune, he is also willing to share. 'Tis a rare occasion to visit Wilmont without him pressing to fly the hawks at least once."

"Have you a preference in birds?"

Stephen did. "Peregrines. At least Wilmont's peregrines. My sister-by-marriage has them trained to such a degree they might hunt on their own."

Edwin raised a doubting eyebrow. "The baron's wife has charge of the mews?"

"Nay, not truly. Gerard's falconer oversees the hunting birds care and training for the most part. Ardith, however, has a great love of peregrines and enjoys the training. The birds respond so well to her methods that Gerard allows Ardith her way with them." He chuckled. "Of course, one must understand that Gerard allows Ardith her way in most things."

Gerard did deny Ardith on occasions when he thought his wife tasked her strength and endurance, like as now when she was carrying. For the next few weeks, until after the birth of her babe, Ardith would find it harder to elude her protective husband's dictates to rest.

Edwin shook his head. "'Tis not wise for a husband to allow a wife to run roughshod."

Stephen leaned back and laughed. "Nobody runs roughshod over Gerard. He is the most obstinate, overbearing, strong-willed man I know. When he gives an order, all obey immediately. He can be reasonable, but once he has made up his mind over something, then arguing with Gerard is tantamount to butting one's head into a stone wall." His amusement died, knowing to what lengths Gerard would go to protect Wilmont and those he loved. "Nay, one does not cross Gerard without paying a severe penalty. The last man who tried lost all, including his life."

"Basil of Northbryre. The tale of his treachery against Wilmont and the king is well-known."

Mention of the man's name still made Stephen's stomach churn. Basil had nearly caused Richard's death, schemed to overrun one of Gerard's keeps, then tried to escape the king's justice by leaving the country—using Ardith and Gerard's eldest son as a shield. Stephen refrained from rubbing at his ear, at the chunk of lobe lost during the kidnapping, an event he yet blamed himself for. If harm had come to his two charges...but none had. Ardith and Daymon had survived unscathed.

"When Gerard received Northbryre's English lands, I went out to inspect the holdings, not so much to see how they fared but to judge any resistance to new lordship. Richard holds a small manor not too distant from here. 'Twas the last time I was in the area, over three years past now."

"Truly? Which holding?"

Stephen searched his memory. "Snelston?"

"Hmm. Not familiar."

"Not surprising. If I remember correctly, the manor's entire fee is three hares and three sacks of grain per year."

Edwin pointed off to his left. "There, beyond the copse of trees is the bridge."

Stephen noted the faint sound of rushing water and the continued good condition of the dirt road, so likely the bridge crossed a stream where fording wasn't possible.

The conjecture proved partially correct. At this bend the stream wasn't wide, nor deep, but made up for the lack in vigor. Water bubbled and churned merrily over the rock bed and the scattered large boulders. A man on horseback could negotiate the steep banks, but not a cart.

The bridge, however, was a sorry sight.

Stephen urged his horse down the bank into the water and crossed over to the other side, where one bridge support in particular appeared ready to give way. Edwin chose to cross the bridge. The beam groaned, but held. Stephen wouldn't wish to test it with two men on horseback.

Edwin rode down the bank and entered the water.

Stephen waved at the beam. "'Twould appear Carolyn has the right of it."

Edwin inspected the underside of the bridge and the support in question, then grunted. "So it seems."

Stephen followed Edwin back across the stream and up the sloped bank. "Where to next?"

"The forester's dwelling."

An important man on any estate, the forester ensured the game in his lord's woodlands wasn't overhunted, mostly by keeping watch for poachers. Any peasant caught taking game on his overlord's land would be severely punished, just as any noble who dared hunt the king's preserves risked censure. The Forest Laws were absolute and unforgiving, and the men who enforced those laws were well cared for.

According to Carolyn's list, the forester's hut should be torn down and replaced.

As they left the road and took a narrow path into the dense, cool woods, Stephen noted the abundance of trees useful for planks. Did Branwick boast a good carpenter, or must he be hired from a nearby town? Stephen made a mental note to ask Branwick's steward. 'Twould make a difference in the cost.

Settled comfortably in the saddle, he followed Edwin down the meandering path. In places, sunbeams pierced the thick canopy overhead. Stephen watched one wide beam dim and then disappear, a warning of clouds traveling the sky.

Edwin pulled up in a grassy glade. In the middle of the glade stood a hut which tilted hard to the side.

Stephen winced at the thought of going inside the dwelling. "Someone lives in there?"

"Nigh on a fortnight ago Carolyn bid the forester to move his family into the keep. Degan still comes out here daily, to do his job properly, but no one sleeps within."

Stephen turned in his saddle to stare at Edwin. "Just how much time do you spend at Branwick that you know the name of the forester?"

"Enough."

"Apparently. Do you not have lands of your own to oversee?"

Edwin shrugged a dismissive shoulder. "The border of Tinfield marches with Branwick on the north. Should I be needed, a messenger will come for me. I can be there and back in the space of a day."

No wonder William favored Edwin. A marriage between Carolyn and Edwin would join neighboring estates, a highly desirable event. Stephen wondered which Edwin coveted more, Carolyn or Branwick—the affairs of which the man knew too much about for Stephen's peace of mind. Which did Carolyn desire less, Edwin himself, or bowing to her neighbor's rule over lands she wished to rule on her own?

Stephen drew a long breath. "Where to next?"

"Back to Branwick. Storm coming up."

Stephen glanced up at the sky over the glade. Indeed,

clouds gathered, but he had one more place to visit before the storm broke and he'd rather do it without Edwin.

Marian's. To inspect the roof.

"Lyssa, 'ware the carrots. Ah, the onions are not ready for picking yet, Audra. Put it back in the ground, if you please."

Marian's voice carried over the stone wall and out onto the road, competing with the rumble of distant thunder. Stephen reined in, hearing but not seeing the three ladies of the house who must be in the garden, hidden by the wall.

"Hurry, girls, before the rain comes or you will be up to your knees in mud."

"Then we could stand out in the rain and wash it off!"

Lyssa's voice, with an imp's response.

"I think not," her mother answered, amused. "Come, a few more weeds and then we are done."

Stephen dismounted and led his horse toward the wall, glad to hear Lyssa's voice. If she was still hurting, she'd not be out in the garden pulling weeds.

"What shall we do with the afternoon, Mama?" Audra asked.

"Mayhap lessons are in order. We have neglected them of late."

"Can we do letters, then? I dislike numbers," Lyssa commented, bringing a smile to Stephen's face. Everart, his nephew, disliked numbers, too. Then Everart was merely three summers old, so his mother only gave him lessons he liked. Not for a few more years yet would he join six-year-old Daymon in earnest lessons with Wilmont's priest.

Marian's twins were a bit taller than Everart, but nowhere near the size of Daymon. About four, he'd guessed at their age.

Stephen tied the reins to a nearby bush and rested his arms on the chest-high wall. Marian and her girls knelt at the edge of the garden where Marian pulled weeds from around a patch of turnips and the girls, by turns, tugged at greenery and played in the dirt.

The sight warmed him clear through, though he was at a loss to explain why. He'd seen other mothers with their children without being so affected.

"You could read to us from your new book," Audra suggested to her mother, then looked his way. "Oh, good morn, my lord!"

Lyssa nearly tumbled into the carrots as she rose and spun around. Marian's head turned. Her gaze locked with his. The warmth turned to heat and settled in his loins. Not even her unwelcoming expression could chill his body's reaction, and he was thankful for the barrier of the wall to hide his physical response.

"Good morn, my ladies," he said. "You tend a lovely garden, Marian."

The slight nod of her head acknowledged the compliment.

Lyssa scampered over to the wall. "We helped!"

Stephen could imagine how much help the girls had been, but he kept his amusement hidden. "So I saw. I am sure your mother appreciates your efforts."

The girls beamed.

Marian stood stoic. "'Tis about to rain, my lord. Surely you should return to Branwick before the storm lets loose."

He probably should. Marian didn't want him here. Still, there was the matter of her roof.

"Your roof is one of the items on Carolyn's list of

repairs. How better to judge the extent of the repair than during a rainstorm?'' he asked, surprising himself. He hadn't planned to wait out the storm here, simply have a look at the thatch.

''One need only look at the corner to see it needs repair.''

Rightly so.

''True, but how much repair? Would you have me lose this contest from lack of thorough knowledge?''

Marian pursed her lips.

Audra tilted her head. ''Will you fix the roof?''

Stephen couldn't imagine himself doing so. ''Nay, merely inform William of the extent of the damage so he can hire a thatcher to make the repair. For that I need to know how much rain falls into the hut.''

''Lots,'' Audra commented seriously. ''Mama puts a pot under the leak so our dirt floor does not become mud.''

''So bad as that?''

''Aye. Come, I will show you.''

Both girls took off for the hut, eager to aid his cause. Stephen willed his body into obedience and passed through the gate. Marian looked most unhappy.

''‘Tis unnecessary, Stephen. My uncle knows—''

''Does Edwin?''

''Aye, but—''

''Then I must know, too.''

Marian's chest expanded during the deep breath she took. He tried not to stare at the rise and fall of her breasts, knowing well what rosy-tipped treasures her worn, gray work gown hid.

She brushed dirt from her hands. ''Very well. Mayhap the storm will not last long.''

She strode toward her hut. Stephen followed, noting

the stiffness of her spine and how the tip of her long braid swayed to and fro, brushing against her bottom in rhythm with her steps.

If he didn't stop noticing Marian's every enticing movement, the day would be long indeed, no matter the duration of the storm. Resolved to attend the chore at hand, he ducked through the doorway.

Inside the hut, the girls stood in the far corner, looking up at the roof. A large, black iron pot lay at their feet. Stephen dutifully walked over to inspect the roof. He couldn't see light through the thatch, but 'twas obvious from the girls' placement of the pot that the rain dripped in here.

Stephen poked at the underside, disturbing a beetle that burrowed deeper into thatch. "Getting thin here."

"How observant of you," Marian commented.

He ignored her sarcasm.

"Why was this not repaired before now?"

"'Twas not bad before now."

'Twas perverse of him, he knew, but he looked to Audra for confirmation. "Is that so?"

Her little head nodded. "We did not need Mama's biggest pot until the last storm."

The next logical step would be to inspect the roof from above. If he used his horse as a ladder he'd be able to get up on the roof. Stephen headed for the door.

"Finished?" Marian asked.

He dashed her hope. "I thought to go up on the roof." The words no more than left this mouth when booming thunder shook the hut and the rain fell with deluge force. "Or mayhap not."

Marian's shoulders slumped, pricking Stephen's anger. Must she make it so clear she wished him gone?

There had been a time she'd joyously welcomed his company, craved his presence as he craved hers.

Audra handed Marian a book, bound in black leather. "Read to us, Mama?"

Marian forced a smile for her little one. "Which story?"

"Jonah!"

"The whale again?" Both girls nodded. "Very well, then, the whale it is."

Marian sat on a rug, her back pressed against the wall. The girls cuddled into her sides. Marian opened the gild-edged pages to a place already marked and began to read.

Stephen settled on a stool near the table. Soon a steady drip of water into the kettle accompanied the melodic lull of Marian's voice. The girls paid neither the rain nor the occasional clap of thunder any heed.

The whale had no sooner swallowed up Jonah when Audra stuck her thumb in her mouth, her long eyelashes fluttering in an effort to stay awake. Lyssa struggled, too.

Stephen shook off his own languor. The warmth of the closed-up hut combined with the patter of rain and lure of Marian's voice were making him drowsy, too. Unwilling to succumb, he rose to gaze out the window. His stallion looked none too pleased for taking a soaking. A long, hard rubdown and special treat were in order later.

"Stephen?" Marian whispered. He turned to see both tykes fast asleep, Marian trapped between them. "Move Lyssa, please?"

Pleased to be of *some* use to her, Stephen knelt beside the girl whose head rested against her mother's breast. To move Lyssa, he must touch Marian. Well, she'd asked for his aid, so must realize she must tolerate his touch, if only briefly.

Stephen slid his hand between mother and daughter, concentrating on not waking Lyssa, on controlling the wayward direction of his thoughts. He didn't dare look at Marian's face when the back of his hand pressed against the pliancy of her breast, fearing he'd see revulsion. Gently, but swiftly, he moved Lyssa to her pallet.

Marian did the same with Audra, then stood up, her back to him. She crossed to the table and put the book down, then put her face in her hands and rubbed at her eyes. Tired? Repulsed? Whichever, she regained her stoic look before turning back to face him.

She wanted him out of her hut; he longed to take her in his arms and kiss her so thoroughly she'd beg him to stay. He grasped for a common thread, some nonthreatening topic. He picked up the book and opened it to the marker—to a splendid illustration of a wave-tossed boat bearing a white-haired man in terror of a wide-jawed whale.

The book was new and obviously purchased from the same monastery as Carolyn's. Edwin not only plied Carolyn with costly gifts, but had seen fit to enjoin Marian's favor, too.

"A gift from Edwin?" he asked, foolishly wanting to know how much she liked the book.

She shrugged. "I admired Carolyn's psalter, so William asked Edwin to purchase one for me. I refused the psalter but relented to a story book of biblical tales."

Stephen felt better about it, but not much. He tossed the book on the table. "How nice of him."

"He is a nice man."

"But old."

"Not so old as one would notice."

A horrific notion struck his brain and came out his mouth before he could stop it. "You fancy Edwin?"

She took one of those sense-muddling long breaths. "Do not be daft. Besides, Edwin has been in love with Carolyn for so long he would not think to look another woman's way."

Edwin wanted Carolyn for herself, then, not to expand his interests or secure further alliance with his neighbor.

"Does Carolyn know?"

"Of course."

"And yet she rejects him."

Marian looked about to answer, then thought better of whatever she was about to say. Stephen guessed at her feelings on the matter.

"You think Carolyn should accept Edwin. Indeed, you wish I would leave Branwick, give up mine own plans so Edwin might yet win Carolyn, do you not?"

"'Twould be best for all."

"All but me, and apparently not Carolyn. She favors my suit. All I must do is win this contest and her father will relent. You had best become resolved to calling me cousin."

With that horrible thought in mind, Stephen left the hut before his temper rose higher, thus raising his voice and waking the girls.

Marian slumped onto a stool, her insides churning.

Whatever made her think she could allow Stephen entry to the hut without suffering consequences? What perverse part of her made her ask for his help with Lyssa? Countless times she'd managed to move both girls to their pallets without waking either one. Still, she drew Stephen near quite unnecessarily, even knowing he would need to slide his hand beneath Lyssa's head.

Merely being in his presence was dangerous, for she

tended to disregard the warnings in her head. It had always been thus, from the very first time she'd laid eyes on Stephen of Wilmont. Why in six years had no other man drawn her as powerfully as Stephen did?

Heartsick, Marian rose and went to the window, looked out to where Stephen's horse had been tied. Gone. 'Twas still raining, though no longer as hard, yet enough so he'd be soaked through by the time he reached Branwick, and Carolyn.

Would Carolyn take advantage? Order Stephen a hot bath to ease his chills? Attend him as he bathed? And after?

Marian closed her eyes against the vision of Carolyn and Stephen together. Yet it played through her mind vividly, for Carolyn had gloated over Stephen's prowess as a lover. There'd been no issue from that coupling, but if Stephen and Carolyn married, there certainly might be. Then her girls and Carolyn's children would not only be cousins but half siblings.

Dear God in heaven, could she keep such a secret? She might have to, unless Stephen lost this contest, as he well might. Edwin knew Branwick nearly as thoroughly as Carolyn, so had the advantage to win and banish Marian's fears in the process.

She fostered that small spark of hope. Edwin stood a good chance of winning the lady he loved, the woman who cared for him enough she'd chosen not to marry him. If Carolyn would only let go of her foolish fears…but she remained adamant.

Marian came away from the window, taking small comfort in having not told Stephen of Carolyn's worst fears where Edwin was concerned. 'Twould be foolish in the extreme to hand Stephen a weapon against Edwin.

Her best hope of preventing the marriage would be to convince Carolyn to accept Edwin. She'd tried before and failed, but it might be worth another attempt. She would do so the next time she went into Branwick.

Chapter Six

The beefy blacksmith's lads took up most of the room in the small hut. Marian felt dwarfed.

"His lordship says you are to come first thing this morn, my lady," Dirk stated, then swung Lyssa up onto his broad-as-a-plank shoulders. "Did not say why, just to come."

His younger brother by a year, Kirk, hoisted Audra up in similar fashion.

She knew why William had ordered the lads to fetch her and the girls on their way into Branwick this morning. She'd avoided going to the keep for nearly a full sennight, far too many days for William's peace of mind. Truly, she was rather surprised he hadn't commanded her attendance earlier.

Marian relented to the inevitable. "Very well. Girls, watch your heads on the way out."

'Twas an unnecessary motherly warning. The boys bent forward and the girls ducked, a maneuver they'd perfected through frequent practice. Marian glanced at the wooden bowls on the table, where the last scrapings of morning porridge began to dry and harden. The vigorous chore of cleaning the bowls awaited her return—

whenever that might be. For her neglect of him, William might well insist she stay for evening meal whether she wished to or not.

The small fire she'd built to cook porridge was already out. The girls had fed the chickens and tied the goat. Nothing of import held her here, no excuse to delay going into Branwick any longer. Marian closed the door behind her and joined the others on the road.

Walking briskly between Dirk and Kirk, she barely kept up with the boys' long strides. The girls bounced along on their high perches, chatting away over her head. 'Twas inevitable Lyssa would suggest a race. Ever amenable, the boys took off, carrying their merrily giggling charges off toward the keep.

Marian laughed and slowed her steps, not bothering to try to match the boys' speed. They would take Audra and Lyssa to the smithy and watch over the girls until Marian fetched them.

'Twas one of the few times she found herself alone. Since the girls' birth, she'd not often been parted from them for more than a few minutes at a time. Rare and precious as gems were these moments to herself.

Not that she didn't love her daughters beyond life itself, but there were times when Marian wished her life had taken a slightly different path, or that someone had been around to share the joys and tribulations of raising the twins. How often, when the girls were infants, had she wished for an extra pair of hands to hold one tyke while she fed or fussed with the other? Even now, though the girls' dispositions ran toward pleasant, both could be demanding and rub hard at a mother's temper. Discipline sometimes suffered for lack of firmness on those days when 'twas easier to yield than enforce a rule or command.

Still, all in all, she'd not done so badly. The girls led a happy life and, except for Lyssa's headaches, enjoyed good health. Marian doubted they'd be any happier or healthier if their lives had been different—if their father had been around to influence their upbringing.

She'd struggled with the notion for most of the week while avoiding further contact with Stephen.

Every time she saw Stephen 'twas becoming harder to keep her hands off him, or inviting his hands on her. Not good. Every time she saw her daughters with Stephen, she wondered if she grievously erred in keeping the father and his children in ignorance of their relationship. Worse.

She'd made the decision six years ago to give up Stephen, to raise the girls on her own. Had she been wrong?

If she told Stephen about his daughters, would he give up his quest to marry Carolyn? Perhaps, or mayhap not. One thing she was sure on—if the people of Branwick learned the girls were base born, the twins would suffer further shunning. Nor would the people be pleased that they'd been misled. They could turn her pleasant life into a living hell.

Marian crossed the drawbridge leading up to the keep's gate. As always, the outer bailey teemed with people going about their morning tasks. Her life within Branwick's sphere could continue on as pleasantly as ever if she kept her secrets and if Carolyn didn't marry Stephen.

Marian quelled a shiver. She'd heard nothing of how the contest went, but was sure someone would have informed her if a winner had been declared or if William agreed to a betrothal bargain with either man.

She passed through the gate to the inner bailey and

nearly bumped into Carolyn, who looked none too happy.

Marian didn't bother with greetings. "What makes you frown so?"

Carolyn crossed her arms and jerked her head to the right. "The pair of them. One would think them friends, not rivals."

Marian glanced over to see Stephen and Edwin, both intently studying a section of the stone wall. With his fingers, Edwin dug a chunk of mortar from between two stones, then called Stephen's attention to it.

"How goes the contest?"

"This contest is a farce," Carolyn declared, then spun around and headed for the keep. Marian followed. "The two of them rise with the sun, attend Mass, break their fast, then set out to inspect an item or two on my list. After nooning, Stephen consults with Ivo, and Edwin has taken to joining them."

"Who is winning?"

"I have no notion. Father will not allow me to discuss the contest with them for fear I will influence the results. Is your roof repaired properly?"

"Aye. The thatcher appeared at my door nearly as soon as the rain stopped, and the roof has not leaked since."

"Good. Father was most distressed when Stephen told him you were using your biggest pot to catch rain. You should have told me the leak had worsened."

"I knew you planned to have it repaired, so must be on your infamous list. 'Twas rather a surprise to have Stephen stop to inspect it."

Carolyn shoved open the door, never losing stride as she crossed the great hall, heading for the ale barrel. "I am amazed Stephen did not haul Edwin over there with him. 'Struth, those two spend more time with each other than they do with me! For suitors, they neglect the object of their suit in most grievous fashion. I should tell them both to go to the devil and choose someone else.''

Marian accepted the cup of ale Carolyn offered.

"I see. Have you another suitor interested?''

"Nay, thank the Fates. Truth to tell, Marian, I am not sure I could survive the humiliation of yet another contest. 'Tis bad enough Father tests my judgment against whatever Edwin or Stephen will advise.''

Marian knew she treaded treacherous ground, but dared Carolyn's ire anyway.

"You could end the contest. All you need do is accept Edwin's marriage bargain.''

Carolyn closed her eyes briefly. When they opened, they reflected such profound sadness Marian almost wished she'd refrained. Almost.

"You know I cannot,'' Carolyn said.

Marian looked about the hall. Satisfied no one could overhear if they spoke softly, she disagreed with her cousin.

"You can. Carolyn, Edwin is not that old. He is neither ill nor frail nor—''

"Nay. I will not take the risk.''

"Is the risk not Edwin's to decide to take or not?''

Horrified, Carolyn pleaded, "Marian, you must never tell him. You made me an oath.''

"An oath I will keep.'' Marian placed a comforting hand on Carolyn's shoulder. She leaned closer. "You should tell Edwin all you have told me. If he is afraid, then he will drop his suit. Truly, I believe he will declare—nay, *prove* to you that you have naught to fear.''

"I could never live with myself if Edwin succumbed.'' Carolyn shook off Marian's hand. "Besides,

Edwin wants full control over Branwick and my dower lands if we should marry. He is much too set in his ways. Best for all concerned if I marry Stephen.''

All, perhaps, except for two little girls.

Marian put down her ale cup. ''I still think you make too much of Edwin's age.''

Carolyn's rejoinder came as a whisper. ''I will not have a third husband die in my bed, especially not a man I care for. I will *not* marry Edwin.''

Marian couldn't imagine waking up to find someone dead in her bed, not once but twice. Carolyn blamed herself because on both occasions her husbands had claimed their marital rights only hours before. Marian blamed the husbands for overexerting themselves.

''Oh, Caro, I just want you to be happy, and I do not think you will find happiness with Stephen.''

Carolyn must have sensed the truth and concern in Marian's voice, for her hard manner softened. ''I know you do, just as I have always wished for you to be happy. We have both made hard choices, then made the best of things. I shall find a measure of happiness with Stephen, you will see.'' Carolyn flashed a wicked smile. ''There is something to be said for taking a young man to one's bed.''

Marian forced a smile against the sharp pain. Carolyn teased, having no way of knowing how much the teasing hurt.

''So you told me.''

Carolyn tilted her head. ''What of you, Marian? You chide me for my choice of husband, yet you shy from every man who comes near you. Many here would dearly love to have you as wife.''

''Hah! They want workers for their fields and mothers for their children. I am content as I am.'' Marian suddenly thought of another way to bring Carolyn to her senses. A bit cruel, perhaps, but to the point. "Of course, if you do not marry Edwin, mayhap the man will need comfort. Edwin looks sturdy enough to me to withstand the rigors of *my* bed."

As Carolyn's jaw dropped, Marian hurried off to fetch her girls from the smithy.

Stephen climbed the narrow spiral stairway in the guard tower at the north corner of the outer bailey. The farther up, the riper the stench. No wonder the four guards assigned to reside here had abandoned the tower, preferring to lay their sleeping pallets out on the archers' walk of the curtain wall.

He opened the door to the garderobe then swiftly slammed the door shut. "I say we recommend an immediate flushing of the shaft. 'Twill need twenty buckets of water, at the least."

Edwin shook his head. "Already been tried. Whatever blocks the shaft did not budge."

Then whatever blocked the shaft must be big and solid. The tower's garderobe was on the highest level, its shaft running straight down the outer wall to empty into the moat.

"Has anyone confessed to losing his breeches down the hole?"

Edwin smiled. "Nay. Everyone's best guess is that some stupid animal climbed up in there to make his home—and died."

"Well, I am not about to stick my face over the hole to confirm the speculation."

"You intend to forgo a thorough inspection this time?"

At Edwin's mock horror, Stephen stepped back and

reopened the garderobe's door. "Care to have a look Edwin?"

Waving a hand before his face, Edwin turned around and headed back down the stairs. Stephen shut the door and followed, his eyes stinging from the smell.

Edwin chuckled. "I suppose 'twill need cleaning from the bottom up. I pity the poor man given the task."

"On that we can agree."

As they'd agreed on so many things over the past week, though until now Stephen hadn't uttered the words aloud. In a more companionable fashion than Stephen had thought possible, he and Edwin made steady progress on Carolyn's list. He spent so much time in his rival's company that he could now tell from Edwin's expression if they agreed immediately on some item or if Edwin was undecided.

For the most part, Edwin resisted confirming the immediate need for some repair simply because Carolyn thought it necessary. The man was having a hard time believing a woman could have such foresight and knowledge, enough to properly oversee a holding as large as Branwick.

Stephen stepped out of the tower and into the outer bailey, leaving the stink behind, encountering other odors no more pleasant but at least tolerable.

Craftsmen's shops lined the curtain wall. From the tanner, the smithy, the cloth dyer and the charcoal maker came the malodorous scents distinct to those various trades. As in every holding of good size, among the pungent odors mingled sweet aromas—bread baking in the common oven, the herbs in the apothecary, fresh cut wood at the carpenter's shed.

Marian walked out of the smithy, a daughter on either side of her, hands clasped and swaying gently as the three made their way across the outer bailey toward the keep. People stepped aside to allow her to pass by. Stephen compared the parting crowd to those he'd seen move aside for nobility—until he saw a woman sneer down at the twins and cross herself.

Ignorant bitch.

The condemnation came hard and fast on a lightning bolt of anger. The crowd parted for fear of two adorable little girls, mistrusted and thus avoided because they were twins.

"Superstition runs deep," Edwin commented, frowning.

Stephen didn't trust himself to answer. His ire yet roiled. If he opened his mouth, he'd be tempted to berate the entire crowd, at the top of his voice, for their lack of wits and cruelty. Perhaps he should. Perhaps 'twas time someone did.

Except it wasn't his place to tell the people of Branwick how they should think or act. William or Carolyn or Branwick's priest must do so for the scolding to have impact. Even then, many would hold on to their deepseated fears.

Had Corwin and Ardith faced the same shunning as children? Stephen was ashamed to admit he had no notion if his best friend had suffered simply because he'd been born at the same time as his sister.

Not all at Branwick treated Audra and Lyssa as less than human. William fair doted on the girls, and Carolyn accepted them. Even Edwin spoke fondly of them, displayed nary a qualm of picking up Lyssa on the night he'd been asked to assist Marian.

Calmer now, Stephen noted that not everyone in the bailey shunned the girls, either. Here and there a hand raised in greeting, a voice called out a good morn. Marian passed through the gate into the inner bailey without mishap.

Perhaps he'd overreacted.

Still disturbed, he turned to Edwin. "How long has it been since you have taken to the practice yard?"

"Several days. Think to end our contest at sword point?"

The jest held a hint of a challenge, and Stephen loved a challenge. Even the verbal sparring with Edwin seemed a contest. 'Twas becoming a matter of honor to see which of them claimed the last word.

"Nay, though you might oblige me by succumbing to unaccustomed vigorous exercise."

"Not a chance, pup."

"Pup, is it? I will have you know a Wilmont trained pup can best a cur of any other breed with ease!"

Edwin's eyes narrowed. "Wood practice swords or steel blades?"

"Wood. I should hate to perchance injure an *old* man with a sharp blade."

"Fetch your gambeson."

Edwin grumbled all the way to the keep. Stephen kept his peace, enjoying the man's discomfort. Dammit all, but he liked Edwin—his rival, the man supposed to be his enemy. At some time in the past week the two of them had reached an accord, which boded ill for his quest for Carolyn. Had Edwin lost sight of the prize? Doubtless not.

Stephen's only thought when suggesting a bout in the practice yard had been to work off his irritation over seeing the girls shunned. Mayhap, in the process, he'd best remind Edwin that their truce was only temporary. Only one man could win William's contest, and Stephen had no intention of losing.

Once inside the great hall, Edwin stomped up the stairs to fetch his gambeson. Though he knew he shouldn't, Stephen lagged behind—to look for Marian.

Girlish giggles from behind the draperies surrounding William's bed gave him her location. Drawn by the irresistible temptation to catch another glimpse of her, Stephen maneuvered around to where he could see the open curtained side of the bed from a bit of a distance.

Marian perched on the foot of the bed, smiling at her girls who talked to William with waving hands and exaggerated gestures, saying something about a race.

'Twas Marian's smile which held him enthralled. Her eyes sparkled, her face lit with joy so profound it near took his breath away.

Her girls were her world, her joys and sorrows. In that moment he knew that if Marian had nothing else—not even a repaired roof—her life would be complete so long as she had her daughters.

"Someday," Carolyn said softly, startling him. He'd been so intent on Marian he hadn't heard Carolyn come alongside. She looked longingly at the girls. "Father so wants grandchildren."

Carolyn was William's only hope for grandchildren, the continuing of his family, heirs to all he'd built. If his delight in his nieces was any indication, the old man would be in heaven with grandchildren.

Stephen's children. His own heirs, too. But he was thinking too far ahead. First he must marry Carolyn, which was not yet a certainty. Still, the thought of having his own wee ones to hold and watch grow wasn't quite so unnerving anymore.

"Twin boys, perhaps?" Stephen chided her.

"Boys would be nice, but I have not the patience for

two so close in age as Marian's. One at a time will do me fine.''

Carolyn grasped him by the elbow and tugged. He resented being led away, though his feet moved.

She waved him toward a bench. "I know we are not allowed to discuss the particulars of the contest, however, I do not think it against Father's dictates to ask if you and Edwin are nearly finished with your inspection.''

Stephen ignored the bench, preferring to lean against the trestle table, reluctant to discuss any details of the contest. Besides, he hadn't much time. Edwin would be down soon, gambeson donned and looking for a fight.

"I should think another fortnight ought to be sufficient.''

"Another two weeks? Why so long?''

"Your list was long, and we have not yet visited the other two holdings.''

Carolyn pouted. "Certes, one would think 'twould take the two of you less time to do the inspection as it did me to make out the list to begin with! Can you not hurry this contest along?''

The request came out in a whine that grated on Stephen's nerves. He dismissed the irritating appeal as understandable impatience on Carolyn's part.

"Would you have me do less than a thorough inspection, and possibly miss some vital point, causing me to lose?''

Her sigh conveyed annoyance. "Nay, but I do not wish to die an old woman before 'tis completed, either. Mayhap, I could ask Father to remove a few items from the list, then you might be done the quicker—'' she ran a finger along his jawline "—and have more time to spend with me.''

So that was it. Carolyn felt neglected. Truly, he'd spent little time with her, and none of it alone. Unfortunately, by the time he finished with Ivo each day, 'twas near time for evening meal. From supper on, too many people, including William and Edwin, hovered in the great hall until time to retire. Since Carolyn and her ladies always went upstairs before the men were ready to bed down, there hadn't been time for private talks, much less a kiss, certainly not the opportunity to arrange a tryst.

Time to rectify his mistake. Time for another gift, perhaps this evening.

Stephen glanced at the stairway. No Edwin yet. The maids near the hearth seemed occupied. The bed curtains blocked William's view of the hall. And Marian's.

Resolved to please the woman he intended to wed, Stephen focused on Carolyn's lovely face, on her wide brown eyes, on a mouth he deemed kissable when not marred by a pout.

"You are right. We should spend more time together." He rose and gently cupped her cheek. "What say we begin now?"

He drew her nearer. Her lips parted, her eyes closing.

He kissed her full on the mouth and felt—nothing.

No lust. No desire. Not a wisp of interest. Damn. That had never happened to him before.

Confused, he broke the kiss. Carolyn slowly opened her eyes; the tip of her tongue tasted her bottom lip.

The sensual action should have tossed him into agony. *Nothing.*

"Aye, we should get to know each other better," she whispered. "Tonight, after all are asleep—"

"Nay, not in your father's keep." He chuckled to hide his panic over what might happen if Carolyn came to his bed and *nothing* happened. "More to the point, not with Edwin upstairs. If he should hear or even suspect we lay together, and inform your father—nay, we must not risk it."

To his relief, she nodded an agreement. "'Twill be hard to wait, but I suppose we must."

"We must." Stephen stepped around her, anxious to escape. "Till later, my lady," he said with a slight bow, and with measured steps, crossed the hall and headed up the stairs.

By the time he reached his bedchamber, his hands trembled.

What the devil had come over him? He'd never kissed a beautiful woman—hell, any woman!—without his body responding in some way. Damnation, all he had to do was *look* at Marian—

Marian. Her presence behind the bed curtain had caused this affliction. Perhaps, as had happened at Westminster Palace, his mind and body had been too aware of a former lover to respond fully to another. That was all. He had to rid himself of the distraction of Marian and all would be well. The possibility of failure to perform his husbandly duty to Carolyn, should he win her, was simply too horrifying to contemplate.

Stephen shrugged into his gambeson, thankful he'd arranged a practice session with Edwin. Perhaps, while they crossed swords, he could figure out how to banish Marian from his head.

Chapter Seven

Wood slapping wood didn't produce the satisfying urgency of steel striking steel. Stephen missed the heft and balance of his sword, the metal hilt warming to his hand, the blade becoming an extension of his arm.

Still, as he fended off Edwin's well-aimed blow, he couldn't complain overmuch. He'd chosen wood practice swords apurpose, knowing his fighting skills far superior to Edwin's—superior to most men's due to the demanding standards of Wilmont's weapons masters. Those knights in charge of training squires, men-at-arms and knights alike settled for no less than perfection.

From the sons of the noble family of Wilmont they'd expected more, and the sons hadn't disappointed them.

He didn't want to injure Edwin. Prove who was the better swordsman, aye, but not hurt his opponent. 'Twould not be wise to make a martyr of his rival.

Damn, but the exercise felt good, despite the heat of the day and the weight of his hauberk. Sweat trickled along the back of his neck and beaded on his forehead. His muscles responded to the pleasurable strain of maintaining his balance while executing the thrust and withdraw of attack and defend.

Edwin pressed an attack with a flurry of quick strokes, driving Stephen back, which he allowed. The maneuver both tired Edwin and pleased the crowd gathered around the tiltyard. Let them cheer and wager their coin on Edwin. Somewhere in the crowd, Stephen didn't doubt, Armand was taking wagers and would be wealthier for it in the end.

Had Carolyn come out to the tiltyard to watch? Had Marian and the girls? He wondered but didn't allow his gaze to stray beyond Edwin's flushed face.

Sensing the nearness of the crowd, Stephen disengaged and swiftly sidestepped, bringing his mock sword around in a punishing but not contest-ending arc. Edwin met the blow with a solid block, his balance wavering ever so slightly.

Stephen took advantage—a slow, feral smile the only warning of his intent. With precision and speed, Stephen let loose, holding nothing back. In a varied attack of swift strokes and sweeping arcs, he pushed Edwin hard, confident his opponent's defense would soon break.

Nothing could have surprised Stephen more than the sound of Armand's high, shrill whistle, a signal used at Wilmont to bring fighting to an immediate end. He nearly obeyed. Except he wasn't at Wilmont and Edwin wouldn't halt, not understanding the signal.

Instead, he executed a series of thrusts to bring Edwin's weapon to the desired defensive position necessary—then swept the mock sword from his rival's hand.

Edwin stared at his empty hand, so stunned Stephen almost apologized. Almost. He turned toward where the signal had come from. Armand crossed the tiltyard at a run.

"My lord, a messenger has arrived from Wilmont. The baron desires an immediate response."

Stephen looked around for a man clad in Wilmont colors of scarlet trimmed with gold. Donald stood near the gate to the inner bailey. Both man and horse looked exhausted.

He tossed the practice sword toward a nearby soldier and briskly headed for the messenger, Armand at his side.

"Hail, Donald! What news?"

Donald smiled and held out a scroll tied with a red ribbon. "Glad it is I am to see you, my lord. Your brother worried you might have already…well…read and then I will explain further if need be."

Stephen took the hefty scroll—one of Gerard's infamous missives. Gerard might be a man of few words, but give him quill and parchment and he rambled on forever.

"You look done in. Come have an ale whilst I read this tome. Armand, have the horse rubbed down and fed."

Armand led the horse away. Stephen untied the ribbon and began walking slowly toward the keep.

What he read chilled him to the bone and halted his steps.

A bit over a week ago, Corwin had been escorting supply wagons to one of Gerard's holdings in southern England. Before Corwin got that far, however, he learned that Judith Canmore, a royal heiress, had been kidnapped by ruffians. Corwin rode off to rescue her, headed north. Neither Corwin nor Judith had been heard from since.

Stephen chafed at Gerard's emphatic order to remain at Branwick in case Corwin showed up there. "Hell-fire."

"His lordship feared you might have already heard of

Corwin's pursuit and left Branwick to try to find them. The sheriffs and barons hereabouts have all been alerted to keep watch for the pair. If it helps, the baron said to tell you Lady Ardith does not fear for her twin.''

The assurance eased his fears, some. The twins shared a bond Stephen didn't completely understand, probably never would. But if Corwin had suffered an injury, or worse, Ardith would know *something* amiss with her twin. Still, his friend could be in deep trouble, and the order to remain at Branwick knotted his innards.

Stephen occasionally disobeyed Gerard's orders, but not without extremely good reason.

''Has the search turned up any sign of them?''

''Not as yet. The baron feels that is good. If Corwin rescued the lady and is being hunted, he may have gone into hiding.''

Having traveled widely and often with Corwin as a companion, Stephen knew of several places where his friend could go to ground. He could give Gerard directions to those worth searching. Feeling less useless, he led the way up the stairs and into the great hall.

Not spotting Carolyn, he approached the two maids who were sweeping out the hearth. He sent one to find Carolyn with a request for a quill and ink, and the other to the kitchen for food for Donald.

With cups of ale soon in hand, Stephen waved Donald to a trestle table. ''Sit while I make my way through the rest of this. I assume you are to return to Wilmont immediately?''

''Aye. I will leave as soon as you are done.''

Naturally. Gerard expected no less.

Stephen sat on a bench opposite Donald and read the rest of the message. Gerard wrote of his wife and sons, and of his hope Ardith would have the babe soon so order might be restored to his household and peace to his marriage. He complained of how his wife balked at his reasonable restrictions.

At the not unexpected news that Richard had married Lucinda of Northbryre in a private, quiet ceremony at Wilmont, Stephen smiled. The two were a good match, though he doubted Gerard was too pleased. He couldn't wait to hear the tale of how Richard broke the news to Gerard.

Of course, Gerard wanted a report on how things went at Branwick. Stephen had no idea how to tell Gerard about the contest without sending his brother into either a rage or fits of laughter. Best he not mention the contest at all.

Feminine voices came from the stairway coming down from the upper floor. The women must have been in the solar. Carolyn carried the writing tools he asked for and strode toward the table. Marian barely glanced at him, then led her girls straight out the door.

He wasn't hurt. Like hell he wasn't.

Mayhap her avoidance of him wouldn't bother him so much if he knew the reason. Every time he broached the subject, however, she negated his concern and pushed him further away. He'd not mention Marian to Gerard, either. What could he say?

The girl I first loved is here at Branwick and she hates me. She's grown into a beautiful woman, a widow with two adorable daughters, lives in a hut in the hamlet where she shouldn't be living, and fires my blood as my intended wife doesn't.

Stephen inwardly shuddered at the last thought.

"Bad news?" Carolyn asked.

"Aye," he answered, relieved she couldn't read his thoughts.

He took the ink and quill; she set the sand on the table.

"Are you called to Wilmont?"

"Not as yet. Where might I find the sheriff in these parts?"

"York, but whatever would you want with the sheriff?"

"A friend of mine is missing." Stephen turned over the last page of Gerard's missive and began his list with directions to a secluded cave near Oxford. "Donald, tell Gerard these are places where Corwin might hide. There are two near here which I will not list, but check myself. I will also have a word with the sheriff in York."

"Um, my lord, I am sure the sheriff of York has already been told."

"Then I will remind him."

A maid put a trencher piled high with cheese, broken meat and bread in front of Donald, ending all argument as the messenger tucked into the food like a man half-starved.

Carolyn slid onto the bench beside Stephen. Though she said nothing she fidgeted—shifting on the bench, playing with the container of sand. 'Twas the drumming of her fingernails on the table that finally set his teeth on edge. He couldn't very well take the mistress of the keep to task while in Donald's presence.

"Donald, I believe your ale cup needs filling. You will find the barrel in yon corner."

Donald glanced at his cup, not even half-empty. He looked about to object before he realized Stephen's suggestion was truly an order.

"Shall I refill your cup too, my lord?"

"My thanks."

When Donald was out of hearing range, Stephen turned to Carolyn. "You have something to say?"

"You intend to go into York?" Her tone could have frozen a rushing river.

"I am."

"What of your obligation here?"

The contest. His friend was in trouble and she was concerned with the damned contest.

"York is only a day's ride from here. I will be gone three, four days at most. 'Tis the least I can do to aid a man who has guarded my back more times than I can count."

"Your brother seems to have the search underway and well in hand. You waste precious time on a situation you can do nothing about. I see no reason for you to leave Branwick."

No reason important to Carolyn. Whether she approved or not, come tomorrow morn he'd be on the road to York. He wouldn't rest well until he heard for himself that the sheriff made an effort to find Corwin.

"I do not abandon the contest, Carolyn, merely postpone it for a few days."

"The last time you told me you would be gone for a few weeks, you did not return for three months!" Carolyn rose from the bench. "I will not wait so long again, Stephen of Wilmont. Be too long gone and you may return to find another man has taken your place."

Stephen watched her flounce off, wondering if that would be so bad. Aye, it would. He'd made too much progress toward his goal to give up now.

Stephen finished the list and then saw Donald out Branwick's gate before he sought an audience with William, a courtesy he must perform to remain in his lordship's good graces. He approached the bedside with resolve in place and court manners firmly in mind.

William wore a frown, not a good omen. "I hear you

are leaving on the morn, something about a friend gone missing.''

Carolyn must have complained to her father. So be it.

He sat down on the stool by the bedside. ''Corwin is more than a friend. We grew up together, trained for knighthood with each other, have fought side by side in more battles than I care to remember. He is more brother to me than a friend.'' Stephen smiled. ''Truth to tell, we are now related. Corwin's sister is the baron's wife.''

''A call of family duty, then.''

''Somewhat.''

William nodded. '''Tis important, duty to family. You have my leave to go, and godspeed.''

Stephen chose not to comment that he hadn't asked William's leave. ''My thanks.''

''Can we here at Branwick assist you in some manner?''

The offer took Stephen by surprise. Truly, he'd been prepared for William to simply bid him good riddance.

''A gracious offer. A few days worth of victuals for myself and Armand would be appreciated.'' Stephen rose, preparing to bid William good day, then thought of another task in need of attention before he left for York. ''In his missive, Gerard mentioned that Richard has married. I should send a gift. Might there be a craftsman on your estate you might recommend?''

William thought about it a moment. ''Truly, lad, I leave such matters in Carolyn's hands. You might have a word with her.''

''Your daughter is not pleased with me at the moment. Mayhap I shall have a look around the merchant shops in York.''

''If you do not wish to consult Carolyn, then you could ask Marian for advice. She would know what gifts are appropriate for a noble couple.'' William's eyes lit up. ''Of course, Marian. Have you seen the lovely embroidery she does? Mayhap you could talk her into decorating table linens or some such.''

Right now he didn't think he could talk Marian into giving him the time of day.

''I shall consider your suggestion.''

''Well you should. Marian is truly gifted. Her designs are only exceeded by her exacting stitch.''

''Talented, is she?''

''By my word, none can compare. 'Struth, she is securing my place in heaven with her deft hand. If you speak with her this afternoon, she might have a design readied for your approval when you return. And while you are out there, tell her I believe another altar cloth is in order. A design in silver and dark green this time, I think.''

Buying William's way into heaven? With altar cloths? A strange notion, but Stephen didn't inquire further, the possibility of a way to connect with Marian driving all else from his mind.

Working together on a project tended to bring the people involved into frequent close contact, and most often fostered camaraderie. Could so simple a thing as having Marian embroider table linens help bring about the much longed for peace between them?

While the girls napped, Marian used the quiet time to work with wax tablet and stylus. The storybook lay on the table, open to the illustration of the first story.

Adam and Eve's banishment from the garden.

The painter had drawn forth a hiss from the snake. Marian was determined to learn how to do the same in needlework.

Gads, 'twould make a beautiful tapestry. Her fingers fair itched for cloth and yarn. To do this picture justice, however, she'd need a large loom in a big room, and far more yarn in brighter colors than Branwick's dyer could supply.

Marian knew Carolyn would allow her the use of Branwick's loom, but she couldn't bring herself to ask. 'Twould mean spending too many days at Branwick. 'Twas easier to ignore those who couldn't accept the twins when not forced to face them every day for long hours.

Yet the temptation lingered to weave a tapestry large enough to hang in the great hall of Branwick Keep, whether of the banishment or some other scene of William's preference.

If of the banishment, she'd also be tempted to make the snake hiss not in victory, but from failure. All human woes could be traced back to Eve listening to an evil snake. How much more pleasant the world would be if not for Eve's weakness.

Marian turned the book to view the snake at a different angle. He certainly was beautiful when colored in green, blue and black. Maybe that's why her attempts to capture him in wax failed so miserably, lack of color.

A knock drew her to her feet. Distracted by the snake she opened the door without first looking out the window. To her dismay, temptation had come knocking, clad all in black, from raven hair to leather boots.

She resisted the urge to answer Stephen's smile, to look too deeply into his bright-green eyes. Her heart beat too fast. She should close the door.

"William sent me," he said, his voice low and mellow and seductive. He looked behind her and saw the girls sleeping on their pallets. "Have I come at a bad time? I could return later."

Marian shook her head. "What does William want?"

He leaned forward and wrapped his hand around the doorjamb. "Might I come in? On my word, I will ask you no more questions about the past and I will try not to wake the girls."

Marian backed up a step, away from the male scent of him she'd remember forever. He took her retreat as permission to enter the hut.

What difference if he were within or without? If he kept to his promise she'd have no reason to throw him out, and she couldn't send him away until learning of William's request.

Stephen walked over to the table and put his fingertips on the illustration she'd spent the past hour studying. He glanced toward the wax tablet, then looked up at her.

"Your uncle said you possessed a deft hand, and I see he had the right of it. Even in wax your snake comes alive."

Alive, but not hissing. Leaving the door open so she might have air to breathe, Marian approached the table, irritated he'd seen the sketch. No one except her and the girls viewed her handiwork until completed in cloth and yarn, until Stephen.

"William's request?"

Stephen's brow furrowed. "He wishes you to make him another altar cloth. A design in dark green and silver, he said. What I find confusing is his belief you are somehow securing his place in heaven with altar cloths."

Marian could hardly believe William had sent a man of Stephen's rank on such a simple errand. Any servant could have delivered the message. Then again, maybe Stephen had just proved the handier messenger.

"The cloths are of a certain size, made to fit the altar in the cathedral in York. For each cloth sent, the archbishop grants William an indulgence." Marian had to smile at William's fanciful vision. "My uncle thinks of each indulgence as one thinks of a coin. He believes if he has enough of them in hand to pay Saint Peter, the saint will allow him unhindered passage into heaven."

Amused, Stephen shook his head. "I suppose, as one grows older, one thinks of such things. I imagine his ill health makes thoughts of the hereafter more immediate."

"One supposes." With his message delivered Stephen could now leave, get out of her hut and take his overwhelming presence with him. "Tell William I will work up a design for his approval."

He nodded at what she thought a perfectly understandable dismissal, but made no move toward the door. He flipped the pages of the storybook to another illustration. Noah leading the animals into the ark.

Stephen's smile widened as he pointed to the corner of the picture. "Now here is a snake of a different sort. No threat to him at all. I wonder if the same monk painted both?" He tilted his head, studying the picture. "Possible. Look here at Noah's face and compare it to Adam's. Very similar."

Taken aback, Marian stepped closer, noting Stephen's acutely correct observation. "Similar, indeed. Yet this painting has a flavor of playfulness the other does not. Look at the lion. He seems to grin."

"As well he should, all considered." Stephen turned slightly and perched on the edge of the table. "So, what types of designs do you stitch on an altar cloth? Not grinning lions, certainly.''

He made himself far too comfortable to suit Marian. His comment on grinning lions hit a nerve.

''The archbishop is partial to crosses evenly spaced between vinelike swirls. I dare not divert from the tried-and-true for fear he might withhold William's indulgence.''

''But you would like to.''

Did he know her so well, or did he guess?

''I would.''

He nodded, as though he'd made some important point. ''Then mayhap, while you stitch the tried-and-true for your uncle, you might design something more fanciful for me. Well, not truly for me but for my brother Richard, as a gift. He just got married.''

Had she heard aright? ''You think an embroidered altar cloth an appropriate gift for your brother?''

He shook his head, slightly mussing his raven locks. A spark of mischief lit his eyes. She swallowed hard against the endearing countenance. Stephen wore his charm as naturally as his own skin, to devastating effect.

''Perhaps table linens or towels or some such. Choose as you think best as a wedding gift. The design, however, must be fanciful. Richard's new wife has led a hard life, without much humor or play. I should like my gift to her appropriate and practical, but bring a smile to her heart when she sees it. Is that possible?''

Marian's head whirled with possibilities. ''Certes. Have you colors in mind? Any preferences?''

He held out his hands, palms up. ''None whatever. So long as the gift pleases the eye and heart, I leave the way of its making to the creator. I shall pay for all materials, of course, plus a bit extra for your time.''

Marian bit her bottom lip to hold her excitement inside. To have free rein over such a project! Already she imagined bold, playful patterns hemming a table-size piece of pristine, tight-weave linen.

"Indigo and saffron make for pleasing designs."

He shrugged a shoulder. "Your choice. Truth to tell, I shall need two gifts, the other a christening gift for Gerard's as yet unborn child. A wool blanket, perhaps?"

Table linens for Richard. A blanket for the baron's child. Stephen paying the costs without restrictions. Near giddy, she crossed the room to a chest in the corner. From it she fetched two small, soft woolen blankets. After partially unfolding each, she spread them on the table.

"I made these for the twins. Would a similar design do?"

His expression changing to thoughtful, almost tender, he ran his fingertips reverently over the lambs on Lyssa's blanket, then the kittens on Audra's.

Marian held her breath. Beyond reason, she wanted Stephen to like his daughters' blankets, lovingly stitched toward the end of her pregnancy when she'd been too huge to move about comfortably.

"Perfect," he said softly. "How about lion cubs for the cub of the lion of Wilmont? A good choice?"

Relieved, and embarrassed for coveting a compliment, she quickly folded the blankets. "Aye. When must it be done?"

"The babe's? Oh two, three weeks, I would guess. The table linens—whenever you complete them. Are we agreed?"

"'Twill take me a day or two to work up designs."

"No need to rush. I leave in the morning for York. I

doubt I will return for four days or so. Soon enough then.''

Marian clutched the blankets. Stephen was leaving Branwick. ''Why York?''

He briefly told her of his missing friend.

Stephen's upset, his anger and frustration, rang clear if not loudly. He feared for Corwin as if a brother. Compassion lifted her hand to his shoulder.

''I hope you find him, if not for his sake, for yours.''

''Do you?''

She couldn't answer, the words stuck in her throat. The touch meant to comfort became a caress, her body tingling with awareness of the man she'd wanted to embrace ever since he'd come back into her life.

Desire swirled in his eyes and her body answered with swift, painful longing. She recognized his intent, yearned for his lips on hers just once more.

He stood, his hands sliding up her arms to caress her shoulders. His arms came around her, entrapping her within. His mouth sought hers, gently, persuasively. She needed no persuasion. She leaned into Stephen, the only man she'd ever kissed, had ever wanted to kiss.

She craved more, far more, knowing what heights this man could take her to. Her knees went weak with the memory of a solitary moment of bliss. She wanted the pleasure again. She wanted Stephen.

He broke the kiss, cradled her head against his shoulder. Even through her hard, unsteady breathing, she felt him shudder.

Nothing had changed. Not in six years.

''I have to go.'' His voice was low and harsh.

It took her a moment to remember he was leaving Branwick for York. But he'd be back, wouldn't he?

''You will come back?''

"On my honor."

The second kiss nearly knocked her senseless. Foolishness beyond belief, but if not for the girls napping on their nearby pallets, she'd be sore tempted to pull him down in the dirt and strip him bare.

She held on to that thread of sanity, the cord between mother and children. It pulled her up short of making a huge mistake.

Marian suddenly understood Eve's downfall. If she'd been alone with the snake, if he'd held out the promise of heavenly bliss, and spoken to her in the voice of an irresistible man—low, mellow, seductive—Eve hadn't stood a chance.

Nor did she if she didn't end this kiss, send Stephen away. She pushed, he backed up. The kiss ended and ripped her apart. He looked as tortured as she felt.

"I will be back," he whispered, then hurried out of the hut.

Marian sat on the stool and buried her face in the soft, woolen blankets now warm from heated bodies and scented with the dusky male scent of the girls' father.

Dear God, what have I done?

She shook with the enormity of her mistake. She'd betrayed Carolyn as well as herself. Not only had she let Stephen into the hut, she'd let him back into her heart. And this time, when she lost him again, the heartache would be so much worse.

Chapter Eight

In the middle of a square of soft ivory wool, a lion cub snoozed, tired from chasing butterflies, stalking beetles and cavorting with his cub mates—the activities depicted along the blanket's edges.

Marian considered the blanket the most creative piece she'd ever done, as well as the most skilled. For the better part of two weeks she'd spent nearly every moment of her free time stitching the cubs, taking great care to keep the yarn smooth and the tension even. After all, the blanket was meant for the child of the baron of Wilmont, who could command the best. Marian meant her work to exceed that expectation.

Even this morning she worked carefully, though she kept glancing at the chest in the corner which contained the fabric and thread the dyer's helper delivered yesterday. The white table linen beckoned hard. To her request for indigo and saffron thread she'd added scarlet and forest green. The pattern she'd chosen, based on the beautiful scrollwork surrounding the picture of Noah and his animals, would be bright and fanciful, as Stephen wanted.

She hoped Stephen approved, but considering what

happened the last time he visited the hut, she wasn't about to get close enough to him to ask. He'd returned from York several days ago, apparently disappointed in not finding his friend. He'd returned to Branwick, but not to her hut. He, too, must have realized their kisses unwise, the temptation for more irresistible. Best he stay away.

"Mama, Carolyn comes!" Audra called from outside.

Through the doorway Marian saw Carolyn bend down to give each girl a brief hug, then shoo them back to play. A large basket containing Branwick's healing herbs and medicinals hung from the crook of her arm. Someone in the hamlet must be sick enough to bring the lady of the keep out to attend the stricken peasant.

Carolyn stepped through the doorway, waving a cooling hand in front of her face.

"Who is ill?" Marian asked.

Carolyn put the basket on the table and plopped down onto a stool. "Carla. From her husband's description of her ailment, she merely needs a physic. Nothing serious."

"Then why did you not send a physic home with the blacksmith for his wife?"

"Boredom and curiosity." Carolyn leaned forward to touch the blanket. "Oh, my. This is precious, Marian. Almost done?"

"I should finish it in a day or two. Tell Stephen I will send it in with one of the blacksmith's lads after I finish."

"Why not bring it in yourself? Father is not pleased about your absence, even though he did recommend your work to Stephen. Your sending the girls to the keep is all that keeps him from summoning you."

Twice now she'd sent Audra and Lyssa with Dirk and

Kirk on their way into Branwick of a morn. After their visit with William, one of Branwick's guards brought the twins home. The arrangement gave Marian extra time to work on the blanket, and allowed her to avoid Stephen completely.

"So long as your father sees the girls on occasion, he will be content. If I am to have this blanket done, I need to work on it. The baron's wife is very near her time. Any word as yet?"

"The last messenger from Wilmont merely brought news of the lack of progress on finding Corwin. Stephen is near distraught over the situation. I wish the man would show up so Stephen would get his mind back to the contest."

Thrice Marian had seen scarlet-and-gold-clad messengers ride past her hut. One of those messengers would soon bring word of the babe's birth.

"How goes the contest?"

Carolyn gave an aggrieved sigh. "Nearly done. All that remains are the three items which require Edwin and Stephen to visit Father's other estates. Stephen balks at leaving Branwick in case his friend should show up." She crossed her arms. "What drives me witless is Father's easy acceptance of the delays. According to him, there is no need for haste."

Marian wished the contest over with, too. Depending upon who won, she would either stay or leave.

The decision hadn't come easily, but all considered, she saw no choice except to leave Branwick if Stephen married Carolyn.

Oddly enough, 'twas Stephen who gave her the means to leave. With the coin he paid for the gifts, she and the girls could set up residence in a town, possibly near a cathedral or abbey. If Stephen was willing to pay for her handiwork, so might others, giving her income to keep the girls fed and clothed.

"Mayhap the next messenger from Wilmont will bring better news about Stephen's friend."

"Either that or word of the babe's birth. Stephen is sure his brother will call him home for the child's christening. Then he would be off again and only heaven knows when he'd return."

Assuming he returned. If Stephen must leave Branwick for an extended period, would he then give up the contest? Or might Carolyn give up on Stephen? Either was possible. Then Edwin might stand a better chance of marrying Carolyn and Marian's worries would be over.

On that bright thought, Marian asked, "How is Edwin?"

Carolyn worried her bottom lip. "Marian, you were not serious when you said you might take up with Edwin if I do not marry him, were you?"

Marian felt a twinge of triumph, but hid the reaction from her cousin. "Any reason why I should not? If you do not want him, he is bound to marry another. Why not me?"

"Because I would hate it if the two of you made a match. I know he must marry again. He needs an heir. I think I could bear his marrying a stranger. But you?" Carolyn shook her head. "'Twould make me miserable. He already likes you so could grow to love you."

Not in an age, but telling Carolyn so served no purpose.

"He could also grow to love a stranger. 'Twould be easy, I think, to become fond of someone who shares one's table and bed every day. You were fond of your husbands, were you not?"

Carolyn shrugged. "Perhaps. Sharing meals and bed play does not necessarily lead to love. Stephen says his parents barely tolerated each other."

"They must have shared something in common. They produced three sons."

"Nay, only two. The middle son, Richard, is base born. His mother was a peasant."

Base born? She'd heard Stephen speak of Richard and he'd never made the distinction. Knowing the advantage and standing Richard enjoyed, she could only conclude Stephen's father hadn't made the distinction either, but acknowledged his bastard and raised him as his own.

Apparently Stephen's mother had been forced to endure her husband's infidelity, and perhaps his parents' intolerance of each other influenced Stephen's view of marriage. But then most nobles married for many reasons other than affection, as Stephen proposed with Carolyn.

Still, Marian wasn't about to let Carolyn get comfortable over Edwin's fate if she let him go, not when her cousin had the unusual chance to marry for love.

"I will take your feelings into consideration, Carolyn, but I must say Edwin is certainly a fine catch for any woman."

"How can you be so horrid?"

Marian looked pointedly at her cousin. "I have a good tutor. Are you not being most horrid to Edwin?"

Thoroughly miffed, Carolyn rose and grabbed her basket. "By the by, I meant to tell you about Father. He improves. He can now flex the fingers of his left hand, which you would have seen had you bothered to visit."

Marian gasped. "Carolyn, that is wonderful news!"

"Perhaps," Carolyn commented, then left on her errand.

Stunned by both the good news and Carolyn's reaction, Marian put aside the blanket. Why wasn't Carolyn overjoyed with William's progress?

If William regained mobility, then he could resume his duties and…oh dear…then Carolyn would be forced to give up the duties to her father, duties she thoroughly enjoyed.

She'd been acting in her father's stead for months. If William could act on his own, Carolyn would again be relegated to the status of mere chatelaine, in charge of only the household. The duty her father thought her most fitted for. The duty Edwin believed the *only* duty a woman should have charge of. Of all the men in Carolyn's life, only Stephen thought her fit for more than overseeing the cooking and cleaning and weaving.

If William recovered, Carolyn would fight all the harder to marry Stephen.

'Twas after evening meal when Stephen approached Marian's hut with a mixture of excitement and dread. Ardith had delivered of a healthy baby boy two days ago, and Gerard called Stephen home to attend the christening, adding an invitation to Carolyn if Stephen wished to bring her along.

Carolyn readily accepted the invitation. Unfortunately William, in the guise of being helpful, suggested Edwin accompany them as escort. Stephen protested the necessity. Edwin thought it a grand idea. William insisted— and so Edwin was going, too.

But at the moment, nearing Marian's door, none of that seemed to matter overmuch. He'd come to collect the present for the babe, which Carolyn told him was near completion and utterly adorable. Problem was he found the blanket's creator adorable and damn near impossible to resist.

Resist he would, however.

He'd given the matter a great deal of thought while in York. His strong attraction to Marian was the result of memories of their brief affair so long ago. She'd been his first lover, and he hers, the trysts sweet and illicit. Naturally, his curiosity urged him to learn if bedding her now would be as memorable.

Their kisses should never have happened, the first sweet and tender, the second hot enough to burn the hut down around them. He'd taken advantage of her effort to give comfort and nearly gone up in flames. Hellfire, he even promised her to return, at her prompting.

He couldn't trust himself alone with her. Marian must have come to her senses, too, for she'd not sought him out.

From here on he'd treat Marian as an old and dear friend, and get on with winning the contest and Carolyn. Away from Marian, he might even work up a wisp of lust for his intended.

Faint candlelight flickered behind the shutters. He need only knock on the door, collect the blanket and pay Marian, and be back in the keep before full night descended.

Stephen took a resolved breath and raised his hand to knock, but before his knuckles landed, from within he heard a young voice shout a defiant "Nay!"

Audra? Sweet little Audra?

"'Tis all there is." Even through the closed door Stephen heard Marian's weariness. "If you choose not to eat the porridge then you go to sleep hungry."

"Hate porridge!"

"You do not."

"Do, too!"

"That will be quite enough, young lady." A pause. "Audra, I warn you, put that down or—"

Stephen winced at the clatter that interrupted Marian's scolding, picturing pots and bowls scattered over the floor. Now might not be the best time to visit. However, he intended to leave on the morrow at first light, so needed to collect the blanket now. Mayhap his arrival might help cool tempers.

"To your pallet!"

"Nay!"

Stephen knocked firmly, wondering if either mother or daughter heard. One did. The inside bolt slid.

"Audra, wait!"

The door flung open. Before him stood the most forlorn child he'd ever seen. Tears streamed down Audra's cheeks, her frown deep and desperate.

He held out his arms. "Come here, little one."

She stood still, studying him with glistening eyes, likely wondering if he were truly friend or foe.

He wiggled his fingers. "Come," he said again, still gently but with a bit more command.

Audra's bottom lip trembled. He couldn't stand it. He picked her up. She wrapped her arms and legs around him and buried her wet face against his shoulder. She breathed hard, an effort to hold back sobs.

Wonderful. Now what did he do with her?

He closed the door and sought out the mother for guidance. Marian sat on the floor between the girls' pallets, cradling Lyssa, a wet rag pressed to the girl's temple. Headache, he realized. Marian looked both angry enough to spit and weary to the bone. No help there.

He'd never seen the hut in less than neat order. The place was a mess, to say the least. Apparently Audra had decided to wreak havoc while her mother was occupied with Lyssa. She'd done an excellent job of it.

Still at a loss, Stephen rubbed Audra's back, wondering what it must be like for Marian, trapped in one room with two young children. He'd go mad. What would one do if both girls went on a rampage at the same time?

The incident reinforced his belief that Marian shouldn't be living in this hut without help. Without protection. Audra shouldn't have opened the door before asking who was without.

He cradled Audra's head. ''You know better than to open the door without first asking who is on the other side, do you not?''

She nodded against his shoulder.

''Swear me an oath you will ask next time, no matter how angry you are.''

Audra took a deep breath. ''I swear.''

An oath too easily given by one too young. Stephen could only hope she'd remember to have a care.

''I assume you came for your blanket,'' Marian commented.

Her anger had cooled somewhat, which only allowed her weariness to come to the fore.

''Aye.'' He righted the pot on the table but ignored the pool of porridge dripping off the edge into the rushes. ''Carolyn told me it was near finished.''

'''Tis done. I will get it.'' She removed the rag from Lyssa's head, shifted as if to put the girl down.

''Stay where you are.'' Stephen tugged Audra's thick, black braid. ''Audra can show me.''

''In the chest,'' she said, not raising her head.

Stephen suspected she wasn't yet ready to face her mother. He squatted down by the chest and lifted the lid.

There, on a field of ivory, a lion cub chased a butterfly. 'Twas a stunning piece of work.

"Upon my word, Marian, you have outdone yourself. Look, Audra, is he not the cutest cub you have ever laid eyes on?"

Audra's arm lifted. She dared a peek beneath. "I like the one in the middle best."

"Do you? Let us have a look then." Stephen flipped open the blanket far enough to discern the pattern. Another cub stalked a beetle with humorous ferocity. Next to him, two cubs tumbled in rough play in a patch of grass. In the center, amid a halo of flowers, a cub slumbered, near angelic in countenance.

He'd done well to listen to William's recommendation. This gift would put him in Ardith's good graces for years.

He glanced over at Lyssa, snuggled against Marian. Her eyes were open and more alert than he'd expected.

"Which is your favorite?"

"My lambs. Did you see them?"

"Aye, and Audra's kittens, too. Your mother was rather proud of both when she showed them to me, with good reason."

Audra's hold loosened. She sniffed and ran a hand across her eyes. "If you move the blanket, you can see the table linen she started."

Stephen did as instructed. Marian had completed only a few stitches in indigo. He picked up a wax tablet from beside the batch of colorful thread.

"Is this the design?" he asked, thinking it looked familiar but couldn't say from where.

Audra's forefinger traced the swirls as she related which colors would go where. "Mama got the idea for it from our storybook."

"Wonderful idea, from wherever it came."

Stephen put the tablet down, handed the blanket to Audra to hold, then put everything back neatly. He closed the lid, then stood up.

Tension yet thrummed between Marian and Audra, but not as heated as before. The two had unfinished business. From experience with his own mother, he knew the faster done the better, no matter who won.

"What say we trade?"

Marian mulled over his suggestion, glancing from Lyssa up to Audra and back again. "The headache eases. You must keep her still with this cold rag on her head."

"Easy enough duty."

Marian smiled wryly. "So you think." With a grace that bespoke of long practice, she rose from the floor without jostling Lyssa. She handed over one daughter while reaching for the other. "Come, you, we have porridge to clean up."

Audra went easily enough, and as the two went about setting the hut to rights, Stephen settled on the floor with Lyssa, a wet rag and the new baby blanket. He set his back hard against the wall and crossed his booted ankles. Lyssa wiggled about to get comfortable, too. Then she wiggled some more. He finally clamped the rag to her head and pressed her head against his shoulder.

She ran a finger over a cub. "Is the baby borned yet?"

"Aye. Two days ago."

She tried to look up at him; he held her still.

"Has he a name?"

"Matthew. Your mother said you must remain still. Does that also mean no talking?"

"It does," Marian answered from near the hearth.

"Ah. Then, little one, I suggest you close your eyes and go to sleep before you get us both into trouble."

Lyssa giggled, but her eyes closed.

Stephen watched Marian move about the hut, putting things away. She gave the task of sweeping up the por-ridge-coated rushes to Audra, who swept slowly and held fast to her sulks.

Then Marian bent over to pick up a bowl and Stephen forgot all about little girls and baby blankets in favor of admiring the woman's beautifully molded bottom.

Friends. Old friends. Nothing more. Except his dear old friend possessed a beautifully molded bottom. She straightened and put the bowl on the table, abruptly halt-ing the beginnings of an erotic fantasy.

"I saw a messenger come this morn," she said. "He brought news of the babe's birth?"

"Aye." He didn't trust himself to say more.

"Carolyn said you would likely be called to Wilmont for the christening."

"We leave on the morn."

She turned to face him, an eyebrow raised. "We?"

"Carolyn is going with me to meet my family."

"Oh." She turned away. "How nice."

"Not very. William insists Edwin go, too, as escort—or rather watchdog."

"I wish you all a nice journey."

Stephen barely discerned she truly didn't when she reached up on the mantel for a stoppered brown bottle. Audra dropped the broom and covered her nose and mouth with both hands. Despite his hold on Lyssa, the girl managed to turn her face into his shoulder.

Marian put a hand on her hip. "Oh, come now you two, 'tis not *that* bad."

"Bleech!" Lyssa commented into his shoulder

A potion, Stephen realized as Marian headed toward him. He fought the urge to protect Lyssa from her mother. 'Twas a potion she meant to give the girl, not poison.

Marian knelt on the floor. "A sip, Lyssa, that is all."

"Mama, must I? 'Tis terrible stuff."

"Would you rather hurt all the night long?"

"Aye!"

Marian pulled the cloth stopper from the bottle and Stephen understood the girls' reactions. The medicine stank, a wholly wretched odor. He was a seasoned warrior, a veteran of many a campaign and encampments. He'd smelled worse without his stomach heaving, but not much worse.

"What the hell is that?"

Marian rolled her eyes. "If Lyssa does not take the potion, then her headache will return full force within hours. 'Tis either this or sit up the greater part of the night, and I have not the strength or patience tonight."

"Fine, then I shall."

Marian's eyes went wide, and Stephen realized what he'd offered. One look at Lyssa's worshipful expression prevented him from taking the words back. Marian's expression was anything but worshipful.

"You cannot stay the whole night!"

"Why not? I have nothing better to do."

"People will talk."

"No one knows I am here." Well, only Armand and Harlan who he'd left checking the supply wagons. They'd not tell.

"Oh, Stephen—"

"Please, Mama? I hate that medicine."

Lyssa's plea apparently caught Marian in the heart. She brushed her daughter's loose hair back. With a sad smile, she relented. "For a few hours then, until the pain is completely gone. And you must lie very still. Understood?''

''Still as stone,'' Lyssa said, but didn't relax until Marian stoppered the bottle. ''My thanks,'' she whispered to him, then closed her eyes.

'Twas utterly foolish to feel so much the hero. He was going to pay for his heroism dearly with sore muscles come morn.

Lyssa lay as quite as was possible for Lyssa. Marian and Audra finished cleaning the mess. Mother and daughter shared a light repast of bread and cheese, which they offered to share with him but he declined. Afterward, when Audra shyly asked for a story, Marian gave the girl a hug and agreed.

All was right within this tiny hut—all but Lyssa's headache and an increasing numbness at the base of his spine.

'Twas far past nightfall when Marian finished reading the last of three stories and insisted Audra bed down. Lyssa had fallen asleep in the middle of the first story.

Marian sank down beside him, on Lyssa's pallet.

''Sore yet?'' she asked. He ignored her amusement.

''Not too.'' Not that he'd admit, anyway. Truly, Lyssa wasn't terribly heavy and fitted nicely on his lap. ''Tis better than having to pour that wretched potion down her.''

''Except the potion helps and allows us all to sleep.''

''There must be another which works and is less horrible.''

''Not that I have found.''

Mayhap there wasn't. He knew Marian had taken Lyssa into London to see a physician, and likely tried every herb and potion known hereabout before making that long, hard journey in search for a cure.

Wilmont was but two days away, and at Wilmont was Ardith.

He rejected the burgeoning notion immediately. Taking Marian along to Wilmont was a bad idea. Too much temptation. He needed time alone with Carolyn.

Except Lyssa needed a cure for her headaches and he was in a position to help Marian find it. Mayhap Ardith couldn't help, but she would try. Ah, hell.

"I know this is sudden, but could you be ready to leave on the morn? You and the girls?"

Marian's confusion wrinkled her brow. "Leave for where?"

"Come to Wilmont with me." At the shake of Marian's head, he explained. "I have told you a bit about Ardith. She truly is a remarkable woman. She also knows more about remedies for illnesses than Wilmont's apothecary. Mayhap she could help Lyssa."

Marian pursed her lips, undecided. "We have tried so much."

"What could it hurt to try again?"

"More poking and prodding. More foul potions. I hate to put Lyssa through all that only to come away disappointed once more."

"Ardith pokes and prods gently, I swear."

She pulled her knees up, wrapped her arms around them and stared at some spot on the far wall. He waited, watching the emotions of her decision play out on her expressive face. It seemed eons before she spoke.

"I suppose the blacksmith's lads can feed the chickens."

Chapter Nine

Marian rode next to the driver of the lead supply wagon, holding tight to Audra, wondering if she'd made yet one more mistake.

She'd been too exhausted last night to make a decision of such consequence, considering only the possible benefit to Lyssa and the practical matters of what clothing to take and of who would feed the chickens and milk the goat.

She'd given no thought to how Carolyn might feel about her going along to Wilmont. Carolyn's pique at having more company on this trip than she wanted, including *both* twins, Marian could deal with.

William's reaction to their leaving proved harder to understand. He didn't like being parted from the girls for long. Strange he hadn't objected, much less thought the idea wonderful.

A good wagon length ahead of her, Carolyn rode bezside Edwin. Mounted on a fine bay, gowned in flowing amber with matching veil, Carolyn rode stiff-backed and silent, every bit the highborn lady on an important journey.

Marian couldn't help compare the meager contents of

her sack with the many beautiful gowns in Carolyn's
trunks. Ah, well. 'Twas Carolyn who'd be on display at
Wilmont, her taste and deportment judged. Marian didn't
intend to become familiar with Stephen's family or attend any feasts or functions, so her one change of work-
a-day garb would serve. She'd meet with Lady Ardith
and discuss Lyssa's ailment, then keep to herself as
much as possible without giving offense.

Edwin rode loose and well. He truly was a good-
looking man with a kind heart. If he amended his views
on a woman's place, and Carolyn disregarded Edwin's
age, the two could make a good match. Both were far
too stubborn for words.

Beyond them rode Stephen and his squire and, at the
moment, Lyssa with Stephen. Naturally, the girls preferred to ride at the front of the company on a magnificent stallion to sitting with their mother. Stephen did
his best to give the girls equal time, though Marian suspected Audra received a bit of preference because she
sat more quietly than Lyssa. Stallions could be skittish
and hard to handle, and it wasn't Lyssa's nature to be
still for long.

Like her father.

He'd amazed her last night with his ability to sit for
long hours, along with his deft handling of the girls and
the situation he'd walked into. Gads, he'd scolded Audra
for opening the door heedlessly, then gently prodded
three irritable females into better temper.

The man *did* have a way with females, one of his traits
that had gotten her into trouble in the first place. If she
hadn't been susceptible to his easy charm, become en-
tranced by his bright-green eyes and humor-touched
mouth, she'd not have lain with him.

But then she wouldn't have Audra and Lyssa.

There lay her greatest fear in making this journey to Wilmont, that someone with a keen eye and discerning mind might make the connection between Stephen and his daughters. 'Twas a risk her weary mind hadn't considered until this morn, until seeing the girls merrily riding with their father.

Before they reached Wilmont, she must have a word with Stephen about riding into his home without the encumbrance of a little girl on his lap. He'd have duties to perform—greetings to his family, introductions to Carolyn and Edwin—all valid and needing his full attention. Best he do so without juggling a raven-haired little girl.

Maybe she made too much of the possibility. No one at Branwick had made the connection, so 'twas unlikely anyone at Wilmont would, either. Still, she'd lessen the risk.

Stephen raised a fist in the air. The wagon's driver pulled the oxen to a halt. Marian knew Stephen hadn't planned to stop until time for nooning, another hour or so yet away.

"Something amiss?" Marian asked the driver.

"Nay, my lady," he answered, amused. "Either Lord Stephen's stomach grumbles early or he spotted something of interest alongside the road. A body never knows how long 'twill take to get from one place to another when traveling with his lordship."

The reason for the delay soon became apparent. Stephen lowered Lyssa to the ground, then dismounted and tossed his reins to Armand. Lyssa scurried off into the woods. Stephen followed and stood guard at the edge.

The driver chuckled. Carolyn turned around in the saddle and glared at Marian, as if it were her fault Stephen inconvenienced the entire company so Lyssa could relieve herself.

Lyssa soon came out of the woods with a sunny smile on her face and a bunch of white flowers in her hand. Stephen scooped her up, and the company was soon on its way again.

When next they stopped 'twas in a lovely glade, the perfect place to stretch stiff muscles and satisfy grumbling stomachs.

Marian no more than lowered Audra down from the wagon when the girl raced for the woods. With a chuckle, Marian began to follow. Carolyn's furious countenance stopped her.

"You *will* have a talk with Lyssa about proper behavior before we reach Wilmont. I refuse to be so embarrassed by one of mine own people again, especially before so august a gathering."

Marian thought to object to the admonishment, then realized Carolyn had the right of it. The girls must now remember and practice the rules for children in a noble household.

Audra and Lyssa enjoyed few restrictions at Branwick because of William's leniency. At Wilmont, the seat of a powerful baron, such leniency wouldn't be tolerated.

As members of Branwick's household, the twins' conduct would reflect on Carolyn, who understandably wished to make only the best of impressions.

"I will have a word with them."

"See that you do." Carolyn flounced off toward where Audra had raced.

Now, while they were stopped to rest, might be a good time to have that talk. She looked for Lyssa, nowhere to be seen.

Stephen strolled toward her, grinning. "Lyssa is with Armand, getting a crust of bread. She is *starving*."

Not surprising. Lyssa lost her appetite when the headaches hit, a good thing because food upset her stomach. She'd not eaten much yesterday and downed only a small portion of porridge before setting out this morning. Still, now she inconvenienced Armand who had better things to do than fetch a crust of bread for a child.

The girls definitely needed a reminder of their manners.

Stephen nodded toward where Carolyn had gone. ''Why is Carolyn so angry?''

''She expressed concern over Lyssa's behavior this morn.''

''Lyssa's…oh, our unscheduled stop?''

''You should have asked her to wait.''

Stephen crossed his arms. ''And risk a wet lap? I think not.''

''She delayed the company and embarrassed·Carolyn.''

''Too bad.''

Why was Stephen being so obtuse? He'd grown up in the household of a baron. Surely he knew the rules of conduct as well as she did!

''Carolyn worries over the girls' behavior at Wilmont, and rightly so. 'Tis one thing for William to permit them freedoms in his household, quite another for them to show less than proper training when in company. They *do* know their manners, but must be reminded.''

''So I should have let Lyssa suffer?''

''I doubt Lyssa's need was so urgent. She did have time to pick flowers.''

He tossed a hand in the air. ''How should I have known? I am not used to traveling with children.'' He huffed. ''Remind the girls of their manners if you must, but keep in mind who is in charge of this company. If I say we stop, we stop, for whatever reason.''

She'd angered him without meaning to. He'd done what he thought best.

"All I ask is you not give in to their whims too readily. Truly, it might be best if the twins rode with me from now on."

Disappointment briefly displaced his anger. "Audra is due another turn. Would you deny her?"

"Nay. She may have her turn."

He placed his hands on his hips, turned to where Audra sauntered out of the woods. "I suppose you know what is best for them."

Marian prayed she did, but there had been times lately when she wasn't sure at all—especially about denying the girls their father's company, and he his daughters. After watching him do so well with them last night, and again today, 'twas obvious Stephen had a natural way with children. His daughters responded to his tender care with affection.

Would it truly be so bad if she told only Stephen and the girls? Could she give them to each other without ruining all of their lives?

The twins practiced staying out of the way while Stephen oversaw the setting up of the tent in which the women would sleep tonight. Both girls would dearly love to take a hammer swing at a stake. While Marian allowed them to watch—with a hand clamped firmly on each twins' shoulder—they weren't allowed underfoot.

Left to Stephen, he'd have put a hammer in their hands and let them satisfy their curiosity. Sitting quietly and speaking only when spoken to had its place, but so did unfettered curiosity and high spirits. They'd ridden in the wagon for most of the afternoon, receiving instruction from Marian—to the amusement of the driver—and must be weary of lessons by now.

"I wish you had brought our storybook," Lyssa complained.

"Lyss-a." Marian's admonishment came softly at the end of her daughter's name.

Lyssa didn't look chastised. "I apologize for complaining, but I still wish you had brought our storybook."

Stephen cleared his throat to choke off a burst of laughter. Time for a diversion, for a bit of freedom before the twins must practice eating daintily.

"Marian, what say we take the girls down to the river? When we watered the oxen, I thought I saw some flowers and frogs on the banks that might interest them."

To the girls' credit, both stood perfectly still, the only sign of their excitement the sparkling in widening eyes. Marian glanced over to where Carolyn had seated herself on a boulder, arranged her skirts into perfect order and watched everyone else bustle about.

Stephen quelled a twinge of guilt for leaving Carolyn behind. After all, since giving Audra her last ride, he'd spent some time riding next to Carolyn. Sad to say, Audra proved the better company. He'd half listened to Carolyn's rambling, then been unexpectedly rewarded for his patience with an intriguing tidbit about Marian. Apparently, several men at Branwick had offered for Marian and, much to Carolyn's annoyance, her cousin turned them all aside.

"Shall we go sit by the river, girls?" Marian asked.

"Aye, Mama."

"Walk, if you please."

Two heads swiveled around and tilted upward. They stared at Marian, incredulous at the order to walk.

"Walk." With the command reinforced, Marian turned to Stephen. "We are ready, my lord. Lead on."

Stephen set a sedate pace through the campsite, pausing where the livestock was staked to tell Edwin of his destination. As the man of highest rank left behind in camp, Edwin must be informed. The girls practiced greetings and curtsies to Edwin before they moved on.

He quickened the pace through the woods, following the path the oxen had efficiently tramped down when headed for water. When he heard the river, he turned around.

"Do you hear the river? See the path?"

"Certes," Audra said, near insulted.

"Good. Last one to the bank does not get to take her sandals off and go barefoot in the water."

The girls streaked past him. Marian tossed her hands in the air and looked heavenward.

"Sorry, could not help myself," he told Marian, not sorry at all, then raced after the girls. He reached the bank to see Lyssa taking off a sandal.

"Audra lost," the tyke proclaimed.

"Not so. Your mother lost."

Audra flashed him a grateful smile. Stephen sat down next to her and shucked his boots and hose. No sense letting the girls have all the fun. Besides, if there was a frog to be caught, the girls would need help. He rolled up his breeches and soon the three of them were mucking about in the muddy water along the bank.

When Marian finally reached them, she set all the footwear to order, then sat down on the grass. Stephen thought to invite her to join in the frog hunt, then watched her lean back on her hands, close her eyes and tilt her face upward toward the fading sunlight.

So at peace. So utterly delectable.

He stood in ankle-deep, cool water, yet his loins stirred. No harm looking at his old and dear friend, he decided, so long as he didn't touch, which would send him up in flames and necessitate a swim.

Why hadn't Marian remarried?

'Twas certainly none of his concern, and he'd put his musings on the matter to rest weeks ago. Except he hadn't known until this afternoon about the offers she rejected, and began wondering all over again about Marian's deceased husband. About what kind of man he'd been. Had he been suited to her or not? Did she reject suitors because she found all the men unacceptable or because she didn't wish to marry again?

Had she found marriage hateful, or loved her husband so much no other man could compare?

Marian was so beautiful, both in face and manner, she could have her pick of the finest crop. She'd get a good deal of male attention at Wilmont. His brother had likely invited most of England's high nobility to attend his son's christening. The king might even show up; the queen stood as godmother to little Everart, Gerard's heir.

He should have left Marian at Branwick. A widow of noble rank, with her pleasing disposition, she would draw marriage-hungry males like bees to honey. If any one of them took advantage of her sweet vulnerability, he'd personally run the man through!

The violence of the thought brought him up short. Who was he to proclaim himself as judge? If Marian found a suitable mate for herself at Wilmont, so be it. Someone constant, unfailingly trustworthy, who could give her and the girls a secure home, protect and love them as they deserved.

Someone very unlike himself.

He'd be a curse to a woman like Marian. She needed

a husband she could rely on for security. 'Twas why he courted Carolyn, a woman who preferred to provide her own security.

"Where are the frogs?" Lyssa asked.

Jolted back to the task at hand, Stephen steered the girls toward the tall rushes. "Mayhap they hide."

"Why?" Audra asked.

"If you were a frog and saw such mighty hunters bearing down on you, would you not hide?"

The girls saw the sense of it and parted the rushes. He watched them search, to no avail, until disappointment set in.

So he set them to an easier task. "Perhaps we had best settle for flowers. 'Twould be more suitable to take flowers back to camp than a frog anyway."

Audra's face lit up, eyeing the proliferation of wildflowers along the bank. "We could take some back for Carolyn. She loves flowers."

"So does Mama."

"Pick some for both ladies, then, but be quick. We lose daylight." Odd he hadn't noticed before. "Off you go."

The girls hurried out of the water and up to the flowers. Stephen headed for where Marian still sat near his boots.

She watched him approach with narrowed eyes, but a smile graced her lovely mouth. "'Twas bad of you, Stephen. Hardly proper behavior."

He sat down beside her. "Ah, Marian, every warm summer day should end with a frog hunt."

"Pray foreswear informing the girls."

"Whatever for? A stream runs near Wilmont, and there I *know* where the frogs hide."

Her smile lost a bit of luster. "We will be at Wilmont by this time tomorrow, will we not?"

"With ease. Why?"

She shrugged. "Merely wondering." Her gaze wandered over his shoulder, toward the girls. "Oh, for pity's sake."

Marian was on her feet before he could turn around. Then he saw Lyssa, a small snake clutched in her little hand, sneaking up on Audra.

"Lyssa, no!" Marian shouted.

Audra turned, spied the snake, screamed and took off running. Stephen laughed...until Audra ran toward the water. He shouted her name with an order to halt. She didn't hear him through her screams.

The river wasn't particularly wide or deep, but every body of flowing water had its deep spots and a current—dangers for a small girl.

Marian flew after Audra like an arrow shot to a target. Stephen stood up, watching the mother gain ground on her daughter. Fright drove Audra down the bank and into the concealing rushes—a place to hide.

Near panic tinged Marian's voice, shouting Audra's name.

Audra would be safe enough if she didn't go too far into the rushes. But if she did and became entangled...Stephen tamped down his worry but began walking toward the river anyway.

Boots and all, Marian heedlessly entered the river, her gown quickly soaking up water. She parted the rushes, called Audra, then went farther out, her search frantic.

Lyssa shot past him. Stephen lunged and caught her by the back of her tunic. He plopped her down on her bottom.

"Sit here and do *not* move!" The order given in the

tone of a commander to troops shocked Lyssa to frozen stillness.

Satisfied she would obey for the nonce, Stephen resumed his walk toward the rushes, determined to remain calm despite his rising heartbeat. Marian had waded out to the farthest point of the rush patch, so far the water reached her knees. Too far with now heavy skirts. One misstep and she'd be in trouble.

Rushes rustled near the bank, too briskly for a small animal's passage.

"Marian, come in! Audra is here."

Audra stepped out of rushes. Marian spun to his shout. She took a step and fell, breaking her fall with her hand. Stephen snapped the ties of his sherte, reached behind him and grabbed hold of both tunic and sherte, and yanked them over his head.

In those few seconds of blindness, Marian disappeared.

His head screamed a denial. The girls' screams weren't silent. There wasn't time to comfort them, only issue a sharp order to Audra to sit by Lyssa and stay put.

Sweet Jesu, let them obey.

Stephen plunged into the river, spraying water, rushing headlong to where he'd last seen Marian. The water turned clear and colder, the edge of the current tugged at his breeches.

"Marian!" He listened hard, and heard nothing. "Marian!"

From downriver came the faint sound of his name. A sweeter sound he'd never heard. He rounded the rush patch—the pebble strewn bottom dropped away from ˮʳ his feet. He swallowed water as he went under, tasting of mud and gritty with sand. Blood pounded in his ears.

He kicked hard, driving upward, allowing the current to carry him toward Marian. What seemed an eternity later he broke surface, sputtering. A hard shake of his head cleared his eyes and senses. A few long strokes took him to calmer, slightly warmer, chest-high water.

"Marian!"

"Here."

He'd shot past her. His relief at finding her was short-lived. With her head barely out of the water, Marian clung by one hand to a fragile lifeline—a snapped branch jutting far out into the river from a fallen log. Water swirled around her, the current threatening to carry her away—or pull her under.

"Hold on!" he shouted, immediately noting the senselessness of the order. Marian wouldn't let go.

Stephen swam to the log, which moved too easily under his hand. He couldn't trust either log or branch to hold tight, and Marian was out farther than an arm's length away.

"Stephen?" No panic, but she was frightened.

"Can you touch bottom?"

"Nay."

He reached out as far as he could while yet holding on to the log. "Can you reach my hand?"

She strained to bring her free arm around, but the current worked against her. The current and her gown. The damn gown acted as an anchor.

He wished he could simply swim out, grab hold of her and head for shore. Not possible. The swirl of the water and weight of her gown would pull them both under.

Stephen saw no other hope but to ease out onto the

branch and get the gown off Marian so she could maneuver. Maybe the branch would hold. Maybe the log wouldn't break free.

"I am going to duck under here and come up behind you."

Stephen pushed out beyond the log. The swirl hit him hard. He ducked under the branch, grabbed hold and prayed. It held.

Hand over hand, he worked his way out to Marian, halting beside her, grasping the branch just above her hand. Blood stained the bark. She must have had a higher hold, then slipped. He squelched the urge to pull her toward him, into his arms. Instead he reached for lacing on the back of her gown.

"We need to get this off you. Do you hurt anywhere?"

"Only my hand. I may have bruised my leg when I kicked off my boots."

Wet lacing didn't like coming undone, especially under cold, numbing fingers, but he managed to undo the knot. The water tugged at the gown as the lacing came out. He slid his hand between her gown and chemise, pushing the heavy material off her shoulder. Marian pulled her arm back, free of the sleeve.

For the other sleeve, she must let go of the branch.

He pulled her up and toward him, wrapped his arm around her midriff. "Let go and pull out of the sleeve. Let the water take the gown."

Stephen braced for the jerk of her weight; she didn't move.

"I have you, Marian. I will not let you go, I swear."

Marian slowly released her hold, giving him her weight in degrees. Still, he grimaced at the strain on his muscles. She pulled her arm from the sleeve, then pushed the heavy gown down from her hips.

The branch broke, giving them up to the merciless current.

Stephen released the branch and tightened his hold on Marian. He'd not lose her now. Not now when he'd just found her again. He flipped to his back, determined to keep Marian afloat, her face above water. Half riding the current, with thrashing legs aiding his backstroke, he headed for calmer water and shore. When sure of the bottom, he stood, turned Marian around and hugged her hard.

''Ye gods, Stephen,'' she whispered, her arms tight around his neck, her chemise-wrapped body pressed along the length of his near nakedness.

He kissed the curve of her neck, so damn glad she was alive and in his arms. ''Hellfire, woman, you scared me.''

''I should not have tried to get up, but I did, and stumbled farther out. Then the current caught me and—'' She shook her head, her forehead grazing his shoulder. ''When I got hold of the branch, I stayed put, knowing you would come for me.''

Triumph seized him, the elated aftermath of a battle hard fought and won. Had he the energy, he'd spin Marian around and shout for joy. Instead, he turned Marian's head and sought her mouth.

The potency of the kiss shot straight to his victory-heady senses, drawing him into a whirlpool of bliss and contentment from which he didn't wish rescue. He could drown in Marian's sweetness and not give a damn.

Within the kiss he rediscovered his first lover, as eager for him as he for her. He could loosen his breeches and have her right here in the water. She'd not say him nay.

She'd welcome his touch, his thrusts, with all the joy of a maiden in the hay.

From far off, he heard his name called. Armand. Those in the camp must have heard the girls' screams and investigated.

Temptation reared so hard it damn near killed him to break the kiss. "We will be found soon."

Desire glittered in Marian's eyes. "How soon?"

Sweet heaven, dare he? "Not too soon."

She wrapped her legs around his waist. "Then do it, Stephen. Take me now before they find us."

Chapter Ten

'Twas amazing to Marian how clearly she'd reviewed her life while dangling in the river from an untrustworthy branch, then vowed to God and herself to set all to rights—beginning with Stephen.

She never doubted he'd come to her rescue, not been the least surprised he found her so quickly. Later she'd tell him about the girls, confess her error in remaining silent all these years. Confess the love for him she'd always felt. After all, how could he become a loving husband and father, give up his wandering ways if she didn't give him the chance?

For right now, she wanted to show him her desire, her burning need, to become his lover again. The rest would follow.

He yet stared at the bank, assessing how much time they had for a coupling.

"Believe me, I am tempted near beyond restraint," he said, his voice rough, "but I will not make love to you like this."

Odd, she'd thought it would be both easily done and rather erotic in the water. "On the bank, then. Stephen, please."

He didn't move. "You are overwrought and know not what you say."

Overwrought? She knew exactly what she wanted! "I *need* you. Is that not clear enough?"

"Ah, sweetling," he whispered, pulled her close and nuzzled in her neck.

Stephen's hot breath warmed her cold skin. His hands skimmed along her thighs, under the chemise, and cupped her bottom. Now here was the Stephen she knew, randy and willing, anytime and anyplace. Finally, he'd unleash himself, pierce her, ease the deep ache only Stephen could ease.

With her legs wrapped around his trim waist, her breasts crushed against his sleek, powerful chest, she couldn't help but feel his deep sigh.

"I cannot, Marian, not like this. I appreciate your gratitude, but cannot accept such a reward."

"What?"

"We have fought a battle for survival and won. Your fear is gone, your elation at victory high. You wish to celebrate, and wish to do so with me, your rescuer."

Marian's ardor cooled considerably as his meaning sneaked past her passion-muddled senses. She leaned back to look at him. He was dead serious.

"Gratitude? Is that what you think?"

"'Tis a natural enough reaction, and I am highly honored."

"I see," she said, horrified.

Stephen thought her no better than a harlot, offering the use of her body as a reward for his good deed.

The insufferable cur.

"So what you say is, in my high state of elation, I would offer to buff the rod of any man who came to my aid."

He frowned. "Crudely put."

He objected to her language, not denied his belief. She nearly choked on her rising anger.

"If Armand had rescued me, would I have offered to swive him, too?"

"Now, Marian—"

"Or Edwin? There is a fine figure of a man. If Edwin had plucked me from the river—"

"Impossible. Edwin is too old. He would have a heart attack in the process."

"Edwin is *not* old, and I tire of hearing you and Carolyn speak of him as such." She pushed against his chest. "Let me go, with my thanks for exposing the frailties of my unstable emotions."

"Marian—"

"Your rescue is complete. I can swim to shore myself. Release me!"

He obeyed. Before she went under she heard Armand call out again, much closer now.

There would have been enough time, damn the man.

She'd not cry. She'd not give Stephen the satisfaction of knowing how deeply she hurt. To think she nearly declared her love, made an utter fool of herself over a man who didn't deserve or want her love any more now than six years ago.

She flipped over and kicked toward shore, surfacing not far from the bank. Armand stood near the edge, Stephen's sherte and tunic grasped in his hand.

"Ah, my lady, 'tis glad I am to see you, too."

Marian thought of just how much of her he was going to see. A thin, wet chemise hid nothing from view. So be it. If Stephen thought her a harlot, why not prove him right? She stood up in water that barely covered her

knees. The squire looked her over once, and turned scarlet.

Immediately contrite for her brashness, Marian turned
around and directed her ire at the man who deserved it.
Stephen looked, too, slower and harder, with no tinge of
embarrassment.

Let him look. Let him see what he tosses aside.

Look he did, thoroughly, missing not one inch of the
near nakedness she flaunted. He took revenge on her
boldness, coming toward her with his easy grace, like
some ancient sea god emerging from the water to claim
a nymph for his pleasure.

Sweet mercy, the man's body yet appealed. So strong,
so damn perfect in form. The rough scar across his
shoulder wasn't a flaw, nor the intriguing notch out of
his left ear. They merely invited a woman's fingers to
explore, to ease any lingering pain from those wounds.

She swallowed hard. He stopped mere inches away.

''My lady, should you ever make me another such
offer, when 'tis me you truly want, I vow I will not
hesitate.''

''Believe me, my lord, I shall not offer again.''

He nodded slightly. ''Armand, my tunic if you will.
The lady is cold.''

She was, but the cold came from within, not without.
Only once before had she experienced this icy emptiness, on the day she'd realized she must not tell her
father about Stephen.

Armand tossed the tunic, Stephen caught it. He
slipped it over her head, the hem dipping into the water.
The tunic smelled of Stephen, but was warm and long
enough so she could walk into camp. She could endure
the aroma for that long.

Marian made for the bank, for the surety of solid earth

beneath her feet. Weariness set in. She craved a hug from her girls, a warm drink and soft pallet—the oblivion of sleep.

"How go things in camp?" Stephen asked his squire.

Armand tossed him the sherte. "All is well, my lord, now that we have found you and Lady Marian. Edwin sits with the twins. The men-at-arms search the rushes. I took one look at the middle of the river and decided to search down current."

"What possessed you to bring my garments?"

"Pure habit, my lord. I have become accustomed to picking up after you."

Stephen slipped into his sherte. "So why not my boots?"

"The girls are guarding them. Truth to tell, Lyssa refuses to move until you come back to release her from her seat."

"She stayed put then."

"'Twas her screams we heard in camp that brought us down to the river. Her voice was so hoarse Audra had to tell us what happened."

Armand's revelation shook Marian wide-awake again. "Lyssa's screams brought you to the river?"

"Aye, my lady. Powerful set of lungs on one so little."

Horrified, she turned on Stephen. "You left them alone? You did not fetch someone to watch over them first?"

He crossed his arms across his now sherte-covered chest. "Fetch someone? I ordered the girls to sit and stay and then plunged into the water after you. There wasn't time!"

"They must have been frantic! No telling what they might have done!"

"They did as I ordered."

"You should not have left them alone!" Marian headed upriver, heedless of anything but to get back to her daughters.

"Marian, have a care!" Stephen shouted.

She spun, her eyes narrowed. "Oh, have no fear. I wish to get back in one piece, so I might properly show Edwin my *gratitude* for caring for my daughters!"

She did have a care, however, more because tramping barefoot though the woods proved hard on the feet. All the while she could hear Stephen and Armand behind her, and after a short while heard the shouts of men-at-arms before her.

Torches lit up the small clearing. Edwin stood over the girls who sat on the bank, well away from the water. Soon she sat on the ground, Audra and Lyssa safe in her embrace, listening to tearful apologies. Marian shushed and reassured them, unable to summon a word of reprimand.

She felt more than saw Stephen come up behind her. The girls quieted, then slowly stood up, their tear-streaked faces tilted upward.

"You have begged your mother's pardon?" he asked gently.

Their "Aye, my lord" came out hoarse and disjointed.

He knelt down and opened his arms. "Come here, then."

The girls obeyed with such swiftness they rocked him back. He closed his eyes and held them fast against him. Raven-black braids hung down their backs, soaking up droplets from their father's like-colored wet hair.

Marian bit back tears, knowing how comforting and reassuring Stephen's embrace could be to one scared nearly witless. Hadn't she availed herself of the comfort before…before…

He kissed both little foreheads. "I beg your pardon, too, for leaving you alone. I know how frightened you must have been, but I am told you obeyed my order even when you might have moved. That took courage, and I am very proud of you both." Stephen met Marian's gaze. "Just as I am proud of your mother for her stead-fast courage. You taught them well, Marian."

The girls learned easily and remembered their lessons. 'Twas their mother who kept forgetting lessons hard learned, needing reminders at least every six years.

As she had yesterday, Marian sat next to the driver of the lead supply wagon. The man was more talkative to-day. She gratefully listened, wishing she had something to do with her hands, too. Something, anything, to concentrate on to wipe her mind free of last eve.

While hanging out on the branch, afraid she might die—which she could admit today—she'd wanted so much to relive the past six years. She'd envisioned Stephen as the man she wanted him to be—her madly-in-love-with-her, hearth-and-home-content husband. They might have lived in a lovely manor with the twins and perhaps a couple of more children after. Her parents would visit and be proud of their daughter.

Lovely, impossible dream.

With the sunrise had come reality, embarrassment and the simple thankfulness of being alive.

She'd already thanked God and every soul in heaven she could think of. She had yet to talk to Stephen, unable to find the words both to thank him and apologize for her truly wanton behavior. Poor Armand couldn't look at her without going scarlet.

She'd been sore tempted to ask one of the wagon drivers to take her home to Branwick. Impossible, of course. Reality was, they were nearing Wilmont and all Marian wanted to do was crawl into the back of the wagon, pull a blanket over her head and become part of the baggage. Reality was, she couldn't.

Reality, too, was that she could also no longer deny her love for Stephen. Of all the thoughts she'd had, which could be attributed to either terror or false hopes, the realization that her love for Stephen had never died remained in her heart and refused to be dislodged.

She should probably thank him for having the sense to turn down her offer. If they'd made love last eve, she might have made demands he couldn't agree to, and she'd be in complete agony today instead of merely suffering.

The wagon driver snapped the reins, urging the oxen up a hill. "You all watch now as we go over. Best view of the castle comin' up."

Wilmont was the largest fortress Marian had ever seen. A huge keep sat on a large center mound, surrounded by two thick curtain walls, lofty towers guarded the corners and either side of the gate. A wide moat separated the fortress from the vast clearing around it—a defensive measure, Marian knew, so those within could readily see attackers from without.

At the moment, the clearing was dotted with colorful tents.

The wagon driver chuckled. "Seems the baron saw fit to invite half of England."

"I like the green one!" Audra proclaimed. "'Tis huge!"

"Should be. Belongs to the earl of Warwick."

Marian thought he must be mistaken. "The earl of Warwick brings a tent to Wilmont?"

"Aye. Most visitors do, unless they like sleepin' on a pallet in the hall. The baron, he likes his privacy. Not too many people allowed up the stairs at Wilmont, 'cept family and the personal servants. 'Course, if the king sees fit to come, then his lordship might give way. Maybe."

Audra poked her head between her mother and the driver. "Will our tent be set up down there, next to the green one?"

The driver smiled at her. "Like that green one, do you? Might be a spot down there yet. We got orders to drop you off at the keep, then go down to set up the tent. I will look for a level spot by the green one."

"Who does the blue one belong to?"

For the next little while, the driver pointed out tents and named their owners. Earls. Barons. England's high nobility. She may be of noble blood, but these people were far above her in rank—and Edwin of Tinfield's and Carolyn de Grasse's.

And Hugo de Lacy's, her father, who would have been invited to these festivities if his daughter had married Stephen of Wilmont. How he would love to rub with earls and barons, possibly obtain some position at court for her older brother through their good offices. She'd denied him a rise in rank.

A pang of longing for her mother and sisters hit hard and nearly drew forth tears. Would she even recognize her younger sisters? They would be all grown-up now. Marian swallowed the lump in her throat, knowing the near death experience of last eve brought all this on. Still, 'twas hard to shake off.

"You all hold on, now," the driver said. "Gets a bit bumpy here for a bit till we get beyond the gate."

Marian faced forward as the wagon driver snapped the reins to urge the oxen over the drawbridge. With Stephen in the lead, Carolyn beside him, the company soon traversed the bailey and the inner yard to pull up at the stairway to the stone keep. A small army of servants surrounded the company, their general a brusk, gray-haired man who Marian assumed must be Wilmont's steward.

"Hail, Walter," Stephen called out. "The lead wagon carries my possessions. The others belong to Lady Carolyn. Have someone find a level piece of ground for her tent."

"At once, my lord. Lady Ardith awaits you in the hall."

"Gerard?"

"Not yet returned from hunting."

Stephen dismounted, then reached up to help Carolyn down, grasping her about the waist—a mannerly yet personal gesture performed toward the woman he intended to marry.

Did his "intention" make Carolyn deserving of a bed in the family apartments? Likely, Edwin would take a pallet in the hall. Which left the tent to her and the girls.

"Lady Marian, if I may be of assistance?"

Edwin stood ready to help her down from the wagon. She could barely look at him, either, remembering her threat flung at Stephen to show Edwin her *gratitude*. The driver unloaded the girls. Determined to get through whatever she must until she could escape to the tent, Marian gathered her skirt of rough-weave brown, slid her feet more firmly into overlarge black felt slippers borrowed from Carolyn, and climbed out of the wagon.

With as much dignity as she could manage, with gracious Edwin's arm for support, she crossed to the bottom stair where Stephen and Carolyn waited. Climbing the steep stairway proved no mean feat. The twins, of course, scampered right up.

Stephen grasped the brass handle on the huge oak door and swung it open. Marian entered the great hall with a shuffle, then stopped abruptly to avoid bumping into Carolyn.

"'Tis magnificent," Carolyn told Stephen, awed.

"Impressive." Edwin's nonchalance didn't ring true; his eyes reflected concern.

Marian perused the hall and understood. Edwin now witnessed the full wealth and power of the baron of Wilmont, against whose brother he contended for Carolyn. 'Twould knock the wind out of any man—or woman.

Wilmont's great hall was designed to impress all who entered. Torches lit up the vast room. Marble carvings graced towering pillars that supported the vaulted ceiling, from which streamed gold-flecked scarlet banners. Weapons of war vied for space with exquisite tapestries along the whitewashed stone walls.

'Twas near time for the evening meal, and though no meat roasted within the massive hearth, Marian could envision an entire cow turning on the thick spit. Due to the heat, the cooking would be done in the outdoor kitchen.

Behind linen-draped tables on the dais sat two thronelike chairs of heavily carved dark wood. Behind them stood several perches, only two occupied by magnificent falcons.

Everywhere milled finely clad nobles, their jeweled chains and brooches atwinkle, gold or pewter goblets in hand, either awaiting the meal or the baron's return from hunting.

Marian released Edwin's arm and whispered, "You have duties to attend. The girls and I will be fine."

He looked at her askance. She shooed Edwin toward his rightful place beside Carolyn, then held out her hands for Audra and Lyssa.

From near the dais, a woman broke away from a group and headed for the doorway at a brisk pace. Gowned and veiled in saffron, her auburn hair pulled back in a single braid, she was utterly lovely. A genuinely pleased smile lit her face.

Stephen released Carolyn's arm and bowed toward the woman. "Ah, Ardith. My dear, I do believe I can once again get my arms around you."

The woman laughed lightly and stood up on tiptoe to hug Stephen. "Did I not know you meant that as praise, I would have the guards toss your handsome hide out the door. Gerard will be sorry he missed your arrival."

"Only if his hunt proves unsuccessful, and we both know how unlikely that is. He could have waited for me."

Ardith backed away. "Oh, you will have your chance. Come now, introduce me to your guests."

As rank dictated, Stephen presented Edwin, then Carolyn, then Marian and her daughters to his sister-by-marriage.

Marian's opinion of the woman rose higher when her smile never faltered for the "lady" clad as a ragamuffin.

"Gerard and I are most pleased you could attend," Ardith said, her statement meant for all but mainly addressed to Carolyn.

Carolyn gave a slight bow. "I fear there are more of

us than you bargained for, my lady. I hope 'twill cause no hardship.''

Ardith waved a dismissing hand. ''With so many about, what matter a few more? 'Tis of no import, I assure you.'' Then she bent over, heedless of ceremony and her saffron gown, to face the girls. ''And who have we here?''

''This is Audra.'' Marian gave Audra's hand a slight tug. Taking the hint, Audra immediately dropped into a curtsey. ''And Lyssa.'' Who followed her sister's lead.

''How adorable!'' Ardith said, glancing between them. ''But how shall I ever tell you apart? Ah, here.'' She reached out to touch Lyssa's forehead. ''You have a mark…oh, dear, a dirt smudge.'' Ardith chuckled. ''Never fear, I shall find some telling sign so I do not mistake your names.''

Lyssa shrugged. ''Most people cannot tell which is which. Only Mama always gets it right.''

Stephen crossed his arms. ''Now hold a moment. Have I ever called either of you by the incorrect name?''

Audra smiled. ''Not as yet.''

A shiver slithered down Marian's spine. Not even those who'd known the girls since birth always named the girls correctly, not even Carolyn. Bah! 'Twas merely through acute observation that Stephen had no trouble identifying the girls, not by some mystical knowledge simply because he'd sired them.

Lady Ardith tilted her head. ''Mayhap that is because Stephen has some experience with twins. I am a twin, you know, though my twin is a brother.''

''Any news on Corwin?'' Stephen asked.

Ardith straightened. ''He and Lady Judith left here for London yesterday. Gerard thought to send a messenger to you, but then realized you would be here nearly as soon as someone could reach you.''

''Been here and gone already?'' he asked, both disappointed and visibly relieved.

'''Tis quite a story, but best left until Gerard returns. We tarry overlong in the doorway when you must all be weary and parched from your journey. The meal will be served upon Gerard's return, but until then, please partake of the wine and ale.''

Ardith took a step, then stopped and stared at Lyssa. Marian's stomach flipped at the intensity of the lady's scrutiny.

''You look puzzled, Lyssa,'' Ardith commented. ''Is something amiss?''

Marian told her racing heart to slow down. A mother herself, Ardith had only noticed a little girl's puzzlement, not the raven hair so close a match to Stephen's. Sweet heaven, if she didn't tamp down her terror at every innocent look or comment, she'd go mad within hours, or possibly give her fears away by her reactions.

Indeed, Lyssa wore an expression of fierce concentration. ''I wondered…'' she began, then glanced upward. ''Mama, would it be bad manners to ask her ladyship if we could see the new baby?''

'''Tis never bad manners to ask a mother to show off her children,'' Ardith answered. ''Is that not right, Marian?''

The phrasing made Marian smile. ''Never. You must be very busy with your guests, so perhaps another time would be best.''

Ardith shook her head. ''Now would truly be a good time, since I should check on Matthew anyway. The tyke is adamant about timely meals. Stephen, dear, would you do me the favor of extending Wilmont hospitality to

Lord Edwin and Lady Carolyn while Marian and I take the girls upstairs?'' She glanced toward the hearth. ''Your mother is looking this way. Best you do the honors there, too.''

Stephen's eyes rolled upward. ''Duty calls.''

''Be gracious, Stephen. She tries hard to change her ways.''

''Only because you insist.''

Ardith's expression turned stern, but she said not a word of reprimand. She didn't have to. Stephen's hands soon rose in surrender.

''Oh, very well. Carolyn, Edwin, shall we?''

Ardith's features softened as the three left. ''I hope I did not overstep, Lady Marian. I merely assumed you would prefer to come with us.''

Marian did, for several reasons, not the least of which was her state of improper dress, which bolstered her desire to get out of the keep quickly, encountering as few people as possible. Perhaps this might also be a good time to discuss Lyssa's headaches. With that over, she and the girls could go to the tent and not have to come back into the keep.

''You assumed correctly, my lady.''

Ardith led the way toward the stairway. Marian released the girls to follow and brought up the rear, shuffling along as best she could. Curiosity turned her head toward the hearth, where Stephen presented Carolyn and Edwin to a raven-haired woman of middling years. The resemblance between Stephen and his mother was striking. His reluctance to greet her indicated the two didn't get along well. Marian wondered why, then decided 'twas none of her affair.

Ardith called over her shoulder, ''Have a care on the stairs. They are narrow and steep.''

Built for defense against intruders attempting to gain the upper floors, the stairway spiraled tightly upward. Marian couldn't imagine trying to fight one's way up them with a sword in hand, encumbered by heavy chain mail. 'Struth, she had a hard enough time climbing them with her only encumbrance her floppy slippers.

Halfway up, after nearly falling, Marian kicked the slippers off and carried them. Better the embarrassment of Ardith seeing her guest barefooted than having her tumble down the stairs.

Marian slipped them back on at the top of the stairs. To Ardith's raised eyebrow, she explained simply. "Borrowed."

"Mama lost her boots when she nearly drowned in the river," Lyssa added.

"Lost her gown, too. Stephen saved her, but not the gown," Audra continued.

"Stephen took off his sherte before he jumped in the water so Mama wore his tunic back to camp."

"But she could not find her boots so she borrowed Carolyn's slippers."

Ardith's eyes went wide, her jaw slackened.

Marian's cheeks burned. "Enough, girls."

Ardith composed herself. "My word, you did have a wearisome journey. No wonder…well, we shall have to find you better fitting footwear, at the least."

"Oh, please, do not take the trouble."

"'Tis no bother at all! And you must tell me the whole of this tale."

Marian's reluctance to relate any of the story caused her to hesitate. Too long.

"Lyssa scared me with a snake, so I ran into the rushes."

"Mama ran into the water. Then Audra came out.

Then Mama fell over. Stephen told us to *stay put* and he dove in the river to rescue Mama.''

"So we obeyed and screamed 'cause we were scared.''

Ardith glanced from twin to twin. "I imagine you were terribly frightened.''

Lyssa nodded. "Then men came running to the river from camp and they looked for Mama but they could not find her. Then Mama came out of the woods. Stephen, too. And then we were not scared anymore.''

"Stephen said he was proud of us because we *stayed put*. Oh, and Mama, too, 'cause we were all so brave.''

Ardith smiled and put a hand on Audra's head. "You were very brave and obedient. I am proud of you both, too.'' The twins fairly beamed. "I must say I am proud of Stephen, as well. He can be very comforting to have around when one is frightened. You see, he once gave me courage when I was badly in need.''

"Did you almost drowned?'' Audra asked.

"Nay, but I was in danger.'' The lady's smile faded, her eyes clouded, as if haunted. "I have been ever grateful Stephen was with me and Daymon that day to give me hope and courage. And even though he was terribly wounded, he came to help rescue us. Would that I could convince him I consider him a hero.''

"Did you tell him?'' Lyssa asked.

"Oh, aye, many times, and will continue to do so until he truly hears.'' Ardith's smile returned. "I love him as dearly as my own brother, but the man can be obstinate! Now, shall we go see if the babe is awake?''

Terribly wounded.

Marian followed along, envisioning Stephen's scarred shoulder, the notch in his earlobe. If he'd suffered those wounds in Ardith's defense, then why didn't Stephen accept his due? Most men thrived on praise for their daring.

He'd certainly performed heroically yesterday. She owed him her life, her praise and thanks, but not her *gratitude*.

Chapter Eleven

Stephen swirled the wine in his goblet, playing the part of attentive suitor, half listening to Carolyn and Lady Ursula, his mother, prattle on about the high cost of silk.

What matter? Some goods commanded a high price. A suit of chain mail, a steadfast horse, a well-honed sword. Salt, jewels, a length of silk. Since both Carolyn and his mother possessed coin aplenty to afford whatever luxuries they craved, why complain?

He envied Edwin, who'd had the good sense to offer to see to the setting up of Branwick's tent and thus escaped this inane discussion. Armand had escaped, too, probably gone to the armory to check on his own pallet and belongings.

Oh, he could probably wander over to some other group of nobles. As a member of the family, he'd be heartily greeted—then fawned over by someone wishing to ingratiate himself to the baron through his brother. No fun there.

His gaze wandered over to the stairway, as it had several times in the past little while. Marian hadn't yet come down. He didn't worry over her, not while she visited privately with Ardith. Marian would ooh and aah over the baby, then Marian might talk to Ardith about Lyssa's headaches, the reason she'd come to Wilmont.

'Twas afterward that worried him, the only reason he remained near his mother, hoping for a private word. If not for Marian's needs, and Carolyn's apparent disinterest in her cousin's plight, he wouldn't bother.

When was the last time he'd *wanted* to speak to his mother? Not in forever. The woman had been the bane of his life since his birth. She'd not wanted to bear him, hardly spoken to him as a child, tried to manipulate him as a young man. He avoided her sharp, merciless tongue whenever possible.

Lady Ursula may have gentled somewhat over the past few years, but Stephen remembered too many shouting matches, too many vicious insults to trust her "changed" nature entirely. She'd agree to aid Marian out of a sense of duty, not compassion, but as long as Marian benefited, Stephen wouldn't quibble over why or how.

Now, if he could only think of a way to tell Carolyn to take herself elsewhere.

"Is that not right, Stephen?"

His attention snapped back. "My pardon, Carolyn. I fear my mind wandered. You were saying?"

She smiled and waved a dismissive hand. "'Tis of no import."

Lady Ursula tilted her head. "Indeed, Stephen, I am surprised that *you* have not wandered off. Our conversation was beyond the realm of your usual interests."

Stephen had to admit the reprimand for his inattention a rather gentle one for his mother.

"I admit distraction. I fear I am simply not accustomed to witnessing so large and agreeable a gathering in Wilmont's hall. 'Tis quite a change from…before."

Before Gerard became baron and established his
rights, before he married and installed his wife as chatelaine. It had galled his mother to hand over the keys,
but Gerard hadn't given her a choice. Ursula lived at
Wilmont at Gerard's sufferance. Stephen firmly believed
that fear of Gerard's power over her, not a change of
heart, checked his mother's behavior.

Lady Ursula managed a tight smile. "You must admit
we have more to celebrate now than when you were
young."

She may have a point, but now wasn't the time to
ponder over past hurts, his or hers.

"Actually, I was thinking Carolyn might have some
interest in returning to her tent before evening meal, to
refresh herself. The roads to Wilmont were dry and
dusty."

Carolyn glanced down at her gown. "Oh, my."

"As I thought." Delighted with his flash of insight,
Stephen signaled for the nearest serving wench.
"Maeve, Lady Carolyn's tent should be set up by now.
Be a dear and show her the way, and assist her if need
be."

Maeve's eyes widened in wonder. His mother's eyes
narrowed.

Carolyn glanced toward the stairway. "Marian—"

"She will be down when Lady Ardith deems it convenient."

Carolyn glanced from Maeve to the stairway. "I
would not wish to disturb her ladyship." She gave his
mother a slight curtsey. "My thanks for your forbear-
ance, Lady Ursula."

Carolyn nearly ran out of the hall to change her gown.

"Stephen, you just sent a kitchen wench to play maid

to a lady. Whatever were you thinking, especially when her own maid is upstairs and could have been fetched?''

"Marian is not Carolyn's maid, Mother, but her cousin, with rank to match."

"But her clothing!"

'Twas exactly as he'd feared, that people would take one look at Marian and deem her beneath regard because of her less than elegant garb.

"We suffered a mishap on the road, and I fear Lady Marian's belongings bore the worst of it. Is it possible to find her a suitable gown and footwear before supper? I do not want her subjected to more embarrassment than she has already endured."

She stared at the stairway. "Lady Marian must be sorely tried to find herself in such straits. Now I know why Ardith took her upstairs to the family quarters. Mayhap Ardith has already seen to Lady Marian's needs." Her brow furrowed. "A cousin of Carolyn's you say?"

"Marian is a de Lacy."

"Ah. Well, then, I shall find something decent for her to wear for tonight, at least."

Ursula headed for the stairway.

"Mother." When she stopped and turned around, he uttered words he rarely used where she was concerned. "My thanks."

She looked at him for a long time before her slight nod acknowledged the unaccustomed civility.

After she disappeared up the stairway, Stephen once more perused the room, contemplating which group might provide the most entertainment or simply cause him the least trouble.

The great hall's huge doors burst open, and in walked

his brother, a falcon perched on his arm, several men trailing in his wake.

Saved.

Gerard, baron of Wilmont—big and blond and obviously in a good mood—searched the room, likely looking for his wife. Stephen angled across the hall to stand square in Gerard's path.

Once spotted, Stephen bowed to Gerard's widening smile. "I fear Ardith is upstairs caring for the babe. You will have to settle for me for company." He noticed the splotches of blood staining Gerard's gray tunic and hands. "What happened?"

"A rabbit should know better than to challenge a horse for right to the road. Stupid creature got stomped on and then flipped up onto my lap." Gerard handed his bird off to a falconer, then punched Stephen's arm. "Come up while I change. You can play my squire."

"Where is Thomas?"

"Cleaning the blood off my horse." Gerard made for the stairway; Stephen kept stride. "How went your journey?"

"Eventful, but I want to hear about Corwin first."

Stephen allowed his brother to lead up the stairs and down the hall to the lord's chambers, slowing his stride when he passed the room used for the children. Muffled giggles told him all was well within.

The largest room on the upper floor, the lord's chamber reflected the personality of its occupants. The large, four-poster bed accommodated Gerard's size; the elegant draperies surrounding it bespoke Ardith's taste. The simple clothing chests mirrored his brother's forthright manner; the carving of a rose, sitting atop a large oak table, hinted at his wife's whimsy. A clay washbasin on a simple stand revealed practicality.

As Gerard washed, he told Stephen a fantastical story of how Corwin had ridden off to rescue Judith Canmore and ended up thwarting a rebellion against the crown of England.

"He is in Westminster now to report on events to King Henry, and to ask royal permission to marry Judith."

Stephen whistled low, shocked at his friend's daring. "A royal heiress for a Saxon knight? Will Henry allow it?"

Gerard rummaged about in a trunk and came up with a white linen sherte. "We shall see."

To a rap on the door, Gerard answered "Come!"

Gerard's squire, Thomas, a brown-haired gangly young man, entered the room and closed the door behind him. Amused, he bowed toward Stephen.

"Talk has it you come home a hero, my lord Stephen. 'Tis not often you jump into rivers to rescue near naked women."

Gerard's eyebrows shot upward. Stephen groaned, wondering how Armand and the wagon drivers had related the tale. Damn, he should have told them all to keep their mouths shut.

"Marian fell in the river and got caught in the current. I was closest at hand to go after her, is all."

Gerard crossed his arms. "I see. Bathing, was she?"

Stephen recognized the stance and tone of voice, accusatory and disapproving. Hellfire, the last thing he wanted was one of Gerard's lectures.

"Nay, Gerard, I was not spying on a woman at her bath. She was fully clothed when she fell in, but 'twas necessary to remove her gown so I could haul her in to shore."

"Necessary?"

"Aye, necessary."

"Hmm. Marian? I thought your intended's name is Carolyn."

"Marian is Carolyn's cousin. I invited her to come with us to talk to Ardith. One of her daughters suffers from severe headaches. She and the girls are with Ardith now."

Thomas handed Gerard a deep blue tunic stitched in silver. "Armand says Lady Marian is exquisite."

Utterly exquisite, whether fully clothed or in a wet chemise. Armand should have averted his eyes when Marian stood up in the water, but how could he be angry at the man for looking when he'd feasted on the sight himself? Stared hard and long at Marian's lush curves, at rose-tipped breasts and the shadow at the juncture of her legs. Instead of divesting her of the chemise and taking what she so blatantly offered, he'd covered her with his tunic.

He knew he'd read her state of mind aright, but perhaps stated his case badly. She'd misunderstood. At no time did he mean to imply she would swive any man who might have come to her rescue. Still, for acting nobly, he now suffered her scorn.

"Armand should mind his tongue!"

Taken aback, Thomas tilted his head. "Armand also says her daughters are pretty, and that Lady Carolyn is quite beautiful. Is he wrong to so describe them?"

Stephen reined in the temper he hadn't realized he'd let show. Why should he be angry because Armand paid the women compliments? But for some reason he objected to the squire voicing his opinion about Marian, probably because of how much of Marian Armand had seen.

The woman was driving him mad, scrambling his

wits. Last eve she'd offered herself up to him and today she wasn't speaking to him.

He wanted Marian so badly the very thought that another man found her attractive fired his jealousy and churned his innards. One way or another he had to banish this craving for Marian. The best way to ease a craving was to satisfy it. He knew every private nook within Wilmont's walls and a few without. 'Twould not be difficult to find a place, only arrange a time.

Except he suspected the lady he craved was no longer willing.

Stephen put his hand on the door latch. "Both women are beautiful, both girls pretty. Armand, however, should not be speculating on the attributes of his betters. Until later, Gerard."

He left the chamber and slammed the door behind him.

Gerard slipped the tunic over his head, wondering what in the devil had gotten into Stephen.

"Thomas, does my imagination run amuck, or is Stephen overly sensitive on the subject of Lady Marian?"

"If so, then our imaginations run the same way."

"I wish to talk to Armand."

"At once, my lord."

Ardith laid the babe in the cradle, then returned to her chair to rearrange her disheveled gown. "There. That should keep him happy for another few hours. I cannot fathom having to nurse twins. You must have been sore and exhausted all the time."

Marian leaned back in her chair, the only other large piece of furniture in the children's room. "I was. 'Struth, I no sooner finished calming one than the other needed feeding or changing, or so it seemed."

Marian glanced over at Audra and Lyssa, who'd taken up position on the thick pallet belonging to Everart, Ardith's three-year-old son. Everart sat with his half brother, six-year-old Daymon, on Daymon's pallet. With wooden soldiers arrayed all about them, the girls warred with the boys, taking turns capturing the nursemaid's pallet that lay on the floor between the contending armies.

While she wasn't sure playing at war a good idea for the girls, the two so rarely had the chance to play with other children that Marian didn't take issue.

Ardith chuckled softly. "Look here. Daymon considers himself a master strategist. He is scheming again."

Indeed, mischief sparked the boy's green eyes, as green as Stephen's. 'Twas a mark of the males of the family, Ardith had explained. Both blond-haired, green-eyed boys resembled their father, while the newest babe, Matthew, bore his mother's auburn hair and azure blue eyes. While one might think Ardith would show a marked preference for the children of her body, she seemed to love Daymon as much as her own.

Unusual for a noblewoman to lovingly accept her husband's illegitimate offspring. But then, Ardith and Daymon had been through some trial together, so perhaps had grown close because of it. Ardith hadn't elaborated on the event for which she considered Stephen a hero.

Unusual, too, for a noblewoman to nurse her babes. Most preferred to hire a wet nurse. Stephen considered the woman remarkable and Marian was inclined to agree.

Daymon let out a war cry and swooped down on the nursemaid's pallet, scattering wooden soldiers over all three pallets and the floor. A thorough victory. The girls squealed their delight.

"Gets it from his father," Ardith commented wryly, then stood up. "As much as I would prefer to hide out up here, I have guests below. First, however, we must find you better-fitting footwear." Marian opened her mouth to object; Ardith raised a staying hand. "I will not have one of my guests falling on her face in the hall. Indulge me."

Marian didn't have time to answer. At a rap on the door, Ardith open it to admit three beautifully garbed women. Marian didn't recognize the two who carried boots, but the third, with a sky-blue gown draped over her arm, was Stephen's mother.

Marian rose from her chair, struck again by the resemblance between Stephen and his mother. Raven hair. Olive skin. Classic features. Only the eye color differed. And expression. Where Stephen tended to smile, his mother leaned to austerity.

Ardith grinned. "Lady Ursula, did you read my mind, then? Is the gown one of Christina's?"

"As are the boots," Ursula answered. "Stephen told me of Lady Marian's plight. Judging by my quick glimpse of her before she came up with you, I thought Marian and our Christina might be of a size."

For me. Marian felt her cheeks go pink.

"I had the same thought." Ardith took the gown and held it up. "I believe we are right about the size. What think you, Marian?"

Stephen shouldn't have meddled, should *never* have bothered his mother on her account. She needed no gown. If she had, however, the beautiful light-blue linen might fit. A pretty color, more lighthearted than the browns and grays she'd been wearing lately.

"I thank you both for your thoughtfulness, however, 'tis not necessary."

Lady Ursula's brow scrunched in confusion. "Stephen said you endured a mishap on the road, that your belongings suffered. He worried you had nothing suitable to wear for evening meal. Was he mistaken?"

She'd brought no garment along suitable for a meal within Wilmont's grand great hall because she didn't plan to mingle with the family or their guests. Stephen wouldn't have known that, however. Had he guessed?

"Well, nay, but I would not deprive another of her gown for my convenience. The girls and I will retire to the tent and take our supper from the supplies we brought along."

Ardith's smile never faltered. "'Tis kind of you to think of the gown's owner, but all of our ladies have gowns aplenty, so you do not deprive Christina. Truly, there is no reason for you to eat alone when you can do so in company. Afterward, mayhap you and I can continue our talk."

While Ardith fed the baby, they'd talked about many things, mostly about their children, and touched on the subject of Lyssa's headaches. 'Twas tempting to accept, yet there were other reasons for declining to sup in the hall, none of which she could explain to Ardith or Ursula.

"I fear the girls have nothing suitable to wear, either. And both will tire soon from the day's journey. I would hate to have them disrupt—"

Ardith waved a dismissing hand. "Daymon and Everart have their supper up here. The children take nooning with us, but with so many guests about, by supper have need to escape all the attention. The girls could eat up here with the boys, with a nursemaid to watch over them."

Then the girls wouldn't be among people who might

shun them, or notice their black hair matched that of
Stephen and his mother. Too, tonight might be her only
chance to talk further with Ardith. Still, the girls feelings
must also be considered. Marian took the few steps necessary to speak softly to her hostess.

"Last night's incident frightened the girls," she told
Ardith. "They have been a scarce few feet from my side
all day. I fear they would be upset."

With a thoughtful expression, Ardith glanced at the
children. "Aye, I see your worry. If they agree, however,
a couple of hours of separation might be good for all of
you."

Marian saw the sense in it, too. And, damn, but the
idea of spending an evening in the great hall tugged
hard. She'd been all of ten and six the last time she
attended a great feast. There hadn't been an occasion at
Branwick to warrant one; both of Carolyn's marriages
had taken place at her husbands' holdings and Marian
hadn't attended. Down in the great hall there would be
food aplenty and entertainments. She hadn't realized, until now, how much she'd missed those enjoyments. She
knew few of the guests, would be just one more lady in
the crowd. What harm could come from spending a pleasurable hour or two among Wilmont's guests, if the girls
were agreeable?

The babe would require a feeding later, and when Ardith came up, Marian would, too, and finish their talk
about Lyssa's headaches. She could then fetch the girls
and retire to the tent, there to stay until the return to
Branwick.

Marian turned to see all four children standing near
the pallets. Naturally, they'd heard most of the conversation. The girls looked worried. Marian set her resolve

and, with a slight hand motion, beckoned the girls to her. They crossed the room slowly. Not a good sign.

She placed a hand on each of her daughter's shoulders.

"Lady Ardith has invited me to sup down in the great hall. As I am sure you heard, the two of you are welcome to remain up here with Daymon and Everart, with their nursemaid to watch over you. Would that bother you overmuch?"

The girls exchanged a glance Marian had become accustomed to over the years, a silent communication between them when a joint decision must be made, a judging of how the other felt on the matter.

Audra looked up first. "Will you be gone long?"

Marian shook her head. "Nay, only for the supper. When next Lady Ardith comes up to feed Matthew, I will come with her. Nor will I be far away, just down the stairs. Should you need me, you need only send for me."

Lyssa looked to Ardith. "Will Stephen be there?"

The question rocked Marian, but she understood. He'd been her rescuer last night.

"Aye, Lyssa, he most certainly will be," Ardith said. "I assure you, we will all watch over your mother most carefully. And I think you will like Gwyneth, who will watch over you. She knows many children's games."

The girls exchanged another look, made a decision.

Lyssa spoke for them. "'Tis all right, then."

Marian bent down and gave them both a hug. The nursemaid was sent for, and Marian approved of the young woman's cheerful demeanor. With the children once more set to play, Marian followed the women out into the hall, headed for Ardith's solar.

"We must rush somewhat," Ursula said. "Gerard has returned so everyone will begin sitting to table soon."

Ardith slowed her steps. "Ah. Mayhap I should go down, then, to ensure proper seating. Marian, might I leave you to Ursula's care?"

"Of course, I—" Marian stopped. "Dear me, I forgot all about Carolyn. She will need my help to make herself ready."

Ursula shook her head. "Carolyn has gone out to the tent to set her gown to rights." She turned to Ardith and rolled her eyes. "Would you believe Stephen sent Maeve out to help? I took the liberty of sending Christina out, too. I do not know what the boy was thinking to assign a kitchen wench a handmaiden's duties."

Ardith laughed lightly. "I doubt Stephen knows the difference. Truly, he may sometimes not say or do the right thing, but his intentions are always good."

Marian entered the solar to change, determined to have a pleasant evening. She shrugged off her problems with the brown peasant-weave, and allowed the sky-blue linen to brighten her mood. For the next two hours she would enjoy herself, forget her cares. Time enough later to take them back up again, when once more she donned the brown gown.

The linen fitted her, if snugly. The boots were roomy, but not overlarge. Marian melted as the maid brushed and plaited her hair, then covered it with a veil.

"Oh, much better!" Ursula declared.

Marian viewed the transformation in the silvered glass and agreed. Much, much better.

Chapter Twelve

Stephen rather liked the honor of sitting at the dais beside Ardith. From this vantage point, he could see most everything happening at the tables stretched down the great hall, note which nobles got along with their seating partners and who didn't. Sometimes the pairings proved amusing.

Carolyn was also so honored, seated at Gerard's left, between his brother and Lady Ursula. The placement told everyone in the hall that the family held Carolyn in high regard, and the "why" of the high regard would quickly become the speculation of the evening. No doubt several persons had already guessed Stephen's intention to marry Carolyn, and then a debate would ensue about the wedding date and over who would be invited.

Stephen marveled at the predictability of his peers, at what messages could be sent and received by the mere chance of where one ate one's supper in whose hall. These nobles didn't know about the contest between him and Edwin, of course, that some doubt yet existed over who would win Carolyn's hand. They simply saw the esteem accorded Carolyn and made their assumptions, exactly as Ardith had intended. Except she didn't know about the contest, either. Still, 'twas nice to know his family accepted Carolyn, and it didn't hurt to have his rival witness their approval.

Not quite so easy for all to comprehend was Ardith's decision to put Edwin of Tinfield and Marian de Lacy in the highest seats at the highest table. As the noblest of rank attending the festivities and a great friend and ally of Gerard's, the earl of Warwick and his wife normally occupied seats at the dais. Neither of those high nobles seemed to mind being bumped down two full placements. Indeed, the earl and his wife seemed to enjoy Edwin and Marian's company.

Stephen hadn't yet figured out Ardith's purpose, but he knew better than to disturb her until after the servants finished bringing in the first course. So he watched Marian's eyes sparkle at some remark made by the earl.

This was how he remembered first seeing Marian so many years ago. Gowned in fine linen, her eyes alight with enjoyment, the girl who smiled easily at a jest. The other Marian, the widow who garbed herself in rough peasant-weave, seemed to have fled for the night and Stephen commended himself for taking a small part in that woman's banishment.

This was where Marian belonged—in a noble hall, suitably garbed and conversing with her peers, not hidden away in a hut in a hamlet. She'd once held sway in her father's hall, charming everyone with her pleasant voice and witty conversation, her genuine interest in whomever she spoke to, even the servants. Yet she'd given it all up or lost it somehow.

The niggling feeling returned that he was somehow at fault. He'd tried to talk to Marian about the rift with her family, find out more about her deceased husband. She refused. He should let the thing be.

Ardith shifted in her chair, turned to watch the doors. They opened and in walked five sturdy lads, each bearing a huge platter on which rested a fully dressed roasted peacock. To the appreciation of those at table, the lads went about the business of serving. Ardith relaxed a bit.

Stephen nudged her elbow. "Good show."

"Let us hope one of the peacocks does not slide off onto someone's lap."

Stephen doubted she truly worried. Wilmont's servants were too well trained for such a happenstance. Still, she watched one of the lads approach the dais to present his bird to Gerard.

"You must explain something to me, Ardith."

"What is that?"

"Why you placed Edwin and Marian so high."

He'd finally distracted her enough to gain her attention.

"Convenience sake, mostly. This way I need only give her a small signal when the time comes for me to see to Matthew, and I thought being partnered with Edwin, someone she knows, would make her feel more comfortable."

"And why does your seeing to Matthew affect Marian?"

"Because she will go up with me, as she promised the girls."

She said it as if he should somehow know all this. His confusion must have shown.

"Ah, I assumed Marian told you of what went on upstairs."

In the midst of introducing Carolyn to Gerard when Marian came down the stairs, Stephen hadn't yet found the opportunity to talk to her. At the shake of his head, Ardith went on.

"Last night's incident badly frightened Marian's daughters. They were reluctant to allow their mother out of their sight. She assured them she would not be gone long or far away." Ardith put her hand on his forearm. "The girls were not satisfied, however, until told you would be in the hall. 'Twould seem they assume that since you rescued Marian once, you could do so again should the need arise. 'Tis quite a trust they have placed in you, and I cannot think of anyone who more deserves it."

The peacock arrived at the lord's table and Ardith turned her attention to her duties once more.

Ardith's words tore at his heart. He could think of several people who deserved her regard far more than he. She simply wouldn't accept that he'd *failed* her. 'Twas his fault she and Daymon had been kidnapped, taken away in the middle of the night by a ruthless enemy of Gerard's. Gerard had left the two people most precious to him in Stephen's care, and he'd failed to protect them.

Stephen twirled his eating knife between his fingers. Ardith had placed Marian right beneath his nose for the girls' sake, so he could watch over Marian, protect her from harm if need be.

A sacred trust, one he didn't want. Too often he failed to meet others' expectations of him, and he hated the thought of disappointing Audra and Lyssa.

'Twas why he'd chosen to marry Carolyn, a woman who expected only one thing from him—an occasional visit to her bed to sire her heirs. Given his unexplainable lack of lust for the woman—hellfire, 'twas the one expectation he'd never envisioned having a problem meeting with any woman.

The earl rose from the bench, held his goblet high and

shouted his compliments to Ardith. The other guests joined in the raucous cheer accompanied by whistling and pounding on the table. Stephen lifted his goblet— and watched Marian, caught up in the glee.

His heart skipped a beat. He ceased to hear the noise around him, see anything beyond the bright smile on her lovely face. With her goblet held up in salute, Marian's gaze shifted briefly to lock with his for one, perfect moment.

As if lightning struck, his senses fired and came alive. What a joy she was to look upon, to speak to, to hold, to—

"Stephen, you had best eat before the meat grows cold."

Stephen looked down to see two large chunks of meat on his trencher obviously placed there by Ardith—and he hadn't noticed.

"My thanks," he muttered, and tried to keep his thoughts where they belonged for the rest of the meal.

Hard to do when Marian's laughter drifted up to snare his awareness, when the flutter of her hand as she talked caught his attention. Harder still when he noticed she never looked his way again, but bestowed her smiles and conversation on Edwin.

Course followed course. He ate, but the food sat hard in his stomach. At the last, he barely tasted the dried apricots and raisins sprinkled with sugar and cinnamon, a dish he usually enjoyed.

Ardith sat back in her chair, placed a hand on her stomach. "Dear me, I must remember I am no longer eating for two!"

"Ah, but you must eat to keep up your energy. For all you do around here you could eat for three and still keep your lovely figure."

"My thanks, but I do believe I shall refrain." Ardith looked down at where Marian sat. "I almost hate to bother her. She is having such a good time."

"Time to go up?"

"Almost."

Stephen didn't mind bothering Marian at all. She was having entirely too good a time in the company of Edwin of Tinfield and Charles of Warwick.

"Say the word and I will fetch her," he offered.

"How gracious of you."

He thought so, then grew impatient when Ardith turned to say something to Gerard instead of moving to go upstairs, but then she wouldn't. *Nobody* rose from table until after the baron did, and Gerard didn't appear ready. He hadn't yet finished his apricots.

Neither had Marian. She plucked a piece of the succulent fruit from her bowl with her fingertips, placed the slice of apricot between her lips, and held it there. Likely sucking on it, rolling her tongue around the fruit to moisten it, causing it to swell.

Stephen closed his eyes and inwardly shuddered. Not even the scrape of Gerard's chair released him from his misery.

Marian bit into the apricot, savoring the sweet flavor. The baron had pushed back his chair and risen, a signal to all that they may do the same. 'Twas greedy of her, but she wanted another hour of fine food and mellow wine and pleasant conversation.

Gad, she sat at table above the earl of Warwick! Ardith had explained her reasons for the seating to the earl, and he and his wife hadn't minded in the least. Such good company they'd been, and Edwin...well, Carolyn was an utter fool to refuse the man's suit. He'd been utterly charming and poised.

The rest of the party at the dais also rose, but none of them stepped down, merely stood about talking. Until Ardith headed for the stairway, Marian didn't need to move, so she plucked the last apricot from her bowl and popped it in her mouth.

The earl's wife leaned forward, her eyes atwinkle. "So, is there a wedding in the offing between Stephen and Lady Carolyn?"

Marian swallowed hard to keep from choking. All in the hall had been privy to the family of Wilmont's honor of Carolyn de Grasse and would make the same assumption as the earl's wife. 'Twas the one disheartening aspect of the evening, that the whole time Marian enjoyed the supper, she'd also yearned to be the woman seated at the dais.

Foolish, of course. Still, she'd been hard-pressed to look at Carolyn or Stephen all evening, so she'd tried to ignore them. For the most part, she succeeded.

"The matter is by no means settled," Edwin stated, quietly and calmly. How hard it must be for Edwin to witness Carolyn's acceptance by Stephen's family. It did Marian's heart good, however, to hear he hadn't given in to despair.

Stephen approached, escorting Carolyn.

Something bothered Carolyn. Her smile was in place, but she wasn't at all happy.

Stephen bowed slightly in the earl's direction. "Charles, I am given to understand you took one too many heron during today's hunt."

With a smug look, the earl rejoined, "I did, an unforgivable feat I am sure Gerard hopes to best on the morrow."

"He does, but I intend to beat you both."

"Ah, a challenge then?"

"Naturally," Stephen said, then turned to Edwin. "You once remarked on the quality of Wilmont's mews. Care to join us on the morn?"

"Delighted," Edwin answered, and Marian guessed he truly was. Even she wouldn't mind a chance to fly one of the falcons perched behind the dais, each one more magnificent than the other.

"Wonderful. That settled, I fear I must deprive you of Lady Marian's company. Marian?"

She leaned over to look around Stephen. Ardith and the baron stood a ways off, waiting. Marian rose, her heart divided between remaining in the hall and returning to her daughters. Return she must, but 'twas harder than she thought it would be.

"I thank you all for a delightful evening," she told the earl and his wife. "'Twas truly enjoyable."

The earl stood and took her hand between his. "Our pleasure, my dear. 'Tis sorry I am you must leave us so soon."

Stephen chuckled. "But my lord, I would never be so mean as to deprive you of pleasant company. I take Marian away, but leave Carolyn in her stead."

Marian moved aside to allow Carolyn by. Carolyn's smile faltered slightly as she leaned over to whisper, "You and the girls are returning to the tent now?"

"Aye."

"Good. We will talk later then."

She'd been right about Carolyn's false smile. Whatever was bothering her cousin? Had something happened, or been said, by one of Stephen's family to put her out of sorts? Could it be serious enough to make Carolyn rethink her plan to marry Stephen?

Marian inwardly scoffed. 'Twould take a miracle to put Carolyn *that* out of sorts.

Stephen put his hand on Marian's elbow. The gesture sent shivers through her entire being. He gave her a nudge toward where Gerard and Ardith waited.

"You look lovely in blue," he said softly.

The compliment shouldn't delight her so. She remembered her ire over his interference.

"You should not have spoken with your mother about my lack of a suitable gown."

He leaned in closer, his breath a warm caress. "Are you truly sorry I did?"

She should push him away, put some distance between them. "I should be."

"You did appear to be having a good time."

"I did. The earl and his wife are delightful, and Edwin is always good company."

"Does this mean I am back in your good graces?"

She'd been horrid to him last eve, rude today. He'd done nothing wrong yet tried to make amends.

"I owe you an apology, Stephen. Might we talk later?"

"We might," he said wryly.

Ardith smiled at their approach. "Marian, you have not yet met my husband. Gerard, this is Marian de Lacy."

Marian dipped into a deep curtsey, then rose to find the baron's green eyes studying her. His regard was intense, yet not frightening. Marian guessed this man could be intimidating if he so wished.

"Lady Marian. I hope your stay at Wilmont somewhat makes up for your journey to get to us."

Obviously he'd heard about last night's mishap. How

far had the tale spread? The earl hadn't mentioned it. Perhaps not everyone knew.

"Wilmont's hospitality is most gracious, my lord."

"I understand your daughters are upstairs with my sons."

"Handsome lads, all."

A smile touched Gerard's mouth. "I believe so, too."

Ardith moved toward the stairs, Marian followed, with Stephen and Gerard falling in behind. Climbing the stairs proved easier this time. Unfortunately, she must give up both the gown and the boots.

Ardith opened the door to the children's room. From inside, Marian heard the nursemaid's lilting voice. The young woman sat in one of the chairs, holding the baby. The other children sat on the floor around her, picking at the food on their trenchers, listening to her story.

The girls must have heard the door, for as soon as they spotted Marian they were up and running. They hit her with force, as they had last night, but tonight there were no tears, no apologies, only relief and joy.

Audra let go, then launched herself at Stephen. He no more than caught her up when Lyssa wrapped around his legs.

With a soft smile he returned their affection, and Marian's heart tore open.

All I need do is tell him.

Stephen would acknowledge the girls as his. Love them. Likely provide for them far better than she could. They would enjoy his affection and the benefits of his wealth.

But not his name. Unless Stephen married their mother, the girls would bear the burden of bastardy, a heavy burden when added to the encumbrance of being twins. Stephen didn't want to wed with Marian. He wanted Carolyn as his wife, a point his family had made very clear at supper tonight.

Carolyn. Her cousin to whom she owed so much, and when wrapped around Stephen last eve, been so willing to betray. No matter how deeply she loved Stephen or believed Carolyn should marry Edwin, she had no right to become intimate with the man Carolyn wished to wed.

Stephen ruffled the twins' hair. "You two look tired. Ready to go to the tent?"

"Are you coming with us?" Lyssa asked hopefully.

He squatted down, his expression disturbed. "There truly is no reason for you two to fear for your mother's safety here at Wilmont. What happened last eve was an accident, and is over. You understand this?"

Two little heads bobbed.

He looked from one to the other. "And you would still feel better if I escorted you to the tent, I take it."

"Aye," they confirmed in perfect accord.

"Then so be it." He stood up. "Marian? Ready?"

She had wanted to speak with Ardith, who now cuddled her baby to her, preparing for feeding. Her ladyship looked weary to the bone.

"Lady Ardith, would you mind if we put off our talk until another time?"

"Not at all. Perhaps on the morrow?"

"Perhaps. We will take our leave, then. My thanks for a lovely supper. Girls?"

She and Stephen waited by the door while the twins did a round of curtsies and thanks to Ardith and Gerard, and the nursemaid, and the boys.

As the four of them left the chamber, she remembered her borrowed gown.

"Hold a moment," she told Stephen, then hurried to the solar, rolled her slippers and gown up tightly and tucked the bundle under her arm. The girls could help her with her lacings tonight, and the gown returned to its owner tomorrow.

Stephen looked askance at the bundle but said nothing. He led them down the stairway, around the edge of the great hall. Marian noted the few heads that turned their way, but no one seemed overly interested. Grateful for the disregard, she followed Stephen and the twins out the door and into the dusk of a summer evening.

The inner yard and bailey were quieter now, most everyone either in the great hall or off attending chores and duties before night descended. Marian fell into step beside Stephen, the girls walking briskly a few paces ahead.

A good time to say what she must to say.

"I need to thank you for coming to my rescue last eve. 'Twas unconscionable of me not to do so earlier."

"As I recall, you tried."

Marian felt her cheeks grow warm. "I need to thank you, too, for not accepting my...gratitude."

"Mind you, I was sore tempted. Still am."

The strike of her boots on the wooden drawbridge rang in rhythm with her pounding pulse. "I was wrong to tempt you, tempt us both. We cannot...allow such intimacy."

"'Twas what I feared you would say. I was rather hoping for another offer."

An offer she'd make in a gnat's breath if they were both free of obligations, if he loved her, if she thought for one moment there might be a future for them together.

"Now who does the tempting? Truly, Stephen, you should look to Carolyn for offers, not me."

She could have kicked herself as soon as the words

were out. They were nearly to the tent before he answered.

"You are right, of course. My pardon, Marian. In the future I will aim my lust toward the proper target."

Marian couldn't help hoping his aim faulty.

She'd no more than tucked the girls into their pallets when Carolyn charged into the tent.

"Have you no care for my feelings at all?"

Carolyn's seething anger took Marian by surprise. She'd known her cousin might need soothing, couldn't think of anything she'd done to warrant Carolyn's ire. Even if she had, Carolyn's implication that she'd done so apurpose wasn't to be borne!

Then Carolyn swayed. Too much wine, Marian realized. Oh, Lord. Whatever her cousin was about to accuse her of wouldn't be graciously said.

Marian glanced over at the girls, now sitting up and wide-eyed awake on their pallets. "Down and to sleep," she ordered, then brushed past Carolyn on her way out of the tent and into the night. Several yards away from the tent, near the huge torch marking its location, she turned around and waited for her cousin. A few heartbeats later, Carolyn came out.

Marian crossed her arms. "What has your braid in a twist?"

"After all I have done for you, how could you be so shamelessly inconsiderate?"

"I have no idea what you are talking about."

"No idea? From the moment we entered Wilmont you have done nothing but call attention to yourself. One would think *you* the woman Stephen intends to marry, not me."

"Nonsense. Who was it who sat up at the dais to-night?"

Carolyn waived a dismissive hand. "For all the good it did me. 'Twas you, not me, who was invited up the stairs to the family apartments, not once but twice."

Marian couldn't be sorry Carolyn hadn't been invited up the stairs for the night.

"'Twas truly the girls, not me, who were invited up the stairs."

"But you did not come down, did you? I fully expected you to return to the tent afterward, in time to help me ready myself for supper. Instead, I am given over to a serving wench who knew nothing of how to serve a lady!"

"Lady Ursula told me she sent a handmaiden out to help you."

"She did, Christina, who took great delight in informing me that *Lady Ursula* borrowed one of her gowns so that *you* might be properly dressed for evening meal. Can you imagine my mortification?"

Not truly. "Because I accepted the offer of a decent gown?"

"Because you accepted not only the gown and the invitation to supper, but then had the audacity to accept the highest chair at the highest table, inconveniencing an earl no less. Could you not have had the decency to sit lower, where you belonged?"

Marian took a deep breath, striving for patience, knowing the wine muddled Carolyn's head. Knowing, too, that when in a petulant mood, Carolyn only heard what she wanted to hear.

"I accepted all at her ladyship's insistence, sat at the high table for Ardith's sake. Besides, the earl did not seem to take offense."

"Nay, he did not. He seemed as taken with you as the rest. I swear, if I had been forced to listen to Lady Ursula compliment you on your deportment one more time, or answer the baron's questions about last night's mishap I might have gone mad."

The hair on the back of her neck prickled. "What questions?"

"Oh, over how the four of you came to be down at the river together, and if I thought you and the girls fully recovered from the mishap."

"That was all?"

Carolyn crossed her arms. "He expressed some surprise that the twins obeyed Stephen's order to stay put. 'Twould seem his middle son is three and does not take to commands easily. I assured him that at age three the girls did not, either."

Marian worried over the baron's curiosity. Had his questions been innocent, or designed to gather information about the girls. Did he suspect? And if he did, would he mention it to Stephen?

Caroline kicked at the dirt, her pout in full bloom. "Then what does Stephen do but march you all through the hall, prompting questions from the earl about the twins."

Marian's heart sank. "I did not think anyone noticed."

"The earl noticed, as did others. They also noticed that when Stephen returned to the hall he spent the rest of the evening up at the dais, speaking to his brother, neglecting me. When the earl deemed it time to retire, he offered me escort to my tent. I was so hoping one of the family would offer a bed upstairs." She shrugged her shoulders. "Anyway, I assume you have had your talk with Lady Ardith so your presence will be less marked on the morrow.''

Marian hadn't wanted her presence marked at all. Despite her ire over Carolyn's attitude, Marian was glad for the warning. She couldn't go back up to the keep. She had exposed the twins to too much scrutiny already. The baron's questions might be innocent, but dare she take the risk?

"You need not worry over the family's distraction with me or the twins any longer. I do not intend to go up to the keep during the remainder of our stay. Beginning tomorrow, you have Stephen and his family all to yourself.''

The statement brought Carolyn up short. "Then Lady Ardith suggested a cure for Lyssa's headaches.''

Marian shook her head. "Not enough time. Perhaps you might speak with Ardith on Lyssa's behalf.''

"I might," she said, then rubbed at her brow. "Then mayhap Lady Ardith will invite me up the stairs.''

Marian put an arm around Carolyn's shoulders, pointed her back to the tent. "Mayhap.''

"Why do you not wish to go back?''

"If the earl noticed the twins and remarked on them, then others will, too. You know how cruel some people can be.''

"To protect the girls from unkind remarks, then.''

Or worse. From someone at Wilmont realizing the girls were base born, and guessing whose base born children they might be.

Chapter Thirteen

Stephen strutted across the hall, his falcon on his arm. He paused long enough to hug Ardith.

She smiled up at him. "I gather the hunt went well."

"Well, indeed. As mistress of the mews, I commend you on a job well-done, but beware, both Gerard and Richard are in a rare foul mood."

"Oh, dear. Edwin and the earl?"

"Content."

Hearing the rest of the hunting party enter the hall, Stephen strode behind the dais, unwrapped the leather jesses from around his gloved arm and urged the falcon onto her perch.

Richard had arrived this morning in time to join the hunting party. 'Twas rare when the three brothers were at Wilmont at the same time and able to enjoy an outing together.

What a pair they were, Gerard and Richard, both big, broad and blond, like their father. Serious, for the most part, and particularly doting where their wives were concerned. He watched his brothers approach, noting the two even walked alike, with long, purposeful strides.

Richard urged his falcon onto the perch. "You can stop gloating now."

Stephen tried not to smile. "I said nothing to anyone but Ardith, and that only to compliment her bird."

"You said nothing of the heron I missed?"

"Nay."

"Or the hare I did not see?" Gerard asked.

"I did not." Stephen glanced from one brother to the other. "In truth, I do not understand what distracted the both of you this morn. 'Twas not the falcons' fault neither of you paid heed. What were you talking about?"

Richard looked to Gerard.

Gerard glanced over at where Edwin and the earl perched their falcons. "Later."

Something family related and private then, Stephen surmised, knowing Gerard's "later" could mean this afternoon or two days from now depending upon his whim. Maybe something he and Gerard talked about last night? Over a keg of ale, the two of them discussed several things—Wilmont's holdings, the state of Stephen's holdings, Corwin's situation, Carolyn.

Toward the bottom of the keg, Stephen related the conditions of William's contest. To Gerard's raised eyebrow, he'd quickly explained there was no offense meant—'twas simply the desire of an ailing father to ensure his lands in good hands when his daughter inherited. Stephen then changed the subject, to Marian and her daughters.

'Struth, he'd rambled on for quite a while about them, perhaps too much, considering Marian all but told him to go to the devil last eve.

He glanced around the room, seeing no sign of her. He'd missed her this morning. She hadn't come up to the keep to break fast. Surely, she would be here for nooning.

Edwin walked up, shaking his head. "I must say, Lord Gerard, I doubted Stephen's boasting on the quality of Wilmont's falcons. I doubt no more."

The earl slapped Edwin on the back. "Now you know the reason I remain friends with Gerard, so I might have the use of these magnificent birds."

"And because I give you a good price on horses," Gerard added.

To the men's chuckles, the earl admitted, "That, too. A good hunt calls for a goblet of fine wine. What say, Gerard?"

"I say why not?"

As the others left, Stephen leaned toward Richard. "Pour me one. I wish a word with Carolyn first."

She hadn't moved from where he left her this morning, seated next to his mother amid a bevy of ladies, most of them daughters of noble houses who served as Ardith and Ursula's handmaidens. The giggling gaggle, he termed the group, young women with little more to do than sit and gossip while they worked with either distaff and spindle or yarn and linen. Under Ardith's tutelage they learned the rudiments of managing a noble household, for when their fathers arranged marriages for them.

Each was beautifully gowned and prettily mannered, but not one of them could hold his attention for long. He tended to drift off into his own thoughts when speaking to them. A problem he'd not experienced with Marian.

She'd hovered at the edge of his mind all morning. Her apology, her embarrassment. His promise to aim at a proper target, Carolyn. He inwardly winced at the thought that at the moment his arrow would fall short.

Unwilling to wade in among the ladies, he stopped at the edge of their circle.

"Carolyn, a word if you please."

The entire gaggle watched Carolyn rise from the bench and walk toward him. He backed up a few steps for a bit of privacy.

"I understand you had a good hunt," she said. "How did Edwin do?"

"Ask him about his swan. I am sure he will be most pleased to give you all the details."

A soft smile touched her mouth. "I imagine he will. My thanks for inviting him along. He does not often get the chance to hunt, and rarely in such grand company."

Her thanks on Edwin's behalf didn't surprise Stephen. He'd been aware for some time that Carolyn liked the man, just considered him a poor choice as a husband.

"Has Marian not come up yet?"

Her smile tightened. "Not as yet, nor do I expect her to. Is this why you call me to you, to talk about my cousin?"

Carolyn's tone warned him to take a less direct tack. "I worried that something might be amiss. Is Lyssa ill?"

Her expression softened immediately "Oh, Lyssa is fine," she assured him quickly, then hesitated before adding, "'Tis just that Marian has her reasons for keeping to the tent."

"Such as?"

Carolyn drew a deep breath and looked around, then said quietly. "If you must know, she is concerned about how much notice people might take of the twins. Even at Branwick, not everyone accepts them. I believe she fears those gathered here might not be so circumspect in hiding their distaste for having twins about.''

Stephen remembered watching Marian cross the bailey with the twins, and the woman who'd crossed herself on their passing. She'd done so behind Marian's back, remained discreet, if ignorant. A baron, or his ilk, would feel no need for discretion with someone not of his rank.

His fist clenched. ''Has some lout made a remark to Marian or one of the twins?''

''Oh, nay! Marian merely wishes to avoid the possibility. She would feel awful if some incident took place which might mar your family's celebration.''

'Twouldn't be Marian's fault if a haughty noble took it upon himself to proclaim his ignorance. 'Twasn't right for Marian to deny herself and her daughters on a chance happenstance.

''Surely Marian will attend the christening ceremony.''

Carolyn shook her head.

Stephen didn't understand the reasoning, nor did Carolyn's comments ring true. Marian was protective of her daughters, but didn't smother them. 'Twas strange she would hide them, as if ashamed of them.

'''Tis not right Marian came all this way to sit in a tent. I will talk to her, let her know she need not worry about how the twins will be treated.''

Her mouth pursed, annoyed. ''Do you think that wise? I would not want the twins or Marian hurt by a careless remark. Too, you must remember Marian never intended to do aught but speak with Lady Ardith about Lyssa's headaches, so brought no garments appropriate for associating with your family and their guests. 'Twould be embarrassing for all concerned if you insist she do so.''

''But she was given a gown yesterday.''

"I returned it to its owner this morn. Truly, Stephen, 'twould be best if you let the matter be."

Claiming the last word, Carolyn flounced off to retake her seat among the ladies.

Stephen headed for where his brothers stood enjoying their wine. He held a hand out as he approached and Richard passed over a goblet. While the others compared the feats of the falcons, Stephen mulled over Carolyn's comments.

'Twasn't right, any of it.

Marian was wrong to hide the twins away as if they were lepers. She should join in the festivities, be here to receive Ardith's praise for the gift she'd made for the babe, properly garbed or not.

He wasn't, as Carolyn suggested, going to let the matter be.

Stephen perched on the edge of Gerard's heavy writing table, remembering the last time the three of them had gathered for a private talk. At that time, Gerard sent him and Richard to Westminster. He hoped this time Gerard wasn't about to send him off somewhere. Too much to do here.

Gerard settled into his chair behind the table. Richard closed the door and took the only other chair in the room.

"Ah, peace," Gerard said on a sigh. "'Tis nice to have guests but not so many."

Stephen chuckled. "Then why did you invite half of England?"

"To irritate the other half, of course."

"Naturally. So why are we up here?"

"To settle my mind on something you said last night." He glanced at Richard before continuing. "I told

Richard about this contest of William de Grasse's. Neither of us has a liking for it, Stephen. 'Tis insulting.''

Stephen checked his ire. Gerard wasn't raging angry, merely irritated, and that on his youngest brother's behalf.

"No insult is intended. True, William believes Edwin the better match for Carolyn, but I think he is willing to allow our marriage if he is assured his lands will not fall to ruin after his death.''

Richard leaned forward. "Did I misunderstand, or did you not tell me Carolyn intends to oversee her own lands when she inherits?''

"She does.''

"Then why test you?''

"In truth, I think William tests Carolyn more than either Edwin or I.'' Stephen told them about William's ill health, his inability to ride his lands. Then of Carolyn's list, and of how he and Edwin were actually assessing her judgment. "I think William truly wants confirmation that Carolyn can oversee the lands, that her grasp of land use and the value of goods and labor is sound.''

"Seems an odd way to go about it,'' Gerard grumbled.

"Mayhap.'' Stephen got up and walked over to the arrow slit. From this vantage he could see most of the bailey and, beyond the outer curtain wall, the tops of the tents surrounding Wilmont, including the tent where Marian hid. "William has known Edwin for a long time, knows how the man would advise Carolyn should she ask for help. He does not know me, so does not trust my knowledge or insight. I imagine he only wants to be assured he does right by his daughter.''

"And you intend to win,'' Richard stated.

Stephen turned around. "Do you doubt I can?"

"Nay. The survey you did several years ago on our holdings proved your ability. Your own holdings are in excellent shape and producing nicely. I just wonder if the woman is worth all the trouble."

"Carolyn is...Carolyn. She is beautiful, opinionated and often petulant. She is not the most loving of women, but neither is she a shrew. I believe we will make a good marriage, for both of us."

"Convenient." Gerard said the word with a hint of disdain. Stephen knew very well what lecture would come next if he didn't head it off now.

"Very convenient, which is how I want it. You both married for love, all well and good. I have other reasons for choosing Carolyn as my wife. Give it up, Gerard."

Gerard looked to Richard for reinforcements.

Richard, bless him, shrugged a shoulder. "Stephen seems to have decided."

Gerard's huff sounded more of frustration than resignation.

"So you win this contest and marry Carolyn. What of Edwin? Will he make trouble for you?"

"I think not. He truly is a decent sort."

Richard rose from his chair, stretched. "You know, Gerard, with half of England's nobility here, mayhap we could prevail upon Ardith and Lucinda to find Edwin a wife. From the little I talked to him today, I agree with Stephen. The man is decent if a bit rigid. If our wives found a woman to turn Edwin's head, then 'twould lay the path clear for Stephen to marry Carolyn."

Gerard leaned back in his chair. "Not a bad idea. Truly, from what I observed last eve, the man could do no better than to look to Lady Marian."

"Nay!" Stephen said, then wanted the word back. His

brothers stared at him, too hard. "The two are friendly, but have no interest in each other."

"A shame," Gerard said. "From what you told me last eve, Lady Marian could use a husband. 'Tis not right for a noble lady to live so humbly."

"So I have told Marian, but she prefers the quiet simplicity of the hut to living in her uncle's keep."

Gerard went on. "And those two beautiful little girls. How sad for them to go about in tunics and sandals when they could wear silk gowns and boots. Marian should marry again, if only for their sakes."

"She has refused several offers, I understand, and I am sure William will see to the girls' bride portion when the time comes for them to…marry."

Gad, the girls were nowhere near old enough to be considering such thoughts. There were games to be played, lessons to be learned, frogs to be hunted before they began to notice boys. And boys to notice them.

Gerard smiled. "Well, mayhap Marian has just not found the right man yet. She truly is a beauty, and Charles remarked on her vivacious manner. Others noticed, too."

What others? "Who?"

"Robert of Portieres for one, and Geoffrey d'Montgomery. Both asked after her this morn."

Both unmarried, both monied. Both highly suitable. He'd known all along this might happen, that other men would look at Marian and want her. So why had he asked his mother to find her a suitable gown so she could come into the hall for all those men to see? To admire? To desire?

Because *he'd* wanted to see Marian gowned in finery, allow her to have a decent supper and give her a couple of hours of pleasure. Wanted her handy because he'd contemplated dragging her off for his own purposes, to satisfy his craving—a craving so deep and consuming he'd lost interest in all other women.

He wanted only one woman. Marian. Body and heart, her love and her trust. His to hold forever as his alone.

Because he'd fallen in love with Marian.

He couldn't say when it had happened, only knew deep in his heart that he loved her beyond reason. Hellfire, he was so close to winning Carolyn, and gone and fallen in love with her cousin.

His wayward heart aside, nothing had changed. He knew himself too well. He was far more suited to an arranged marriage than one based on love.

Marian would expect a marriage akin to what his brothers shared with their wives, and Stephen just didn't have it in him to fulfill those expectations. At some point he would fail Marian, prove himself unworthy of her.

Useless to pursue this line of thought. Marian wouldn't have him anyway, had told him last eve to look for offers elsewhere. Except he didn't want another woman's offer. He wished he could go back to the river and claim Marian's offer, which he'd "nobly" turned aside.

"Stephen?"

He looked up at Gerard. "Hmm?"

"Robert and Geoffrey. Should I make their interest in Marian known to Hugo de Lacy?"

"Why?"

"'Tis how marriages are generally arranged, through the woman's father."

Typical Gerard. See a problem—solve it. Except Gerard didn't see the true problem. Nor could Stephen tell him why, merely discourage him, for now.

"Since when have you taken an interest in arranging marriages?"

Gerard tilted his head. "Why not? Is there some reason why Robert or Geoffrey should not approach Hugo?"

Several reasons, both his own and Marian's. "I fear Marian and her father had a falling out of some sort, so he may not have her best interests at heart."

"Any notion of what they argue over?"

He had his suspicions, but repeatedly respected Marian's wishes not to discuss it. "Nay, only that the bad feelings are years old."

"Then perhaps 'twould be best if I speak with Marian, after the christening ceremony perhaps."

His chest tightened. "Marian does not intend to come, I am told."

"Why ever not?" Gerard asked.

"Not sure." And he wasn't. The more he thought about the excuses Carolyn gave him, the more he thought them inadequate. "I intend to talk with Marian about it, convince her to come."

Gerard softened his voice. "If all else fails, ask her to come as a favor to me, actually to Ardith. She likes Marian, enjoys the girls. She would be hurt if Marian stayed away."

Stephen's gaze slid toward the arrow slit and the tents beyond, trying to remember that Gerard strove to aid Marian. If he wasn't in love with the woman, he'd applaud Gerard's efforts.

Except he was in love with Marian, and no matter how many times she negated his concern, he knew their affair was at the root of her rift with her father.

Mayhap 'twas time he stopped being respectful, so damn noble.

"I will tell Marian. In fact, if you have no further need of me, I will go now." Stephen headed for the door, then stopped. "I nearly forgot. Would either of you mind if I borrowed Daymon and Philip for a time? I promised Audra and Lyssa a frog hunt, and thought the boys might like to go, too."

Gerard looked to Richard. "Any objection?"

"Nay, none, so long as they are back before evening meal."

Stephen nodded and closed the door behind him.

Gerard held out his hand to Richard, palm up. "Give over."

Richard dug a coin from his leather pouch and slapped it into Gerard's hand. "Very well, so Stephen is in love with Marian, I will give you that. But the other? 'Tis beyond belief."

"Think you? Wait until you see Stephen coddle those two little girls and then tell me I am wrong."

Chapter Fourteen

"Hail in the tent! Anyone there!"

Marian started at the small voice from outside.

"Mama, that sounds like Daymon," Lyssa said, and ran to open the tent flap.

Without stood two boys, one of them Daymon. Stephen stood behind the boys, a large sack dangling from his hand. He looked troubled, unusual for Stephen.

"Might we come in?" he asked.

She'd rather he didn't, but the three had obviously come for some purpose.

Marian stepped back. The boys scooted inside without a problem. Stephen needed to duck.

Daymon addressed the girls, waving a hand at the black-haired boy at his side. "This is Philip. Uncle Stephen said you liked to hunt frogs and Philip and I know where to find them. Would you like to come?"

The girls, understandably, looked apprehensive about taking part in another frog hunt. The last ended badly. Still, both wanted to go, having been confined to the tent for most of the morn. 'Twas also necessary to get them into water again soon, so they'd not harbor fears too long.

Audra looked up at Stephen. "Are there snakes?"

Philip's eyes went wide. "You like snakes?"

Audra shivered. Lyssa shot Marian a wary glance.

Stephen ruffled Philip's hair. "Nay, Audra does not, so we hunt only frogs." He faced the girls. "'Tis a stream we go to, not a river. The stream is shallow, barely reaches your knees with no current to speak of…and lots of frogs."

"Are you coming, too?" Lyssa asked, though the plea and hope reflected in both girls' eyes.

As they had last night, the twins looked to Stephen as protector, someone to rely upon if something went awry. Marian stifled unwarranted resentment that they looked to someone other than their mother to fulfill their needs. 'Twas natural, she supposed, they would look to a big, strong male who'd already proven himself capable, for protection.

"I would not think of allowing you to go frog hunting without me," he stated, then smiled. "We will even take your mother along, if she is brave enough to consent."

She needed no courage to go near the water. Spending time with Stephen, however, 'twould wear on her spirit. Only for the girls' sake would she flirt with temptation once again.

"I say lead on."

Stephen shooed the children out of the tent, then handed her the sack. "I paid Christina for these, so they are now yours. We will wait for you."

He ducked out of the tent before she could open the sack—and object. Within lay two gowns—the blue she'd worn last night and one of amber—and a pair of boots.

Stephen shouldn't have purchased them. 'Twas thoughtful of him, but…maybe she would keep the boots.

Marian slipped off Carolyn's felt slippers and put on the boots. No sense being impractical. Having no use for the gowns, she'd give them back to Stephen after the frog hunt.

Daymon and Philip led the way across the clearing, Audra and Lyssa keeping up with their quick strides. Marian noted several more tents had been set up since yesterday. The bright rounds of brilliant color were scattered haphazardly in the grassy field, a field now chopped up by the numerous wagons and horses parked near their owners' tents.

Marian bit her bottom lip when the children disappeared into the woods. "The boys know where they are going?"

"Daymon knows the land surrounding Wilmont as well as I do. Philip is learning."

"I gather the two boys are friends."

"Philip is Richard's ward. They arrived this morning."

So now the whole family was gathered in the keep. The three brothers and those they cared for. Tomorrow they would christen the newest of them, baby Matthew. But not all was well. Stephen was upset about something.

She wouldn't ask. 'Twas none of her affair.

She liked Stephen's family. Ardith certainly ranked among the nicest of women, and while Stephen's mother might be a bit stiff and curt, she possessed a lovely smile and helpful manner. Even the baron, for his formal ways, seemed an amiable and fair man. All of the boys were certainly cute with sunny faces, even this newest lad, Philip. She suspected Richard and his wife would prove affable, too.

No matter. They were Stephen's family, which Carolyn might one day be a part of, not she.

The path through the woods wound about to a rock-bottomed, gurgling stream. The children were already barefooted and splashing along the edge. Stephen waved her over to a large boulder to sit upon. He stood next to her, arms crossed and feet spread, watching the children.

"Carolyn told me you remained in the tent this morn because you feared the twins' presence in the hall might pose a problem. Not so, Marian. No one would dare make a heedless remark on their being twins. Gerard would take it as a slight against Ardith and show the miscreant the gate."

Marian's guard rose. 'Twas the baron's scrutiny and possible remarks she wished to avoid.

"Your family has been kind to us even though we intruded. 'Tis best I not court trouble."

"You did not intrude. I invited you, which makes you a guest, and due the respect and courtesy given all guests at Wilmont. Gerard and Ardith expect you to attend the christening ceremony on the morrow, and there is truly no reason why you should not. Not because of the twins nor from lack of proper garments. Even now Ardith's maids stitch gowns for the girls."

Have all attending see her daughters draped in costly silk, their raven tresses tied in ribbons? Let someone note the affection between Stephen and the two little girls with hair the hue of his? 'Twas far too great a risk.

"Besides," he continued, his voice gruff, "'twould be a good chance for you to meet your…suitors. Both Robert of Portieres and Geoffrey d'Montgomery made inquiries of you last eve. Gerard asked me if he should send word of their interest to your father."

Marian leapt up from the boulder, shock and fear roiling her stomach. "What did you tell him?"

His eyes narrowed. "I told him you and your family are not on good terms, that your father may not have your best interests at heart. But I could not tell him why because you continually refuse to confide in me! Time to give over, Marian, or the next ceremony you attend may be your wedding to a man not of your choosing."

Any man not Stephen wouldn't be of her choosing. Except Stephen chose Carolyn.

"You must tell your brother to desist. 'Tis none of his affair."

His ire lessened, his expression softened. "Nay, it is not Gerard's affair, but mine. I realize your separation from your family a result of our liaison, yet you continually tell me 'tis none of my concern. It is now, very much so. What happened between you and your father?"

Marian closed her eyes, bracing against new tears over an old wound. She'd cried her eyes out nearly the whole way from Murwaithe to Branwick, Carolyn's assurances of little comfort. And again when the girls were born, so scared and wanting her mother desperately, still wanting Stephen to somehow *know* and come for her. Useless tears, all.

"'Tis my own doing. I defied him, wounded him deeply. He will never forgive me for it."

Stephen put his hands on her shoulders, inviting closeness, confidences. "Look at your daughters. Is there anything they could possibly do to make you stop loving them?"

Audra and Lyssa were having a grand time. Philip had found a frog and prodded it with a stick to make it jump. The girls squealed with each leap. Raising them had been her greatest joy and heaviest burden. They could make her laugh and toss her into the depths of despair. She'd been frustrated, angry, ready to give them away at times. But she never would. They were hers, born of her body, the lights of her life. Nothing they might do could ever make her stop loving them. Disapprove of their behavior at times, aye, but the love was always with her, always would be.

She understood the point Stephen sought to make.

"My father may yet feel some love for me. I hope so. But what I did was unforgivable."

He squeezed her shoulders, took a deeper breath. "So I thought with my mother, but do you know, I believe she may have finally forgiven me for being born."

She reached up and put a hand over his. "Come now, how can a mother hate a child for simply being born?"

"When she hates the father for getting her with child," he said quietly. "She barred my father from her bed after he dared bring Richard to Wilmont and acknowledged him as his son. I understand Father allowed her to punish him for a while, then ordered the bolt removed from her door and insisted she resume her wifely duties. To my mother, I was the child who should not have been." He laughed with no humor. "Truly, Richard is assured a place in heaven for he has already known hell. She reminded him at every turn that he was bastard born, the lowest of the low. And me, she mostly ignored me, as if I did not exist."

Marian shook her head, unable to imagine such a harsh childhood, glad her daughters were spared such scorn. Still, she understood Urusla's reasons for hating her husband, not that those reasons condoned her mistreatment of her younger son.

"I imagine your mother must have been horrified when your father acknowledged Richard. To have proof of her husband's infidelity so blatantly presented to her and always present must have been difficult for her to live with.''

''Not difficult—impossible.''

''What happened to soften her, then?''

''Several months after my father's death, Mother decided she would rid Wilmont of all bastards, including Richard and little Daymon. Gerard would not stand for it. He packed her up and placed her in Romsey Abbey, would not allow her to return until she understood that bastards were not to blame for their circumstance of birth, the fathers were.''

And the mothers. Marian pursed her lips from uttering it aloud. She was as much to blame for the girls' conception as Stephen. Sweet Mother, she'd been utterly shameless in the hayloft, hot for the coupling, too wrapped up in her love and desire for Stephen to consider the consequences. She'd been so young, so foolish.

''Ursula no longer berates Richard?''

''Nay. Gerard demands she mind her tongue, more now for Daymon's sake than Richard's.''

She squeezed his hand. ''And you?''

''Well, with me things took a while longer, but we can now speak without fighting. I doubt we will ever be fond of each other, but we have reached a sort of peace. Is there no way you can find peace with your father?''

Only one way, by naming the sire of her girls. She'd debated the wisdom of that so many times, sometimes knowing it the right thing to do, at others assured the words must never pass her lips. For the girls' sake, for her own, which was best? She wished she knew.

''Father wants a confession of me, one I am unable to give him. Until then, he will not forgive me. There can be no peace between us.''

"Confess what?"

Her heart skipped a beat then thudded against her ribs. She shook her head.

"Marian—"

"Look, the children are too far downstream. We should go after them."

She tried move. He held her in place and gave out a long, sharp whistle. Both boys stopped where they were and turned around.

Stephen shouted, "Daymon, come back this way."

"But the frogs—"

"Daymon!"

With no further argument the boys obeyed and the girls followed.

"Let me go, Stephen."

His sigh was long and heavy; his thumbs massaged her collarbone. "Not this time. I will not fail you again, Marian, I swear."

"There is nothing—" her voice cracked, the tears too hot and close to withhold "—nothing…"

Stephen's arms came around her, enveloped her in his warmth and strength. She leaned into him, her knees threatening to buckle. She grabbed fistfuls of his tunic to keep upright, clenched her teeth to stifle sobs.

Gads, but she was tired. Tired of fighting her inner battles, weary of standing firm in her beliefs of how to best protect the girls, herself. Tired of being alone.

"There is always something to be done, some way to right a wrong, or at least to try. Tell me, Marian. Let me help."

If only he'd loved her all those years ago, parted from her with sweet words. If only he'd sent some message to let her know he considered her special. If only he'd been interested enough then to want to right a wrong—

a wrong he didn't know about. Because she'd been too young and proud.

So where was her pride now? She stood within the circle of Stephen's arms and didn't want to leave. Dare she tell him, let him share some of the burden? Stephen might not love her, but he cared for the girls. He'd do nothing to hurt them.

His hands cradled her head, tilted her face upward.

"Tell me," he whispered, the command in his voice and the sorrow in his eyes her undoing.

How did one tell a man he was a father? With a bit of preparation or straight out? What would he think, say, do?

"Several months after you left…when I could no longer hide…" She closed her eyes, groping for words.

He kissed her forehead gently, firmly. "Go on."

"I refused…refused to name the man who had… gotten me with…child."

Stephen's brow furrowed. "Your husband—"

"I never married."

"But then…"

She felt him stiffen, watched his face go blank. He looked up toward Audra and Lyssa. Marian clutched his tunic and prayed, as she had never prayed before, that she'd not made yet one more mistake.

"They are mine," he whispered. "The girls are mine."

Marian swallowed hard, her heart caught in her throat. She could only nod.

He looked back at her then. "The girls are mine," he repeated, his voice stronger.

"They are."

Rocked to his core, Stephen didn't know whether to shout for joy or scream in horror.

Marian hadn't married, he'd been lied to.

They are mine.

Why hadn't she told him? Why hadn't she sent for him?

Audra and Lyssa are mine.

He'd left Marian without a word of farewell, not his fault. He'd returned to Wilmont and worried somewhat over whether or not…but her father hadn't come demanding a marriage, so he considered himself safe. All the while Marian had been carrying, and suffering and— all his fault.

Sweet Lord, I am a father!

So now what? Tell everyone? Hell, he'd shout it from Wilmont's highest tower! Nay, not yet. Not until his insides settled down, his heartbeat slowed. Not until he had some answers from Marian.

First he had to sit down before he fell down. No, first he had to kiss Marian. Except he couldn't kiss Marian because he was furious with her. If he hadn't provoked her into telling him she might never have done so, allowed him to go through life never knowing about his daughters.

How dare she!

He glanced at the girls again. All four children stared straight down into the water, unaware that the earth had shifted to provide room for a stray piece of heaven.

What kind of a father would he make? He nearly staggered under the duty he now assumed. Responsible for Marian, the girls. Of all the explanations he'd expected, this news hadn't been among them.

Hellfire, could he be a decent father, a reliable husband?

He gazed into Marian's beautiful pewter eyes and found worry and doubt. He had to set her mind at ease, tell her he wouldn't fail her again, that all would be well just as soon as he figured out where he was and what he was going to do next.

Tell the girls. He should tell the girls, give them a hug, let them know he loved them. Or maybe he should tell Marian that he loved her. Good start.

"Stephen, I think you should sit down."

Grand idea. Maybe if he sat down his head would stop spinning and his thoughts settle.

Marian led him over to the boulder. "I know this must come as a surprise...."

He plopped down on the rock and scoured his face with his hands, as if the action would make everything clear.

"Hellfire, Marian, surprise does not begin...I never dreamed...when your father did not come to demand a marriage... Why did *you* not send word? I would have come!"

"At the time I was not sure you would remember my name!"

He shouldn't be angry with Marian. He could think of several reasons she might not have been willing to name him as her lover, and he wasn't ready to hear them confirmed.

"So you told your father you were carrying, but refused to name...me as the child's sire. What then?"

She looked downstream where Lyssa sat on the bank, laughing at Philip, who delightedly showered Daymon and Audra with water.

My daughters. The thought made him giddy all over again. The girls would be—he counted years—five. Then he counted months—somewhere near Yuletide if he guessed the month of conception aright. He'd thought them younger by a full year.

"Father flew into a rage," Marian said, dragging him

back. "He demanded the name of my lover over and over. I refused." She took a deep breath. "He vowed he would not harbor a harlot or her bastards, swore to send me out the gate if I did not give over. Carolyn happened to be at Murwaithe. She was as horrified at my father's threats as I. She offered me shelter at Branwick and I snatched the chance. The following morn we left Murwaithe. I said no farewells."

No wonder Marian put up with so much from her cousin, considering Carolyn her savior, of sorts. How frightened and upset Marian must have been.

He understood the false tale of Marian's widowhood, to spare her disgrace and save the girls from scorn.

"'Twas Carolyn's idea to claim you a widow?"

"Aye. William knows what happened, but no one else at Branwick."

So William sheltered his niece, and might have done better by her, to Stephen's way of thinking. At least William had taken her in. What would Marian have done if Carolyn hadn't taken her to Branwick? Would Hugo de Lacy have shown his pregnant daughter the gate? No way to judge—he didn't know the man all that well. Marian thought her father capable of such harshness or she wouldn't have left Murwaithe.

So many people to tell, so much to set right.

Audra came toward him at a run, her tunic and braid wet from the children's play. *Mine.* Gad, every time the realization struck he suffered another shiver of joy mingled with terror.

"Mama, Lyssa rubs at the back of her neck."

Marian's mouth pursed into a straight line. "The beginning of a headache. We must get Lyssa back to the tent."

Stephen pushed away from the boulder and headed

for where Daymon and Philip stood over Lyssa. Only three days had passed since Lyssa's last headache.

"Does she get sick so often, then?" Stephen asked.

"Not usually. I had hoped she would be spared another until we returned home, at the least."

Home to Marian meant Branwick, a hut in the hamlet. That was about to change, but he'd discuss living arrangements with Marian later, when he figured out what they might be.

Lyssa tore up a fistful of grass and flung the blades toward the stream. Tears streamed down her cheeks. She glared at Audra.

"I told you not to tell! We do not have to go back yet!"

"Do, too," Audra retorted.

"Do *not!* Please, Mama, 'tis only a little hurt. Can we not stay a while longer? I do not want to go back to the tent. I want to stay here!"

Marian bent down and brushed at Lyssa's cheeks. "You know 'twill only get worse. Best we do what we can early on."

Lyssa looked ready to argue. Marian put a forefinger on the girl's lips.

"You *know* we must, Lyssa. Mayhap, when the pain is gone, we can come back."

He reached down; Lyssa lifted her arms. "Certes, we can. The stream and the frogs will still be here."

Lyssa laid her head on his shoulder. His daughter. He'd held her before but not like this. Not as his own. Ye, gods.

Marian set the other children to putting on footwear, and they were soon headed back through the woods. As they stepped into the clearing, he sent Daymon ahead to tell Ardith why he was bringing Lyssa to the keep.

Daymon shot off like an arrow from a bow, Philip beside him.

Marian protested. "Oh, Stephen, we need not bother Ardith. She has so much to do with the baby and her guests and—"

"So I give her one more task to attend. She will not mind. Besides, if she has some notion of how to cure Lyssa, why not let her try it now?"

Marian didn't look happy, but she didn't argue further. He knew she wasn't used to having others make decisions where the girls were concerned. The moment she admitted he was their father, however, she gave him rights. Rights he intended to claim fully.

As they passed through the bailey, several heads turned his way. 'Twas all he could do not to shout out the news, answer the questions on their faces.

He found Ardith waiting for them on the keep's stairway. "Bring her up to the children's room," she ordered, then turned to lead the way.

The great hall was as crowded as Stephen had ever seen it, people everywhere. He followed Ardith along the wall, the quickest path to the stairs. His foot was on the first stair when he glanced toward the hearth. His brothers were in deep discussion with Robert of Portieres, one of Marian's new suitors.

After what Marian had just told him, he felt completely justified in telling his brothers to inform any future suitors to take their interest elsewhere.

Marian put a hand to his back. "Not yet. We need to talk more first. *Please,* Stephen."

Stephen climbed the stairs, his curiosity high. Marian couldn't have guessed his thoughts. So what did she believe she stopped him from doing? Telling his brothers?

If Marian thought he'd keep his daughters' existence secret, she'd best think again.

Chapter Fifteen

The nursemaid gathered up all the children except the baby and took them to play elsewhere. Ardith left to mix a potion. Lyssa sat on Stephen's lap, her back to his chest, her eyes closed. Marian didn't know if the lavender oil he rubbed into Lyssa's temples truly helped the headache, but her daughter's expression reflected no pain.

Marian sat in the other chair, tamping down her hopes. Over the past two years she'd dosed Lyssa with feverfew, meadowsweet and valerian, none of which worked well. Ardith meant to try a potion made from hawthorn berries, willow bark and rosemary.

If the potion relieved Lyssa's pain, then coming to Wilmont was worth the trip, no matter what else happened.

Lyssa gave a contented sigh and Marian had to smile. She'd given little thought to how the girls would react to learning Stephen was their father. She rather expected they'd be angry at her for keeping it secret, but they'd already taken Stephen to their hearts and would welcome him into their lives.

How much of their lives would he be a part of? Would

he always be around to rub Lyssa's head with lavender oil, or would he only come around to play with the girls occasionally?

Marian felt as if she'd opened a door that couldn't be closed. By giving Stephen his daughters, she'd changed all of their lives irrevocably. Some changes might not be for the better, but as she watched Stephen's fingers caress Lyssa's head to ease her pain, Marian couldn't be completely sorry.

Ardith bustled into the room, a cup in her hand. "Here we are. Tsk. Stephen, you were supposed to soothe the child, not put her to sleep."

"Here now, Lyssa, open your eyes or you will get me into trouble," Stephen teased.

Lyssa's eyes popped open. Ardith handed her the cup.

"'Tis warm, and I tried to make the potion more palatable by adding honey. It may yet taste awful but should ward off your headache."

Lyssa took a sniff and wrinkled her nose.

"Drink it down," Stephen encouraged her. "The sooner the hurt is gone, the sooner we can go back to the frogs."

Even the promise of frogs didn't take the wary look from her daughter's face. Marian got up, took the cup from Lyssa and tried a sip. Not tasty but not intolerable.

"You have had *much* worse."

Lyssa relented and drained the cup of the brew.

Ardith pointed to the nursemaid's pallet. "Now a nap. We should know within an hour or so if we have found our cure."

Stephen tucked Lyssa under the coverlet. He hovered over her for a moment, just looking. Marian remembered how, when the girls were babes, during those rare moments when both slept peacefully, she'd simply stare at them, wondering how she managed to give birth to two such beautiful, angelic creatures. Was Stephen, knowing he'd sired them, now awed in the same manner?

Ardith peered into the cradle at Matthew. "This one will be squalling about the time I want to check Lyssa. I had best go down to the hall till then. I assume you wish to remain here?"

Marian nodded. "Just in case she needs me. My thanks, Ardith, for your help. I know you must be terribly busy."

As always, her ladyship's smile held warmth. "No trouble at all." She headed for the door. "Stephen? Coming?"

"In a moment."

Ardith left the room, leaving Marian alone with Stephen and two sleeping children. Marian walked over to the pallet and bent over Lyssa, who had fallen asleep almost immediately upon lying down.

"Mayhap the lavender oil helped," Marian whispered, believing Stephen's gentle massage had the greater effect.

"You wanted to talk," Stephen said, his voice soft in deference to the sleeping children. Marian realized how many of their talks had been in low voices so as not to be overheard.

Marian approached him but remained out of arm's reach—her arm's reach. 'Twas far too tempting to lean on him for support, to take succor within his embrace. She couldn't think clearly when he held her. Only look at what she'd confessed earlier.

Down in the hall, she'd stopped him from going off to tell his brothers about his daughters, fearing he'd blurt out the news for all to hear. Perhaps she'd been too hasty. She didn't think Stephen would do anything to hurt the girls, not apurpose anyway. Still, she had to be sure.

"I am rather proud of my daughters—"

He interrupted with a forceful, "Our daughters."

Marian accepted the reminder with grace. "'Twill take me some time to remember. I am not accustomed to sharing them."

The corner of his mouth turned upward. "Understandable. Ever since you told me I have been thinking of them as *mine*." He glanced over at Lyssa. "I cannot help wonder how they will think of me when we tell them."

On that score she could ease his mind. "They have become very fond of you. I doubt calling you 'Father' will be a chore for them."

"When do we tell them?"

"When the time is right, I suppose."

"Later today? Mayhap tonight?"

Marian understood his impatience. She also knew the telling must be done carefully.

"As I said, I am proud of our daughters. They have coped well with being twins. For the most part they ignore the stares and snubs from those who cannot accept them, who think them strange and loathsome for a misfortune of their birth. When we tell them of you we give them another burden to bear, that of being...base born. I should like as few people as possible to know of it."

Stephen's eyes narrowed. "I intend to acknowledge Audra and Lyssa, Marian. Surely you realized I would when you informed me they are mine."

"To the girls and, if you wish, a select few of your family. I see no reason to tell anyone else."

"What of your family?"

"They need not be told."

"Not even your father? Would he not be relieved to hear the truth after all these years?"

Probably. Then he'd try to force a marriage just as he would have done six years ago. Marian wanted no part of it now as she hadn't then.

"Especially not my father." How to make Stephen understand? "You told me about Richard, of how he suffered as a child. That is what I wish to avoid with the girls. Did your father truly do Richard a favor by acknowledging him to all?"

"But that was different. Mother made Richard's life hell because she hated the reminder of Father's liaison with a peasant woman, even though the woman died. Better to look to Daymon. The boy has little to complain of."

"So you say because Daymon is the baron's acknowledged son, everyone treats him with as much respect as they do Everart."

"Well, nay, there are differences in the boys' stations."

"Exactly."

He stared at her a moment. Just when she thought her point well taken, he said, "Not quite. Everart is the heir, so is given deference. Daymon is treated more as a second son would be. Gerard will see to Daymon's upbringing and livelihood in much the same manner as little Matthew." Stephen ran a hand through his hair. "I fail to see what this has to do with us, anyway. Neither my father nor Gerard were free to marry the mothers involved. That is not the case with us. From the moment we wed and I acknowledge the girls, they bear no taint and are entitled to all of their birthright."

Marian's heart did a happy flip, then sank straight to her toes. He'd simply assumed they would wed. She'd

once wanted to be Stephen's wife and lover with all of
her young heart, and a piece of her yet yearned for him.
Sweet Mother, but it hurt to have him so near and speaking of a life together—as a convenience, for the girls.

If only he loved me.

Their physical attraction to each other had burned
bright and hot from the beginning. Even now, if she put
her lips to his he would kiss her back. He'd even told
her last eve he yet lusted for her.

She'd learned long ago the difference between lust
and love.

"If I had been willing to marry you for the girls' sake
alone, I could have given my father your name. I had
my reasons for defying him, for giving you your freedom
then. Those reasons have not changed." He flinched, as
if she'd slapped him. If she didn't go on she wouldn't
get it all out. "'Struth, you are not free to offer for me,
having already spoken to Carolyn's father about marriage. You cannot cast her aside for your convenience
without doing her irreparable harm."

He shook his head as if coming out of a daze. "Carolyn and I are not betrothed."

"Not formally, but your family proclaimed your intentions last eve by inviting her to sit at the dais. I will
not have her shamed or made the subject of gossip,
which will surely happen if you do her honor one day
and discard her on the next."

He walked over to the chair and sat down, hunched
over with his forearms on his thighs, staring at his
clasped hands between his knees. "If I could do right
by Carolyn, what then?"

Her insides churned and her heart bled. She took a
resolving breath, gathered her pride.

"I still must refuse."

"For the reasons you defied your father."

She nodded.

"Would you mind telling me those reasons?"

Marian closed her eyes, allowed her chin to drop. She'd never told anyone. Stephen wasn't just anyone, but the man she'd adored, still loved and couldn't have. Maybe he didn't deserve an explanation, yet if she gave him one, he might desist in this madness. He may as well have the truth and the whole of it. In the telling she might find hope that her own heart might heal.

She sat in the other chair.

"After you left, I spent…weeks waiting to hear from you. I could not believe you could leave me without a word, that what we shared meant so little to you."

"I explained—"

"I know. I did not know then you and your father had been called away. Truly, it now matters not, nor did it then if I am honest. 'Twas not until I realized I had mistaken our lust for love that I came to my senses. You must forgive me for being young and naive."

His head came up, his expression drawn. He said nothing. Marian swallowed the lump forming in her throat. She'd get through this without crying. She *would*.

"Shortly after Yuletide I began to suspect I carried. I put off telling my parents until my gowns grew too tight. Father demanded I name my lover, but I could not bring myself to tell him, knowing he would try to force a marriage. You see, by then I had realized two things. First, your father could have easily refused my father. You were the son of a baron, and I the daughter of a minor lord. Your father could have sent my father away, insulted and angry."

"I doubt it would have come to that."

"Mayhap not, but I wasn't willing to hear I had been

rejected once again, whether by your father...or you. I had also come to see that you and I would never suit. We would both have been miserable."

He leaned forward. "How can you be so sure? You never gave us a chance to find out."

"Think on it, Stephen. We were both a mere ten and six, I the lass who dreamed of a knight who would make me his wife, build me a strong manor and give me children, and you...the lad with visions of adventure in his heart. You wanted to visit Italy, climb mountains, sail the seas. You would have soon hated me for trying to bind you to a normal life, and I would have hated you for not loving me enough to give up your dreams."

Unable to sit still, Marian got up and walked over to the cradle. Matthew's lips were pursed, twitching. Hungry, she realized. He'd be awake soon.

She swallowed that annoying lump again. "I dreamed of hearth and home, crops and stone walls. You wanted to follow the flight of an eagle, just to see where it landed. You still do. 'Twas why you chose Carolyn to wed, because she does not care if you stay away for months at a time, prefers it actually."

Marian found the courage to face Stephen again. "I could not be happy with such an arrangement."

Stephen put his hands on his knees, pushed up to his feet. With hands crossed behind his back, he walked slowly toward her, his expression thoughtful.

"Marian, if Carolyn had not whisked you off to Branwick, what might you have done after your father threatened to show you the gate?"

Caught off guard by the question, Marian shrugged. "I—I suppose I might have gone to some town...and, oh, found somewhere to live."

"Think on it, Marian. You were a mere ten and six,

a noble lass with no funds, forced to live in squalor and beg for meals, and carrying. Would you have truly walked though the gate, or realized you were sentencing yourself to ridicule and starvation, and your child along with you?''

Marian shuddered to even think about it. Now that the girls were older, and she'd realized she could make a living with her needlework, she might be able to live on her own and still care for the girls. But back then?

He glanced over at Lyssa. ''Do not misunderstand me. I am glad you had somewhere to go, people to care for you and the twins. But I believe Carolyn did you a disservice. If she had not interfered, I wonder if you would not have seen the sense in naming your lover. Once done, my father would not have shown your father Wilmont's gate. And believe me, Marian, I would have remembered your name.''

Marian pursed her lips, thought chasing after thought in a whirlwind. She'd never considered Carolyn's offer of shelter as interference, but as a kindness.

I would have remembered your name.

Perhaps, but in lust, not love. And for how long?

From the cradle came a mewing sound, a baby about to wake.

Stephen smiled, a sad smile. ''I will let Ardith know her youngest will be calling her sooner than planned. You will let me know when you think the time right to tell the girls, will you not?''

''Certes.''

He headed for the door.

''Stephen.'' He stopped, turned. ''I know you think I did wrong, but I swear, you would have balked at a forced marriage as much as I.''

''Perhaps. But I cannot help think we might have

come to some arrangement, mayhap even chased a few eagles together. Would that have been so bad, Marian?''

Three hours and too many goblets of wine later, Stephen paced Gerard's accounting room.

"So there you have the whole sorry story," he told his brothers. "Marian does not want me. She is willing to allow me a part of our daughters' lives, but rejects marriage. If I did not love her so much I might strangle her. Damn, but she is a stubborn one." He waved a goblet in the air. Luckily, he'd already emptied it. A shame to waste good wine. "How does a man make a woman like that see reason, I ask you?"

Richard and Gerard just looked at each other, and if he wasn't mistaken, Gerard held back laughter. Neither answered.

"Harrumph. Some help you two are. Since you both have opinionated wives, one would think you might have figured out how to handle them by now. Especially you, Gerard. You and Ardith have been married for what, nigh on three years? And you have never been averse to giving me the benefit of your wisdom. Why withhold now?"

Gerard folded his arms on his writing desk. "I do not suppose that somewhere in all this you thought to tell Marian you love her."

"Ha! Of course I thought of it. But tell her? Nay. She would not believe me, I swear. My declaration would fall flat, coming far too late to her way of thinking."

"And why is that?"

Stephen plunked the goblet down on the desk, slammed his hands down next to it and leaned forward—then leaned back more upright. How much wine had Richard fed him?

"Because Marian would think I uttered the words because I want her to marry me."

Gerard raised an eyebrow. "That is what you want, is it not?"

"Certes! But Marian will think I say I love her only because I want the girls, which I do, but I desire Marian, too." He gave his head a quick shake, a bad mistake. "Did I make sense?"

Richard got up from the chair and put a hand on Stephen's shoulder. "Come, sit down. Have another wine."

Grand idea. One more goblet of wine and he'd likely pass out and wouldn't have to grapple with Marian's stubbornness or his brothers' amusement anymore.

Richard handed him a full goblet. "So what do you intend to do?"

Stephen took a healthy swig. "Pass out and let Gerard tell Marian I love her."

Gerard smiled, shook his head. "Hardly a good idea."

"Why not? You are the baron. Steady as a rock, not off chasing hawks…eagles. She might believe you. She sure as hell is not going to believe me!"

"Then you need to find a way to convince her."

Stephen shook his head, which was beginning to hurt. He may have to ask Ardith for some of that potion she'd used on Lyssa—the brightest spot of the entire day, besides learning the girls were his. Watching Lyssa skip out of the keep on her way back to the tent, her headache gone, had almost lowered him to tears.

Convincing Audra and Lyssa that he adored them wouldn't be hard. Their mother, however—

"Marian is not about to let me swive her any time soon. Besides, your stables are too crowded. Always someone about."

Gerard groaned and bowed his head. "You talk to him, Richard. I give up."

Richard hauled up onto Gerard's writing table. "A tumble in the hay is not what the lady wants."

"She likes it in the hay. Goes wild. At least she used to. Could try a bed, I suppose."

Richard sighed. "Marian wants proof you love her, not of your lust."

"She is the only woman I am *able* to lust for. Is that not proof enough?" Stephen slapped a hand on the table. "That is when I should have known and told her, when I kissed Carolyn and *nothing* happened. Damn, missed opportunity."

Gerard's head came up. "Nothing?"

"Not a whimper."

Richard cringed. "And with Marian?"

"I could swive her whilst standing in a cold river."

Richard stared at him, disbelieving, then waved a hand in the air. "What Marian needs to know is that you are willing to give up chasing eagles. If not, then you had best learn to live without her. One or the other, Stephen. You cannot have both."

Very carefully, Stephen set the goblet down. "Hearth and home, crops and stone walls. Settled and staid, like you two."

"Oh, 'tis not so bad," Gerard said. "'Struth, you need not become chained to the hearth. Ardith comes with me when I make my yearly tour of Wilmont's holdings."

Richard nodded. "Lucinda adores trips into Cambridge."

Stephen rubbed at his face, knowing the problem ran much deeper. "Even if I could convince Marian I am willing to lead a more normal life, she may yet not trust me with her heart. I believe she loved me once, and she suffered for it. Why should she take the risk again?'' He got up. ''And Marian is right about Carolyn. I cannot, in all honor, simply shunt her aside because I find another woman more to my liking. The two are cousins, and Marian would think me the veriest cad if I shame Carolyn.''

After a few moments of silence, Gerard suggested, ''You could lose the contest to Edwin.''

Lose the contest. For a moment it seemed a perfect solution.

''Nay, Marian would see though that ploy. Then she would think me not only the veriest cad but a dishonest knave. Somehow, I need to get Carolyn to reject me.''

''Well, you could take Carolyn to your bed, and if *nothing* happens—''

Stephen tossed his head back and laughed. ''Oh, Gerard, I have had too much to drink, but not *that* much! Can you imagine Carolyn telling Marian of how I tried to bed her and could not perform husbandly duties? I think not.''

Richard rubbed his chin. ''This morn, when we talked of finding Edwin a wife, mayhap we should have talked of finding Carolyn a husband. What of Edwin?''

''Never work. Carolyn rejects him because of his age.''

''How old is he?''

''Not sure. He has a few silver strands in his hair, though.''

''Means nothing.''

''Does to Carolyn. Edwin also has this notion that a woman cannot oversee her own lands.'' Stephen frowned. ''I believe this contest has proved to him she is more than capable, but the man is not likely to admit it.''

''Not even to win Carolyn? Does Edwin love her?''

He blew out a long breath. "I believe he cares a great deal for her, but even if he softened his stance, there is still his age." Stephen picked up his goblet, set it back down. "I need a walk to clear my head. Mayhap I will go visit Lyssa, see how she does. Mayhap Marian is ready to tell the girls." He headed for the door. "My thanks for listening. You may tell Ardith and Lucinda the news, but for now, no others."

"You will be back for evening meal?" Gerard asked.

"Sure. Why not. I hear Ardith is having boar roasted, my favorite. I would not wish to disappoint her."

He closed the door quietly behind him.

Richard sank into the chair. "Must be serious. I cannot recall ever seeing Stephen this dejected."

"I do. 'Twas right after Ardith and Daymon were kidnapped. Stephen, Corwin and I were forming a plan to go after them. He sat there with his shoulder all wrapped up and his ear still bleeding, inconsolable because he felt he failed Ardith. No matter that he attacked five armed men with his bare hands, nearly got himself killed. He could barely sit a horse, yet he rode out with us and accounted himself well. To this day he feels unworthy of Ardith's regard." He waved a hand at the door. "And now he feels he failed Marian, is unworthy of her love even though he wants it so badly he would give up all he holds dear for her. Thickheaded, stubborn, obstinate—"

Richard laughed. "Sounds like you. So what do we do?"

"Nothing, unless he asks us to. We have both pulled him out of trouble before. This time he needs to do it on his own."

"And if he cannot?"

"Then he just may take that trip to Italy he has always talked about and we may not see him for years."

Chapter Sixteen

He found Marian sitting in the shade of the tent, leaning against a support, her eyes closed.

I love you, Marian. I swear it.

But how to make her believe? Impossible? Nay, there must be a way.

Richard believed Marian didn't want a tumble in the hay, but she'd sure craved a swiving in the river. He could still feel her legs wrapped around him, taste her skin where he'd kissed her neck—before he'd been too damn honorable to take advantage. He'd not make that mistake again. If Marian ever showed the least sign of surrender, he'd give her what she wanted, wherever she wanted it, for as long as wanted it. Satisfy her so thoroughly she'd beg for more.

He knew Marian desired him with all the fire he remembered so well. If he reminded her of how well their bodies melded, how delicious and satisfying their joint ecstasy, might she yield? Or would she again tell him to seek offers elsewhere?

Could a woman like Marian give herself to a man she didn't love? He thought not. So if she allowed him entry to her body, that meant she'd already given him her heart.

Stephen prayed he was right. She'd turned aside offers of marriage, not wanting or loving those men. Hard to believe that over all these years she'd never coupled with any other male, but Stephen was willing to wager he'd been her first and last lover. Only lover.

Strange, but fate had brought him back to Marian. Through the years, his wanderings, other women. Back to the first, the best, and now the only.

If Marian made love with him, then there was hope for a future between them. If not…

Dear Lord, let me do this right.

He lowered down onto the grass beside her. She opened her eyes, sleep softened and wary. He picked up her hand and raised it to his lips.

"Hail, mother of my children. Girls in the tent?"

She pulled her hand away, sat up straighter. "Nay. On our way out of the keep, the earl of Warwick's wife invited them to play with her children."

Stephen glanced over at the huge, emerald-green tent a good ways across the field. "Lyssa must not be ailing if you let her go."

Marian smiled so fully her eyes sparkled. "She is. I cannot tell you what a relief it is to have finally found a potion to ease her headaches so quickly." She tilted her head. "I have you to thank, in part. Ardith may have brewed the potion, but 'twas you who brought us to Wilmont. My thanks."

Gratitude. Not a bad thing. He'd take whatever help he could get.

"Seemed the right thing to do, at the time. Little ones should not suffer so." He glanced again at the earl's tent. "Will the girls be back soon?"

Her smile faded. "I know you are anxious to tell them, but I fear you must wait a while longer. The girls will have evening meal with the earl's children. I am not to collect them until after supper."

Splendid. How terribly thoughtful of the earl's wife to have left Marian on her own. Carolyn was at the keep. The tent was empty save for several pallets. Nice soft pallets.

"A few hours one way or the other does not matter. Just so we do not put it off too long."

"You told your brothers?"

He'd told his brothers far more than he should have, but both could be trusted to keep a confidence.

"I also told them they could tell their wives, but no others. In that I will respect your wishes."

Pleased with his answer, Marian leaned back on her hands, stretching the bodice of the rough-weave gown tight across her bosom. His fingers itched to reach out, stroke a nipple to hardness. His loins quickened. Within the space of a breath his privates strained against his breeches, begging freedom, urging a mating with the woman spread out on the grass.

"I fear Ardith will look down on me now, knowing the girls were born...as they were."

"Not Ardith, nor Lucinda. Both became lovers to my brothers long before they married. They cannot fault you for surrendering to desire when they did not resist."

"A small consolation. Both surrendered to men who they then married, while I—" She blushed, then got to her feet. "The gowns of Christina's. I want you to return them to her. I will fetch them."

Stephen wasted no time following her into the tent. Marian held out the sack.

He crossed his arms. "Those are yours. Wear them or

no, I will not take them back," he declared, vowing if he could get Marian out of the wretched peasant-weave she insisted on wearing, he'd steal it and burn it.

"I have no use for them."

"There is evening meal tonight and the christening ceremony tomorrow. You must attend both."

"Carolyn will toss a fit. She already believes we take up too much of your time and inconvenience your family too much."

"Carolyn can think what she will."

"Stephen—"

He grasped her shoulders, heartened that she didn't pull away. "No more, Marian. We both know I can no longer consider marrying Carolyn. Her opinion does not matter. Only you and the girls matter now."

Her pewter eyes glistened with moisture, tears he wouldn't let her shed. If he had his way, she'd never cry again.

"Carolyn will hate me for ruining her plans."

"She has no cause to." He slid his hands up to her neck, his fingers brushing hair soft as silk. He'd give most anything to spread the long strands out to fall soft and teasing against his bare skin. "I will do right by Carolyn. She will suffer no shame or embarrassment. I do not know how as yet, but there must be a way. 'Tis not as if there is any affection between us."

"She wants you."

Not like I want you. Now and forever.

"She wants a man to give her children and allow her to oversee her own lands. I am not the only man in England who might fulfill those requirements. Now you have pleaded your cousin's case and not changed my mind. No matter what else, I cannot marry Carolyn."

Hadn't he this morning informed his brothers of the

opposite? What a difference a few hours and an earth-moving confession could make.

She searched his face. Did she see how much he wanted her, see his resolve to set all to rights?

"I know I have much to make up for," he whispered. "Give me time, give me a chance. We have lost six years. I would rather not lose another day."

He heard the sack of gowns fall, felt the heat where her hands landed on his chest, but mostly he noticed how she sucked in her lower lip, held it between her teeth, then soothed it with her tongue.

"You ask me to fly when I do not have wings."

"Then let me carry us both." He grasped her right hand, kissed the healing scratches on her palm, and gambled his future on a fragile assumption. "Two days ago, in the river, you were willing to put the past behind, begin again. Have you truly changed your mind?"

"If memory serves, 'twas you who told me I was not in my right mind."

"One of the most foolish errors I have ever committed. What were you thinking, hanging out on the branch, that made you so bold?"

Marian remembered most every thought racing through her head when her hand slipped on the branch—the vows she made, her decision to take the chance Stephen now asked for.

Heaven knew she wanted to with her whole heart, and her body urged her onward. Already her knees were weak, her woman's depths warm and wet.

Dare she hope he could find a way to do right by Carolyn? Could the eagle truly come to roost? Could she learn to fly, perhaps close to the ground? If she didn't try her wings now, she might never get another chance.

She pursed her lips, took a breath. "At first I was sure

I was about to die, but the longer I hung on to the branch, the more firmly I believed you would come rescue me. I vowed to God and myself that if I lived, I would tell you about the girls, and that you… we…deserved another chance. I decided to begin by letting you know I still wanted you.''

He kissed the palm of her hand again. Did he know it sent shivers up her arm and down her back?

''I heard. And I wanted you so badly I could have taken you right there in the river. I *should* have taken you right there in the river.''

Yet he'd refused her, damn him. Made her angry and gotten her all confused and obstinate again. ''Then what was all that drivel about gratitude?''

'''Twas not drivel, not all. Only some. Truly I should have just shut my mouth. I seem to get into mighty messes when I talk too much.''

She remembered Ardith's comment about how Stephen didn't always say or do the right thing. Mayhap she had the right of it.

''Your intentions are good,'' she whispered.

''Not always.'' He lowered his arms to encircle her. His hands clasped in the small of her back, he pulled her full against him. ''I came to see you with the sole purpose of seducing you. Hardly noble or honorable of me.''

The evidence of his intent already reached out to her, hard and ready. The Stephen she knew and loved—randy and willing, any time and any place. In the hay or the river or now a tent.

Heaven help her she was ready for him, too.

''Think you we have time?''

His mouth descended, his kiss hungry as if starved. She thrilled to the mobile warmth of his mouth, the kiss imbued with the promise of ecstasy. No longer a lad, now a man, Stephen had likely kissed other women with such ardor, made other promises. She couldn't bring herself to care so long as he kept his promise to her.

When he finally backed away, 'twas with a shaky breath. "I will tie the tent flap."

Marian made quick work of her gown's laces and kicked off her boots. By the time Stephen finished, she stood before him in only her chemise.

He pulled off his tunic as he strode toward her. He tossed it aside; his sherte followed in its wake. His arms came up, Marian held out a staying hand.

"Before we commence, I need to see what you mean to poke me with."

Stephen stopped, remembering those words from another time, another place. Marian had always been the bold one when it came to sex, even the first time, when he'd taken her virginity and lost his own.

"Surely you remember."

"I remember the lad. I wish to see the man."

Six years ago his fingers had fumbled with his lacings, worried over whether Marian would like what she saw or back away in horror. This time his hands trembled because he knew what came next. He pushed his breeches down far enough to allow her a thorough inspection of his staff and the sacs hanging beneath. It damn near killed him to stand still.

"You have, um, grown rather magnificently." She looked up, this time not questioning but teasing. "You know what to do, where to put it?"

With far more confidence now, he said, "Damn right I do."

"Show me, then."

He shook his head. "First I get to see the woman."

She acknowledged the change with a smile and pulled the chemise off over her head. No longer a girl. Her breasts were bigger, the tips darker. Her hips were fuller, giving her shapely form more definition. Her stomach rounded slightly, streaked with thin white lines. The body of the woman who'd borne his children tempted him to touch and possess as much as that of the untried girl.

"Lovely. Exquisite. Take your hair down."

She gave a little laugh and undid the tie. "You never cared before."

"Never took off boots and breeches, either."

He stripped down, watching Marian untwist her braid, then shake out the strands so long the tips mingled with the hair surrounding the entryway he'd soon breach.

She knelt down on a pallet. "No hay this time."

He knelt before her. "We will make do."

They came together, skin against skin, man against woman. The years and fears faded away, soothed by exploring hands, burned off by kisses. She moaned when he nuzzled in her neck, leaned into his hands as he kneaded and suckled her breasts, drew in a sharp breath at the first stroke of his fingers through her moist heat.

She cupped him with both hands, petting and stroking, driving him near mindless until he had to pull away. He meant to pull her into another long, lingering kiss. Marian laid back on the pallet and spread her legs.

The hair there glistened with droplets of her woman's dew. He leaned forward and used his thumb to spread the moisture around the nub of her need. Her back arched, her breathing quickened.

"Stephen, please."

"Let it go, Marian."

"Come with me."

"Indulge me. I always did love watching you come apart."

"Kiss me."

So he did, but not where she expected. She arched up off the pallet with a long, broken gasp, then came down with a cry akin to pain. Her eyes glazed over, then closed. A flush spread across her upper chest and breasts, her nipples standing proud to poke through the veil of her hair.

Stephen covered her and slid his aching member into her pulsing pleasure. Her legs came around him, pulling him in tight. He rose up on his hands and timed his thrusts to her rhythm. Deep and hard he stroked, holding back his release with every ounce of willpower he could muster. For his efforts he enjoyed the reward of taking her over the edge once more.

He thrust deep again, and again. On the verge of spilling his seed he began to pull out, something he hadn't known to do six years ago. Marian felt the movement and gripped him tighter, holding him inside.

"I want it all, Stephen. Either we are together for all time or we are not."

For all time. Forever. Whatever he had to do to make it so. If Marian asked for proof of his resolve, knowing the possible consequences, then he'd not withdraw.

He thrust again, gave in to the physical urgency for release and his heart's cry to prove his love. He came hard and long, his member thrumming against Marian's soft sheath. Impossible for her not to feel the hot liquid pumping into her, not to know he gave her all he had to give.

She closed her eyes and sighed. "There. That feels *so* good."

He lowered to his elbows and planted soft kisses all

over her face before capturing her mouth. He kissed her over and over, tasting her, initiating gentle swordplay with her tongue until his body began to cool, until he knew he must roll off to allow her to breathe freely again.

She rolled with him, onto her side, as averse to separating their sweating bodies as he. He pulled the coverlet over them, wrapping them in a cocoon that entrapped their heat and the aroma of lovemaking.

Replete, he closed his eyes and held Marian close, content to remain right where he was until forced to get up. Like the end of the world. Or the tent falling down. Or Carolyn returning—which might be the end of the world. She'd kill him. Death wasn't in his current plans. Worse, she might take her ire out on Marian.

He shook Marian gently, roused her enough to open her eyes and push the hair from her face. Waking every morning to those sleepy pewter eyes and her soft smile was going to be sheer joy. But first they had to marry.

She stroked his chin. "I like the man."

He kissed her forehead. "The woman is utterly incredible. You drain me dry, Marian. I may never recover."

"An hour at most and you will be ready again. Or has age slowed you down?"

"Not me. Not yet, anyway."

The quip widened her smile, then she pulled him down for another kiss, soft and gentle, and incredibly stirring. Not long later, when she squirmed deliciously against him, he knew he wouldn't need a full hour.

He'd tried to be careful of her earlier but she hadn't let him. He ran a hand over her stomach, over those thin white lines earned while bearing his daughters.

"Do you think we might have gotten you pregnant again?"

"Would that displease you? You did try to pull away."

"Only because I thought you might want to wait until all was settled and sure. 'Tis not displeasing to know you have the confidence in me to take the risk...yet, I do wonder how you knew what I was doing."

"Ah, that. Well, after I gave birth, I made it my business to know exactly how things worked. An old herbswoman told me of several ways how I might take a lover without...consequences, including the method you tried."

He'd assumed she'd remained celibate, talked himself into believing she would only take someone she loved dearly to her bed. He knew she'd turned down offers of marriage, but the other?

"Apparently the method worked."

"Oh, quite well."

She jested. Maybe. He couldn't tell. If not he didn't want to hear about her other lovers, just as he didn't want to tell her about the other women in his life.

Too many others. Women he'd been careful of, however, because he'd also made it his business to learn how to take a lover without consequences.

Still, he couldn't help wondering who the hell else Marian might have instructed to pull down his breeches so she could judge the quality of his parts.

Stephen lay back on the pallet with his forearm over his eyes, and took comfort in having passed Marian's inspection and then giving her good benefit of his parts. 'Twas enough, for now.

She ran a fingernail over his stomach, making him quiver, stirring his loins.

"What do we do about Carolyn?"

Somehow talking about Carolyn while lying naked next to Marian didn't feel right, probably because he'd been to bed with Carolyn, once, at Westminster. Not a fact he would ever bring up. Would Carolyn? If the two women ever made comparisons…he shivered, more from where Marian's hand had wandered down his inner thigh than anything else.

"Gerard offered to find Carolyn another husband, someone young and forbearing of her views."

"What about Edwin?"

"Too old, too set in his ways."

"Not too old. There is vigor in him yet."

He moved his arm to look at her face; she was looking elsewhere, at his parts. The woman simply loved sex, pure and lusty. Had she ever asked Edwin to pull down his breeches?

"How would you know?"

"Edwin is but six and thirty. The gray in his hair speaks of experience, not feebleness." She finally met his gaze. "When you are *so* old, must I find a new lover?" She slid her palm along the underside of his solid staff. "Will you yet be lusty, or gone feeble?"

Suddenly six and thirty didn't sound so old. He knew of men older who'd sired children, the earl of Warwick for one. Stephen knew the man had seen his fortieth year, yet his wife had delivered their latest child, their fourth, only two years ago.

"I plan to be lusty well into my dotage."

"Past thirty, then." She wrapped her fingers around him, squeezed, ran her thumb over the tip to spread around the single drop of liquid.

"Well past."

"Nice to hear. Besides, Carolyn loves Edwin. She

uses his aversion to change as an excuse to—'' She pursed her lips.

Carolyn in love with Edwin? Beyond belief! Except Marian believed differently. Had she cause?

"An excuse to what?"

Her eyes narrowed. "You must swear never to say a word of what I tell you to either of them."

His curiosity piqued, Stephen rose up on his elbows. "I so swear, my lady."

She took a deep breath and worried her lower lip. "You know Carolyn has buried two husbands." He nodded. "Both were quite old, near as old as William. She now fears marrying a man older than she because, well, both of her husbands died in her bed after claiming husbandly rights. She fears she will kill Edwin if she marries him."

Stephen's first reaction was to laugh aloud, but the expression on Marian's face stopped him cold.

"She thinks she will kill Edwin if she makes love to him."

Marian nodded.

"Are you saying that all Edwin has to do is take Carolyn to bed and do nothing more than not die and she might relent?"

The corner of her mouth quirked. "Well, he might want to be a bit more active. The thing is, Carolyn is not about to swive Edwin. She truly fears for him."

Stephen laid back down, his hands beneath his head. If he could convince Edwin to tumble Carolyn, that problem might be solved. Nay, first he'd have to make sure Edwin understood how much Carolyn wanted control over her lands. Surely, due to the contest, Edwin now knew her knowledgeable.

Marian's hand moved lower, down to under his sacs,

fondling, driving Edwin and Carolyn to the farthest reaches of his mind.

Marian sure wasn't worried about him succumbing, not when she wanted him again so soon, and was making steady progress in ensuring her needs met. Insatiable wench.

Mercy, what the woman did with her hands could push a man right over the edge of madness. He let her play as long as he dared.

"Marian, you do intend to buff that rod sometime soon?"

She laughed. "Crudely put."

"Aye, and I have been hoping you might see your way clear to do the buffing ever since you mentioned it the other day."

She slid over him and took him into her. He grasped her hips and arched upward; she sat up and pushed down. She hissed at the fullness of his possession; he moaned low at the depth of his penetration.

Marian threw her head back and rose up ever so slightly before lowering down. Over and over and over. Stephen knew he wasn't going to last long, so put his thumb to her sensitive nub. He girded his loins and made deliberate circles around the nub, pushing her toward release, heating her sheath until she melted around him.

Marian's pleasure drew him up and in, caressed him in the most intimate way possible. He gave himself up to the pleasure and the joy, the love and the woman. He could have sworn the earth moved beneath him, that thunder rumbled across the land.

'Twasn't until several moments later, with Marian sprawled atop him, his breathing beginning to return to normal, he realized the moving earth and thunder had been real, in a sense. Horses, many of them, must have ridden past the tent.

He had to leave before someone discovered what he and Marian had indulged in for a good part of the afternoon. He truly hadn't meant to linger so long.

"Marian, we must get up, get dressed."

"Must we?" she complained.

"Greedy wench. Come, move that beautiful rump of yours."

He caressed one lovely cheek to take any sting out of the order.

She rolled off with a moan. "You get dressed. I intend to cover my head and sleep."

"No time." He got up and pulled on his clothes as he came across them. "Evening meal is not far off."

"Not hungry."

"You need to eat to keep up your strength. I will send Christina out to help you dress and fix your hair so you had best be ready." Fully dressed, Stephen picked up the sack and drew out the two gowns—the light-blue gown Marian wore last night, the other a lovely shade of amber. He tossed the blue on a pallet and shook out the amber. "I like this one."

She laughed lightly. He looked over to see her lounging on her side, propped up on an elbow, all that gorgeous hair flowing down around her. She smiled indulgently. "If you say so, my lord."

He liked the sound of it. He tossed the amber gown down atop the blue, then picked up her old peasant weave and stuffed it into the sack.

"What are you doing?"

Stephen pulled at the ties securing the tent flap. "I intend to burn this rag. See you at supper."

He escaped as she screeched a protest.

He flung the sack over his shoulder and headed for the keep, plans forming in his head for his talk with Edwin. Once done, then all he had to do was get Edwin and Carolyn together in a place of privacy—naked. His chamber would do nicely. Or perhaps the tent.

First he'd tell Gerard to inform Robert of Portieres and Geoffrey d'Montgomery to look elsewhere for wives. Lady Marian de Lacy wasn't available. She belonged to him now. She'd become the wife of Stephen of Wilmont as soon as he freed himself of Lady Carolyn de Grasse.

Or rather Carolyn disavowed him. How strange to realize his entire future might depend upon the swiving skills of a thirty-six-year-old man.

Chapter Seventeen

Marian wore the light-blue gown to supper to let Stephen know he had no right to tell her what to wear. She might be the mother of his children and again his lover, but not his wife and subject to his orders—a longed for state of affairs but not a certainty.

Seated next to him on the bench, all she need do is lean left to whisper the admonishment to Stephen, but feared some expression or action might alert Carolyn to how Marian had spent part of the afternoon. Writhing either under or over the man Carolyn still considered hers.

Because of the grand feast planned to follow the christening on the morrow, tonight Ardith served a plain supper of venison stew in a rich brown gravy on bread trenchers. 'Twas so thick with meat and generously seasoned no one seemed to mind.

Honored on the dais were Corwin, Ardith's brother, and his bride to be, Judith Canmore, the royal heiress whom Corwin apparently rescued from traitorous rebels. The king granted the pair permission to marry in reward for good service to the crown. A Saxon knight and a royal heiress. An unheard-of match. Yet there the two sat, looking as happy as any couple could be.

The earl and his wife once again occupied the high seats at the highest table, followed by Richard with his wife Lucinda, then Stephen with Carolyn and—for some reason not clear to Marian—she and Edwin.

By rights, the two of them should sit far down the tables, neither of them holding high enough rank to warrant a place at the table with the family and the earl. 'Twas more than unsettling to sit at Stephen's right, facing Edwin and Carolyn.

Marian heard the scrape of the baron's chair as he rose. She tucked away her eating knife without guilt for leaving so much food on her trencher. The serving wenches would gather up the trenchers and take them out to the gates. Some peasant would enjoy a good meal.

Carolyn leaned forward. "Marian, before you leave to collect your girls, I wanted to tell you not to expect me back at the tent tonight. I probably will not see you again until the morrow, at the christening."

How very odd. "Why is that?"

Carolyn's smile could only be called smug. "Lady Ursula has invited me to remain for a private gathering of the family. 'Twould seem they intend to celebrate Corwin's good fortune and Ursula believes 'twill be quite late before everyone seeks their pallets, so I shall remain in the keep for the night."

Edwin went a bit pale. Marian wanted to reach out to him, tell him to ignore Carolyn's gloat over how well she'd been received by the baron's family, over her growing closeness with Stephen's mother. She knew how the man felt—jealous and rejected—every time he witnessed Stephen and Carolyn being paired as a couple, every time the subject of their marriage came up.

She knew because she felt it, too, as now, wishing she were the one to accompany Stephen to the gathering as his intended bride. Impossible, of course, until Stephen was free of his obligation to Carolyn.

Stephen leaned toward her. "Actually, Marian, you and the girls are invited, too. Ardith plans to speak with you about it in a few moments."

Marian's heart did a joyous little flip.

Carolyn looked abashed. "Nay, I do not believe she does. I already declined the kindness on Marian's behalf." At Stephen's disapproving look, Carolyn explained. "Marian has been shown many kindnesses because she is my cousin, and so might be your kin if…when my father approves our marriage. I assured your mother that further deference was unnecessary, and your mother agreed to pass my wishes along to Ardith. Besides, Marian must collect her daughters soon."

Stephen tilted his head, studying Carolyn. "You have become very accustomed to making decisions for Marian. One would think you felt you had the right."

Carolyn looked crushed. "I was merely thinking of Audra and Lyssa. The twins are used to an early bedtime. If they do not get proper rest, they will be unfit to attend the christening tomorrow."

The point was well taken. Marian knew that without proper rest her little angels could turn she-devils. Still, the decision had been hers to make, not Carolyn's.

With a start, Marian realized fully what Stephen had hinted at earlier. Had she truly become so weak-willed she'd let Carolyn rule over her completely?

Maybe so. Ever since Carolyn offered succor and shelter at Branwick—which Stephen suggested was interference, not an act of kindness—Marian had allowed Carolyn her way in most everything. The tale of her widowhood to begin with. Even in small things, like Carolyn's reproach over the girls' manners, Marian usually bowed to her cousin's wishes.

Marian winced inwardly. 'Twas not all Carolyn's fault she seemed so high-handed. Marian had accepted direction without question, unwilling to argue overmuch with the cousin on whom she depended for the very meals on her table.

"Marian, what say you?" Stephen asked. "You *are* invited and welcome to join us if you wish. The twins, also."

Stephen's defense of her, the hope on his face that she would join his family's gathering, made it easier to refuse. His family now knew the girls were his daughters, and would see them in a new light at the ceremony. Marian wanted Audra and Lyssa rested and well-behaved, little angels in the darling gowns Christina had delivered to the tent.

"My thanks, Stephen, but I did promise the girls I would collect them after evening meal. They will be weary from a long day at play, so I had best get them to their pallets early."

"You are sure?"

Marian wished she could hug him openly for his care. All she could offer him was a smile and reassurance.

"Quite sure. You have seen Audra at her very worst. We do not wish to court such surliness again, do we?"

"Heaven forbid, nay," he agreed with a light laugh, then addressed Edwin. "I hoped to have a word with you this noon, but Corwin's arrival distracted me. Might you have a few moments now?"

Marian did her best not to blush over what had claimed Stephen's time before Corwin's arrival. She'd been riding atop Stephen, in the throes of ecstasy, when the large company that turned out to be Corwin, Judith and their escort thundered past the tent.

"If you wish," Edwin said softly.

Stephen rose off the bench. "If you will excuse us, then, ladies?"

Edwin followed Stephen's lead, getting up off the bench as if the weight of the world bore down on his shoulders. She wished she had words of comfort for him, but there were none.

Carolyn scooted down a space to the seat Edwin vacated. "I am glad to hear you have the good sense to agree with me. I cannot imagine what havoc the twins might wreak if both were surly."

In good conscience, Marian couldn't refute Carolyn. "You did take liberties in refusing the invitation for us, however."

"I was merely trying to be helpful," she said, and Marian thought her cousin truly believed it.

She thought to press the point, but the earl and his wife were getting up, readying to return to their tent. Best she go with them, fetch the girls and get them bedded down.

"Shall I send your pallet up to the keep?"

Carolyn shook her head. "'Tis not necessary." An odd smile touched her mouth. "Stephen has offered me the use of his chamber for the night. 'Twill be pleasant to sleep in that large bed. I rather believe he means to share it with me."

Marian wanted to scream a denial, but the words hit her gut so hard she couldn't breathe.

Stephen wouldn't. He *couldn't*. Not after making sweet love to her this afternoon. Not after all their talk of beginning again, of second chances.

Just because Stephen offered his chamber to Carolyn

didn't mean he planned to share the bed. 'Twas what Carolyn might hope for, but it wouldn't happen.

Calmer now, she stared at her cousin. "Carolyn, you are in love with Edwin. How can you love one man and take another to bed? I have never understood that."

She shrugged. "I loved Edwin before I wed my second husband. Look about you. How many of these wives may have loved one man yet submitted to the husbands chosen for them, given them heirs? 'Tis not unusual."

"Except *you* have a choice. Why not submit to the man you love, marry him and give him heirs?"

Carolyn's eyes darkened briefly. "You know why not. Besides, sharing a bed with Stephen is no hardship. The man is quite lusty."

Carolyn would know. Hadn't she freely admitted—nay, bragged on—how satisfying her one tryst with Stephen at Westminster had been? Had Stephen made love to Carolyn since?

Marian banished the repugnant vision before it fully formed. She might have to live with knowing Stephen had bedded Carolyn, but 'twas useless to dwell on it. Too, if Carolyn had shared Stephen's bed at Branwick, she would surely have said something. So just the one time then, before Stephen and Marian had been reunited in a palace bedchamber, months ago. Long before this afternoon when they'd reclaimed each other in the tent.

Marian got up, resisting the urge to claw Carolyn's eyes out, knowing both her anger at Carolyn and mistrust of Stephen unwarranted. Stephen wouldn't make love to her and leave her, not again.

The earl's wife approached. "Ready, my dear?"

Marian forced a smile for the gracious lady. "I am."

"Good. Charles is anxious to get back to the tent."

Marian followed the earl and his wife out of the keep, trying to keep her imagination from running amok.

Stephen wanted a chance to make up for all the years they'd lost, put the past behind and begin again. She just wished that somewhere in his pleas he'd said he loved her. 'Twould then be so much easier to put these niggling doubts to rest.

Stephen dipped two large cups into the ale barrel, handed one to Edwin, then sought out the far, dark corner of the hall. Edwin looked him askance but didn't comment. Once assured of privacy, Stephen set his resolve to see his plan through. His entire future could depend on Edwin's cooperation, Carolyn's submission.

"Have you plans for this eve?" he asked the older man.

Edwin held up his ale cup. "Have a few of these. Perhaps ask Armand to guide me to a dice game. Your men-at-arms seemed fond enough of gambling while at Branwick, so I assume there must be a game or two about."

Stephen smiled. "Highly likely. Harlan goes nowhere without his dice. I do, however, have another suggestion for you, an amusement you might find more....entertaining."

The corner of Edwin's mouth quirked upward, but his expression belied any hint of amusement. "Since I already have invitations from two of the serving wenches, your *entertainment* might lack in appeal."

The two of them had done much verbal sparring during the contest, and Stephen had learned to like and admire Edwin, who for all his pompous attitude was truly a decent sort. Confident he and Edwin understood each other, Stephen couldn't resist chiding the man.

"Are you any good at it?"

Edwin raised an eyebrow. "Not that it is any of your business, but I have had my share of practice and more years than you in which to perfect skills."

"I am not proposing a contest here, Edwin. I merely suggest that the lady I have in mind for you may not be easy to please. Are you up to the challenge?"

Edwin took a long swig of ale. "I could manage *if* I were interested, which I am not. Nor do I appreciate your implication that I need your help in finding a woman willing to share my pallet."

"Not if you are willing to settle for a serving wench. I, on the other hand, can put you in a soft bed with a woman so special, so beautiful, you will beg my pardon on the morn for being irritated with me."

"Not interested."

"Not even if the woman is Carolyn?"

Edwin stood thunderstruck, then his eyes narrowed and he growled, "I knew you were young and brash, but I never took you for cruel."

He turned on his heel. Stephen caught him by the shoulder.

"I would not jest with you over such a thing, my friend. If you still want Carolyn, then you may have her with my blessing. All you need do is convince Carolyn to have you."

Edwin turned back; Stephen released him.

"Why? I find it hard to believe you are suddenly eager to drop your suit—unless another woman has caught your fancy. Are you so fickle?"

He should have known Edwin would take insult on Carolyn's behalf. 'Twas also rather disconcerting to have Edwin determine the cause of his change of heart so accurately.

"I fear so, but I am not so fickle as you think. When a woman captures a man's heart, what is he to do but try to make her his own? I never understood why you have been so constant with Carolyn. I do now."

"So you think you can simply hand Carolyn over to me and all your obligation to her disappears? Knave."

Stephen sighed inwardly. Knave he might be, but he was still doing the right thing.

"You must promise me you will allow Carolyn some say regarding her lands. Be honest, now. This contest we took part in did nothing but prove she knows what she is about. True?"

"True," he admitted so begrudgingly Stephen nearly laughed. He couldn't hold back a smile.

"Well, then?"

Edwin tossed a hand in the air. "Even if I agree, there is this ridiculous impediment of my age. I am but a few years older than she, but all Carolyn sees is my graying hair. 'Tis a curse of the men in my family to go gray young, no more."

"Do you know how Carolyn's husbands died?"

"Hearts gave out, so I am told."

"Did you know they succumbed in Carolyn's bed, after claiming husbandly rights?"

After a moment's thought, he admitted, "Nay, I did not. Who told you this?"

"Marian, who got it from Carolyn. I am under most strict orders to never breathe a word, but I think in this case the telling is justified. Have a care you keep it secret, however, for if Marian ever finds out I let the confidence slip, I am a dead man."

Edwin finally smiled. "'Tis Marian, is it not, who has captured your heart?"

And body and soul. "Aye."

"I wondered why you spent so much time out at the hut. Here I thought you fascinated with the twins when 'twas the mother you were after."

"The mother is fascinating all on her own, believe me."

"You take on a full family should you marry her. You will lose more of the freedom you cherish so highly than you would if you married Carolyn. Can you do right by them all?"

Stephen thought back on the first time he'd seen the twins, at the stone wall at the hut and remembered thinking that their father would need his wits about him as the girls grew up. Now he was the father who must guard the girls against knaves like their own father. He might even feel some sympathy for Hugo de Lacy if the man hadn't threatened to show his daughter the gate. Stephen couldn't imagine what might prompt him to such harsh measures with Audra and Lyssa.

And Marian? If all worked out, maybe he could make up the lost years to her, bring her lifelong joy. Mayhap even teach her to have some fun again. She certainly deserved it after all she'd put up with since he all but abandoned her. If only Carolyn hadn't interfered, Marian might well have broken down and told her father the truth.

Would he have made her a good husband then or, as Marian suggested, balked at a forced marriage and made her life miserable?

Put the past behind, begin again.

"I intend to make a good life for all of us. First, however, I must ensure Carolyn suffers no hardship or embarrassment. I would prefer she set me free, not me disavow her."

"Your plan is flawed. I doubt Carolyn will allow me her bed."

"You have more of an advantage than you know. Marian also told me Carolyn loves you. She refuses you her bed because she fears you will succumb in the same manner as her husbands. She is not disinterested, only afraid."

"Nothing wrong with my heart, or the rest of me, either."

"I do not doubt you. Now convince Carolyn."

Edwin swirled his ale. "You mentioned a soft bed."

Stephen nearly shouted for joy at this first battle won, but knew the war only begun.

"Carolyn is attending our family gathering tonight. When done, I will deliver her to my chamber, telling her to leave the bolt undone. Then I will come fetch you. By the time you arrive, she ought to be disrobed and in bed."

"Ha! She will be waiting for you and get me. The woman will not be pleased."

"Did I not tell you the woman may be hard to please?"

"I will not force her, Stephen."

"The idea is to seduce her." Stephen thought of his latest encounter with Marian. "Mayhap instead of talking you should drop your breeches and show her what you have to offer. Insist she listen to the steady beat of your heart. How can the woman resist?"

Edwin raised an eyebrow. "We are speaking of Carolyn."

"We are also speaking of a woman in love. Where do I fetch you?"

Edwin nodded toward the hearth. "I have been sleeping on a pallet over there."

''Then we trade beds. Make good use of mine, Edwin. And do try to live through the night.''

Several hours later, Stephen stood outside his chamber door, heard the bolt slide behind Edwin. The only bit of conversation he heard clearly was Carolyn's gasped, ''What are you doing here?''

The two of them were talking now, but the thick oak door muffled the words. No sense standing out here in the passageway. He should go downstairs to Edwin's pallet and get some sleep. Morn would come soon enough, and then he'd have his answer.

Except his feet wouldn't move.

He looked up and down the passageway. All the doors were closed, everyone gone to bed. His part was done and there was nothing more to do than wait and worry over Edwin's success, or lack of it.

He put his ear to the door. Still talking.

Get into the bed, Edwin!

Stephen leaned against the wall and gave a brief thought to slipping out the gate and going to Marian, then dismissed the idea, tempting as it was. 'Twas far too late to be wandering about outside the walls. Marian was probably asleep. The girls, too. He doubted he could wake Marian without waking the twins.

Best to go down into the hall and stretch out on a pallet.

Stephen put his ear back to the door. Silence. Carolyn hadn't screamed. Edwin hadn't come flying out of the room in a rage. All good signs.

He forced his feet to tread the passageway, taking care to do so quietly so his footsteps wouldn't echo and give his uncouth behavior away. Not that Edwin or Carolyn were likely to hear if they were engaged in what Stephen hoped was a rousing, convincing bout of bed play.

After easing his way down the stairs, he sought out the pallet and lowered onto it, rather envying Edwin. Gads, all the man had to do was live through the night to prove his good health and stamina to Carolyn. Edwin loved Carolyn. All he had to do was tell her, and live, and she'd believe him.

Not so with Marian. No amount of sex, no matter how satisfying, proved his love for her. The two of them had engaged in bed play six years ago, then he'd left her alone, carrying and without support. Marian recognized a good tumble, knew the difference between lust and love, that words were merely words.

So how to prove to her that he loved her now? That he was willing to try to be the responsible, steady man she needed?

How to wipe away six years of neglect? She might be willing to forgive him but might never forget, might not ever trust him fully. Being a good father to Audra and Lyssa would aid his cause. Tomorrow, without fail, he'd claim his daughters, begin to provide for them. Little silk gowns. A keep built of stone. Meat for their meals. Frog hunts. Their birthright—which also included the right to know their mother's family.

He needed to make things right with Marian's father. She must miss her parents and siblings. Surely, mending the breach between Marian and her family would prove his willingness to take his responsibilities seriously.

But would either prove his love or gain her trust?

Somehow he'd do both, if it took him six years or a lifetime. He just wished he knew how.

Chapter Eighteen

The bailey smelled of heaven.

Marian guided Audra and Lyssa past the huge roasting pits where beef, venison and pork turned slowly on spits tended by broad-shouldered lads. From the bake ovens wafted the aroma of rounds of bread. Huge cauldrons contained soup, bubbling out the aroma of wild onion.

The twins had never seen the like of preparations for so large a gathering. Marian allowed them to gawk and answered their endless questions, but kept them moving toward the keep.

The girls had slept well and partaken of a light meal of bread and cheese. Marian knew they'd behave and mind their manners. Not having slept much, she was far less sure of her own ability to face whatever awaited her in the hall.

She'd tossed most of the night, wishing Stephen were beside her so she knew where he spent the night. She'd bounced between anger over his faithlessness and guilt over her mistrust.

Near the stairway, she let go of the girls' hands. They scampered up the stairs while she followed at a more sedate pace, holding up fistfuls of amber silk so she didn't trip on the hem.

Most of the guests were already gathered in the hall, garbed in the finest of their finery. The amber gown Stephen had given her suited Marian's rank, not so high as most but hardly as low as the serving wenches who scurried about in rough-weave. Marian inwardly winced at the thought of her old gown, hoping Stephen truly had burned it.

"I began to wonder if I must come out to wake you." Stephen's low voice drifted to her, his hand landing on her shoulder as he took his place at her side.

She took comfort in his immediate presence, that he'd watched for her arrival. "We lingered in the bailey overlong."

Audra swung her arms around in an exaggerated stirring motion. "We watched the girls make soup!"

Stephen raised an amused eyebrow. "Did you?"

"Uh-huh," Lyssa replied. "And the cow go round and round and round."

"Sounds as if you two are well-rested and ready for a full day. And you, Marian?"

She should say "Fine" and let it go at that. "I tossed a bit last night."

He chuckled. "So did I. I have not slept on a pallet on a cold, stone floor for some time." He leaned toward her, his warm breath teasing her ear. "Had I known you were restless, I would have given in to the temptation to visit."

Those few words brightened her mood as several hours of solid sleep couldn't have done.

"I might even have allowed you the visit."

He squeezed her shoulder. "Nice to know," he said, then removed his hand and turned his attention to the girls, gazing at his daughters with pride in his eyes. His entire manner with the twins fair screamed his love for his daughters.

Unable to watch them converse without tears forming, Marian looked about for Carolyn, but waited until Stephen and the girls finished their talk before asking after her.

Stephen glanced toward the stairway leading up to the family chambers. "I assume Edwin not only lived through the night, but Carolyn is ensuring his good health yet this morn."

Marian's jaw dropped as the implication set in.

"Edwin and Carolyn? You jest!"

He shook his head. "Nay. 'Struth, if they do not vacate my chamber soon, I will have to disturb them. I need to change... Ah, here they come now."

The smile on Carolyn's face lighted up the room.

"'Tis hard to believe. I have been trying to get Carolyn to...you know...for months."

"I must confess I gave Edwin an advantage. Once he knew her fears he was able to deal with them."

Her ire sparked. "You told him what I told you."

"Someone should have told him long ago. All the secrets did was keep them apart. Now look at them."

Marian couldn't disagree. Carolyn, her hand slipped though the crook of Edwin's arm, looked so happy as to burst. Was it her imagination or did Edwin appear taller, more self-assured?

"I need change my tunic," Stephen said. "Be back anon."

He strode across the room, collected a hug from Carolyn along the way, then disappeared up the stairway.

Marian put a hand to her midriff, her heart beating so hard it threatened to bruise her ribs. Edwin had gained

Carolyn's bed and obtained her surrender. Had he also claimed the prize he most sought? Was Stephen now free?

"Come girls, make your greetings to Carolyn and Edwin. Show them how lovely you look."

The girls loved their new gowns so needed no more prompting. They even walked sedately and curtsied prettily. While Carolyn, garbed in the gown she'd worn yesterday and now a bit rumpled, exclaimed over the girls, Edwin grasped Marian's hand and kissed it lightly. Carolyn gave her a more effusive greeting. Caught up in a hug, Marian couldn't resist prompting Carolyn to reveal more.

"Does this mean what I hope it does?"

Carolyn came away with a blush. "So I too hope. We will talk more later, in private."

Marian was sure her curiosity would drive her witless before they had a chance to be private. But 'twas a telling sign that Carolyn wasn't rushing off to change her gown, as if not caring anymore what impression she made on Stephen's family, or anyone else for that matter. Not like Carolyn at all!

Stephen came down the stairs looking every bit the highborn noble as he had when arriving at Branwick, garbed in black from head to toe. A scarlet sherte peeked out from the beneath the neckline and sleeves of his silk tunic. Silver threads glittered along the trim like stars shining at midnight. A silver circlet banded his head in an effort to hold captive his raven hair. He looked splendid, and if fate proved kind, he was hers.

"Gerard and Ardith are nearly ready to come down." He held out his hand. "Shall we?"

Stephen meant to take her up front, to stand beside him amidst his family, thus making an announcement to the high nobility of England that contradicted everything they'd already assumed. Her heart skipped several beats as she slipped her hand into his.

Audra pointed to the stairs. "Look, Mama! The babe is wrapped in the blanket you made!"

Stephen squeezed her hand. "I gave the blanket to Ardith and Gerard this morn. I knew they would love it beyond reason."

Ardith had arranged the blanket so a portion of it draped over her arm. Marian stared at the lion cubs cavorting over the fine weave wool, nearly overwhelmed that everything could come together in one place at one time—her dreams come true.

Too easy. Too fast. And it scared her witless.

Stephen kept Marian and the girls at his side throughout the ceremony and feast. Afterward, he introduced her to Corwin and Judith, and made the rounds of family and guests as was expected of the baron's brother on such an occasion. If anyone in the hall misunderstood his message about who he intended to marry, then they'd gone witless. If anyone thought him a knave for the sudden switch in brides, they need only note Carolyn's arm linked through Edwin's and see the joy in her eyes to know that the lady was in no distress.

As for his daughters, he picked them up and hugged them often, inviting all to notice their raven hair and olive-toned skin that matched his. To banish any lingering doubt, when in midafternoon the nursemaid collected Gerard and Richard's boys to go upstairs for a nap, he sent the girls along, too.

To all Marian was polite. Her smile warm and her manner gracious. Was he the only one who felt the shimmer of unease that lay beneath the surface of Marian's smile, who saw the hint of something amiss in the depths of her eyes?

Not even Edwin and Carolyn's private and quiet confirmation that they planned to wed as soon as they returned to Branwick seemed to banish Marian's disquiet.

He was sore tempted to whisk Marian upstairs to his chamber for a nap of their own. 'Twasn't possible, so he settled for guiding her toward the far end of the hall where he'd had his talk with Edwin last eve.

She rubbed her eyes with the heel of her hands. "Dear me. I had forgotten how wearing these festivities can be on both body and mind. I doubt I will remember the names of all of the people you presented to me."

Was that the problem? Was she merely weary?

"They will remember you, which is all that matters."

"I will do better...next time." She gave him a soft smile. "Carolyn and Edwin seem happy, do they not? You will have to tell me how their ending up together in your chamber came about."

He bobbed his head. "'Twasn't terribly hard, though I did need to convince Edwin to take a risk. Again, I apologize for taking liberties with your confidences."

She reached up to rearrange the ties on his sherte, a fussy, kind of wifely thing to do. He rather liked it.

"In this case, you are forgiven," she said. "Once Carolyn's fears reached the right ears, then they could be dealt with openly. I wish I had possessed the wisdom, and maybe the courage, to reveal them to Edwin myself."

"You were being loyal to Carolyn, is all. I, on the other hand, felt no compulsion, not when it stood between us."

"*Us.*" The word came out soft and reverent. "'Tis

strange, is it not, that we are again lovers after all this time?''

''Oh, more than lovers I would say.''

Her smile widened. ''Parents of twins.''

Of two adorable daughters who now slept upstairs and still didn't know he'd sired them. Soon, now, they'd wake, and then he'd wrap them in his arms and call them his own. 'Twas both exciting and unnerving, wondering over their reaction.

''And perhaps parents again if our union proves as quickly fruitful as last time.''

''Perhaps. After we are…married we can further the cause.''

Stephen caught the hesitation. She'd done so twice now, both times when speaking of future events. Why should she be unsure of the future? Was Marian the only person in the hall who still harbored doubts over her place in his life?

Was that what she needed, to hear the words? If 'twould take the hint of doubt from her eyes he'd gladly say them.

''After we are married, I may keep you tied to a bed until ensured our cause furthered.''

She laughed lightly. ''No need for restraints, my lord. 'Twill truly be my pleasure to suffer your husbandly attentions.''

He gathered her in his arms, wishing they could stand on the steps of Wilmont's chapel, say the words and be done with it. Marian deserved better, however. She deserved all of the excitement and attention due a bride of noble birth. The gifts. The feasting and good wishes of friends and guests. To have her family gathered around her. For Marian to have a proper wedding, they needed her father's blessing.

He'd go to Murwaithe and face Hugo de Lacy, but wouldn't mention his plan now. Today was for celebrating, and he wanted Marian to smile, not worry over what might be a strained meeting with her father. So, what to do to bring joy to Marian's heart?

"Do you think the girls might be awake?" he asked.

"'Struth, with all the excitement, I will be surprised if they slept at all."

"Then let us go tell them. My patience is at its end."

Marian nodded her agreement. He grasped her hand and headed for the stairway that wound up to the family quarters. He'd have run up the steps if his knees didn't begin to tremble, if his heart didn't pound so hard.

Mercy, he was a battle-hardened soldier, had faced horror and death with less trepidation than facing two little tykes. His tykes. Would they be happy to learn he was their father? Or horrified? Or not care? What if they rejected him?

He paused at the top of the stairs. "What if they do not want me?"

Marian's smile eased his mind. "They will. The girls will be surprised, and possibly angry with me for keeping you a secret. Fortunately, young children tend to forgive those they love easily."

True enough. The girls' youth worked in his favor. They'd forgive both him and Marian for past mistakes if from this day forward their parents loved and cared for them. He had only to look as far as his own willingness, as a child, to forgive his mother's neglect of him if only she'd uttered a kind word, found some quality in him worthy of her time and affection. He'd been much older than the girls were now when he'd given up hope.

"Which one of us tells them?"

Marian sighed. "I do. 'Tis best the girls hear the tale

from me, I think. I would also prefer to do the telling without other ears around to hear. The tent, mayhap?''

"My chamber is closer. We will take them there.''

Stephen took the few steps to the children's room and opened the door to the sound of young voices. Not only were his daughters awake, but in the midst of a game with his nephews. His apprehension subsided when the girls looked up, smiled, and ran toward him. Everything would be all right. It had to be.

"Did you have a good nap?'' Marian asked, the cheer in her voice somewhat forced. The girls seemed not to notice.

"We slept—a little,'' Audra offered.

"'Tis more than I hoped for. Come,'' she said, herding them toward the door. "Stephen and I wish to have a talk with you.''

Stephen led them down the hall to his chamber. As he closed the door, Marian lifted the girls up onto the bed and sat down between them.

Lyssa ran a hand over the wolf coverlet. "Oh, this is soft. Is this your chamber?''

"It is,'' he answered, noting the slight flush on Marian's cheeks. Because she realized she sat on his bed? Or was she thinking, as he did, about how soft and caressing the fur would feel against bare skin.

Now wasn't the time for erotic thoughts, but the vision of Marian sprawled naked on a wolf fur burst forth in carnal splendor.

Tonight, Marian. Tonight, he promised himself, she'd share his bed, writhe on his furs, become his wife in all ways but the utterance of the words.

She took a composing breath and wrapped her arms around the girls. "I have what I believe will be good news for you.''

Marian glanced up at him, and he hoped she found the reassurance she sought. Certes, he admired her courage and composure considering what she was about to do.

"I know this will come as a surprise," she continued. "Indeed, I never thought I would be telling you this, but…well, a long time ago I made a grave misjudgment, and because of it I deprived you of your birthright and…your father."

Lyssa's brow scrunched. "What is a birthright?"

"The privileges and inheritance you are entitled to due to your rank. You both know you are of noble birth."

"Because our father was of noble birth?"

"As am I."

"Was our father a great noble?" Audra wanted to know, making Stephen wonder what Marian had told the girls about their father. Surely, they must have been curious and asked.

Marian hesitated, then tried to smile. "Your father hails from one of the highest noble families in the kingdom." She gave the girls a squeeze. "'Tis now time for you to meet him."

His heartbeat fluttered.

"But our father is dead! Everyone says so!" Lyssa protested.

Her smile faltered. "My darlings, I must beg your pardon for allowing you to believe that tale. Your father is quite alive and will now take his rightful place in our family."

Marian looked up at him, giving the girls the only indication they needed to identify their father. Time seemed to stand still as the twins exchanged a glance, as if holding a silent discussion and arriving at a mutual decision. He reminded himself to breathe.

Audra slid off the bed, slowly walked toward him and stopped beyond his arms' reach.

"You are our father?" she asked.

The lump in his throat nearly choked off his answer. "Aye."

Her eyes glistened. "Did we do something wrong that made you leave us?"

His heart split open. "Ah, sweetling." He swept her up into a hug she didn't return. She held herself stiff and away.

Patience. Give her time.

"You did nothing wrong. Your mother—" Nay, he'd not blame Marian. He bore responsibility, too. "I have been remiss in the past, but no longer. Now that 'tis possible for your mother and I to marry, we begin a new life, the four of us."

Her expression melted into one he recognized well, that of Marian when about to take him to task.

"Our hut is awfully small."

His daughter's hint of anger jarred him. He'd expected surprise and puzzlement, and he'd hoped for happiness. Right now he'd settle for acceptance.

"I have manors aplenty from which we can choose a home. Mayhap the four of us can visit them to see which you might like best."

"Mayhap."

He walked over to the bed, sat next to Marian and turned Audra sideways on his lap. "And mayhap we can be just friends for a while longer, until you become used to having a father."

Lyssa crawled up onto Marian's lap. "But if you are our father, we should call you Father, true?"

Sweet Lyssa, my thanks!

He chucked her under the chin. "When you are ready, then certes you must call me Father. I shall be honored when you do."

Marian's smile told him he'd said the right thing. Only time would prove her right or wrong. And now they had time, the four of them, to get to know each other better, to form a family.

A fist pounded on the door. "Lord Stephen?"

He recognized Armand's voice, wished he could tell the squire to go away, but the knock and shout were too urgent to dismiss.

"Come!"

Armand opened the door and stepped inside the chamber. "My lord, a runner has arrived from Torgate and requests to speak to you forthwith."

Torgate, one of his holdings, marched along the border of the king's cherished New Forest in southern England. The steward wouldn't send a runner to Wilmont without pressing reason.

"Trouble?"

"Brigands."

The difference in Stephen's demeanor gave Marian pause.

With his brothers at his side, he stood in the bailey listening intently to the messenger who'd run for nearly two full days with little sleep and no food, hoping to find Stephen, knowing help could be got from the baron if that failed. When the runner refused succor until after his tale was told, Stephen let the man ramble.

Stephen stood with arms crossed and feet spread, assuming the appearance of a powerful overlord, one now angered on his villeins' behalf. She'd never seen this side of him, as the man not only in command but entitled to, and receiving, the runner's respect and confidence in his ability to right a horrible wrong.

The runner told of fields set to fire, of the sheep herd mutilated or scattered, of a tenant who'd been killed when defending his daughter against a brigand's evil intent.

Stephen snapped out the question, "How many?"

"Near as we can tell, my lord, there be five."

"You are not certain?"

"Nay. The brigands strike at dusk in groups of two or three, never all together."

"What has been done?"

The runner gave a report on the attempts to catch the miscreants, to no avail. One brigand had been badly injured, but no one knew if the wound later proved fatal.

Stephen glanced at Gerard. "I will take Armand and Harlan with me, if you will allow."

Gerard nodded his permission, then looked skyward, toward the late afternoon sun. "When do you wish to leave?"

"As soon as I change into chain mail and my horse is readied."

Marian didn't hear the rest of their conversation, too busy dealing with the realization that Stephen meant to go after the brigands himself. Meant to leave Wilmont within minutes.

He couldn't leave, not now!

Stephen could get himself hurt or killed, just when they'd found each other again, just when the girls learned they had a father. She'd left the girls in the children's room with Stephen's nephews, with the group of them delighted they were actually cousins. They would be upset if Stephen left.

When Stephen headed toward the keep's outer stairway at a brisk pace, Marian followed, nearly running to catch him.

"Stephen, hold. We must talk."

He slowed and held out his hand. "Come up and help me change. We can speak there."

Marian grasped his hand and held her peace, indeed, didn't have breath to speak while struggling to keep up with his long, purposeful stride. As she closed the chamber door behind them, Stephen crossed the room and bent over a large trunk. He pulled out a gleaming conical helmet and tossed it toward the bed. It landed on the wolf fur with a soft thump.

She stared at the helm she'd known he must possess but never seen him wear. He bent over the trunk again. A chill swept through her at the distinctive sound of rattling iron. He pulled out his heavy chain mail.

Marian stilled the tremble in her hand and found her voice. "I would like you to reconsider going to Torgate."

"I fear I cannot. You heard the runner."

"Certes, the brigands must be caught and punished, but 'tis not necessary for you to do so yourself."

He spread the mail out on the bed and ran a hand over the armour, checking for breaks or weak links. "Who better than me? I am the overlord, after all."

A villein swore loyalty to his overlord in return for a promise of protection, but that didn't mean the overlord must be the man to wield the sword.

"Could not Armand and Harlan take a group of Wilmont's men-at-arms to Torgate? You need not go."

Stephen's head came up slowly. He stared at her as if her words dealt him a blow.

He *wants* to go, she realized. The prospect of a journey, the thrill of the chase, called to him hard—harder than any whisperings of remorse over leaving her, leaving the girls.

"'Tis my duty." He glanced down at his chain mail. "I have never been one to carefully attend my holdings, but when there is trouble I always see to it. My people expect it of me. *I* expect it of me."

Marian heard and understood, but now others must come first.

"What of your duty to Audra and Lyssa? Should not their needs hold sway? We tell them you are their father, give them a gift they never thought to possess—and then you leave on an errand easily done by others. Your leaving tells them they are not important to you."

"That is not true!"

"They are but five, too young to appreciate duty. They will only know you abandon them when they need you most."

He crossed the room to stand before her, his warm, strong hands landing on her shoulders. "Then I will explain why I must go, and assure them I will return and fulfill my duty to them as every lord fulfills his duty to both his family and villeins. Our daughters have relied upon you for their entire lives for support, and will look to you for it now, not to me." He caressed her neck, her cheeks, tilting her head back. "But this is not truly about the girls, is it? The concern I hear, the worry I see— dare I hope they are for me?"

Her fears ran deep, and unspeakable. She closed her eyes against the oncoming tears. "I do not want you to go." *Do not abandon me, not again!* "I shall…miss you."

His arms tightened around her. Marian clung to his tunic, breathed in the heady scent of virile male wrapped

in silk. Her head whispered that her fears were ground-
less; her heart remembered six lonely years without him.

"Marian, I will be fine. No brigand will lay a hand
on me."

She reached up to caress the ear missing a chunk of
lobe. "What of a sword? A dagger?"

"I promise to practice great care to come home to
you whole and unbloodied."

Sometimes good intentions weren't good enough. Her
worries made no dent in his resolve, however, and further harping would only sound like childish whining.
Marian dried her eyes.

"How long will you be gone?"

"As long as I must to ensure the holding and people
safe." He kissed her temple, his lips warm, his breath
stirring wisps of her hair. "Come help me into my ar-
mor. The sooner gone, the sooner returned."

Stephen pulled his silk tunic and linen sherte over his
head. She hadn't meant to touch the scar across his
shoulder, hadn't intended to press against his smooth,
bare chest to beg another kiss. She certainly hadn't
planned to end up sprawled on his bed atop the soft wolf
coverlet, his fingers making quick work of her gown's
lacings.

"We have no time for this," he said, his kisses and
caresses drawing her downward into a whirlpool of
swirling heat and mind-fogging bliss.

"Think on it as saying fare-thee-well, and do it
right."

"With you I cannot seem to do it wrong."

And he didn't. His possession came hard and full, in
swift and thorough measure. Her body responded as always, desperately grasping his, reaching for that perfect
moment when passion reached its peak. Marian tumbled

over with a cry of pleasure melded with pain. He followed close behind with a groan of completion mingled with sapped strength.

He nuzzled in her neck. "You are welcome to my chamber while I am gone. 'Twould be pleasing to think of you here, warming my bed."

Remain at Wilmont for weeks, residing in Stephen's chamber, missing him dreadfully, with little to occupy her hands or mind? She'd go mad.

"Carolyn told me she and Edwin leave on the morrow for Branwick. The girls and I will go home with them."

"To the hut?"

Marian dismissed his undisguised objection. "'Tis our home until you find us another."

He brushed sweat-dampened wisps of hair from her forehead, his touch gentle, his expression concerned. "At least do me the favor of residing at the keep."

"If you wish," she said, not intending to do any such thing, but unwilling to argue with Stephen right now. He was leaving, off to bring a band of brigands to justice, off on an exciting adventure.

As she watched Stephen transform from splendid lover to warrior knight, her deepest fear once again coiled around her heart. True, the girls would be upset at Stephen's leaving. The man she loved could be hurt or worse. But what she feared most, had seen a hint of earlier, was his true desire to be gone.

Once he was far away from her, with time to think on what he was giving up, would he have a change of heart? Would the freedom he cherished so highly overpower his good intentions?

Would his eagle's wings fly him back to her or would he soar far beyond her reach?

Chapter Nineteen

Marian stared at the uncle she'd thought she knew well. William of Branwick. The man who'd been married to her mother's sister, and who apparently corresponded with his sister-by-marriage, Edith de Lacy, far more often and deeply than mere greetings at Yuletide. The man who'd just given Marian the surprise of her life.

"You *knew?*" she managed to ask.

"We suspected." William shifted against the bolster of his bed. "Believe me, your parents will be relieved to hear the matter will at long last be resolved."

Marian sat down on the corner of the bed, her legs too wobbly to trust.

Only an hour ago they'd returned to Branwick. Carolyn and Edwin had informed William of their decision to marry and asked his blessing, which he promptly gave. Then the girls had given William their version of how the journey and visit to Wilmont had gone. After William sent the girls out to the kitchen to fetch treats, and Carolyn and Edwin left to begin planning a wedding ceremony, Marian told him the rest of the story.

To hear he already knew…suspected…Stephen was

the girls' father, 'twas a jolt she hadn't been prepared for.

She and Stephen had been so sure they'd kept their trysts private, their attraction to each other concealed.

She found her voice again. "How did you know?"

"By the time your mother suspected Stephen, Hugo had already threatened to toss you out the gate for defying him. Then you had the audacity to leave Murwaithe, sending him into another rage. He told me that since I had you I could keep you until you came into your right mind." He chuckled. "Then the twins were born in a timely fashion and possessed glorious black hair. Edith wanted to come get you, but Hugo refused to chase after his errant daughter. So we agreed you should stay here, under my care, until you either married some other man or relented and named the girls' sire."

Astounded by the revelations, Marian asked, "So the three of you discussed all this by messenger? How did I not notice?"

"You *were* more deeply interested in other things at the time—before the birth with food and sleep, afterward with the babes. In most else you took little notice or care."

Marian admitted she'd wallowed in her misery, then thrown her whole self into motherhood, determined the girls should never want for lack of a father.

"'Tis surprising Father did not go to Wilmont with his suspicions."

"Unless you were willing to point a finger at Stephen, Hugo saw no sense in confronting a man as powerful as the baron of Wilmont on suspicion alone. If Stephen denied involvement with you, 'twould leave Hugo without recourse." William waved a hand in the air. "What is done is done. You and Stephen will set all to rights as soon as you marry. When might that be?''

Marian shrugged and told him of Stephen's journey to Torgate, and why. "He will return when the matter is settled.''

During the two-day journey from Wilmont to Branwick she'd managed to quiet her fears over Stephen's safety. Over whether or not he'd chase an eagle or two after ridding Torgate of the bandits she wasn't quite sure. But Stephen would come for her, eventually, if only for the girls' sake.

Eager for a change of subject, she patted William's knee.

"How are you feeling these days? Any more improvement?''

"Some. Actually, after all you young people left for Wilmont, I needed to find other amusement. So I had Ivo build me a litter. A couple of days ago we harnessed it to two horses and took a walk around the bailey. Felt good to be out and about.'' He paused, then smiled widely. "Go tell Ivo to harness it up again. I believe the girls and I shall take a ride.''

Marian got up, knowing her daughters would be thrilled, then thought of one more question she needed to ask.

"You must have been stunned when Carolyn came home from Westminster with the news she wished to wed Stephen of Wilmont. Suspecting his relationship to the girls, would you have let them marry?''

He hesitated, then said, "I debated long on whether or not to even allow him the gate, then decided his presence here might do two things—give Carolyn a chance to compare another man to Edwin, who I knew she was fond of, and might give you and Stephen a chance to reconcile. 'Twas an opportunity for all of you to come to your senses I could not resist.''

A chance to compare.

''Then you knew you would declare a contest before Stephen even came.''

''Oh, nay, that was a whim, a rather good one I might add, to stall for time. I thought to give the men something to do while you ladies sorted out their qualities. I must say we all did learn a bit from the contest. Agreed?''

Edwin had learned to appreciate Carolyn's skills. His consent to allow her the freedom to use those skills was essential to their happiness—as well as the condition of his health in bed.

Marian had seen Stephen in a different light—as a man capable of steadfastness and good judgment, with the ability to be a proper husband and loving father. That he might not always do or say the right thing, but his intentions were usually good.

What had William learned? Stephen? Not that it truly mattered, considering all had turned out well in the end, or would be well after Stephen came to fetch her and the girls.

''Agreed. I will have Ivo harness the litter.''

Marian strode out to find Branwick's steward, vowing to allow William a great deal of time with the girls in the following weeks, before Stephen returned and took them all off to wherever he'd chosen for them to live.

Where might that be? Stephen owned several holdings scattered throughout the kingdom, estates which he must visit from time to time, a responsibility which would take him from her side on occasion. Too, every knight owed forty days of service each year to his overlord, a duty Stephen owed Gerard.

No matter how much it bothered her, 'twasn't possible for Stephen to keep to hearth and home all of the time, be around whenever she might have need of him. 'Struth, no husband of wealth and property could and still be a proper lord to his people.

And Stephen possessed a free spirit, a wanderer's soul, subject to whims of fancy. If she tried to hold him too tight, she'd smother the essence of the man she professed to love.

Marriage to Stephen gave the girls the protection of their father's name, and Marian a measure of the security she craved. All in all, she'd rather live with Stephen than without him, loved him too much to do otherwise, would adjust to whatever changes she must. Stephen would have his share of changes to adjust to as well.

'Twas how most marriages began, was it not?

Already three brigands dangled from the roadside tree, a warning to others who might contemplate villainy that the lord of Torgate tolerated none. The fourth brigand sat atop his horse—too fine a piece of horseflesh not to be stolen—with his hands tied and a rope looped around his neck, looking anywhere but at his fellows.

Stephen had never given the order for such severe punishment before, but with these men he felt no qualms over making so harsh a judgment. Not a one of them had shown a bit of remorse for his misdeeds. If allowed a lesser punishment than death, they'd only move on to the next holding to plunder and kill and ravish again.

A female just into her womanhood stepped forward from the crowd gathered to watch and cheer as each brigand received his punishment. Stephen looked into hazel eyes that reflected no joy of youth, only deeply held pain. Every time he saw Nettie, he thought of the degradation Audra or Lyssa might someday face, and his ire rose another notch. Nettie had asked permission to mete out this last brigand's punishment, and he saw no reason to deny her request.

Still, knowing her a fairly timid soul, he felt duty bound to let her back out if she chose. "Are you sure you wish to do this, Nettie?"

"Aye, my lord," she said quietly, and looked up into the face of the man about to hang. "He killed my father, then raped me. Aye, I am sure." Her eyes narrowed. "And I want his horse afterward."

The spark of anger and outrageous demand gave Stephen hope she'd recover from her ordeal. "The horse is yours." He handed her a willow switch and stepped back. "Hit hard enough to make him bolt."

Nettie nodded, then adjusted her grip. With a mighty swing she smacked the horse's rump. The crowd cheered as the horse took off from beneath its former master. The rope went taut; the brigand's neck snapped. Nettie dropped the switch and flew back to her mother's open arms.

His duty here was done. Almost. He wished he hadn't agreed to stay tonight to preside over a feast prepared in his honor, but Torgate's residents wanted to show their gratitude and celebrate the brigands' capture and demise. So be it. He could rein in his patience for a few hours more, then be off at morning light.

He'd been separated from Marian for a mere sennight. It felt like forever.

The crowd began to disperse. Stephen accepted the thanks of those who passed by him, then headed toward where Armand and Harlan waited for him.

"A decent few days' work, my lord," Harlan said. "Your tracking skills are to be commended."

High praise from the gruff old knight who'd taught him how to follow a trail.

Armand rubbed his hands together. "No one will expect us back so soon. What say, Stephen? Perhaps a visit to London on the way back is in order."

There was a time he'd have agreed in a heartbeat. He loved the city, from the grand entertainments in Westminster Hall to listening to the hawkers at dockside. Just strolling the streets could prove exciting.

"Not for me," he said, drawing surprise from both companions. "You two may do as you wish, but I am for Branwick."

For a quiet hut on the edge of the hamlet. To Marian, whom he doubted had obeyed his wishes to reside at the keep. Stubborn woman. But he loved her anyway and couldn't think of anywhere he'd rather be than with Marian.

Harlan rubbed his white bearded chin. "Branwick, hmm? Well now, there is young Edwin who might yet have a coin or two to wager."

Young Edwin? Naturally, to Harlan most everyone was young. Age was all a matter of one's perspective, Stephen supposed.

A spark of interest lit Armand's eyes. "There is the little dairy maid who must miss me by now."

Amused, Stephen shook his head. "Neither of you are obliged to go with me. With our duty here done, you may return to Wilmont, even by way of London if you choose."

Harlan shook his head. "Best not let you go alone. You know how the baron worries over you."

Someday Gerard might stop worrying, like on the day the ocean turned into an ice pond. Stephen better understood his brother's concern, however, for he now had worries of his own about those little darlings he'd protect with his very life if it came to it. Love did strange things to one's perspective.

"Then I welcome your company." He glanced over his shoulder at the brigands. "Armand, see to it that Nettie has taken charge of her horse. Harlan, inform the steward the brigands are to stay up but three days, no more. I hate the sight of dangling bones."

Stephen then turned his sights north, where his next task awaited him—to prove to Marian that he'd changed, that she could trust him, love him. 'Twould take far longer than a few days, he didn't doubt.

Marian heard the pounding of hoofbeats and the jangle of tack long before the riders reached her hut. She set aside a partially decorated table linen to look out the door, telling herself 'twas foolish to look for Stephen so soon, but hoping all the same.

As she passed through the doorway, Armand and Harlan flung up hands of greeting, never slowing their pace. With a flourish, Stephen reined his black stallion to a halt at her stone wall. He'd come for her. Finally. With an undignified whoop of joy she ran across the small yard and out the gate, giving Stephen barely enough time to dismount before she slammed into him.

He picked her up, swung her around once, then lowered her for a kiss that melted her insides and stole away her breath. Hardly proper behavior for in the middle of the road, but she couldn't bring herself to protest.

Snug against Stephen, she listened to the beat of his heart, reveled in his firm embrace. "'Tis good to see you, my lord."

He chuckled. "Mayhap I should go away again just so I can return."

Marian's racing heart slowed. She knew he teased her this time, and yet, only a few days ago the jest might have raised either her ire or panic. Perhaps she'd make him a good wife after all.

He hugged her harder. "Ah, Marian. You have no notion of how much I missed you, and the girls. Are they here?"

She tamped down the unwarranted, truly loathsome jealousy that he should ask after his daughters so soon. Naturally he wanted to see them. He loved them.

"At the keep with William. I thought it best they spend as much time with him as possible before you returned. Shall we go fetch them?"

"Not as yet. We need to talk first."

Marian braced for the worst—that while he was gone he'd regretted his hasty decision to marry her. She shouldn't have let him go off without her, given him time on his own to regret his impulsive decision.

Then she took a deep breath, upbraiding her tendency to make hasty assumptions where Stephen was concerned. 'Twas a bad habit she'd formed six years ago and needed to break.

"Did all not go well at Torgate? Catch the brigands?"

"Caught and punished. Did the twins come to understand why I had to leave Wilmont so suddenly? They seemed to take the news well when I stopped to say them farewell."

On that she could ease his mind. "They were far more upset at finding out their mother is not perfect. We have had several talks since over how grown people can make mistakes."

He kissed her forehead. "But you are perfect."

She couldn't withhold a huff of disdain. "I am so far from perfect as to be laughable. Please do not expect it from me, as I will try very hard not to expect perfection of you.''

He smiled then. ''Agreed. Might I assume you have forgiven me for leaving you, too?''

'''Twas selfish on my part to want you all to myself. I know you have other obligations, not just to me and the girls, duties that will take you from us on occasion. I may not like it, but will strive not to hold it against you.''

His fingers slid along her jaw, his expression puzzled. ''Obligation? Sweet Jesu, Marian, you are not an obligation, but my life. Without you the rest means nothing. I love you, Marian, and will do whatever I must to prove myself worthy of you.''

Her knees went weak. She stopped breathing. The man didn't know it yet, but he'd just given her the greatest gift of all. His heart. 'Twas a thing she'd hoped for but not expected. Whatever else happened, she would cherish the gift, hold it close and keep it safe.

''I love you, Stephen. Whatever else—''

He cut off her words with another kiss, his hands moving over her in possessive, persuasive caresses. She needed no persuasion. Her body fired under the power of a kiss fueled by love declared without reserve, then trembled at his body's declaration of his need for more than kisses.

By the time his mouth released hers, Marian was ready to tear off his tunic and tug loose his breeches. Shameless. In the road, yet. The hut was empty.

What would making love be like when under the influence of such heady emotions?

Breathless, he asked, ''Whatever did I do to deserve you?''

''You came back to me.''

Confused, he asked, "That is all?"

She tried to think. "Love me and always come back to me. 'Tis all I require of you, my love."

Amusement touched his mouth. He cupped her bottom and pulled her hard against the bulge in his breeches. "All?"

"Whatever else you might wish to do to further my happiness will be gratefully accepted, my lord."

He glanced up the road toward the keep. "By now Armand and Harlan have reached the keep. Everyone knows I am here, including our daughters. Have we time?"

Marian tightened her hold around his neck. "Enough."

He swooped her up into his arms. "We should really be deciding about where to live, how best to approach your father for his permission to marry."

Wasn't he going to be as shocked as she'd been when hearing that news? "All in due time. You have husbandly duties to perform first."

He set her down on the table. She leaned back on her elbows and gave him what she hoped was a come-hither smile.

Sweat broke out on his upper lip. He fumbled with the ties of his breeches. "I am not your husband yet, my love."

My love. She'd never tire of hearing the words. "In my heart you are, always have been, I think." Very slowly, she inched the amber silk of her skirts upward. "Unless, of course, you would prefer to think of us as lovers."

"Not me," he declared. "I cannot wait to hear the vows which bind you to me, make you my wife. Then no matter what I do you are obligated to share my bed, my life.''

Gladly. 'Twas what she wanted, too. ''Then come give me your oath of forever and ensure I believe it.''

He slid into her slowly, completely. ''Us. Together for all time.''

Marian took him in, as sword to sheath, tight and to the very hilt. Joined. Together again, this time forever.

Stephen flung her high, beyond heaven, where only he could take her. As they soared, Marian believed.

* * * * *

AWARD-WINNING AUTHOR

GAYLE WILSON

presents her latest
Harlequin Historical novel

ANNE'S
PERFECT HUSBAND

Book II in her brand-new series

The Sinclair Brides

When a dashing naval officer searches for the
perfect husband for his beautiful young ward,
he soon discovers he needn't search any
further than his own heart!

Look for it in bookstores in March 2001!

Available at your favorite retail outlet.

Travel back in time to America's past with wonderful Westerns from Harlequin Historicals

ON SALE MARCH 2001

LONGSHADOW'S WOMAN
by **Bronwyn Williams**
(The Carolinas, 1879)

LILY GETS HER MAN
by **Charlene Sands**
(Texas, 1880s)

ON SALE APRIL 2001

THE SEDUCTION OF SHAY DEVEREAUX
by **Carolyn Davidson**
(Louisiana, 1870)

NIGHT HAWK'S BRIDE
by **Jillian Hart**
(Wisconsin, 1840)

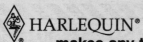